CRESCENDO

L. MARIE WOOD

MOCHA MEMOIRS PRESS

COPYRIGHT NOTICE

OTHER L. MARIE WOOD TITLES

About Horror: The Study and Craft

Acknowledgments

Thank you, Mom and Mike, for wearing several hats, editor, beta reader, stunt double included.

Shelley Roth, thanks for letting me edit at your house.

This is my first love, reader, thank you for diving in.

REVIEWS FOR CRESCENDO

"...A TREAT TO THE SENSES."

"Crescendo is a riveting, yet horrifying tale of one man's descent into insanity, and author Wood straps the reader into his or her seat and refuses to let go until the very last gasp, shiver and groan is delivered in vividly rendered detail."

- Denise M. Clark
Author of "Cross the Line" and "A Man's War"

"...SHOULD BRING A SMILE TO ANY HORROR OR MYSTERY FAN'S FACE."

"There's a wicked atmosphere which grows page after page right until the end...

Crescendo has plenty of disturbing imagery and nasty scenes that will give most readers a jolt."

- Buried.com

"...A VERY SATISFYING READ!"

"Crescendo literally sweeps the reader away from the very first page. The torturous journey of the main character is captivating. L. Marie Wood quite skillfully pulls the reader into the world of the supernatural, making each and every sentence feel almost palpable. Fantastic book and a very satisfying read!"

AllAboutGhosts.com

"WOOD HAS PRODUCED A KILLER NOVEL."

"Wood has earned her place amongst the greats with her debut work."

Jeffrey Menzise, M.A.
Clinical Psychology, Howard University

"[Wood] shows us how quickly a comfortable, normal life can be changed into something quite beyond normal."

Barb Wright
Murder and Mayhem Book Club

For you, Michael

cre·scen·do kr 'shen-'dO

1 a: a gradual increase...
    1 b: the peak of a gradual increase: Climax

The night's divine countenance a blinding sight be.

PROLOGUE

He stared at the television screen, oblivious to the gunfight typical of every Mafia movie made in the '70s of cut-rate, Mario Puzo variety. He was distracted. The sunlight was fading and the day was drawing to a halt as the crisp wind blew and children zipped up their jackets before returning home. But he didn't see any of the activities that were happening outside his window. He had pulled the drapes closed, shutting out the October afternoon and drenching the room in darkness, the picture tube that cast a cone-shaped ray of light over the floor providing the only illumination.

October. The beginning of fall. Shorter days. Nippy, chafing wind. Gray. He never saw the beauty of fall the way other people did. The leaves changing color, taking a long drive along a winding country road to view the colorful foliage as it blanketed the ground, making the landscape an earthy kaleidoscope, these things did not appeal to him. When he saw the changing landscape, he thought of dead leaves that crunch under foot and bare trees with their fingers pointing accusingly at the sky, damning God for their condition. When the brisk wind tousled his hair he felt, instead, the cold fingers of Mother Nature, so cold they burned, scraping the soft skin of his cheek, punishing him for coveting her warmth. And for him, winter was worse.

But that wasn't what was wrong with him then as he sat in his bedroom with the darkness of night closing in around him. As the wise guys shot at their rivals, shielding their Don like pawns on a chessboard protecting their king, he stared at the television set—through the television set—seeing that day again and again, as if it had been captured on instant replay.

He had just gotten back to his office. At 10:00 a.m., he felt the walls of his gray cloth cube closing in on him, as usual. He walked across the street to a little bookstore and browsed the magazine rack. Settling on the daily newspaper, he then went to a neighboring coffee shop and bought a cup of Chai tea, heading back to the office with both hands full.

As he sat down, frowning at the ten emails that had come in while he was gone, he thumbed through the newspaper, finally deciding on the *Lifestyle* section. Pulling out the section and skimming the first page, he realized that the diversion was exactly what he needed. There was nothing heavy in it. No fatal accidents on the highway; no politics, no coverage of the previous night's football games to get his dander up. Just good old neighborhood happenings and movie listings. He didn't feel like engrossing himself in anything that would take more concentration than a story about a local hero or a cat stuck in a tree. But he never got the chance to read the story about the 102-year-old woman who lived in his town, not ten minutes away from his single-family house, who had won the National Garden and Landscaping award that year. He didn't see the picture of her garden full of winter mums, or her wrinkled, watery-eyed, pleasantly smiling face surrounded by a shock of white hair above the caption that read, "At 102, Myra still tends to her garden daily." Instead, a memory masked in the haze of a dream filled his mind.

It was like a nightmarish screenplay playing in his mind, the storyline pieced together by a sentence or a look. Thoughts, memories, wretched clarity jostled him. Images flitted in and out of his consciousness, filling it, pushing past the monotonous thoughts that normally flooded his mind, such as what he was going to have for dinner and his mental checklist for the weekly meeting at 3:30 p.m. Even when he raised his ever-cycling thoughts as a shield to deflect the intrusion, the images still trickled in slowly until they took over his mind completely. The wicked smiles, blinding in their lucidity, descended upon him without pause.

They taunted him.

Gliding from side to side like a vulture surveying its next meal dying on the ground below, these truths cast their shadow over him, moving in and out of focus, only turning to face his mind's eye for a second, teasing it.

He knew.

It was this understanding that had paralyzed him behind his desk in an office filled with chattering project managers and accountants, sustaining the buzz and paperwork that made up life in Corporate America. It was this same understanding that stood before him then, blocking his view of the dance of death portrayed on screen, pinning him to his chair, his limbs immobile and motionless, his eyes dried by the air that hung thickly in the room, his lids unable to blink. It was the dreadful knowledge of what would bring him to his demise, to his inevitable fate, that weakened his knees and made his bladder contract.

He knew.

He had known, even then.

And as he sat, staring impassively at the television screen while the imposing shadow of the inevitable engulfed him in its wake, he realized with painful clarity that he had known all along.

CHAPTER I

The clouds hung thickly in the darkened sky that night. Black smoke bellowed upward, polluting the air with the smell of burning oil. And there was one other smell, dancing seductively in front of him, horridly playing at his nostrils. The smell of burning flesh. It surrounded him, settling heavily on his clothes and filling the air with its scent, thickening it. He lifted his legs high as he ran toward her, like he was running against the ocean current, his knees almost touching his chest. Still the viscous air encircled him, hindering his movement.

She's dying.

He tried to silence his inner voice but it kept whispering to him, relentless in its efforts to make him hear, to make him understand. It spoke only two words, the voice even, devoid of emotion. But he wasn't. The words sent him into a panic, pushing him forward, throwing him headlong at the burning car.

The flames kicked upward and the air gave them life. He sucked in black smoke—smoke as thick as tar—as he ran, his legs propelling him forward by some unseen force. The car, its windows darkened from the heat and smoke, was covered in a majestic shade of orange. The flames blanketed the car, contouring the shape of the windshield and hood. The flames were mesmerizing as they shimmered up to the sky like sensuous fingers reaching for a lover.

He could see her.

Through the flames and smoke engulfing the car, he could see her looking at him.

She was screaming.

Fire licked out at him, pushing him back. He blinked rapidly, his eyes stinging from the smoke. Through the haze he saw her turn to look at him, her agonized scream abandoned. She looked at him through the darkened glass with a kind of resolute peace on her face.

Groping hands pulled him away from the car, directing him toward the emergency vehicles. As he stumbled backwards awkwardly, he watched her staring out at him. Her eyes seemed to look right through him. Her face was dirty, but not burned even though flames engulfed the car. Her eyes were clear as they looked at him from the burning car. There was a sadness in them that tore at his heart. He saw something else in them also, something flickering there, just below the surface. As he watched that sense of calm was replaced by something much less tranquil. Her face seemed to darken. A smirk formed on her lips and her eyes glistened with condescension. Some intangible knowledge flamed within them. Her stare was unwavering, derisive at its base. A feeling of inexorable fear brewed within him, spreading from his stomach down to the base of his feet and up through his arms to the tips of his fingers. A gasp rose in his throat.

His legs stopped moving and he found himself being dragged by two people, one on either side of him. Their hands grabbed him in the pit of his arms, thrusting him backwards and away from the fire. He felt the heels of his shoes digging into the soft ground beneath them as he was pulled, but it was distant, inconsequential. The woman kept staring at him even as the flames grew hot around her. The smell of her hair, singeing at first, then burning off completely, filled the car, its bitterness mingling with the stench of burning leather. Her face had grown heinous, her expression grotesque as the fire burned her skin. But he couldn't look away. He could only stare back at the woman in the car, watching as her life was being taken away from her, staring at her disconcerting countenance in the midst of it all, because of it all.

"You have to stay back here, sir," a voice admonished. He turned towards the voice and, for the first time, noticed that the people that had dragged him away from danger were firefighters. They had stopped dragging him and set him on his feet to stand a considerable distance from the burning car. As he stood amidst a crowd of people, police officers blocking off the scene, onlookers oohing and ahing at the spectacle in front of them, her eyes called out to him, beckoning him to her, inviting him to the dance. One firefighter had left but the other one still lingered, speaking to him curtly, but politely, holding his arm tightly, urging him to comply.

"It's not safe for you to be any closer than you are right now."

"No! I have to help her! She's—."

She's dying.

He tried frantically to pull away from the firefighter and make his way back to the car. Back to her.

"She's dying!" he exclaimed, giving life to the voice in his head. "Her and the baby."

His voice hitched as he spoke, the words bubbling up from a hidden well inside him, spilling over into the smoke-laden air. The baby? He would have no way of knowing that she was pregnant. Where had that come from? He caught a glimpse of the car again. The woman still stared at him, her face ruined now, but turned toward him, nonetheless. A chill came over him as, suddenly, he knew the origin of the damning words he had just uttered and it made his blood run cold. She had spoken through him.

He struggled against the firefighter, losing strength with every lunge. He finally doubled over and coughed violently, his body shaking as he fought the smoke invading his lungs.

"Take it easy, fella."

A middle-aged fireman looked at him compassionately and led him to an ambulance. He looked back at the blazing fire. At the woman's demise. The pregnant woman. A steady stream of water doused the fire, but he knew in his heart it was too late. He could still see her silhouette, charred and rigid, in the front seat. They were looking at him.

And he smiled back at them.

CHAPTER 2

James bolted up, sitting rigidly straight in bed, knocking his pillow that had been balanced precariously on the edge of the bed into the dark abyss below where it disappeared from view almost completely before hitting the floor. He was shaking fiercely, trembling from a coldness that seemed to permeate his bones. Andrea was asleep next to him, his movement only disturbing her enough that she switched positions and let out a disconcerted moan.

The room was impenetrably dark. He could see the shape of the armoire across from the bed, the doors still open to reveal the darkened picture tube of their television, but that was growing faint. It seemed that the armoire and the wall behind it were one structure, the armoire's doors reaching out from its base like hands of the condemned. The room seemed to be darkening somehow, like a cloud had covered the moon, blocking all of its light. It felt like the walls were closing in making the darkness of the room seem tangible, physical. The desk and chair were faintly visible in the dim light; their bone finish was more reflective in the dark than the oak and pine furniture in the room. He couldn't see the floor, couldn't see where the carpeting began under the thick blackness that surrounded him, covering the room like fog. The atmosphere in the room seemed wrong. Almost sinister. James blinked against it, trying to clear his vision.

He tried to focus on something in the room, on things that he could see well enough to discern a shape. He looked at the armoire again, trying to make out the angular lines of the crafted top. There was a silk floral arrangement sitting on top of the armoire—pumpkin roses, red and yellow daisies, and russet-red berries with sprigs of eucalyptus in a wicker vase. James squinted, trying to make out the base of the vase or the shade of one of the flowers, but saw nothing. He turned his attention to the sides of the armoire once more, determined to see something of the shape that was visible, although faintly, minutes before. Nothing.

Suddenly a dim stream of light penetrated the room from a window behind the bed.

A window that wasn't there a second before.

James stared in awe as the wind ballooned cheap curtains the color of crimson outward in wide shimmering bursts, blowing their frayed ends over the bedpost. One of the sheers grazed his back, caressing him like an impassioned lover. James jumped, not from the touch of the curtain, but from the reality of it.

He looked at Andrea, expecting to see the shape of her body under the sheet turned to the side, her hips tilted backward waiting to spoon with his own, her hands folded under her head. He recoiled awkwardly when he saw her sitting up in front of him, wide awake, staring right at him. He realized quickly that it wasn't the shock of her being asleep one second and awake the next that startled him. It was her, the way she looked.

There was something wrong with her.

James had always loved Andrea's brown eyes. The softness they held when she looked at him, the playful jubilance in them when she told one of her silly jokes, the lift in their corners when she smiled. He could see none of that now; only empty sockets that seemed like inordinately large holes, holes that once hugged her beautifully shaped eyes.

Paralyzed by shock and indescribable fear that some part of his mind tried to tell him was irrational, James stared at his wife who seemed to relish his reaction. She smiled a heinous version of her usually vibrant smile and licked her lips with a bloody tongue. She hissed,

"You're mine now, Jimmie."

A bony, claw-like hand clasped his forearm and James found that he couldn't shake its grasp. Underneath Andrea's skin he could see something wriggling, moving. It traveled down her arm, over the top of her hand, and separated as it moved through each of her fingers. Andrea let out the most terrifying laughter James had ever heard as he felt his forearm become hot. The veins in his arm pulsed and his skin grayed as whatever was in Andrea transferred to him. He screamed from the hollow of his stomach as he changed.

He didn't feel his teeth bite into his tongue, filling his mouth with the tinny, metallic taste of his own blood. He saw only his wife, his precious Andrea, laughing at him as her long, jagged nails curled, reaching for his eyes.

CHAPTER 3

James' eyes snapped open. He looked around disoriented, surprised that he could see at all. He turned over and saw Andrea lying peacefully on her side, her back facing him. She was sound asleep. It was Saturday morning and sunlight pierced the room from the window behind the chaise in their reading nook. James looked behind him quickly, half expecting to see the mystery window set innocently in the wall behind the bed, confirming that he was still embroiled in the nightmare. It was gone.

Andrea awoke to her husband sitting up in bed whipping his head around, surveying the room.

"Are you okay, honey?" she asked in her groggy, 'it's too early to be awake' voice. James looked at her, dazed, disbelief spreading over his face.

"James?"

Andrea put her hand on his forearm. His first reaction was to yank it away, not wanting to let the thing inside her travel through his skin. Panic flashed across his face, alarming her.

"James, what's wrong?" Andrea asked, concern creeping onto

her face, replacing the fog of sleep that seemed suspended in front of her. She blinked her bleary eyes and stretched. James looked at her, desperation filling him as he scanned her face. Her beautiful eyes stared back at him, gradually gaining focus as she pulled herself out of sleep. They were normal.

Her hands, her soft skin and manicured nails, were normal. Not claws and cold, scaly skin, but the hands of his wife of three years. He looked into Andrea's eyes and sighed in relief.

"It was just a dream, that's all," he said, not sounding convinced. "I didn't get much sleep last night."

James sank back into his pillow, somehow comforted by the sunlight that brightened the room. Everything in the room looked normal in the light of day. The armoire's doors stood open revealing the picture tube but it no longer seemed like an ominous pool of blackness like in his dream. The armoire itself looked pleasant, as though it belonged in a country home surrounded by bright yellow daisies and wicker furniture. He stared at it, daring it to change back into the hulking structure that loomed at the foot of his bed in his dream. Nothing happened. James sighed as he nestled deeper into the bedcovers, succumbing to the fatigue that had played around his senses all night—a sigh that was both one of relief and acquiescence.

Andrea stroked his hair as he drifted into an inhibited, fitful sleep. As he dozed, his eyes shutting against the room, James could feel the darkness surrounding him. He was vaguely aware that the room had become impenetrably dark, almost like the moon had eclipsed the sun. James saw Andrea sitting behind him, her body pressed against his, raking her talons through his hair, drawing thin slivers of blood as they pierced the soft skin of his scalp. He saw her mouth open, contouring into a devilish grin, revealing pointed, yellowed teeth. Blood dripped from her mouth like raindrops falling from the sky. It pooled on his shoulder, the stain spreading on his white nightshirt.

He saw all of this on the backs of his eyelids, like a movie reel playing in an old, dilapidated movie theater whose only patrons were the kind of people who needed the privacy of a dark room to do what they do.

Instinctively his eyes fluttered open and he immediately felt foolish. The same sunlight that brightened the room before he shut his eyes shone in the room still, casting brilliant colors off the white and silver vase that sat on the desk—a wedding present from Andrea's mother. He turned over and looked at the rest of the room. The sunlight was still coming in from the window behind the chaise, drenching the room in warmth and light. Everything seemed normal.

He looked at Andrea and noticed for the first time that she was asleep. The light from the window backlit the slender frame of Andrea's sleeping body, making her look like an angel. James stared at her, watching, listening. Her steady breathing was rhythmic, hypnotic. A shudder rippled through him as he realized that he had been dreaming when he thought she was awake.

Yet the room looked the same as it had in his second dream.

James took a deep breath, inhaling and exhaling slowly, trying to clear his mind. *I'm really awake this time*, he said to himself. He could smell the linen spray Andrea used on their sheets, could feel the warmth of the sunlight as it heated up the room. This time it wasn't a dream.

Or was it?

James grinned in spite of himself as his mind played devil's advocate. He nuzzled the pillow, ignoring the screams of terror that reverberated in his head.

James slept as the last Saturday of his life carried on, unaware and unconcerned. Everyone except one woman went on about their lives, shopping in the mall, having coffee at the corner cafe, having sex in the warm sunlight that caressed the backs and legs of entwined lovers. It was a normal day for everyone else except Carmen.

CHAPTER 4

"Miss?"

A gray-haired woman looked questioningly at the girl in front of her who seemed to be daydreaming. She was staring at the wall, just below the ancient advertisement for Newport cigarettes; her brow furrowed, wrinkling the otherwise smooth skin of her forehead. She looked too young to have the troubles that showed on her pleasant, dimpled face. The poor girl looked as though a storm was brewing behind her tortured eyes.

Sighing, Pauline shifted her weight behind the counter. There wasn't a line waiting behind the girl, but she was anxious just the same. She didn't have time for any foolishness; her body language expressed her impatience. She put a hand on her ample hip and repeated,

"Miss?"

Carmen turned her gaze to the woman who seemed to be looming over her, zooming in and out of focus. What she could make out was that the woman was scowling. Her face was contorting into wicked expressions. Her face went from normal to demonic, writhing as it changed, ripping through the vestiges of her human face until only raw evil remained. The thing—the woman—was talking, but Carmen didn't hear anything. An audible gasp escaped Carmen's lips as she blinked and took a step backwards, almost crashing into a potato chip display. As her right hand rose reflexively to cover her mouth the woman's face returned to normal, showing only her discontent, but nothing more sinister. Carmen looked at her in disbelief, not believing her eyes.

Pauline leaned forward and said, "Look, if you don't want the stuff—."

All of a sudden, Carmen could hear the woman speaking again, the odd droning beep that had filled her ears before disappearing. The woman's rough-edged voice spoke hurriedly, agitated. It was all Carmen could do not to scream. The woman snatched back the bag that had been packed with a 2-liter bottle of soda, chips, and a paperback and started to unpack it.

Carmen stuttered, cleared her throat, and said,

"I'm sorry. What do I owe?"

Pauline eyed her suspiciously, beginning to wonder if more than a case of the blues was affecting the young woman at her counter. She repacked the bag slowly, keeping her eye on the woman as she worked.

"Comes to $9.76," she said, her voice guarded.

She tried to mask her uneasiness as she stood in front of the young woman, who was not more than a girl, really. But something about her made Pauline nervous. She watched the woman warily as she dug into her oversized purse for money to pay the bill.

Carmen conducted the rest of the transaction on autopilot. Her mind was cluttered with incoherent thoughts, all of them feeding off one another, mixing like paint on a pallet. She couldn't seem to focus on one of them long enough to understand it, to see why it was filling her with a sense of dread. Every time she thought she had pinned one down to review it, just when she started to form an opinion of it, it floated away and was quickly replaced by another jumble of thoughts. She felt confused and disoriented as she fumbled around in her purse, trying to get enough money together to pay the bill. Indiscernible images kept hanging in front of her eyes, only giving her clear sight for a second or two before another vision replaced the last one. She blinked rapidly, trying to wipe them away. When that didn't work, she tried rubbing her eyes, squeezing them shut. Still, they loomed.

Pauline watched as the woman struggled in front of her. Carmen finally handed her a $20.00 bill, barely looking in Pauline's direction as she did so. Pauline thought about skimming a couple of dollars from the change, especially given her patron's state of bewilderment. The girl would never know the difference, Pauline thought. But something changed her mind. It was the sudden dullness in her eyes. They were so lackluster that they appeared bone dry. They sent a chill down Pauline's spine, and coming from a woman who shot a man in the head at point blank range when he tried to rob her store, that was saying a lot. Not even the splatter of blood and God knows what else on the Fritos corn chips was enough to make her feel the consternation that she felt looking into that girl's eyes. She felt like someone was walking over her grave.

So, she gave the young woman all of her change and watched her pick up the bag and make her way to the front door as though she was in a trance. She pushed the door open, sounding the bells hanging on the wreath hook, turned, and passed the picture window on the right side of the store. Pauline held her breath unconsciously as the girl passed, bracing herself for what, she didn't know. When the woman turned to look at her through the dirty glass Pauline jumped in spite of herself. A flash of embarrassment reddened Pauline's cheeks but left as quickly as it came when she looked at the girl again. The sight of her made all of the color drain from Pauline's face.

An involuntary gasp escaped her lips.

The girl suddenly looked pallid, wan. She was thinner than she had been moments before, no longer shapely but gaunt. Her eyes had sunken into their sockets. Her skin had darkened and yellowed since she left the store. She looked sickly. Pauline's hand fluttered up to her neck as it never had before when their eyes met. There was an emptiness in them that was troubling. There was nothing there, no sign of life, no vibrance. They were more than just insipid and dull. They looked lifeless.

Pauline's heartbeat banged in her ears as the pace quickened. She tried to pull her eyes away from the young woman but couldn't. Before reaching the edge of the picture window the girl offered a thin smile to Pauline. Pauline returned a smile that was born more out of madness than congeniality. They stayed that way for what seemed like hours, smiles plastered to their faces, eyes watching each other. Finally, mercifully, the young woman walked beyond the picture window and out of sight. A sigh of relief left Pauline's lungs as she gazed out to the busy street, a street ignorant of the exchange that had just occurred between the two women.

As her heartbeat gradually returned to normal and her mind relaxed, Pauline realized why she had been shaken so. Her mind had a difficult time wrapping around it, but she knew it to be true the moment it dawned on her. Looking at the young woman as she walked in front of the picture window was like looking at the living dead. A film of sweat blanketed her brow.

Carmen's daze broke a block past the store. She walked briskly to her new apartment, ran up the stairs two at a time, and locked the door. She felt like something was after her. Paranoid? Maybe. But why? She had just moved to New York from Washington DC a month before and hadn't met enough people to make enemies. About the worst thing she had been guilty of had been jaywalking in Nyack her first week. Even though jaywalking is a crime in

Washington DC, cops rarely reprimanded you for it. Apparently, they did in New York.

Carmen had only worked for a week or so. She hadn't had that many customers, but that was to be expected in her business. A psychic's success is contingent upon word-of-mouth advertising, so she was giving it some time. She'd had three customers in the week that she hung her shingle on the door— a man looking for love, a woman wanting to know what would happen in her complicated love life, and a woman who wanted to summon the spirit of her adopted mother so she could find out who her birth parents were. So what if two of the readings had been bogus. Nobody believed in that shit anyway, right?

Carmen put the bag down on the kitchen counter and turned around, surveying her meager studio. She hadn't brought much with her when she left DC, and still hadn't had time or money to decorate her digs. But her shabby bedspread and worn-out pleather sofa were not important to her then. She could feel a presence in her apartment.

She walked around slowly, unsure of what she might see and if she really wanted to see it at all. She circled the floor space between her bed and the dining room table (a card table with folding legs), straining her eyes to see something that wasn't there, something that sat just beneath her consciousness, watching her with perfect clarity. She went into the bathroom tentatively and yanked the shower curtain back. She repeated the process with her two closets doors. Nothing.

She walked toward her bed, shaking her head as she went. *I have to lighten up,* she thought, trying to shrug off the odd feeling that had plagued her since she entered the supermarket. It was as if something had touched her soul, examining it, fondling it while she walked up and down the aisles. The feeling of being touched— of hands on her skin—was so strong she turned around to face the person trying to get her attention. She found the aisle empty. Chuckling self-consciously, she tried to ignore it, to chalk it up to a "medium" moment. Sometimes that happened to her. Spirits wanting to communicate with the living thrashed around in limbo on earth, banging against the barrier that separated the world of the dead from the world of the living, trying to break through.

Spirits touch people all the time, but only those who were sensitive to it knew what was really happening. Most people attribute the sudden breeze that tickles the back of their necks to a draft from an unseen window somewhere in the house. They mistake the temporary pressure on their shoulder blade for a muscle spasm. They easily explain these things away so that they don't have to deal with the supernatural truth that the dead do exist in the same space and time as the living. Carmen tried to do the same thing that most people did: she ignored the odd feeling of being touched. She pushed it out of her mind while she shopped, thinking instead of her plans for the evening—a movie and Chinese carryout. It worked until whatever had touched her in the aisle way crept into her mind again at the counter.

Sighing, Carmen turned on the television and flopped down on the bed, resting her knee on the unmade sheets. The feeling was still there, lingering just under the surface of her skin, waiting for something. She looked around again and saw nothing.

"I'm starting to believe my own bullshit," she said aloud to the empty room, her laugh sounding high pitched and tinny to her ears.

She flipped through the television stations absently, finding nothing of interest on the tube. She kicked off her shoes, took off her clothes, and snuggled into the bed. The sheets felt cool to her unprotected skin, the chilly folds touching everything that wasn't covered by her underwear. As she struggled to get comfortable against the tangles of her bedcovers, a cold breeze whipped around the room. The fact that the windows weren't open popped into her mind but passed as quickly as it had appeared, as if carried by the soothing gust of air like a feather. The air smelled rich and heavy, robust like Italian food. She mused fleetingly that the neighbors must have been making a pot of their homemade pasta sauce like they did every other week. She made a mental note to go by the Wickers' house and try it this time, since she had turned down an invitation to do so the week before.

"It's the best this side of Sicily," Marian Wicker had boasted, flashing her a near toothless grin as she stirred the thick, red, fragrant sauce with her weathered wooden spoon.

Carmen nestled the pillow and inhaled, almost tasting the pasta. A smile tickled the corners of her mouth as she anticipated her evening meal. The smell of oregano and basil caressed her nostrils and lulled her into the most meaningful rest she had experienced since she moved.

Carmen was asleep before she realized it, and dead before sunrise.

CHAPTER 5

When I look out at the chaos building on the streets, I tell myself that I am safe here. But where is here? Here, in the alley that I am cowering in—why? Here in the shadows of my mind?

I should be out in the midst of it all, reveling in their energy, smelling the adrenaline in their sweat. Instead, I cower here, in this membrane-like vice with you, an unwilling witness to my latest conquest.

A woman's body lays bloodied on the ground, surrounded by morbid onlookers, mortified yet intrigued by the carnage in front of them. They think she jumped from the roof of the six-story building looming behind her, as if standing over its victim in victory. The crowd, morbidly curious yet inherently afraid, stared at the woman, her mortality reflected in her cold, unseeing eyes. They chatter incessantly about the whys and hows, their voices betraying their apprehension. Yet I feel calm.

I am not afraid, shocked, disgusted, or any of those adjectives one uses to describe their reaction to the listening ear of a fellow voyeur. The sight of her, this young woman whose shapeliness would have once caught the eye of any man but was now reduced to a grotesque mass of blood, skin, and bones, did not sicken me. On the contrary, it excited me. At first, I thought the sensation was sexual. The tingling I felt in my loins when I looked into her ruined eyes was similar to arousal, but there was something more. Her eyes, depressed into her eye sockets like a Neanderthal reincarnation, seemed to look at me longingly, complacently, at peace through the bloody film. Her broken face, a tangle of protruding bones and muscles, still held its compelling beauty.

But that wasn't it.

The feeling was more of familiarity, of promise, and of genesis. In here. You, too, felt her allure.

I watched as the crowd was ushered away from the remains. I saw the EMS unit bag her lifeless body and put it in the ambulance. I felt a gust of wind on my face as the ambulance passed, a kiss blown sweetly in the night air to land on my flushed cheek. She left me then, charioted down the avenue to the hospital deliberately, but decidedly slower; the sense of urgency dissipated as the ambulance carried its DOA.

I watched it all.

And felt rebirth. And a silky warmth between my legs.

CHAPTER 6

The darkness of night met James as he awoke at 3:30 a.m., Sunday morning. Reluctantly, he sat up, squinting against the unyielding and unusually bright moonlight that danced across the floor. His body felt rested. After what seemed like never-ending dream cycles, he had fallen into a blissful, dreamless sleep.

He rose from the bed carefully, trying not to awaken Andrea. He was too rested to will himself back to sleep, too restless to stay in bed. His stomach rumbled, cramping painfully as he stood. He was hungry. Why shouldn't he be? He had only eaten one time that day —a thin ham and cheese sandwich that had been consumed hours before. He stretched and twisted, his torso swiveling on his waist as he tried to crack his tense back. The thought of another sandwich made his stomach rumble even more, so he turned towards the bedroom door to make a dash for the refrigerator. As he turned, his eyes falling on the contents of the room, he noticed clothing strewn on the floor near the desk chair.

James looked at the sweater, jeans, and sneakers in confusion, the garments thrown indiscriminately across the floor. One of the sneakers lay on its side in a corner and James could see dirt caked in the sole. Some of the dirt had dropped onto the cream carpet. An illogical fear rose in the pit of his stomach as he retraced his steps from the day before.

He had awakened to greet the afternoon refreshed. Even though he hadn't felt tired he found himself lounging in front of the television after lunch on the cusp of sleep.

He was watching an old movie on cable, some Frankenstein iteration where the monster terrorizes a small town in search of a bride. After only thirty minutes of the movie, James felt his eyelids growing heavy and shutting against his will. He slept hard, lying on the sofa in the family room as the day changed from sunny afternoon to starry night in front of his closed eyes. When he awoke it was only to put the plate and glass, he had left on the coffee table in the dishwasher and carry himself up to bed.

He tried to think about what he had been wearing before making his sandwich. He had donned 10-year-old sweatpants with a hole in the inner thigh and a college T-shirt to bum around in. The most he had on his feet were socks. James prided himself on being a neat man, at least neat enough to keep him out of trouble with Andrea who insisted upon a tidy living area. It was one of her 'Rules of the House', as she called them. She had also insisted upon buying the cream carpet that was laid throughout the house against James' wishes.

"It might be pretty, but it's not practical," James had said that day in the carpet store. He was dismissed with a simple wave of the hand, an 'Oh James, it'll be okay', and this sexy thing she does with her eyes that gets her anything she wants whenever she wants it.

He would never have thrown his clothes around and kicked dirty shoes into the corner and risk Andrea seeing them. Where had the clothes come from?

James stood between the bed and chair staring at the clothes lying in a mound on the floor. A draft blowing gently from the window behind the chaise made him aware of a sticky wetness just below his navel. His hand instinctively rose to touch it, feeling the thick liquid against his skin. Some of it had already dried, white flecks lifting off his skin as he rubbed at it. As he wiped it off, a flashback full of red and white circling lights and graffiti on a piss-darkened brick wall filled his head. He staggered forward and gripped the arm of the chair, barely keeping himself on his feet.

A pungent, tinny smell permeated the air, surrounding his head and shoulders, choking him. He threw himself over the back of the chair, trying to find clear, lighter air to breath. He reached down to pick up the sweater, but instead his hand snagged the belt loop of the jeans. He looked at the dingy knees and felt so sudden a euphoria that his legs felt weak. His conscious mind screamed as he pressed the crotch of the jeans to his nose. He was suddenly mute. His senses were deaf to the will of his mind, functioning completely separate from him as he watched. The feeling was akin to a soul floating above its dying body, watching as the shell it had lived its life in died on the ground below. He could see everything that was happening in the bedroom. He saw Andrea sleeping on her side of the bed, saw himself standing next to the chair, the weight of his chest supported by it as he leaned. He saw the soiled jeans in his clenched hands, the crotch pressed firmly under his nose.

He could feel his consciousness, his awareness being displaced by some other mind as strong as his own. Stronger even, although he was afraid to admit that. He felt his mind fight valiantly to remain in his body, its rightful dwelling, only to be ousted by the stronger being. He felt his mind shrink away then, cowering in the wake of its determination, taking his essence with it.

He was inhabited.

The new being, the interloper, made a new home of his body, tantalizing his nerves with new commands, filling his mind with taboo thoughts. Thoughts he would accept as his own, allowing their warmth to course through him.

Aware of what was going on but unable to do anything to stop it, James watched—felt—his body savoring the dank, familiar smell, transporting him to a place that existed outside of his conscious memory. He was terrified, helpless to move the pants away from his face, not completely sure that he wanted to anymore.

Amidst his fear he felt refreshed.

The memory of Jane Doe filled his head as he sank to the floor.

CHAPTER 7

James woke up with a crick in his neck. Blinking open eyes that felt glued shut, he found himself in his office—a little room hidden off the back of the house, decorated in cherry wood, dark paneling, and old family pictures framed in mahogany with hand crafted silver and brass trim. The room was a throwback to the den that his father had spent most of his time in, and where he had chosen to end his life. James had always admired his Dad, even after he'd found him slumped in his favorite chair, with his shotgun leaning on his right thigh; the natural extension of his blood-spattered left hand. James had patterned his office behind that den, using some of the furniture that witnessed his father's demise. "You and me? We're one in the same," his father had been fond of saying. Maybe so, when it came to the seclusion and design of his office, James conceded. Maybe so.

The large mahogany desk with ornate handles and leg bases dominated the room. A black writing mat flanked by burgundy leather rests covered the bulk of the free space on the desk. A matching pen cup and paper clip holder littered the desk along with stacks of miscellaneous papers—bills, magazines, sections of old newspapers. A simple banker's lamp sat to the right of the writing mat on the desk, illuminating the almost empty desk calendar whose date hadn't been flipped since Thursday, November 8, 2001.

A reupholstered love seat sat across from a television and VCR on a modest wooden stand. A battered coffee table from his college dorm room sat on top of a moth-bitten forest green and maroon imitation Oriental rug that was probably as old as he was. Bookshelves lined the walls holding books of many genres. Some well-read copies of Stephen King's novels sprinkled with other horror suspense writers like Dean Koontz and John Saul lined the first two shelves, the obligatory Clive Barker edition on the end. A particularly precious copy of Sophocles' Oedipus Rex sat alone on the third shelf above the others, its spine creased and worn, its cover old and yellowed.

On the walls hung family portraits that spanned as far back as the late 1800s. His father's portrait hung on the far right wall, at James' right hand if he were seated behind the desk. He watched over the room with a look of foreboding. James would sometimes find himself in a daze staring at the likeness of his father, drawn to it, unable to look away. Unable to blink.

His great-great grandfather's portrait hung behind the desk. The frame that held the impressive rendering was so heavy, one would think it was made of pure gold. The eyes, like those of many portraits, looked as though they were keeping watch over his brood, as he was rumored to do, even in death.

James walked over to the VCR to check the time. 7:30 p.m. He had missed almost an entire day. He walked back to his desk pondering when he picked himself up from the floor, when he put his clothes on, if he had spoken to his wife, and how he had gotten to the office. He sat back in the desk chair feeling the imprint accept him as it always does, the warm seat inviting him to lounge. He breathed deeply, looking around the room. Everything looked the same as it always did; dark and covered with a light film of dust. Andrea rarely cleaned the office. She told him that she didn't like going into the room because of the paintings.

"They're creepy," she said the day he hung his father's painting. "I feel like they're staring at me."

As James glanced over at his father's portrait, he decided he agreed with her. They were staring and disliking what they saw.

James raised his hand to the top of his head and stretched, reclining in the chair. When he brought his hands down to rest on the table, they brushed against a pad sitting in the center of the writing mat. The top page was full of words in handwriting that James barely recognized as his own. He ripped the page from the pad and looked closer at it, trying to read the words written in hasty, amateurish scrawl.

For protection. For me.

The phrase was repeated across the page, on every line, covering almost all of the white space. The letters were written in varying sizes; some cursive, some block, some slanted, some upright. Some sentences started with capital letters, some with lower case letters. The words formed a rhythmic meter as he read them, resounding in him like an accentual verse of poetry or a divine incantation, repeated there, echoing hypnotically in the chambers of his mind. *For protection. For me. For protection. For me. For protection. For me.* James shook his head, trying to mute the mesmerizing sound.

His hands curled around the edges of the paper as he peered at the writing. His grip was tight and damp, crumbling the corners of the paper. His eyes ran across the phrase line by line, word for word, trying to make sense of it. The terrible chant droned on in his head, matching his pace.

James suddenly dropped the piece of paper, freeing his hands of it, as though burned by the fibers. The phrase, visible even as it cascaded to the desk as though written in bold, continued to chant in his head, getting louder as his anxiety heightened.

Everything spiraled out of focus while James stared at the piece of paper; the desk rotated in front of him, carrying the sheet with its nonsensical phrase further and further away until it was nothing more than a white rectangular blur. The walls around him spun, blurring the faces of his ancestors as they went by, the colors merging together as they whirled. James reached for the armrests of his chair to steady himself. His hands descended well past where the armrests should have been, into the darkness that seemed to rise from the floor and blanket everything in its wake.

Everything was gone.

The office, the desk behind which he sat only a moment before, the banker's lamp whose illumination he saw out of the corner of his eye underneath its green cover - everything was gone. He was seated in a wicker, low back chair on a wooden porch facing a forgotten outer borough street. It was just past dusk and the evening sky was changing from violet to midnight blue. The night was still.

Behind him, boarded windows and doors covered with graffiti marked a house that had once belonged to a shut-in old woman who muttered to herself all day as she paced in her garden. Sometimes she would venture into the street stopping traffic as she ranted and raved about the dogs that kept coming into her yard and urinating on her plants. "They're killing them!" she would scream in a high-pitched voice that cracked and broke at its height, like a teenage boy experiencing puberty. Spittle sprayed from her mouth as she yelled, her head slightly upturned as she shouted her words to the air. She would pace in the middle of the quiet street seething about what the dogs (mangy mongrels, she had called them) had done to her precious garden. She wandered several streets over in search of the phantom dogs that were ruining her tomatoes and herbs. She always came back empty handed, though, and it was no surprise to anyone watching her. There weren't any dogs within three blocks of her house, hadn't been any for years. And the garden that she was so protective of was nonexistent. It may have produced plump tomatoes and fragrant herbs at one time or another—the dirt patch was still blocked off from the grass bed, at least somewhat—but that was long ago. All that remained was an overgrown patch of weeds and twigs rimmed by a wire fence whose paint had long ago chipped away, exposing the metal underneath to the elements.

Aside from hunting down phantom dogs and the occasional trip to the local supermarket, the woman never came out of the house. Whenever anyone saw her, she always looked the same: an old woman who might have been considered pretty before time and suffering weathered her looks. She would be dressed in a coat that was two sizes larger than her frame with turned over nurse's shoes covering her feet. She wasn't particularly dirty, just disheveled. Her torn housedress added to her mystique. Her graying hair would be gathered up in a bun, more hair hanging in wayward wisps than drawn up. She was wild-eyed and paranoid, always casting a glance over her shoulder in search of the stalker that was following her.

Sometimes she would stop and stare at a child that had been walking behind her eating candy or reading a comic book as he strolled on the sidewalk, not paying attention to the woman standing in front of him. She would stare at him, her gaze unwavering, as he approached her, oblivious. When the child finally looked up to see the crazy lady from the house on the corner staring at him, he would be paralyzed with fear. The comic book would undoubtedly fall to the ground, the candy either swallowed wrong or hitting the ground with an audible crack as it broke into little pieces. She would just stand there, watching. The child would run away, moving as fast as his legs would carry him, abandoning the comic book or candy on the street. Still, she watched. Some people thought she took pleasure in terrifying the children in the neighborhood, randomly picking one to stare at and torture in silence. But she never cracked a smile at the fear on a child's face, never once chuckled as a child scrambled away from her. She only stared.

Most times the woman kept to herself, preferring to look at the ground when she walked instead of making eye contact with a neighbor. She would rather talk to herself than speak to someone on the street. And that was all right. People had come to expect that kind of behavior from her. They had never known her to be any other way. No one ever paid any attention to her, good or bad. Her eccentricity was tolerated. She was just the crazy old woman who lived in the house on the corner.

She had been dead for days before anyone knew it. The only reason she was ever found was because her neighbor complained about a horrible smell emanating from her house. Mr. Parker went to Ms. Boone's house that day, half expecting to find that she had caught one of those dogs she had been complaining about for years and left its body outside to stink up the place. He knocked on the door to tell her as much. When she didn't answer he looked in the window and saw her lying face down on the floor between the living room and dining room.

Things went the way things go after that. Some long-lost relative came to claim whatever was left, and apparently there was a lot, despite appearances. Old Ms. Boone, who was Lillian Boone of the New York Boones, thank you very much, had a meager ceremony attended by Mr. Parker and his wife, Mr. Washington from the corner store, and two Boone relatives. As it was, Mr. Parker and his wife only went because they had lived next to the old kook for more than 20 years and thought it was only right to see her off. The Boones went so that they wouldn't feel guilty later. After all, they were inheriting the woman's estate, and after taxes that would come to somewhere around two million dollars. It seemed like the right thing to do. No sooner than Ms. Lillian Boone was brought to her final resting place at Cedar Grove Cemetery did the Boones of the New York Boones fly back to New York to spend their newfound money.

Mr. Parker found out that Lillian Boone had left New York years before following behind a man who had promised her a life of luxury. She didn't need any of the money he could give her; she had her own. What she wanted was a life filled with love, children's feet pitter-pattering down the halls, a white picket fence surrounding the house, and Golden Retrievers lounging on the lawn. Instead, she got a gigolo out for a buck, an apartment in Northeast Washington, and maxed out credit card bills. She moved to the Silver Spring, Maryland neighborhood some 20 years before she died, heartbroken and slow witted. The family thought that she hadn't returned to New York because she was angry at the way they had treated her man friend. None of the Boones were nice to him, not even civil. They were rarely, if ever, pleasant to people who didn't run in their circles, and they didn't treat Lillian's beau any differently than anyone else they came across that wasn't cut from their cloth. The family thought Lillian held a grudge against them because of it, that she was angry with them for not accepting the man in her life and treating him with kindness instead of condescension. But that wasn't what Mr. Parker thought. Mr. Parker thought Lillian never went back to New York because she was empty-handed.

After Lillian Boone's death, the house was abandoned. The Boones never did anything with it. No new tenants moved in, and the state didn't request that the Boones' do anything about the disarray it had fallen into—there wasn't a homeowner's association established in the neighborhood to mandate that the homeowners perform basic upkeep on their property. There really wasn't a need for one, there or anywhere, back then. People cared more about their property then. They looked at their houses and lawns as extensions of themselves. So, the men worked all day in the hot Saturday sun mowing the lawn and drinking beer. The women washed the windows regularly and planted gardens that added splashes of reds and yellows, giving color to the brick fronts and white molding. They did it because everyone else was doing it, not because someone told them they had to. Because it made them feel presentable, the way donning a tuxedo changes a man's stride and posture.

The families that lived on the street considered the house an eyesore, but no one ever tried to do anything about it. If you had asked Evelyn Patterson—the only resident left in the neighborhood who lived there when Lillian Boone was alive—why no one ever tended to the Boone yard she would tell you that there was something about that house that made everyone shy away. A strong-willed bear of a woman who shot pool with her husband's work buddies, and smoked two packs of cigarettes a day, she wasn't one for skittishness. She would never be the woman standing on furniture to avoid a mouse, no; she would be the woman ridding the trap of the rodent's carcass. In spite of her stern demeanor the Boone house troubled her, gave her pause, made the hairs on her forearms and neck stand on end if she got too close. The Boone house got to everyone on the street. Even her.

Evelyn would have told you that there was something strange about that house, even after Lillian was dead and buried. Something that seemed to emanate from it, surround it like a force field. She would have told you this from personal knowledge. She had walked the sidewalk in front of the house once in an effort to allay her fears about the house. Fears that were never uttered, but present in all of the residents on the street. She made it as far as the front door on the sidewalk before she stopped. She would tell you that she tried to lift her leg and take the next step, but something wouldn't let her walk forward. Instead, some force tried to make her turn to the left and start up the walkway to the house. To the front door. She would say that a scream escaped her lips as she pulled herself out of the house's grasp. She'd recount how she ran back to her house covered in a film of pungent sweat and shaking like a leaf caught in a breeze. She'd tell you how she swore to never return to that house, no matter what. How she'd vowed never to so much as cast a wayward glance towards that evil place. She'd tell you all of that if she was still able to talk. She lost her voice to laryngeal cancer a decade before. Nowadays all she did was putter around the house, rarely stepping foot outside. Much like Lillian Boone did in the years before her death. Evelyn often thought of this when she sat in her window. She had broken her vow of not looking at the Boone house a year after the surgery. Now, nine years later, she looked at it often, sometimes all day long. It was all she had left.

Evelyn would have only been echoing the sentiments of everyone else that lived on the street. No one wanted to go near the Boone house. Neither kids nor adults. They thought it was haunted like every abandoned house from the beginning of time has been rumored to be. That is, if you listened to the children in the neighborhood or gave any credence to the town gossip. People said they could still hear old Ms. Boone yelling about the dogs, or better yet, could smell the urine in her garden. The rumors rolled on and on, picking up speed as they went, packing on more fodder over the years. People stopped walking on the sidewalk in front of it, crossing the street before reaching the house. This was especially so after hearing Evelyn's story, the facts surrounding it sounding more sensational with every telling. They were afraid that old crazy Ms. Boone would come running out at them, whether they'd admit it or not. Everyone has a hint of Evelyn Patterson in them, after all.

As the years passed and the firsthand accounts were padded heavily with embellishment and imagination, people avoided the side of the street where the Boone house stood all together. Unless they were one of the two unfortunate families to border the Boone house, no one ventured down the road that way. The street itself was a circular through street with exits on both sides. If you didn't want to see the Boone house you didn't have to. After a while even the cautious glances people would sometimes cast at the dilapidated house tapered off. They were terrified of what they might see.

The neighborhood started to fall apart in the years after Lillian

Boone's death. Drugs infiltrated the quiet neighborhood, and with them came reckless abandon. Anyone who cared about the aesthetics of the Boone house and the surrounding area moved away in search of a new town, preferably one impregnable by the craziness going on in the world. The houses they left behind were filled with a different kind of people, ones who didn't care about what their house looked like, inside or out. Ones who couldn't give a damn about the Boone house.

The winos and drug addicts who haunted the town at night started breaking into the house to squat. They used the back door, loosening a board that had been shoddily thrown up to block entry into the house. They slept on Lillian's left behind mattress, waiting for morning to come so they could hustle for their next fix.

James sat with his back to the old house in stunned silence. He was almost certain that he had never been there before yet everything seemed so familiar. The dingy smell of urine, stale potato chips, and rotting garbage was repulsive but expected. But that wasn't the only thing that made his hands grow cold and clammy, or made his stomach quiver in anticipation. As he took in his surroundings the feeling of déjà vu resonated sourly in his chest. The old Victorian house itself was familiar to him. From the wrap-around porch he was sitting on to the short picket fence surrounding the patchy grass and trampled, overgrown garden. He knew this place.

He stood up to take a look around, walking off the porch and onto the concrete walkway that led to the house. The grass on either side of the cracked walkway was tall and overtaken by weeds. Crickets chirped from somewhere in the thick, adding music to the otherwise quiet evening.

Someone came out of the shadows, almost bumping into him. A drunk staggered into the walkway in front of him, filling the air with the smell of regurgitated liquor. James recoiled from the smell. He stepped backwards quickly, raising his right hand to his nose reflexively, trying to block out the sour smell. The stench was nauseating. He could feel his stomach turning over. He started to back away; to step into the shadows and disappear from sight so the man could pass. He didn't want to run the risk of colliding with the man and getting a full whiff of his odor. That was one reason. The other reason wasn't as obvious to him. Call it instinct, call it gut, call it whatever you like. Something inside him told him to move away. To hide.

The wino looked him squarely in the face, recognizing him. He mumbled a greeting that James couldn't make out and stumbled by, rushing to an overgrown shrub to vomit a second or third time. James started to walk away from the man and away from the house. Listening to the man struggle and pant was making bile rise in his throat. He had almost crossed the street when he heard the man speak again.

"Back again."

James turned back and looked at the man incredulously, but he was already staggering into the tenebrous night. For a long while James stood there, half on the sidewalk and half in the street, looking back at the house. The man was long gone but his words hung in the air.

Back again.

The world seemed to be getting darker as he stared back at the house, his vision growing dimmer with every second that passed. He could still see the plywood boards that covered the windows from where he stood, though not as well as he had before. The boards were thrown up haphazardly, barely covering the glass of one window and overflowing onto the shutters on another, as though a child had done the job. A dim light was shining behind the window. He stared at it, was drawn to it. *Was that light on before?* he wondered as he approached the porch steps, his legs seeming to move on their own, step after step bringing him closer to the house. He drifted closer, unaware that he was even drawing near the window until he was so close his nose almost hit the protruding board.

There was something moving on the other side of the glass.

James started to pull at it suddenly knowing that he had to see what was behind the board, no matter what it was. The thought that it might only be squatters rustling around occurred to him, but he dismissed it almost as quickly as he had thought of it. There was something in there pulling at him, talking to him, yes, he could now hear the voices that had been talking to him just under the surface of his sanity since he had found himself in front of the strangely familiar house. They were whispering to him, almost chanting, telling him to pull the board down and go inside.

He tugged at it until the board broke free. For a moment the light was so bright it blinded him. James blinked as the brightness gave way to a dull beam. He peered through the gummy window, wanting to see. Needing to see. There was a body on the floor lying face down between the living room and dining room. James could see an old woman with pale, lifeless skin staring at him. Her face was turned toward the window frozen in a grimace of pain. Her mouth was open as though she had tried to scream when she took her last breath. Her left nostril was caked with dried blood, and a brown stream of it led to her contorted mouth.

The woman lifted her head and fixed her gaze on him. He stared back at her, the voices in his head getting louder as they spoke inaudible words to him. He was transfixed to the window as though his head was locked in a vice, and his eyes were held open by toothpicks. He couldn't pull his eyes away from the woman on the other side of the glass.

The old woman rose to her feet revealing a nightgown that was rumpled and moth bitten. The front was streaked with what looked like dried blood. She took a tentative step towards the window then three unnaturally quick and sure ones until she was looking right at him. The woman, long dead, stood as close to the window on the inside as James did on the outside. Only the glass separated them. *What if the glass breaks and she grabs me?* James thought, suddenly panicked. But still, he could not move.

The woman's skin seemed to rot in front of James' eyes. She stared at him as if she knew who he was. Like she knew his very soul. Sweat poured down James' immobile face as he stared back, unable to tear his eyes away from her. Fear enveloped him, invading the air around him with its thickness. He felt claustrophobic under its weight.

The woman's eyes rolled into the back of her head as she fell to the floor with a dull thud that made James sick. He squeezed his eyes shut, willing himself to wake up from the terrible nightmare.

The voices stopped.

Hope crept into James at the sudden silence. He allowed himself to indulge in the idea that he was waking up. He fantasized that he was in his own bed with his wife. He told himself that as soon as he opened his eyes he would be at home, waking up to a leisurely Sunday morning. The memory of this terrible nightmare would begin to fade in the light of day and would be completely forgotten by the time he finished his first yawn. He stood a second longer with his eyes shut against the dream world where a dead woman had come back to life and stared at him through a dirty window. He squeezed them even tighter, praying that the bright morning sun would fill his eyes instead of the derelict house that had crowded his vision a moment before. The face of the dead woman crept into the darkness of his mind staring at him as she had from behind the glass. He shuddered at the clarity of the vision, powerless to wipe it away.

It will all be over when I open my eyes, he told himself. Even as he said it in his mind and aloud, he didn't believe it. He could still feel the heaviness of the air around him, closing in on him, crawling on his skin like a spider.

When he opened his eyes, he found himself still standing in front of the house, but it was different somehow. He had made his way to the back door and was standing in the tall grass that rimmed the walkway. The back of the house showed the same wear as the front did; shutters hung lopsided from the sides of the windows, the paint on the window frames and molding was chipped, and the steps to the back door were warped and splintered.

James' knees felt weak as he looked at the house. A sense of dread, new and cold, ran across his body. He wanted to leave.

He considered shutting his eyes again but decided against it. He could feel the air on his face as he had when he was in the front yard wishing his way back home. He could feel blades of grass and the tough stalks of weeds brushing against his legs. Everything felt real. He didn't know what that meant, but he knew that shutting his eyes wouldn't work. This dream was different. This dream didn't seem like a dream at all.

It was completely silent, both in his head and around the house. Even the crickets had stopped singing their night song. The silence was louder than the continuous chanting that had occupied his mind before, obliterating all conscious thought. Somehow the silence frightened him more.

James stood in place for a long while watching and listening. No one came out of the house, and as far as James could tell, he was the only person on the outside of the house. He approached the steps tenuously, realizing that he had no other choice but to go in. Whatever was happening wouldn't end until he went inside.

The back door creaked open. The board that had barricaded it had been torn free and thrown on the ground next to the steps. He entered the kitchen stepping carefully. The floor was a huddled mass of snoring squatters competing for space. He walked slowly through the kitchen following the path that led to the living room, trying not to disturb their fitful sleep. A body lay in the middle of the floor between the living room and dining room. James approached it, his body tense, assuming the body was that of the old woman. He stood under the separator beam, afraid to take a step into the living room, but knowing he had to. The voices started again and James was dismally aware that they were no longer coming from his head, but from within the house. He turned around to see the squatters piled in behind him, red-eyed and dirty, chanting at him in a bloodcurdling drone.

The mass of bodies was lurching closer and closer now. James turned to run, intending to go out through the front door. Surely, he could kick it down, even with the flimsy board nailed to the molding outside. But a middle-aged woman blocked his way. She was wearing a sweater and jeans, the front of both were soaked in blood. The right side of her head was misshapen and her light brown hair was matted with blood.

She looked at him, her right eye a mass of broken capillaries, and smiled.

CHAPTER 8

"It's good to have you back, Jimmie," the woman said, her voice raspy and detached, rising above the squatters' mounting chant.

"Who are you?" James asked, paralyzed, unable to back up for fear of being engulfed by the squatters, and unwilling to move forward into the dead woman's arms.

"Oh Jimmie," the woman laughed, her smile stretching across broken teeth and discolored, bleeding gums.

Her face was ravaged. Blood streaked her cheek and lined her forehead. Exposed tissue peaked out of the top of her head. Her right cheekbone had been crushed. Her nose had shifted impossibly to the left. A sickly blue-green tint colored her skin, just beneath the surface.

Her left eye was undamaged. It pierced him, begging him to remember. James stared at her unwillingly, the same feeling of immobility that he had felt outside the window returning with renewed strength. The corners of her eyes softened, the look almost endearing. James felt his breath catch in his throat as he watched her face contort, forcing the remaining skin to form an expression of familiarity. A deafening scream rang in his head when knowledge dawned on him, crashing to the ground like a glass breaking in the silence of night. Her face held a gruesome smile of invitation.

Warmth beat upon his neck as the squatters closed in on him. They grabbed his arms, holding him in place as the woman approached him. She unbuttoned his shirt and ran her cold hands down his chest.

"No!" he yelled futilely, unable to raise his own hand to push hers away. His skin felt feverish underneath the cold flesh of her hands. A chill shot through him as she touched his chest, her caress feeling like tiny sharp pricks piercing the tender skin of his areolas. The cold seemed to bore through his skin to his very bones.

Her palms were hard, all of the soft tissue below the thumb and sides of her hands had worn away. James could feel the bones in her hands raking his skin, rubbing it raw as she ran her hands across his chest.

"No," he said once more, hoarse with fear now. She smiled at the sound of his voice, cracked and defeated, revealing teeth that were smeared with fresh blood.

She leaned towards him as a lover would in anticipation of a kiss. James tried to recoil, pulling his head backwards with all the strength he could muster, but he only succeeded in offering a twitch in the way of actual movement. His voice, though, came back rich and full.

"Get away from me!" he bellowed, his voice deepening with emphasis.

She stopped in front of him as the rumble in his voice subsided and regarded his face. For a moment their eyes locked in recognition, although James would never fully understand the emotions that danced behind hers. A fetid odor emitted from her mouth as she laughed, louder than before; the sound that came from her diaphragm and pushed through her mouth with force, pushing her breath out in heavy gusts. She laughed freely, almost gleefully, but not without a tinge of sarcasm. The sound was chilling.

The momentary feeling of control that James found when the woman stopped coming towards him melted away as her laughter intensified. He could feel himself shaking against her and hated himself for it.

And then, she stopped. Her face, upturned while she laughed, lost the sickening smile it had held, and looked at him again with a quickness not possessed by the living. Her eyes stared at him more intensely, her face more determined now. James could hear the fear in his voice when he said beseechingly,

"What do you want from me?"

As his shouted, protests gave way to shrieks of fear, the woman's mouth closed over his.

CHAPTER 9

"Oh Jimmie," he heard as he stood over her, stroking himself. She lay beneath him, her nipples sitting atop her soft breasts, alert and ready for his mouth to suck them. Her light brown hair was spread across the pillow framing her enraptured face. He ran his finger slowly between her breasts and down to her navel as he pleasured himself. He enjoyed making her wait, making her beg for it.

She arched her back as he pressed his lips to her neck. Her moans broke the silence of the room, bouncing off the walls and echoing in his ears, arousing him. He kissed her mouth, their tongues dancing together slowly in step. His hand slid beneath her, tracing her spine and cupping her buttocks. Her hands caressed his back and shoulders, gently pressing him downward in expectation.

His alertness heightened as he felt her hands on his back. The sensations were so vivid. Her hips grinding against his, the softness of her breasts pressed against his chest, her breath against his skin; everything grew more intense. Her nipples seemed to stab at him in their erectness. Her hands felt as though they were kneading circles in his trapezius muscles, rather than just caressing the skin on top of them. A burning sensation spread through his shoulders, down his spine, and over his buttocks.

The burning increased; his skin was flushed and hot. He could feel beads of sweat rising on his forehead. And he liked it. He tilted her hips toward his and entered her, sinking instantly into her warmth. He closed his eyes and rolled his head back in ecstasy.

Her hands were strong and deliberate as they massaged his back. They plotted circles beneath his shoulder blades, cresting with every thrust and touching the base with every withdrawal. Her index fingers walked his spine. They pressed harder and harder as he pushed into her, matching pressure for pressure, pain for pleasure. James called out, his voice a mixture of rapture and pain, a sound that rivaled ones made during the throes of birth and death at the same time, the intensity palpable. It was more than he could bear. Her hands seemed to rub his skin raw and strum the muscles underneath. Yet he couldn't stop. It made him nervous, this inability to stop himself, to pull away from her. He didn't want to leave her warmth no matter how much he wanted release from the sweet pain of her touch. He wasn't sure if he wanted release from her hands at all. He pressed into her harder, faster, as the pain mounted, faster still as his own voice rang in his ears, crying out. His mind clouded, filled only with the pleasures of the body and the pain attacking his senses. He was obsessed with it. Soon he knew nothing more than the enfolding warmth of her loins, and the hot needles of her fingers. The squeaking mattress, the headboard slamming against the wall with every pump, all of those sounds were muted. There was only her. There was only the pain and the pleasure.

Then it stopped. Her caress became gentle, feminine. Her soft hands ran across his shoulders like satin. His skin responded, goose bumps dotting his arms and back in the wake of her touch. The anxiety had vanished, dried up like the sweat that stood on his brow only moments before. His mind tried to hold on to the memory of his burning back, aching from the touch of skin against it. He wanted to use that memory to sober him up, to snap him out of the hypnosis within which she controlled him, kept him imprisoned. But then he felt her against him again, coaxing him back to the moment. Her hair tickled his chest as she teased him. He could feel the heat of her breath surrounding him again, could smell the tangy sweetness of it in the air. And he was aroused.

He felt her take his breast in her mouth. He opened his eyes and saw her sucking on a nipple, circling it with her tongue and biting it gently before engulfing it again into her mouth. Pleasantly surprised at the inclusion of another woman, he smiled and prepared to make room. Before he could move, he felt an uncharacteristic tingling sensation in his pecks that paralyzed him. He moaned in spite of his confusion and felt his nipples harden. He felt her hands run across his breasts, patterning them lightly. His mind rushed between confusion at the change in his body and his desire to see what other pleasures his body would reveal. She switched positions, perching on top of him. He moved easily with unaccustomed grace as he settled into the warm bed sheets. She kissed his lips sweetly, her tongue probing his mouth, finding his tongue and circling it slowly. He felt light, uninhibited, and sensuous as she caressed his slim hips, and gently pressed her pelvis against his. His body seemed out of his control. It felt different to the touch. His skin, smoother now, was hot with excitement. He touched his breasts and felt round, supple skin. He pinched his nipples playfully, out of both arousal and to determine whether or not he was awake.

She replaced his hands with hers and rolled his nipples between her fingers.

"You like that, huh?"

She whispered so quietly he questioned whether she had spoken at all. Her hands were caressing his inner thighs, thighs that felt soft and feminine like never before. He could feel himself tingling, a light film of sweat forming on his forehead and stomach. The sensations were so new! She lowered her body and he thought he knew what was coming next. He couldn't feel it, but he was sure his penis was rock hard and throbbing, anxiously awaiting the sensation of her lips as she engulfed the head. Instead, he felt the gentlest of licks on a knobby, pulsating piece of flesh.

He wanted to sit up and see what was going on, his mind rebelling against the sensation he most surely felt, but his passion overtook him as he nuzzled the pillow. His mouth agape, he moaned in a voice that was not his own. The tongue that confused and pleased him at the same time stroked his clitoris rhythmically as a finger played at the base of his labia. His breathing increased as he felt himself approaching his climax. His heart raced from the anticipation. His muscles began to tremble uncontrollably as he coasted towards overwhelming release.

"Do you like that, Jimmie?" he heard faintly, distantly. Just as he was about to succumb to his desire a shrill, mocking laugh penetrated his thoughts. His eyes snapped open, and for a moment, he saw the concave silhouette of her head—Andrea's head—laughing on top of the decaying body that was straddling him, holding his legs in a vice grip.

He flipped her over, pinning her under his weight. Feeling his upper body strength return, he reached for the neck of the nightmarish visage. As his hand closed around her neck James saw her change. Her skin was no longer decaying and her head was not misshapen. All traces of Andrea faded out of her face. The woman beneath him seemed to change while he watched, her skin growing flush and tan, her eyes darkening. She looked back at him with sparkling eyes that danced in amusement. She wet her lips expectantly as she watched him, her ridiculing laughter still echoing from her seductive lips.

"What's the matter Jimmie?" she cackled. "Cat got your tongue?"

His vision was blurred by his emotions. He could barely see

who was underneath him. He did not feel himself thrust inside the woman, angrily slamming his pelvis into hers. His hands squeezed tighter around her neck as he thrust into her. He pressed his thumb into her esophagus, his grip growing stronger as his pleasure mounted. He didn't hear her screams nor feel her hands clawing at his arms. He only felt her loins stroke him as he moved in and out, in and out.

As her breath left her and her glassy eyes stared up at him, he rode her, grunting with each pump, and musing about the wonderful fuck he was giving her. He pulled out in time to ejaculate on her lifeless face. As he rested, still straddling her, he noticed her bloodshot eyes and the trail of blood that ran down her chin.

And screamed.

CHAPTER 10

James awoke with a gasp that was audible only in his head. He tried to sit up but found that his arms and legs were pinned to the bed. He tried to lift his head from the pillow but couldn't. He tried to stretch his legs but wasn't able to do that either. Panicking, he tried to call out, to wake Andrea from her slumber so that she could help him, but he had no voice. He could hear himself screaming in his head but all that escaped his lips was an almost inaudible moan, airy and strained, as his breath pushed relentlessly at the roof of his mouth.

He was completely immobile; the paralysis affected every part of his body including his eyes. He couldn't move them up or down or from side to side. A numbness had come over him, his skin felt dull and detached. His arms lay in what would have appeared to be a casual position: one resting inches away from his hip, the other bent comfortably underneath his head. He could feel the strands of his hair pressing against the palm of his hand. He tried to grab at them but couldn't move his fingers.

He started to hyperventilate as, after a couple of seconds that felt more like minutes, he still couldn't move. His breath came sharply, pushing out of his mouth and cutting the outside air. He imagined his chest rising and falling with every breath but couldn't tilt his head enough to see if it was happening. Again, he moaned, the sound like a deafening roar in his head but a mere whimper in reality.

The sun shone in the room from the window behind the chaise lounge setting the tone for the day. A film of sweat coated James' body as he lay motionless. He could feel his uncovered toes warming in the sun's rays that filtered in through the sheer drapes. He tried to wriggle them. Nothing happened.

Crazed now with a desire to move, James sighed as loudly as he could, forcing the air out of his lungs. The effort caused nothing more than a faint whistle to emanate from his lips. Encouraged that the sound was louder than the muted moans he had been able to emit earlier, James sucked in air and exhaled as loudly as he could repetitiously. The whistle grew louder and louder with each breath but it still wasn't loud enough to rouse Andrea from her sleep.

James tried to move one of his limbs again. This time something happened. He moved his hand a little on the bed, the sheet rumpling underneath his fingers. He tried again and moved it a little more. He tried to shift his eyes and got a little movement from them, changing his view from straight ahead at the ceiling to the molding between the ceiling and far wall. He kept trying to move, exercising his muscles to coax them out of the paralysis that met him when he opened his eyes.

His mind raced as he tried to work his muscles. Part of him knew that what was happening to him wasn't permanent, that a nerve in his neck was causing this and he would soon be able to move normally. But another part of him thought that he would forever be in this state of immobility, that some unknown illness had taken over his nervous system and rendered him motionless overnight, without warning. It was this same irrational side that sent a wave of fear over him when a shadow was cast in the room unexpectedly. He tried to tell himself that a cloud had covered the sun and that bright sunlight would illuminate the room again within seconds, but the irrational side wouldn't listen. Instead, it filled his mind with evil images from the netherworld, chthonian four-legged beings: bestial, animalistic creatures that resembled a sordid cross between lizard and lion except for their deformed human heads crawling towards him, their underbellies gliding just above the ground. As the shadow moved across the room, James envisioned the atrocities creeping up on him, just below his view, their talons tangling in the carpet, their mouths open revealing sharpened canines whose conical shape was wide at the gum and finely tapered to a point at the base. He shuddered, feeling the fear rise within him as he lay vulnerable on the bed, unable to fend off any attack that might come.

He could hear voices now, jumbled voices, all of them chanting the same tune but at different speeds, and with different inflections. They echoed in his mind, bouncing off the walls, reverberating off each other, clashing and distorting. The sound was maddening, moving in and out of earshot, fading, and then blaring deafeningly. The sound was erratic, as though it was coming from a rudimentary rotating speaker.

The voices grew louder as the room darkened. James was sure the voices belonged to the diabolical creatures lurking at the foot of his bed preparing to pounce on his prone body. He tried to move again with no luck. Sweat broke out on his skin, heavy now, the effort exhausting him. The voices grew louder, closer in his mind. His eyes were shrouded by the darkness, its blackness covering them like a blindfold. He could feel the creatures closing in, could smell their putrid breath—he could feel their sickening warmth on his skin. Waiting. Biding their time. He screamed in terror, the sound quieting all others as it filled him, obliterating the thoughts in his mind, clearing it, until there was nothing but the blinding white light of fear.

The sound broke through his mind and out into the darkness of the room. James' voice went from silent to piercingly loud as he freed himself from the strange paralysis that had kept him silent and still. The mix between dream state and waking life had been odd enough. Coupling that with the inability to move or speak had left him shaken.

James sat up with a start, rising to his feet beside the bed in the same movement. The cry of fear died on his lips as he looked into the blinding light of the sun, unveiled again. He scanned the room, desperate for confirmation that he was awake, and not embroiled in another multi-faceted nightmare. He didn't see any sign of the beasts he had been sure were lurking at the foot of his bed, watching him. In the light of day, the image of the creatures didn't seem so monstrous; the idea of them struck him as silly then, when the room was filled with light. In fact, the experience itself didn't seem so frightening as he stood looking back at the bed to which he was confined only moments before.

The pungent smell of adrenaline and sweat wafted up to his nose. His skin felt warm and clammy from the sweat. The heat of his skin was oppressive. He inhaled deeply, welcoming the air into his lungs. He exhaled slowly, trying to calm himself down.

The room looked normal. The armoire was open revealing a blackened picture tube as it had been before. A copy of a well-read Vivian Schilling novel laid open on the chaise lounge, its cover shining in the sunlight streaming in from the window behind it. Everything seemed to be in order. He turned to his wife's side of the bed, terrified that she would pull him back into the frightening reality that things were far from normal. But her side of the bed was empty, the bed sheets crumpled and bunched at the foot of the bed. Normal. Andrea typically rose early on the weekends to take in the mornings with a cup of Hazelnut coffee and her bootie slippers.

James' shoulders began to relax as the morning opened up to him. A breeze trickled in from the open window, reassuring him in its caress that he was awake. The warmth from the sun on his face turned cold as soon as his senses became aware of it. He braced his hands on the side of the bed, suddenly shivering. How many dreams had he had? He couldn't sort them out; they all ran together in his mind. As he sat, his legs trembling as they hung off the side of the bed, the door opened and Andrea raced into the room.

"James? Are you all right?"

Concern spread across her face, pinching her forehead and pursing her lips. She moved to him quickly, kneeling in front of her husband who looked like a child scared of the boogeyman hiding in the closet.

"My God, James. You're shaking. Are you all right?" she asked more insistently this time.

He waited a long time to answer, studying her face. She looked normal. Her silk robe folded across her body, contouring to her breasts, holding them snuggly in the navy material. The silk created a V on her chest allowing him a glimpse of cleavage as she knelt in front of him. Her face, though concerned, was as he remembered it.

This was Andrea. His wife.

As he began to believe what he was seeing, just when he was starting to believe that he was really awake, a feeling of trepidation and remorse hit him profoundly, making tears well in his eyes. He wanted to tell her, to get it over with and reveal what had been tormenting him for months. God, maybe it would end the nightmares.

"Honey?"

Andrea stared at James, keeping eye contact with him, hoping to bring him back to her and away from the mystical world that had been plaguing his dreams. "James?"

"I'm okay, babe," he lied. He would tell her. Just not today. Not when the love in her eyes shined so brightly the morning sun seemed dim.

"I heard you screaming," she sighed as she rose from her knees to sit next to him on the bed. She put her arms around his shoulders and hugged him. "It was the scariest thing I've ever heard."

James couldn't take his eyes off her. It was as if he was seeing her for the first time. The morning light framing her face, the gentleness of her eyes as she looked at him with love. How could he ever tell her? How could he have ever betrayed her?

"Was it another dream?" she asked, unaware of the shadows covering his eyes.

Images rushed back into his head. Misshapen silhouettes, an abandoned house, impenetrable darkness. He dropped his head into his hands.

"Yes," he said as he rubbed his forehead, trying to erase the memory.

"They're getting worse, aren't they?" Andrea's voice was thick with worry.

"They're just dreams."

Even as he dismissed them to Andrea, he knew they weren't just dreams. It wasn't that simple. Not for him. They were more than that. Memory mixed with imagination, mixed with clairvoyance, hell, he was willing to buy any explanation. But to say it was just a dream? Just involuntary sensations and images? No.

His dreams didn't fade like dreams were supposed to. Their power didn't diminish in the minutes after he woke up; they didn't drift away. These dreams weren't transitory the way his childhood dreams had been. When he was a boy, nightmares of some boogeyman or another would wake him from his sleep and thrust him into the blindness of night, his eyes clamoring to adjust to the darkness before the thing from his dreams got to him. By the time his mother made it to his room the memory of the monster was all but gone. The tears would dry up more from bewilderment than from subsided fear. The dream—the intensity of it—the cold grip he had been held in, would be gone almost as soon as he woke up.

But not these.

These dreams caused him to wake up from a fitful sleep with

his head aching. His mind would be cluttered with images, disjointed yet horrific. He couldn't shake them no matter how hard he tried. Where normal dreams would fade in the early moments of alertness, the images from his dreams lingered in his mind, milling there until they found an empty corner in which to curl up and rest. He likened them to memories rather than concoctions of his imagination—memories of terror, as though he had lived the horrors himself. Nothing from them was ever lost; no emotion, no feeling ever lessened as the sunlight of a new day flooded his eyes. In his dreams the colors were always as vivid in his mind as they would be if he were seeing them in an awakened state. They remained as such when he woke up, as lustrous as when he first saw them in his sleep. The dreams echoed in his subconscious, thumping melodically like the acoustic bass of a mariachi guitarron. They were always there, just beneath the surface.

He started to wonder if they were really dreams after all.

What was happening to him was anything but random. Something wanted him to know of its presence.

"Maybe we should see someone about this, honey," Andrea said as she laid back on the bed and turned toward him. His back was dripping with sweat. "These dreams seem like they came from out of nowhere."

James heard his wife talking but he couldn't respond. Her voice usually had a soothing effect on him, lulling him into a sense of security rivaled by nothing else in his life. But this time it sounded like it was coming from the end of a tunnel, muted and distorted. He was daydreaming about Susan. The way her eyes danced when she saw him walking to their secret spot or at the small restaurant, they loved just twenty miles outside of town. The way her body felt hot under his touch. The closed casket at the front of the church.

"James?" Andrea was sitting up now, concern once again appearing on her face, mingled with something else this time. Fear.

He had to tell her. And him.

"I'm okay, babe. I just need to clear my head. That's all."

James got up and walked towards the bathroom. "I'm going to go out for a little while. Maybe the fresh air will do me good."

James disappeared into the bathroom while Andrea stared at the closing door.

CHAPTER 11

Sweat dripped from Pete's nose as he mowed his lawn. His ears were filled with experimental jazz, a tape that Susan had left in the Walkman the last time she used it. He grumbled, the combination of his rising body heat and chaotic sounding riffs not sitting well with him. The day had warmed while he had been pushing the outdated mower up and down his three-quarter acre lot. Dirt flicked up from the mower mixing with his sweat, dotting his face and hair. The dirt trapped itself between the collar of his t-shirt and the nape of his neck, rubbing against him and irritating his skin. He scratched at it occasionally, bothering it, until it turned painfully red. That, along with the flies that couldn't seem to resist his musky smell, was making the chore of mowing the lawn unbearable.

More than once, Pete considered giving up and going inside, leaving the rest of the lawn for another day. He had never been much of a landscaping kind of guy. He didn't possess the green thumb that Susan had. She had planted a garden full of flowers whose names he couldn't pronounce, making their house a showcase. Since she had died the flowers and shrubs had been neglected; wayward bushes with branches pointing toward the sky framed the house. The flowerbeds were overrun with weeds that were slowly choking the life out of the once colorful bulbs. Pete hadn't bothered with the lawn in weeks and wouldn't have been working on it that day if the boy who had cut it the last time—when was that? July? —had been available. But the kid, a tall, gangly young man with sandy brown hair and freckled shoulders that turned copper in the sun, had gone back to school, up to some college near Ithaca, and he was on his own. Pete decided he'd better cut the grass before the first freeze which, by the way the morning had felt, wasn't far off. The grass had grown tall and unhealthy, his lawn transformed from the belle of the street to the eyesore. So, he had sucked it up that Sunday morning and kept at it. By the time he had decided that the music forcing its way through his ears was driving him crazy he was almost done with the yard. Wiping grit and sweat from his brow and feeling the air blow over his moist skin, he figured he had about four more rows to go before all was said and done. He promised himself a cold one if he could finish it in fifteen minutes, knowing he'd drink the beer even if the lawn took him another hour.

James' car pulled into his driveway when he turned to mow another line of unruly grass. James looked frazzled, disheveled, and tired. A smile played at the corners of Pete's lips as he turned the mower up the hill on the side of his house, seemingly oblivious to James' approach.

James' hands were clammy as he walked up the steps to Pete's house. He had driven around for an hour trying to make sense of what his gut was telling him he had to do. But now, as he stood in front of the house, hearing Pete's lawnmower on the other side of the house, almost done with his Sunday morning chore, he wasn't so sure.

He stood staring at the door as Pete and the lawnmower rounded the side and started mowing the front lawn.

"Jim! I didn't know you were coming by," Pete said as he turned off the mower and walked towards his friend.

"Neither did I," James said as he looked away from Pete. He couldn't believe that he was standing in front of his best friend's house getting ready to tell him about what happened between himself and Susan. Pete had just started to come back to life since Susan's death. When Susan's remains were found in her car just outside the city, James didn't think that Pete would make it. Hell, he didn't think he would make it either. God, what was it about her?

"Jim? What's up, buddy?" Pete asked, wiping sweat from his forehead. "You look like you've got something on your mind."

James looked up at the cloudless blue sky and said, "Maybe we should go inside."

The house was dark even though the sun shone brightly outside. The stale air smelled of old pizza. James cast his eyes around the living room, startled to see pictures of Susan removed from the walls. The little knickknacks that had been carefully placed in the curio and on the coffee table were gone. James remembered the time he and Susan made love on the coffee table, sending the miniature figurines crashing to the floor. One of them shattered when it hit the hardwood floor; an elephant with clear glass tucks. "James," she had squealed, "we broke the elephant's nose!"

"Do you care?" he had whispered hotly into her ear before nibbling her lobe and tracing his lips down her neck. With a child-like giggle she said, "Not right now," and threw her head back as James kissed the hollow of her neck. The sound of her laugh still hung in the air.

The drapes had been pulled closed. He had never noticed their dark color before. Heavy forest green material hung from a solid mahogany rod. The drapes didn't allow even a sliver of light to break into the room. The furniture's light brown hue seemed muted in the dim light, the oak wood abandoning its radiance. The living room was in such contrast to the way that it had looked when Susan was alive that James felt strange standing within it, as though he had just walked into the house of a stranger. Susan had loved light and floor to ceiling windows, summer breezes and bright colors. Orange was her favorite color and she would wear a different shade of it every day of warm weather. She was vibrant; alive. This room was not Susan's. It looked like Pete was trying to deny her existence.

James hung his head, realizing how he had failed his friend. Since Susan's death, James hadn't visited with Pete, hadn't done anything with him - no football games or boxing matches on the tube, no trips to City Island for fresh seafood like the ones they had been known to take on a moment's notice before the accident; nothing at all. James hadn't talked with Pete about Susan to help him work through it after the funeral. He hadn't so much as brought over a six-pack of beer and cried off the loss with him. He didn't do anything. In the beginning he had been too wrapped up in his own grief and his need to conceal it. Then the nightmares came. He didn't see Pete withdrawing into himself. He assumed that Pete would get over it the way everyone else would—everyone except him—if he thought about it at all. He could only see his own grief. And his nightmares.

"So, what's the deal, man?" Pete called out from the kitchen. He came back into the living room holding two cold beers. James drank half of his quickly before saying a word.

"I have to talk to you about something."

"Yeah? So, what's up?"

James and Pete had been friends since their years at the University of Maryland. Coming from similar backgrounds, they were both wet behind the ears when it came to big city life. The idea of going into Washington DC terrified them. Then one day they took the wrong bus on Rhode Island Avenue. They meant to catch the bus that would take them from their campus to American University. Back then there were only two things that could lure them out of suburban Maryland and into the streets of Washington DC: the ability to purchase booze before they were 21 and the potential for sex. This time it was the potential for sex that called to them; the sorority party on American University's campus was rumored to bring girls from several of the colleges in the area. They fantasized about hooking up with girls from Georgetown, George Washington, Howard, or maybe even George Mason. Their heads were crowded with the vision of girls, all shapes and sizes, everywhere. They boarded the bus eagerly, ignoring the scrolling sign that named the intersection of Georgia Avenue and Florida Avenue as its last stop. They ended up in the middle of northwest DC near Howard University's campus, across town from where they needed to be, and in the middle of the city elements they tried so hard to avoid. James and Pete made it out of there unscathed that night, a little frazzled and excited but nothing more. They had been inseparable since that day. Pete knew things about James that no one else knew and vice versa. He was one of the only people that James trusted. James ran his hand through his hair, realizing that what he was about to say to Pete would change things between them forever.

"Pete, I have to tell you something. About Susan."

Pete's breath caught in his throat. Susan danced in his mind like she had every day since her death. He felt his eyes fill with tears at the mention of her name, but he blinked them back. Pete sat down in an armchair that was cattycornered to the sofa, his eyes fixed on James as he sat down in the armchair opposite his on the other side of the coffee table. Pete watched intently as James pulled at his jacket. He inhaled deeply, held the air there for a moment, then exhaled audibly.

"Pete, it's about Susan and—," James stopped. Could he really go through with telling him? Something in his mind was screaming for him to leave, telling him to make up some excuse and run out of the door, back to his car, and drive away. And he wanted to. He wanted nothing more than to leave the house with their friendship still intact. Somehow, he knew, though, that the nightmares wouldn't stop until they both knew the truth. Pete and Andrea.

James squared his shoulders to Pete and looked at the dull, scuffed hardwood floorboards between his feet, boards that used to possess a lustrous finish.

"Pete, Susan and I—," James paused, his voice threatening to retreat into his body. He breathed heavily, calming himself enough to finish.

"Pete. We-we had an affair."

James kept talking, spilling over with apologies and excuses, but Pete didn't hear any of them. He sank back into his chair, certain that his face showed shock and anger brimming just beneath the surface. That wasn't far from what he was feeling. A sense of resignation seeped into him like rum rolling down his throat, warming him as it traveled through his body.

He already knew about the affair.

He saw them one day when he was driving back to the office from a client visit. Holding hands and strolling the small-town street, neither of them knew they were being watched while they window-shopped in the quaint, new age manufactured town, nor when they shared a kiss in front of a fountain. They were just two nameless lovers spending a warm spring afternoon together. Two lovers who happened to be married to other people.

Pete sat in his car that day watching them walk out of view as his emotions spiked between shock, sadness, and anger. He opened the car door to pursue them, having every intention of bashing his best friend's head in. But Susan, he just wanted to look into Susan's eyes and ask her why. He found himself standing three steps away from his open car staring at the place where they had stood a minute before, holding hands and strolling as if they didn't have a care in the world. Tears streamed down his face as he stared at the empty spot, nothing more than scenery for his dreams now. He was unaware of when he had gotten out of the car, when he had stepped into the street, whether or not he was stopping traffic. He didn't know, didn't care about any of those things. The only thing he cared about, the only thing that was real to him at that moment, was the smile on Susan's face as she nestled her head on James' shoulder.

How could she betray him like that? How could he? Those questions and others echoed in his mind every minute after he saw them. He couldn't get his mind off seeing the two of them together looking completely normal; seeming to fit perfectly against the backdrop of Nyack's tree lined streets and antique shops. He kept seeing them, standing in front of him sometimes, off in the distance other times, laughing and giggling; sharing secrets with each other. Pete became convinced, after the movie replayed itself in his head over and over, picking up gestures and movements as it went, that they were laughing at him as they strolled by. He imagined that they were chuckling about how naïve he was, how oblivious he had been to what was going on right under his nose. He heard both of their voices ridiculing him with their laughter, but Susan's laugh seemed louder to him. What used to sound melodic, a lilting soprano carried delicately on the air to grace his ears, sounded shrill and harsh to him now. She laughed and laughed and laughed at him, sometimes looking right into his eyes as she did it.

It was a troubling daydream, one that he couldn't seem to stop running over and over in his head. With each showing his temper rose and his blood boiled within him. Just when he thought he would explode, the dream would stop. Seconds later it would start up again, each time more imaginative than the last. Sometimes Susan would be scantily clothed, resembling a prostitute, in high-heeled shoes and a miniskirt. Sometimes Pete would see Susan and James walking toward him, James' exaggerated erection protruding from his pants pressing so hard against the zipper that the pants looked as if they might split in the center. The daydream was relentless. And he couldn't stop it.

While James offered apologies Pete thought about the day that he confronted Susan about the affair. It was the day after he saw them in Nyack. It was the day she died.

Pete was pulled away from his memories when something that James said crept into his thoughts. He cut James off, agitatedly waving a hand in front of him. He said,

"Wait a minute. What did you say?"

"I said that the nightmares started right after Susan died. Pete, I've seen such horrible things. And the worst part is that I'm not sure whether I'm asleep or awake half of the time."

"Do you think this is a dream?"

Pete lunged at James, hitting his calf on the coffee table and knocking it over. He reached James before he was able to stand up; James' hands were on the armrests and his buttocks hovered above the seat, just barely off the cushion when he was hit. Pete threw a right cross that landed flush on James' jaw, whipping his head to the side, and throwing him back into the chair. The force of the punch propelled him backwards so hard that even after he hit the chair, he kept moving, knocking the chair and himself onto the floor. As quickly as he had come, Pete walked away from James and faced the window.

As James righted himself and rubbed his swelling cheek Pete said, "You tell me, after my wife has been dead for months, that you were carrying on with her? What did you expect to prove by telling me now? What? That you could satisfy her better than me? That you could fuck her the way she wanted and I couldn't? She's dead, James. And fuck you for bringing her back to me like this."

James recoiled, not expecting Pete to respond that way. Some part of him, the part that hid behind humility and sensibility, knew that Pete was right. The rest of him wrestled with the truth. Had he only admitted the truth about the affair to make the dreams stop? Could he really be that self-absorbed? *Yes*, the coward in him whispered, defeated. Meekly, he offered,

"I thought that I owed you the truth. I thought—."

"Our friendship meant so much to you that you slept with my wife!" Pete cut in. "And you have the nerve to come here and throw it in my face!"

"No, Pete. I just thought that if I told you the truth it would help us. That it would help me," he confessed.

"So, you told me so you could clear your conscience and stop the boogeyman from coming to your door every night. It's not that easy, buddy. You can't screw a man's wife, come into his house after she's dead to apologize, and expect that everything will be back to normal."

"I didn't mean it that way. I—."

"I don't care how you meant it. You slept with my wife! You were supposed to be my best friend."

Pete paused there, letting the words sink in. The silence between them was deafening.

"I don't give a damn why you told me, Jim," Pete continued, pacing the floor as he talked. He turned his head and walked towards James, enjoying the look in his eyes as he self-consciously recoiled, moving just enough for Pete to notice before he regained his composure and stood his ground. He stared at James, his eyes boring through him, and gave voice to the question he had wanted to ask since he saw them that day in Nyack, "Why don't you try telling me why you did it."

James was dumbfounded. There wasn't an answer for a question like that. He couldn't tell his friend that he did it because he was attracted to his wife and couldn't control his urges. He couldn't say that he was sorry another time—if Pete didn't already believe it, he never would. What could he say to somehow make this right? He opened his mouth to speak but shut it quickly, not having uttered a word.

Pete snorted derisively and started walking toward the kitchen. As he passed the front door, he said,

"Get the fuck out of my house, Jim."

James walked towards the door, the weight of the lost friendship sitting heavily on his shoulders.

As he opened it to leave, he heard Pete say sarcastically from within the kitchen,

"Give my love to Andrea."

CHAPTER 12

James walked into the house at 7:15 p.m., almost ten hours after he left that morning. Andrea was making pasta in the kitchen; the smell of oregano and basil filled the air. James stood in the foyer and took in the smell. He hadn't eaten all day, but he wasn't hungry. The sweet and spicy smell of the pasta sauce hung in the air, but it didn't rouse him. His stomach was full of butterflies, fluttering from one side to the other. He had been feeling uneasy the whole day, even before his encounter with Pete. Not even Andrea's homemade sauce could sway him that night.

He turned to look at himself in the oval mirror that stood to the left of the front door. The wood that surrounded the mirror and made up the antique mahogany hallstand was looking a little worse for wear. Andrea inherited the 18th century piece from her grandmother. Although its handcrafted crown and frieze once captured the eye of every guest that attended the annual Mason Christmas party, its intricate detail was beginning to look worn after over a hundred years of use. James pondered the aging hall-stand for a moment as he hung his keys on the left brass hook (left hook for him, right hook for Andrea—another one of Andrea's rules of the house). As he studied the details of the hallstand, he was drawn back to the reflection of himself, a vision he wanted to avoid.

His face looked haunted. Dark circles ringed his eyes, perspiration crested the top of his forehead. His jaw was swollen and bruised; it was sensitive to the touch. After he left Pete's house he drove to a supermarket parking lot, parked the car, and sat there for hours. Disconnected scenes flashed in his mind. He saw Susan in his arms in a hotel room, and Pete shooting a three-pointer at a community center pick-up game. The images started to meld, intermingling with each other, superimposing themselves onto each other. He saw himself passing the ball to Susan and her shooting the three-pointer. He saw himself holding Pete in a loving embrace. Many times, to his chagrin, he saw himself sitting in a chair across from their bed, watching as Pete and Susan made love. Shaken by the incoherent thoughts, he sat in his car trying to sort things out before returning home.

He tried to come up with an answer that would satisfy Andrea when she asked him what happened to his face. As he turned to walk into the kitchen, he mulled over a couple of responses to her questions; all of which sounded suspicious, even to him. He eyed the stairs in front of him and thought about running up, jumping in the shower, and changing into some fresh clothes. Maybe he would come up with an explanation for his swollen jaw by that time. Sighing, he realized that there was no answer that would suffice. Nothing he could say would placate Andrea in the long run. He was tired of avoiding the truth. It was weighing on him in more ways than he cared to acknowledge.

Before he walked out of the foyer, he caught his reflection in the beveled edge of the mirror again. He watched in horror as his face distorted and he found that he had no control over his muscles. A dark shadow loomed just past his reflected image, starting in the center of the cream wall, and spreading out in all directions like oil dropped into a pot of water. Within seconds the wall was covered in a gray film that pulsated like smoke rising from a lit cigarette. Flashes of light blinded him. He squeezed his eyes shut, suddenly aware of a terrible pounding in his temples. The pain drove him to lay his head on the hallstand abruptly, knocking the keys off the brass hooks. He heard the clanking as they hit the floor, but the sound was muffled and far away. The room felt different to him when he knelt to pick up the keys. It was colder; the air felt harsh on his face. As he raised his head and blinked his eyes open, he saw an unfamiliar floor covered with cheap tan carpeting. He found himself sitting on a black sofa draped with a multicolored throw. A television droned on to his right, one of those 24-inch jobs with tinny, baseless sound and terrible reception, despite the hanger antennae that hovered lopsidedly above the box.

The apartment was small, nothing more than a room. There were grocery bags sitting on top of the kitchen counter. A woman's coat was draped over the back of one of the folding chairs that were tucked under a card table in the makeshift dining room.

A floor length mirror hung on the back of the front door. James looked at it, seeing a reflection that, at first, he didn't recognize. A man sat on the same sofa upon which he sat. He was dressed like James, his olive-green camp shirt and khaki pants wrinkled from a day of wear. The man sat with his legs crossed in a wide bridge, his foot fidgeting, keeping time. His arms were spread across the back of the sofa with a casualness that made it seem like he was as comfortable in the unfamiliar surroundings as a frequent guest would be. The man's face—James' face—held a cocky smirk. There was a flicker of knowledge, of understanding glinting in his eyes that was disconcerting. The man on the sofa was definitely James, but he couldn't have looked more unlike himself. His surroundings were as foreign to him as the attitude displayed on the reflection of his face. His eyes shot around the room looking for something familiar.

The reflection of himself started to rise from the sofa slowly and deliberately, taking a step toward the mirror. He stood close with his shoulders tilted back slightly and squared. James watched in horror, seeing himself straighten his shirt and put his hand in his pocket without feeling it. He tried to concentrate on feeling the material of his shirt under his fingertips or the warmth of his pants pocket. He felt nothing. He had unknowingly tilted his head upward to look at his reflected image when it stood. He realized then that he was sitting and not at eye level with the eyes in the reflection. The man standing before him couldn't possibly be a reflection of himself. Where, then, was his image in the mirror?

Something had changed. James no longer felt like he was looking into the mirror at a reflection of himself. Instead, he felt like he was looking out into the room from a space opposite the sofa. He didn't know what had changed—maybe it was the light coming in from the window, different now, no longer behind him, but in front of him—*had it shone that way before?* Maybe it was the absence of feeling where his legs should have met the leather sofa, replaced now with a nothingness. James' mind reeled as he thought about all the things that were suddenly different somehow.

James, suddenly feeling his legs folded beneath him, tried to stand but he couldn't. Feeling the disadvantage of his position, he strained against himself, trying to force his muscles to respond, but they remained motionless. He tried to raise a hand to his face to wipe away the sweat that had formed on his forehead, but he couldn't move his arm either. James shuddered, if only in his mind, realizing that he was stuck in the same paralytic state that he had woken up in that morning. But this felt different. He could feel the breeze coming in from the window the way he had felt the sun's warmth on his feet that morning. This time he was seeing things, actually seeing them, not just imagining that creatures were lurking beyond his view. The man in the mirror, who so closely resembled James that it made his skin crawl, was standing right in front of him. He was so close that James could hear his breathing.

James shifted his tongue around his dry mouth, forcing himself to swallow.

A smile spread across the man's face as he looked at James. The smile held contempt and evil easily, but it also held admiration and sensuality. It terrified James. In that moment he knew that the man in front of him was not himself, couldn't be. In the same breath though, he realized with paralyzing clarity that it was.

The man turned his head away from James, allowing his eyes to fall upon the form lying on the bed. They shone menacingly as they took in the contours of her frame. His lips parted in excitement. James saw her also, a beautiful young woman lying asleep on her bed. Her breathing was regular and steady. She was oblivious to the intruders in her apartment. James tried to bang his hands on the floor to make a sound—any sound— that would jar the woman out of her sleep, but his limbs were useless. He felt pinned in, surrounded by invisible walls—six of them, encasing him.

His breath rose in a mist in front of him. The air in the imaginary box seemed colder than it had been only moments before. A tickle formed on his thigh, and without thinking, he reached to scratch it, finding that he could. He raised his other arm, making sure that the return of his movement wasn't a fluke. His arm stretched out before him. James found his voice and called out, screaming warnings at the woman. She continued to sleep, unfettered. He tried to stand, intending to stop the man before he woke her, but his head bumped into what felt like a wall. He looked up and saw nothing. He raised his hand above his head and touched what felt like thick glass, cold from the breeze flowing into the room from the open window. Incredulously, he brought both of his hands up and banged them against the barrier that he couldn't see. A guttural scream rose from his diaphragm and out of his mouth when the realization that had dawned on his subconscious mind minutes before made its way to his conscious self: he was trapped in the mirror.

James watched helplessly as the man approached the woman, a mere spectator to the game that was about to unfold before him. He felt a burning sensation in his chest as the man touched the woman's skin softly, as though he was touching the arm of a lover after intimacy. He pulled his hand out of his pocket and revealed a 10-inch chef's knife. The edge reflected the light of the diminishing day casting glints of splintering light through the small room. The woman on the bed remained unmoving, entranced in a deep sleep.

The man knelt in front of the woman, taking in her face so that he could remember every feature. He traced the form of her cheek with the blunt edge of the knife, hovering just above the skin. Gingerly, he skipped over the scattered moles that dusted the top of her cheeks like freckles, patterning her face. He placed the point on her neck ever so slightly, barely touching the skin. Confident that this was the worst one yet, James screamed out from inside the mirror, trying to jar himself from the terrible nightmare he was embroiled in. The sound of his terror was loud inside the prison of the mirror but didn't penetrate the silence of the room. He was forced to watch the horror unfold.

The man stood over the sleeping woman for what seemed like an eternity, positioning the knife on the hollow of her neck. James sat screaming as loud as he could, throwing his hands into the air, begging for the nightmare to end. He kicked his feet out, almost straightening his legs completely, as he pushed against one of the clear walls that imprisoned him. He struck the invisible wall, his heel ramming against it hard with each kick. James jumped as the almost imperceptible bump sounded on the other side of the mirror. James fell silent and still, amazed that he was able to affect any change of events in the nightmare.

The man looked at the mirror. His eyes, this time awash in excitement and expectancy, glistened with moisture. The man chuckled aloud, a sound that resembled James' rich laugh more closely than he was willing to accept and threw a playful wink at the mirror. He raised the knife high above his head and plunged it into the soft of the woman's neck quickly, the slow relish he had displayed earlier giving way to brute violence. A second later the woman's eyes snapped open, her mouth forming the scream rising in her chest, but no sound came out. The man, who had backed away from the bed the moment the blade cut through her flesh and into the mattress beneath her, watched the woman writhe and grope at her neck, trying to remove the knife. For what seemed an eternity, the woman screamed silently and flailed her arms; her last attempt at saving herself.

Soon she laid still, blood pooling around her and soaking into the mattress. The man emerged from the shadows when it was over and looked down at his victim. A visible erection protruded from his pants as he dipped his finger in her blood and traced his hand along her lifeless body. He brought the finger to his face and stared at it longingly. As his hand descended towards his open mouth, James screamed and clamped his eyes shut, unable to watch anymore.

When James opened his eyes, he was on a rooftop overlooking the city. The wind flowed across his damp forehead, the crisp air chilling him. He didn't see the darkened figure standing at the roof's edge at first. The man stood looking at the ground below in amusement. He lifted one foot and dangled it over the lip of the roof playfully. He turned his head and looked at James, his jovial smile betrayed by hateful eyes that revealed his malice. James wondered, looking back at the man, if he meant the disdain his eyes showed, if he would kill him if given the chance. The look seemed so natural; the contrasting emotions were perfect on his face. It made James' blood run cold.

James looked at the man in awe. The man could have been James' twin; the resemblance was uncanny. It was like looking into a mirror.

The man smirked and turned back to the city below, looking out at the streetlights that illuminated the night. He stood watching the night, breathing the cold air, reveling in the serenity of the sleeping neighborhood. As an afterthought, he turned his attention to a massive bag that lay next to him. He had pushed the bag flush against the brick border that squared the roof. Smiling, he knelt to lift the heavy bag, bringing it to his chest. He cradled it, holding it over the edge of the roof. As the head lolled backwards and an arm dangled, almost touching his knee, James realized that it wasn't a bag that he was holding, but a body. James walked towards them slowly, needing to know if the body the man held in his arms, like a mother would hold a child, was the woman from the apartment. As he approached the man, he could smell the pungent smell of blood and adrenaline. He looked at the woman's face, her hair matted with blood, her cheeks splattered with droplets of crimson that looked as black as tar in the night. As he stared at her face, lovely even in death, her eyes snapped open. James recoiled quickly, slipping and falling on the dirty rooftop, barely catching himself from falling through the skylight. He sucked air in and out of his lungs rapidly, his chest heaving up and down as he made eye contact with the woman. Her eyes were empty, dead.

The woman smiled at James, the sadness on her face so profound that James had to swallow back a sob. She turned her head to the man who held her twelve floors above the ground.

The man looked down at the woman, kissed her lightly on the lips, and dropped her. She fell swiftly and silently, the sickening pound of her body hitting the earth sounding after only about ten seconds. James gagged when he heard it, bile rising in his throat quickly, choking him.

The man turned to James and stared. His eyes, illuminated by the moon, were hard and cold. James shivered as he stood to face his double, meeting his gaze. The man, surprised by James' gumption, laughed aloud. It was a deep, throaty sound, pushed from his diaphragm, solid. It chilled James.

"Don't laugh at me!" he yelled, anger welling up in his chest with every laugh. The man continued, his countenance fading into a shadow, physically disappearing save for his scornful laughter. James charged the shadowing man, his legs moving of their own volition. He hadn't consciously decided to attack the man, but he felt he had to do something for the murdered woman, even if it was too late. A flash of disappointment seared his thoughts, burning all others away. He had been too much of a coward to save her. He stood by and let her be killed—watched her die. He wouldn't stand by any longer, he vowed. Her death would be avenged.

As he gained momentum, he stretched his arms out in front of him. *He'll never kill another person;* James swore to himself. *And he'll never laugh at me again.* James charged the man, meaning to push him over the edge to join the doomed woman on the unforgiving concrete below. When he should have reached him, should have felt the resistance of his body against his forceful hands, the world turned black. He screamed soundlessly as he floated in the nothingness surrounding him.

It felt like he had just fallen from a high altitude and landed on his feet. As he stood up from bended knee, he realized that he was screaming. James opened his eyes expecting to see the man standing over him, ready to take him as his next victim. Instead, he found himself standing in his foyer next to Andrea's grandmother's hallstand. Jazz was playing in another room and the smell of Italian spices hung in the air, faintly. He was facing his front door, staring at it as it came into focus. He knew where he was but stood disoriented just the same. He remembered standing in front of the hallstand and facing the stairwell only a second before. Then what? He remembered knocking the keys off the hallstand... His left hand rubbed his temple absently as he tried to piece the memory together. He brought his right hand up to run it through his hair and found that it held the keys that had fallen to the floor. The room came into focus and seemed to brighten with that discovery. James turned to the mirror and almost screamed when he saw the protrusion of his pants and the circle of dampness just above and to the left of the bottom of his zipper. His hands shook so badly the keys jangled on the ring.

Andrea came into the foyer, glass of soda in hand, and said, "Hey! I thought I heard you come in. There's some pasta left on the stove for you."

As James turned to her the phone rang. Andrea turned away from him in time to miss the look of utter confusion etched on his face.

"It's probably Ann, James," she yelled as she ran into the kitchen. "She's having a hard time since the separation. I have to get this."

James didn't acknowledge her. Within seconds he heard his wife chattering on the phone with a friend, happily recounting current events and planning their next lunch date. He chuckled at the sound of Andrea's voice, light and happy, without a care in the world, while his world seemed to be closing in on him, suffocating him. He looked at himself in the mirror, the tortured look in his eyes scaring him more and more. He caught a glimpse of the clock hanging on the wall in the day room. He stepped back from the mirror, his eyes wide and his arms hanging stiffly from his sides when he saw the time: it was 8:25 p.m.

CHAPTER 13

Pete's anger burned anew when James confessed, smarting like the sting of a cut whose scab had been torn away. He knew the story. He knew that James and Susan had an affair. He saw them with his own eyes. But that didn't make it easier to hear James speak the words. All the anger, the feelings of betrayal, and the pain came rushing back in. His head ached as he remembered them holding each other, oblivious to the world around them. They were so arrogant. How dare they carry on like that in open view? It was as though he and Andrea—their spouses, for God's sakes! —meant nothing to them. Perhaps that was what hurt the most.

Pete had his share of betrayal in his life. His father left the family when Pete was nine years old. He only moved two blocks away and saw Pete every other weekend, but in Pete's mind, he had still broken his promise.

One day when his parents were still together, Pete and his father were playing catch in the park. Pete asked his Dad if he would ever leave them. He didn't know where the question had come from; it had just come out of his mouth from some hidden place in his mind. His father looked at him inquisitively, wondering where such a thought had come from also, especially from such a young boy. Pete remembered the words his father said clearly, as if he had spoken them the day before.

"Where'd that come from, Pete? You know I love you and your mother. I would never, ever leave you," he said while cocking his hand back for the next pitch.

Three years later his parents separated. A year later they divorced. Pete never forgave his father for that.

When he saw Susan and James in Nyack, brazenly embracing each other like they belonged to one another, it made him sick. His wife. His best friend. He felt like he could kill them both. He could almost see himself running across the street and taking them both out before they even knew what had hit them. He wasn't ashamed of the rush he got from the thought of it. Anyone would have felt the same way.

But he didn't do anything that day. He got back in the car and drove away without even letting them know he was there. He was surprised that he could drive at all; his vision was clouded by tears that stung his eyes and rolled hotly down his face. He was ashamed of his reaction, his weakness. He chastised himself for crying over the pain.

"You're acting like a baby!" he shouted in the empty car as he banged his hands against the steering wheel. It was the wrong reaction to the emotion he felt. He was more angry than sad, so why was he crying? They didn't deserve his tears.

He thought about going over to James' house and having a little talk with Andrea, maybe telling her what he saw. He drove to her neighborhood, made it all the way to their street before stopping three houses away. Andrea was outside watering the lawn. She couldn't see him parked behind another car on the street, but he could see her. He watched her for a while, envious of her ignorance, admiring her beauty.

Pete had always been attracted Andrea. From the moment he

met her in Manhattan when she and James had just started seeing each other exclusively, he couldn't get her out of his head. When James said he was going to marry her, Pete thought his chances were shot. He was single then, only dating Susan at the time. Sure, he was happy with her, but something about Andrea gave him pause. It might have just been sexual; he couldn't deny that he liked the way she looked. She was tall and shapely, fit. She was fond of wearing form-fitting clothing. Nothing that could be considered distasteful or deliberately tight; the clothes just contoured to her shape, hugging her in a way that few women experience. She was stunning. Always. Even when she was running errands on the weekend or working in the yard, as she was that day, she looked flawless. Her face didn't need any makeup; her eyes and cheeks were enhanced by nature itself rather than mascara or blush. Her hair was silky, black with light and medium brown highlights dancing throughout. It looked styled even when it was pulled into a casual ponytail. She was beautiful. Pete was infatuated with her.

Truth be told, part of the reason that Pete wanted to move to Rockland County was to have an excuse to see more of Andrea. He saw her in the mall, in the supermarket, stopped at a light. He was satisfied with that until his world turned upside down.

At first, he was hurt. How could Susan have betrayed him? With James, no less? Pete had thought their bond was unbreakable. How could he have been so naïve? Then the pain was replaced by anger. Who the hell did they think they were? The two closest people to him in the world did the most unspeakable thing that could ever be done. Then he realized the irony in it. He had been betraying Susan with James' wife in his mind since before they were married, wanting her, craving her touch. But he had never acted on it, hadn't even come close. That made all the difference in the world.

Pete thought about what was happening to James. The dreams he had described, the difference in his behavior since Susan's death. Pete had noticed the change in him but he was too angry to care about it. *Fuck him,* Pete thought often. *He deserves whatever he gets.* But as James' erratic behavior intensified, as the dreams started to crowd his waking mind, Pete started to pay more attention to what was happening, studying him. The dreams had come right after Susan's death, creeping in slowly but rapidly building momentum, gradually picking up speed. At first the dreams came two nights a week, then three, then four. Now James was having nightmares every time he shut his eyes. Sometimes he was afraid to sleep, terrified of the monsters he would meet in the darkness behind his closed lids. James was being tormented. Pete had come to believe that the dreams were punishment for what James had done to him and Andrea, his guilt manifesting itself while he slept. Pete considered it poetic justice. James had ruined his marriage and destroyed a long-term friendship with his eyes wide open to the consequences. His callousness had damned him. Pete liked it. The price of his and Susan's betrayal was steep indeed.

Something else nagged at Pete's mind as he went over the timeline of James' downfall. There was something more than just the guilt that was tearing at James, eating away his sanity. There was something else behind door number two.

Pete started recollecting the stories that James had told him when they first became friends in college. James had talked a lot about his father when the suicide was still fresh in his mind. James said that his father was found in his office, slumped in the chair he had done most of his reading in. A shotgun lay against his right leg, settling there after the blast. James' father had put the shotgun in his mouth and blown the back of his head off. Some of his brain matter was splattered on the back of the chair; some had projected over the back of the chair onto the carpet. His eyes were closed, his forehead relaxed. Only the burns at the corners of his lips betrayed the carnage behind his head.

James had been the one to find him.

"I couldn't believe what I was seeing," James told him that

night in the dorm room. James was sitting on the floor, his legs outstretched in front of him and his back leaning on the bed frame. He held a beer, his sixth, casually in his hand, enjoying the buzz he had worked up. The room smelled of weed and liquor, even after they had sprayed air freshener inside the room, outside the door, and on the throw rug. The window was open, but it didn't seem to pull any of the smells out. The combination was nauseating.

"I heard a loud bang coming from downstairs," James went on to say. "I opened my door and heard my mother snoring. I remember thinking that she would sleep through a bomb as long as it didn't hit her in the face." He chuckled uneasily, avoiding eye contact with Pete.

"The door was closed, but I could see the light shining underneath. I didn't know then that what I heard was a gunshot. I didn't know what it was. Something made me stop outside the door. I stood in the hallway with my hand on the doorknob for at least a minute before going in." James paused, shaking his head. He looked past Pete at the wall behind him, suddenly sitting up stiffly. His eyes had glazed over, watching the memories play in his head like a movie on a screen. It was as if he was standing in the hallway in front of the door to his father's office again. He could almost feel the cold doorknob turning warm from the heat of his hand.

Pete saw the tension building on James' face, saw his eyes glistening with fresh tears. He shifted in his seat, waiting.

James swallowed hard before continuing, "I've thought about that moment a lot. I didn't know what I would find on the other side of the door. I wasn't frightened. I wasn't concerned. I didn't feel anything, not really."

"But you heard the shot?" Pete asked tentatively. He couldn't think of anything else that a shotgun blast sounded like other than a shotgun blast.

"Yeah, but you wouldn't think that it was a shotgun blast, especially if it was coming from inside your house. It just doesn't cross your mind, at least not consciously. I'm sure on some level I knew what happened from the moment I heard the shot. But the thought never really took shape in my mind. My body just started moving when I heard it, hardly thinking at all. I knew Dad had the gun, but in my entire life I had only seen it twice. I guess I forgot it existed."

Pete nodded and took a swig of his beer. He didn't really want it, but he felt like he had to do something with his hands.

James continued, "I finally turned the knob and opened the door. The room was shadowy; he had only left the desk lamp on. His chair was facing the door like it always did. Everything seemed okay.

"I saw him sitting there with the shotgun on the floor between his legs. I still didn't get it. His face looked normal from where I was standing, almost like he had fallen asleep. His chin rested on his chest and I could have sworn I saw him take a breath. I know now that it was a trick of the light or my eyes not focusing, or both, but it seemed real to me then. Maybe I didn't want to accept what was right in front of me."

It was James' turn to drink. He downed his half full bottle in three big gulps before he continued.

"Then all of a sudden, I saw it. It was like the dim lighting got brighter and brighter, illuminating the scene for me. I was para-lyzed. Where I didn't before, now I saw the blood on the chair and the dark spots on the floor. I saw the brain matter stuck to the back of the chair. It was like the shadow that had blocked my view of my Dad's head moved, and I saw the whole thing in full color. The back of his head had been blown away, man. It was gone."

He stopped and turned away self-consciously, afraid that the tears he felt gathering in his eyes would spill out in front of Pete. Pete was glad for the break. It was the most horrible story he had ever heard.

James turned back after a while and said, "If I'm grossing you out man, let me know, okay? You don't have to hear this if you don't want to."

"No, man. I'm all right. Get it off your chest."

James nodded and continued, "I don't know how long I stood out there before I went in. I felt like I had to go in. I owed it to him. I took a couple of steps into the room but I fell to my knees when I got in front of him. His mouth was slack. I could see the burns on the inside of his lips from the barrel. Jesus, I could still smell the gunpowder in the air.

"I just started screaming. I was crying and yelling and cursing at him. I was so pissed at him for doing it. I couldn't believe he had left me to find him like that. Mostly, I couldn't believe he left us. After a while, my Mom woke up and came downstairs. I don't know how long I sat there with him before she came in, but the skin on my face felt constricted and my eyes were sore. I didn't even hear her when she came in. I don't know if she screamed or shouted. I didn't know she was in the room until she touched my shoulder. She was shaken and tears had wet her cheeks. We stayed like that a long while—me on my knees in front of Dad's chair and Mom standing over me.

"I remember looking out of the window and seeing the sky starting to lighten, burnt orange and gold breaking through the midnight blue of night as the sun began to rise. Mom saw it too and made me get up and leave the room. Before long the house was full of medical and police people, most of which were crammed in the tiny office with Dad. A policeman with the kindest eyes I've ever seen sat with Mom and me in the living room, blocking her view of the gurney as they wheeled Dad out of the house. But I saw him. I could make out his shape in the black bag that held him. I didn't see him again after that."

James sat back and leaned on the bed, spent from telling his story. Pete was intrigued. As horrible as the story was, it was the most interesting thing that had ever happened to anyone he knew. He wanted to hear more, but he knew better than to press too hard.

"Damn, man, that's terrible," Pete started. He had to say something to get him talking again. "How did you get through that?"

"I don't know. It was tough, but we got through it somehow. Mom was great. She was stronger about it than I was. I used to have nightmares every night. I would see him sitting there every time I closed my eyes." James stopped abruptly, as though forcing back the memories of his dreams. "But Mom helped me work through them," he continued. "And now I'm here."

It was going nowhere fast. Pete needed to know more.

"Did you ever find out why he did it?" Pete asked. James stood up and got another beer. He didn't say anything. He drank a couple of swigs. The silence in the room was making Pete feel uneasy. He was afraid he had made a mistake.

James sat down in silence, thinking about his answer carefully, trying to judge what he should and shouldn't say. Suddenly, he leaned forward, looking at Pete imploringly.

He said, "Pete, you can't tell anyone about this, okay? I'm trusting you."

Pete almost jumped off the chair at his chance.

"I would never say anything to anyone, James. I would never do that to you, man. We're friends. You can trust me."

That seemed to satisfy James. He answered Pete's question.

"My Mom said he was sick. Mentally ill, although she didn't say it that way. She said he was sensitive; that he let his emotions control him. She said he was suggestible. That if any idea, any inkling to do something got in his mind, it would fester. It would build and build until he would finally do it, whatever it was. It didn't matter how dangerous it was, how foolish or impractical, he would do it.

"She said I was like him when it came to stuff like that. She said it could be a good thing if I used it right. She was trying to make me feel better, I guess. She wanted me to find something in common with him, something positive to remember him by. She didn't want the image of his brains blown all over the office to be the only thing I associated with him. I know what she was trying to do, but I just can't get past what happened, you know? I saw him sitting there, dead in his office. I can't erase the image from my mind."

James rubbed his forehead and took another drink. The beer wasn't having any effect on him anymore. The topic was too sobering. He was just drinking to have something to do.

"She thought that's what had happened to him that night," he continued. "He got an inkling to shoot himself so he did it."

He stopped there. Pete knew there was something James wasn't telling him, but he didn't know how to get it out of him. That was the last time James talked about his father. To him, at least. He never found out what it was that James was hiding, but he had learned enough.

Pete never thought he would use that information. Sure, he tested James' limits, found out what he could and couldn't be talked into doing. Harmless stuff, really. Just sowing some wild oats.

Pete had meant what he said when he told James he could be trusted. Then. It would have stayed that way if James hadn't betrayed him the way he did.

Things were different now.

Pete watched as Andrea rolled up the hose and went back inside, oblivious of her husband's whereabouts. She had no idea what he was up to. Pete decided that he wouldn't tell her. *No*, he thought, *it'll be more fun to watch how things unfold*. With a little prodding and the precise placement of emotional land mines, James would clear the way for him. He would do that and more when all was said and done.

As Pete recounted his visit with James earlier that day, he knew he was right.

CHAPTER 14

When Andrea walked out to the foyer after her phone call James was still standing there, clutching the keys, and staring at himself in the mirror.

"James? James, what's the matter?" she asked as she approached him. James didn't turn around or answer her. She continued, "That wasn't Ann. It was Samantha. She's got a new guy and she wants us to meet him..." Her voice trailed off when she saw his discolored jaw and disheveled clothes. Her eyes watered as she stared mutely at him, unable to form words. It was evident that something more than dreams was affecting James.

"James, what happened to you?"

James continued to stare into the mirror, seemingly through himself at something just beyond his reflection.

Or just beneath it.

"James," Andrea repeated. Her husband's eyes looked vacant and his face was so still, he didn't appear to be breathing. She shook his arm to get his attention.

"What?" he asked, shouting. The sound of her voice came from far away, as though they stood at opposite sides of a tunnel.

"What happened to you?"

James slowly started to become aware of his surroundings. He realized how odd he looked standing in front of the mirror staring at himself. He was sure Andrea had seen his chin. James couldn't clear his mind to talk, to say anything at all. He couldn't find the words to tell her what happened between Pete and him earlier that day. He certainly wasn't lucid enough to tell her about the affair. *My God, what just happened to me?* he wondered, terrified of the response. Images of the woman's blood-soaked pillow flooded his head.

"James?!?"

"Nu-nothing happened Andrea," James responded, stuttering unconsciously.

"Look at yourself! Your chin is black and blue, your clothes are wrinkled, and you look scared to death. Don't tell me nothing happened!"

James pulled his eyes away from his reflection and turned to face Andrea. She was shaking. Her hairline was slick with sweat. Her eyes screamed at him to tell her the truth about what was happening. If only he knew the truth.

"I know I look bad. I went over to Pete's house today and—."

"What? He gave you that chin? Why would Pete do something like that to you?"

James searched for the right answer. He had to tell her about Susan, but could he do it? It would ruin everything he considered dear in his life. He was afraid of Andrea's reaction. That fear, mingled with the strange experiences he'd just had, were enough to push him over the edge. He put his hands on Andrea's arms and rubbed her gently.

"James, please just tell me what's going on here," Andrea said, her voice cracking from the weight of it all.

"I—I have to talk to you about something. This is not easy—," James started. The phone rang mercifully and he jumped at his chance.

"You should get that, Andrea."

"No, let the machine pick it up. I want to know what you have to tell me."

"No, this can wait. You need to get this call. It could be Ann. You know how much she needs you now."

Andrea hesitated. James averted his eyes and started to walk toward the stairs to their bedroom.

"I'm going to take a shower and change clothes. We can talk about this later."

"As soon as I get off, okay?" Andrea conceded and walked into the kitchen to get the phone.

Wearily, James climbed the steps, realizing with each rise that his life would be different the next time he took them.

CHAPTER 15

James climbed into the shower, cursing himself for starting the conversation with Andrea. He was angry at himself for hinting at some big discussion. Now he was trapped. He had to talk to her. He had to tell her the truth. He thought of her eyes, her worried eyes, as she watched him change. She saw the differences in him as much as he did. Maybe even more. James had become distant since Susan's death. Jumpy, edgy. The dreams started one day out of nowhere, not long after Susan was found burning in her car just outside of New York City in a sleepy river town off the Hudson. In an eclectic town called Nyack.

Nyack was one of the places that James and Susan truly loved. They would drive down to the village to go antiquing, take in a show at the Helen Hayes Performing Arts Center, or have lunch in Piermont. Other times they would just drive the country roads out of town, looking at the grand houses that lined the Hudson, paying homage to times past. On an especially lazy day, they would spend time milling around a farmer's market erected on an expanse of land off the road. There was something to satisfy every mood. That was the magic of Nyack.

When James and Susan were in Nyack, they felt invisible. Even though their cozy location was only twenty minutes away from Monsey—the village in which they both lived—it was worlds away. Most people drove past Nyack on their way over the Tappan Zee Bridge into Westchester County, or further down to the Bronx. Not many people stopped in the little, understated town. And if they did, it was mostly just to fill up the gas tank before braving the bridge. No one had time for the slow-paced village, its Main Street packed with art and antique shops. It wasn't fast enough to draw any attention to it; it wasn't big enough to catch anyone's eye if they weren't looking for it. It's one roadway, which was bordered by cafes and storefronts, dead-ended into the Hudson River. A boat ramp was erected at the end of the three-mile-long street. Side streets branched off Main Street, leading to colorful cluster communities with winding roads that all lead back to the main drag. It wasn't chic, at least not in a New York City kind of way.

Likewise, Nyack natives rarely ventured out further than Nanuet, a town just north of Nyack and only a little bigger. Nanuet was the home of the mall, and everyone in bordering towns (Nyack, Spring Valley, New City, Ramapo) flocked to it on the weekends. But there was little else that lured a Nyack native out of their comfortable town. The way Nyack natives saw it, they had everything they needed in their quaint little town, from food and culture to history and entertainment; from soup to nuts. And that was just fine to James and Susan.

They had a favorite bed and breakfast with a view of the Hudson. Mitchell Manor. It was a nice place with great innkeepers, and the best part about it was that it was rarely full. Often times they found that they were the only guests in the house for a night. There was a romantic Italian restaurant a block away that had incredible food. James and Susan ate there often, building a rapport with the owner. Their getaways to Nyack were like little tastes of heaven. When Susan was found dead there, James couldn't fathom it. It almost crushed him.

Was it that he loved Susan more than he loved Andrea? James taunted himself with that question often. Every time he tried to suppress it; it reared its ugly head.

James and Andrea had been married for ten years. They met at a small café in Manhattan that overlooked the west end of Central Park during the summer before Andrea's senior year at NYU. James had just graduated from the University of Maryland that May and was working in the city with an accounting firm. After six months of dating, James knew that he had found the woman he wanted to spend the rest of his life with. He asked her to marry him on their six-month anniversary, and to his surprise, she said yes. They got married a year later and, a year after that, moved to Monsey, a quiet suburb in Rockland County, trading congested city streets for winding country roads. The county was only thirty minutes outside of New York City, but it seemed worlds away from the skyscrapers that formed the famed skyline. Monsey was secluded and homey. The only congestion they found was on Saturday afternoons when Route 59 was grid locked with weekend shoppers heading to the Nanuet Mall. They moved far away from the city's fast pace and didn't miss a second of it.

James and Andrea made a nice life in Monsey. They bought a house and filled it with all of the sought after things that people worked all week to get. They took nature walks in the woods behind their house, and discovered a stream hidden in the wooded lot adjacent to their property. They woke up on weekend mornings and nursed cups of coffee while watching deer in their backyard. Life was good for them.

Their marriage had its ups and downs like every marriage. James and Andrea argued sometimes and he'd sleep a night on the sofa every once in a while, but they would make up the next day. It was as simple as that. They didn't have any serious issues between them. James couldn't help but wonder why he had created one.

Pete and Susan moved to Rockland County about a year after James and Andrea had settled in, buying a house in nearby

Chestnut Ridge. James was excited. With Pete living closer, they were able to see more of each other. They spent time at each other's houses without the wives and watched the game on Sunday. They had barbeques together. It was just like it had been at college, but better. Andrea and Susan got along as well, sometimes running off to the mall and leaving the 'boys' to their sports shows. Life was good. Until one day, James and Susan bumped into each other in Nyack.

Window-shopping for a gift for Andrea, James strolled the quiet Nyack streets two summers before, looking into the windows of antique stores and art galleries. Feeling noncommittal about the pieces on display, James made his way down to the pier. As he stared out at the murky Hudson River, he heard his name being called from somewhere behind him. When he turned to face the voice, he saw a vision that warmed the nip of the fall air circling around him. Susan walked towards James, her hand shading her eyes from the glare of the setting sun as it merged with the darkness of the river. Her hair, tousled by the crisp air, framed her face gently. He was seeing her as he never had before. In the light of the fleeting day, James thought her elegant, sensual, and comely.

What he felt scared him.

He remembered it so well. Susan walked towards him, the wind ruffling her long skirt with every step.

"Hi James. What brings you to Nyack, of all places?" she asked, lighthearted sarcasm playing in her voice.

"I'm looking for a trinket for Andrea. Something to add to her antique collection." James looked at his shoes. He felt foolish talking about his wife with a woman that was stirring him to his core. What was going on?

"Well, this is the place to do it, that's for sure. There must be at least twenty antique shops in town. I'm sure you'll find something."

"Yeah."

The pause was awkward; the silence between them was so

thick, it was suffocating. A coy smile spread across Susan's lips as she looked at the sun disappearing on the horizon.

"I used to come here when I was a child," she said as though entranced by the magnificent yellows, burnt oranges, and glowing reds that shimmered in the distance. "We would take a day trip to Bear Mountain, then have dinner here in Nyack on the way home. I used to love the look of the leaves turning color, blanketing the banks of the river, and looking at the stately houses lining the country roads. It was magical to me. But then I got older and submerged myself into city living, prowling the streets until 4:00 a.m. I forgot about the sleepy town on the other side of the river. It's a world away from Manhattan's fast pace."

Susan took a step forward, her eyes reflecting the fiery show over the water.

"I had forgotten about Nyack's charm until Pete and I moved back here. The week we moved up here, I made the drive into town. The old feelings came back. The warmth of the place filled me so full of emotion that I almost cried. I felt Nyack in my soul again, reclaiming its hold on my heart. I felt as one with it again."

James was lost in her words, wrapped up in the passion of her voice. He watched her face as it reflected the sun, her smile wondrous and full. And loved her.

"The pier is actually my favorite spot in Nyack," Susan said, smiling.

"Really?" James asked, wanting her to keep talking.

"Yup. While my family walked up and down Main St., I came here to read and watch people as they went about their day. Sometimes I came here to think. I can't think of any other place where I feel this comfortable."

James stared at her profile as wisps of hair patted her cheeks gently. She was serene. She belonged there. And at that moment all he wanted to do was to stay there with her. Susan turned to him, smiled, and looked away from his intense gaze.

"What? You didn't think a city girl like me would like a place full of grass and trees and, heaven forbid, water?" She chuckled. It was so self-conscious and innocent a sound that James had to restrain himself from turning her to him and kissing her.

Where was this coming from? He was happy with Andrea, so why was he looking at another woman? Why would he be looking at his best friend's wife? James sighed and looked toward the river, hoping that what he was feeling would pass as quickly as it had come. But had it come quickly? All other questions were pushed out of the way once that one surfaced in his mind.

He remembered the first time he met her. James, Andrea, Pete, and Susan met in Manhattan for dinner. It was a great night. James laughed more than he had in years and so had Andrea. He remembered thinking that Susan was a beautiful woman, and how lucky Pete was to have gotten her, but that was the end of it. Or was it? James didn't know and the idea was nagging at him.

James had fallen for Andrea hook, line, and sinker when they met. Since then, he hadn't so much as looked at another woman. After meeting Susan that night, he felt the faintest pang of guilt balling into a knot in his throat. He remembered looking around guiltily, feeling like he had allowed his face to betray his attraction to her. His cheeks burned hot with embarrassment as he looked at everyone at the table. Luckily, no one else seemed to notice. But he knew.

The couples only got together a handful of times. James was able to convince himself that he wanted to space their visits out because Pete and Susan were dating.

"They need time together without the intrusion of other people," he would tell Andrea when she mentioned getting together with them. He made himself believe it too. But that day, under the darkening sky in a town all but forgotten by city folk, he realized that there had been more to his reasons than met the eye.

What was it? He thought she was attractive. So what? A lot of men would. Was that enough reason to distance himself? *Why tempt yourself?* his mind had countered. He felt strangely around

Susan. Inappropriate. That was the bottom line. So, he suggested that he and Andrea do things with other friends from time to time. He would see Pete alone, without Andrea or Susan. This went on before and after Pete and Susan were married. James and Susan were friends by association only. Until then.

He was deep in thought when Susan said, "Well, I'd better get going. I have one more stop to make, and then I've got to get home."

"Really? I was hoping you could show me around a little. Maybe recommend a restaurant. You know, someplace that I could take Andrea one afternoon."

Where had that come from? James chastised himself for saying it, but he hung on the dead air between them, waiting for her answer. Susan smiled and looked at James. He tried to read her face, needing to know what she was thinking. Did he see the same mix of confusion and desire in her eyes that was brewing in his? He smiled lopsidedly at the thought, the very inkling that Susan might be feeling the same way that he was. It was ridiculous, he knew. Or was it?

Susan looked up at the sky and said, "The sun's going down. I wish we had met up earlier. I would have taken you to see Helen Hayes' mansion and some of the old churches in the village."

"I'm sure you would have been a great tour guide."

Her angelic voice was like music to his ears as she laughed. "Maybe another time."

"I'm going to hold you to that."

"Please do," she said as she leaned into James. Her lips grazed his cheek ever so slightly. The touch sent chills down his spine. Hadn't she kissed him before without this happening to him? What had changed?

"Please say hello to Andrea for me."

"Will do. Say hey to Pete for me too."

"I will," she said as she backed away from him. With one last smile, she turned to walk up the slight hill that led to the pier, and back to the sidewalk. James watched her until she was out of sight. He turned back to the water, the sky darkening with every second, and asked aloud, "What's wrong with me?"

James was coaxed back to the present by the warm water from the showerhead splashing his face. A sob rose in his chest, startling him. He felt hot tears spill out of his eyes. He cried for Andrea, and the pain that she would feel when he told her about the affair. He cried for the friendship that had died earlier that day when he confessed to Pete. He cried for Susan and the terrible death she had suffered, succumbing to the flames that engulfed her car. And he cried for himself. For all of the losses.

James felt alone and small. He was on edge from the lack of sleep and the nighttime torments that were starting to creep up and manifest during the light of day. And, probably worst of all, he felt he deserved the desolation and confusion that bounced off the walls of his consciousness.

His mind drifted back to Susan and the way she had looked that day at the pier. He remembered walking back to his car, the gift that had brought him to Nyack forgotten. He couldn't get Susan out of his mind. There was something about her that held his attention, captured his thoughts. It was more than her beauty. She had an earthiness about her that was warming, comfortable. It intrigued him.

They met several times after that, each encounter planned. One workday Susan called him at his desk, offering to give him the tour he had asked for that day on the pier. As if walking on air, James left the office early and drove out to what was now their meeting spot, parked the car and walked Nyack with Susan, seeing it through her eyes. Things progressed quickly after that. They bonded. They had more in common than they knew. They could talk about anything and everything or say nothing at all. James had never felt more comfortable with another person.

The first time they made love was forever etched in his mind. James felt the warm water of the shower trickling down his back as

Susan's hands had that night. She caressed him with strong, sure hands, tracing his body slowly, as if committing each contour to memory. When he entered her, she gasped in his ear, holding him tightly to her chest, wanting to feel him as he moved. He thought of his wife as he slept with Susan, her face floating in front of him. Guilt crept in, but the sound of Susan's voice wiped it away. Ecstasy erased the visage as quickly as it had appeared. The sunlight bathed Susan's skin, adding a glow to her creamy tone. Her hair spread across the pillow wildly. Her head was turned to one side and her eyes were clamped shut. Her mouth was open in a soundless moan. She was exquisite.

When he climaxed, an inexpressible sadness came over him. Guilt pulsed in the pit of his stomach. He had slept with his best friend's wife and cheated on his own. The wind was taken out of him as he collapsed on the bed.

He looked over at Susan, afraid that he had ruined the moment for her.

Instead, she looked up at him, her face clear and serious, and said, "We made the decision to do this, Jim, because we wanted to. We had to."

James nodded almost imperceptibly as he reached his arm out to Susan. She pressed her head to his shoulder, snuggling as close as their bodies would allow. They laid in silence, both of them wrestling with the transgression. It was never mentioned between them again.

When the water turned lukewarm, James got out of the shower and toweled off. He stared at his face in the mirror. He looked weary, and he felt as much in his bones. As he dressed and descended the stairs to the family room, the weight of what was to come almost drove him to his knees. He threw himself on the sofa and sank into it, wishing he could hide from reality.

Andrea's voice was muted as she wrapped up the call in the kitchen. When she entered the family room, she had an odd expression on her face. But that wasn't what James noticed. What he saw was the badly misshapen silhouette of a head, the face shrouded in darkness. His eyes, wide in fear, struggled to focus on the person in front of him, advancing towards him. Pushing his back deeper into the sofa, he let out a choked shriek, as the being sat down next to him, its features still unclear. He imagined the creature's mouth moving, its reptilian tongue whipping in and out of its mouth as it spoke, taunting him, smelling him in the air. He could hear a voice in the distance calling his name, but he dared not turn away from the horrid creature in front of him. He stood quickly, knocking a vase off the end table as he backed away. It stood with him, drawing nearer. His name was being called louder and louder.

"James! James! James!!"

It reached out to touch him. James felt his legs collapse as he let out an anguished scream.

"James!!!"

James blinked his eyes and saw Andrea kneeling in front of him. He had fallen to the floor, his head inches away from the end of the coffee table.

"James? What happened?"

James stared at Andrea, her face streaked with tears as she leaned over her husband on the floor.

"James, for God's sake, what is going on?"

CHAPTER 16

James could feel his fear coursing through his body like ice water in his veins. He stammered, "Andrea, I don't—I don't know what's happening to me. I saw the most horrible thing. Your head was—was—."

"What? What happened?"

"You had no face! Your face, it just wasn't there. I kept trying to see it, but the face was dark. So dark."

"Honey, let's get you on the sofa, okay?"

Andrea helped James onto the sofa and grabbed a blanket to cover him, hoping that the warmth would calm him down.

"Now, tell me what you saw."

"I told you. I couldn't really see anything. The face was gone. And the head was misshapen, concave. Like someone had hit you..." His voice trailed off, his dream flashing before his eyes. Then a terrible memory revealed itself. He sank into the sofa and sighed heavily. His shoulders turned inward, shuddering.

"What is it, James?"

"I know who the woman is."

"What woman?"

"The faceless woman with the misshapen head. I dreamt about her last night too."

"She's from a nightmare? Honey, she's not real, then. It was just a terrible dream. Maybe the stress from today with Pete brought her back to you, but honey, she isn't real. I'm not hurt."

"That's not it, Andrea. She's not from the nightmare. She is the nightmare." Andrea folded her legs beneath her on the sofa and looked at James, bewildered.

"I don't understand," she said.

James shook his head slowly. He hadn't thought about the woman in years but somehow, she was showing up in his dreams. Why?

"We never talked about this, you and I. I guess I didn't want to think about it anymore. It was just too painful. It was easier for everybody involved to just ignore it, to act like it never happened. But it did happen, Andrea. And it's rearing its ugly head in my dreams. I don't even know when I'm awake or asleep anymore. The dreams seem so real."

"I'm listening."

"My father. He was having an affair with a woman that worked with him. They had to have been carrying on for years. I can remember going to the office to visit him and when she would walk into the room, it became oddly quiet. They didn't have much to say to each other. 'Hello.' 'Goodbye.' 'Can you get this file?' 'Are you going to be in the meeting later?' Nothing out of the ordinary. But there was something about it that made me take notice. It was like they were deliberately carrying on small talk, mimicking normal office behavior for my benefit. This went on from when I was a kid to when I was in my teens."

Andrea nodded silently. James continued,

"The story goes that one day my Dad met her—her name was Karen, I think. Anyway, he goes to meet her at their favorite hotel. It was in Tarrytown, if I remember the story right. Just before the Tappan Zee Bridge in Westchester County. He beats her there, gets some beer, goes into the room, and gets settled. A little while later, Karen comes in and they go at it as usual. When they were done and getting dressed, Karen asked Dad when he was going to divorce Mom and marry her. Apparently, she had been asking him about it for a long time and Dad had just been placating her. So, he tried it again. 'Soon honey. Just be patient. James is still at home. As soon as he leaves for college, I'll do it', he said. She didn't buy it that time. She started going at him about how she's going to tell Mom about their relationship, threatening him."

James paused. He was beginning to shake with the knowledge of what came next. Andrea put her hand on his shoulder and said,

"Just take it slow. We've got all the time in the world."

A voice seeming to come from somewhere in the room asked, "Do you?"

James jumped and looked from side to side. The voice was genderless and even toned. It seemed to hiss at him. James looked at Andrea and realized that he was the only one that heard it. His body quivered as he curled into her embrace.

"Honey, you don't have to tell me if you don't want to."

"I want to. I have to tell you now. I should have told you about this before."

He took a deep breath and gained his composure before continuing.

"My father lost it when she started talking about telling Mom. He pushed her back on the bed. She got right back up and stood toe to toe with him. I don't know whether or not she taunted him, but he punched her."

Andrea gasped as James continued.

"It gets worse, Andrea. Much worse than you could ever imag-ine. He punched her in the face, knocking her back on the bed. The punch dazed her long enough for him to have time to break off a leg from one of those cheap motel chairs. He went over to her and, God, he beat her with the chair leg. He hit her in the head, arms, and her whole torso. Even after she was dead, he kept hitting her with it, disfiguring her so badly she was unrecognizable.

"When he was done, he put the chair leg down next to her on the bed, sat down, and cried over her body. After a while he got up, showered, and came home to us. He was in good spirits that night, even though Mom wasn't. She had gotten home an hour earlier than he had and we were having pizza for dinner. Mom was in a mood, but she had been up and down for months by then, so it didn't seem out of the ordinary.

Dad came in, grabbed a piece of pizza, and talked with me for a couple of hours. We reminisced about old times and things we used to do, like going to the water park, and hitting a few balls around a field. When I was a kid, we used to do everything together. Even now I can remember how cool it was to be with my Dad. He used to tell me all the time that we were the same, that I was so much like him it was scary. That really meant something to me, you know? I loved that I was so close to my Dad. But things started to change, I guess, when I was about eight years old.

"At first, I hated it, but then I realized that Dad really was busy and that he needed time to himself. That's what he told me and that's what I believed. Every once in a while, he would mention our similarities, trying to make conversation. There was an emptiness in his eyes when he said it. But the night he died was different than it had been for a while. We hadn't talked like that in years.

"Then he said he had some work to do, poured himself a rum and coke, and went down to his office. I found him dead in his chair later that night."

"Oh James, that's terrible. I'm so sorry you had to see that."

"The note is the thing that always stuck in my mind, except last night when I saw it in my dream. It was the same one he left but I didn't know what it was, didn't recognize it at all.

"The note was simple. It said, *For protection. For me.* Mom destroyed it before the police came, and we never talked about it. When the police found Karen's body and the chair leg next to her, they were able to figure out that Dad had killed her. They compared the bloody fingerprints on the chair leg against those taken from him at the morgue. There was a one hundred percent match.

"Everyone on our street looked at us with pity in their eyes. It was nauseating. I was glad when I left for college. At least I would escape their loaded stares. Mom and I never talked about Dad's suicide after that. All she ever said was that Dad was mentally ill, and that we should just let him rest in peace."

Andrea sat back taking all of it in. After a few minutes of silence she said, "That is an incredible story. I can't believe you went through all of that." Andrea rubbed James' shoulder as she spoke. "That's enough to make anyone have nightmares."

"But the nightmares haven't been about the suicide. I haven't dreamt about that in a long time. I don't know why I'm seeing Karen in my dreams. I barely knew her."

Andrea fell silent again, her mind flooding with questions, each bounding off the other.

"What do you think the note meant?" she finally asked. "Do you think that he wanted to protect your mother from suffering the same fate as his girlfriend?"

"Maybe. That's what I thought at first. For years, even. But now I'm not so sure."

"What do you mean?"

"What if Dad didn't kill Karen?"

"What? You said the police found the evidence. His fingerprints were all over the murder weapon."

"I know, but his and at least twenty other people's fingerprints would have been on that chair. It was in a motel, after all."

"Yeah, but none of the other prints would have had blood on them."

"What if the killer wore gloves?"

Andrea looked disbelievingly at James.

"Hear me out. The story that I just told you came from my

mother. She told me this just after he died and said she would never discuss it again. She claimed that Dad told her about the affair and the murder right before he killed himself. She said he confessed everything. It was the middle of April. Mom usually went to bed early; her allergies always got the best of her during that time of year. Dad went downstairs at about 10:30 p.m. Mom had already gone upstairs. In fact, you could hear her heavy breathing from the bottom of the stairs. I just don't believe that she woke up, talked to Dad, and went back to bed knowing everything she would have known."

"So, what are you saying?"

James hesitated. He had never said what he thought out loud, let alone to another person. He hadn't even allowed himself to entertain the thought for long. Could his mother really have been capable of murder?

"What if Mom followed Dad to the hotel? She might have known about the affair. Or at least suspected it. It had been going on forever and Dad was never at home. Maybe she waited for both of them to get in the room, and then watched to make sure that she had the proof she needed. If she overheard what Dad was saying about leaving us and marrying Karen, that might have been enough to throw her over the edge."

"Yeah, but murder? What about your father? Do you think he would have stood there and let it happen?"

"People always said that Dad was suggestible. Maybe she used that to her advantage. If she broke into the room in a jealous rage, broke the chair, and attacked Karen, he might have been too shocked to react. Or maybe she made Dad do it."

"What? How could she do that?"

"Mom had a hold over Dad. She was strong-willed. She wanted what she wanted when she wanted it. She was able to get him to do what she wanted him to do. It was like he couldn't say no to her. Maybe she used that. Maybe it was a combination of her power over him, and his mental state at the time. If what people said about him was true, I don't see why she couldn't have pulled it off."

"And you think he may have killed himself because of the guilt?" Andrea fidgeted uncomfortably on the sofa, the conversation taking a turn to the surreal.

"I don't know what I'm saying, Andrea. I only know that the story Mom told me was too perfect. It was wrapped like a gift under the tree on Christmas Day. How could she know so much about it?"

"Maybe because your Dad talked to her before he killed himself," Andrea said, louder than she meant to. She was feeling very antsy, the hairs on the back of her neck were standing up. James' mother a murderer?

"Do you know the incredible mind control she would have had to use over him? It would be akin to what Charles Manson did to those kids. Do you think your mother was capable of something like that?"

James shook his head slowly and looked down at his hands. It did sound far-fetched. He wouldn't have even considered that his mother had anything to do with it were it not for her saying that people could get his father to do things for them by planting the seed of thought in his mind. Did he think his mother would have exploited it? Not before the affair. But after his father had betrayed her, all bets were off. If Andrea had a lover and he had the chance to get rid of him and keep his hands clean, would he? James wondered. He flinched as his mind offered an answer all too readily. It was human nature, like it or not. You hit me, I'll hit you back harder.

"I know it's hard to believe. That's why I've never told anyone what I thought before. It doesn't make sense. My mother killing someone? Or forcing my Dad to kill another person? It sounds like the plot of a B movie."

Andrea snickered, trying to camouflage her apprehension.

"The story just seemed so... scripted. Disingenuous."

"I don't know," Andrea sighed, stretching her legs out in front of her.

"Neither do I, but how else would Mom have found out that story. That level of detail?"

"Maybe she pieced it together. Embellishing a story is not unheard of."

"Maybe."

Andrea sighed heavily and stretched her back.

"And Karen's coming to you in your dreams? Why?"

"That's the part I don't understand. After I went away to college, Mom started to see things."

"Things? Like what?" Andrea asked, pulling her knees up to her chin.

"One night when I was home on break, I was up late watching television in the living room. It was 1:30 in the morning when I heard Mom yell, 'Get out of here! Leave me alone!' Then I heard a door slam."

"Who was she talking to?"

"That's the thing. I asked her who she was talking to the next day and she said, 'You don't see them, Jimmie?' It froze me where I stood. She never called me Jimmie. Nobody ever called me Jimmie. That was my Dad's name. He was Jimmie. I am James or Jim. Dad only went by Jimmie."

Andrea nodded slightly. James had been adamant about that when they first met. She made the mistake of calling him Jimmie once. She only did it the one time, but that was enough. They were walking on her campus one Sunday, getting lost in the fall foliage that crunched under their feet. She was feeling so comfortable with him, loving every minute of their budding romance. It just fell out of her mouth. She was reveling in the cool air as it combed through her hair, the sunlight peeking through the trees. She was holding his hand and it felt warm entwined with hers. Their arms swung effortlessly in the cool breeze as they strolled along the pathway toward the student center. Andrea thought the weather was perfect for a day outside with her new guy. She thought it signified the beginning of something real. Then she said it.

"Isn't this a beautiful day, Jimmie?"

She was still swinging her arm lightly as they had been before when she felt the dead weight of his as it hung limply at his side. He had stopped walking and was staring at her with eyes filled with wonder and dread.

Andrea remembered looking at him, confused as to what made him stop.

"What is it, honey?" she asked as she took a step toward him.

He took a step backwards as she approached, letting go of her hand. The smile that was on her face faded as she stood awkwardly in front of him. The happiness she had experienced only a minute before seemed old, faded like a memory from years ago. Now the air felt cold and unyielding, the sun's rays deceptive and cruel.

She asked again. "James, what's wrong?"

"You called me Jimmie, didn't you? That's what you said, right?" He tried to keep his voice even.

"Yeah, but what's the matter with you?" She reached out to him again and he flinched but didn't pull away.

"My name isn't Jimmie."

A smile spread across her face. She thought he was playing with her. She nudged him playfully and said, "I know who you are, silly. You're my Jimmie."

James' face remained stern as he put a hand up to silence her.

"No," he said firmly, "my name is not Jimmie. Please don't call me that."

"How come?" Andrea said, her smile still shining brightly.

"That was my father's name."

Andrea lost her smile again and stared at James in silence. He looked at her, his eyes emotionless. He could see that she was confused. James didn't really understand why he cared so much either, but it was important to him. He was not going to be like his father, nothing could make him. There was no better place to start than with the name.

After a minute or two James touched Andrea's shoulder and said, lightening his voice, "It's no big deal. It's just that, well, my Dad's dead, and I have a thing about him keeping his name. Just call me James or Jim... okay?"

He hoped that the explanation would be enough for her. Her eyes still questioned, but she said nothing.

Andrea nodded, although she still didn't understand. James smiled at her reassuringly as he put his arm around her. It was infectious. She felt a smile forming on her lips as he leaned down and kissed her on the cheek. He pulled her closer to him as they started back down the pathway.

Nothing more was ever said about it.

"The way she was looking at me was strange too," James continued. "It was like she didn't really see me at all. She was looking through me at something behind me. It was scary."

"What did you do?"

"I called her again, only louder this time. She snapped out of it and asked me what I was yelling about. I told her what she had said, but she didn't remember any of it. Then she told me to let the past lie and walked into the kitchen."

"You think she was talking to Karen and your father?"

"I don't know. She never told me. She had a couple more episodes like that before she died. One time she even threw a pot of boiling water across the room at whoever or whatever she was talking to."

"That's eerie."

James sat back on the sofa, clearly spent. He furrowed his brow and shook his head slowly.

"Something still bugs me about my dream though. When I saw Karen, she was in this old, abandoned house. She kept calling me Jimmie. Andrea, she said, 'It's good to have you back, Jimmie.'

CHAPTER 17

James and Andrea sat up for hours talking about his father, Karen, and his mother's potential involvement in Karen's death. Could she have really killed his father's lover in cold blood? James wasn't sure either way, wasn't sure that he should even be thinking about those long-buried ghosts. All three people involved were dead, long dead, and there was no need to rehash the past, especially when he would never find out the truth. But he knew that really wasn't true. The questions had always been there, he guessed, tucked away in a little corner of his mind. But somewhere, deep in his subconscious, he knew the answers too. He just didn't want to wake the beast that would speak in confession.

They finally made their way up to the bedroom and went to sleep. James slept well for hours, better than he had slept in months. At about 2:30 a.m. he awoke to the sound of a loud crack. He sat up in bed, his back arched, his body still. He listened. Nothing. His eyes scanned the room searching for movement. He peered through the darkness trying to determine if anything was out of place. A sliver of moonlight draped the back of Andrea's vanity chair, drenching it with its bright light. The rest of the room was dark. Normal.

James wrestled with wanting to go back to sleep and the need to investigate the cause of the sound. He was vaguely aware that he needed to get back to sleep if he planned on going to work later on that day, Monday morning blues already clouding his mind. Before work intruded in his groggy mind, he remembered that Monday was a holiday. Columbus Day? Who cared? He was off and that was all that was important at 2:30 in the morning.

That problem solved, his mind jumped back and forth between sleep and finding out what caused the noise, one voice raising a point, and another identical voice countering it, the banter sounding loudly in his head. Listening to the faceless echoes of himself, his eyelids became heavy, and he started to settle back into the folds of sheets and blankets. His shadowy bedroom became a blur just beyond his closing eyelids. Before he succumbed to sleep, just as his eyelids were about to close, he saw something move beside the armoire.

He opened his eyes quickly, scanning the room, more franticly this time than before, because he saw the thing, whatever it was, moving in his direction. Again, he saw nothing out of the ordinary. After a couple of minutes of sitting in bed, his eyes wide open like a frightened child after a nightmare, he decided to try sleep again. He dismissed the movement as a trick of light, one of those shadows that appear on the wall as soon as nightfall sets, to scare children and jumpy men. *It's nothing,* he told himself as he sank down in the covers and turned on his side. But as he rested his head on the pillow and shut his eyes, he wasn't so sure.

James awoke the next morning with a feeling of dread surrounding him so strongly he almost didn't want to open his eyes to face the new day. As he lay in bed on the cusp of alertness, he heard voices. Snarling, growling voices in the distance. They were talking about something, the language was indecipherable, but the inflection was clear. James knew they were talking about him, looking at him even though he couldn't see them. He listened as they rumbled on, the menacing chorus filling his ears. The sound was deafening. He tried to open his eyes if for nothing more than to see his tormentors, to lay eyes on the creatures making those horrible noises. About him. To him. But he couldn't move.

The voices were coming closer and closer, more disjointed, more wicked. He could make out the pattern of a language now. Chinese? Vietnamese? He couldn't tell. The voices were so angry. He wanted to move away from them, to be anywhere other than in their path. He tried desperately to open his mind's eye, to sense who or what was talking to him. But he couldn't do anything. It was as though he was paralyzed. Again.

The voices swirled around James, taunting him in languages he didn't understand. He heard more languages now, French, Italian, Spanish, German, and others. They were coming from all sides, above and below him. He was terrified at the intensity with which they spoke. The voices crescendoed, rising and falling rapidly, driving him to the point of insanity. The languages twisted and turned around each other like writhing snakes.

When he thought he couldn't take anymore, a voice speaking English broke through, barking incongruent sentences at him. The phrases were so discordant and the intonation was so much like the other ones that, at first, James didn't realize that he could understand the words. The moment he began to recognize the language being spoken as English. The voices fell silent. His eyes snapped open and his body spontaneously caved into the mattress, as though it had been dropped from the ceiling. He tried to remember the words that had been shouted at him but couldn't, the memory of their sound fading by the second. A single word echoed in his head, playing at the edges of his consciousness, torturing it.

Jimmie.

CHAPTER 18

Pete sat in James and Andrea's kitchen nook nursing a cup of coffee and watching Andrea toast bagels. He decided to keep the long-standing date that he, Andrea, James and Susan had started for three-day weekends. On the third day, they would meet at James' house, throw some steaks on the grill, and play cards in the evening until about 8:30, when Susan and Pete would go home. It was always a fun time. That day would have been the first time they had done it since Susan died.

The good times they'd had weren't Pete's real reason for being there though. What he really wanted to do was to put pressure on James. Pete knew that James wouldn't be expecting him, not after what happened the day before. That was, if James remembered about the tradition at all. Pete also knew that the coward hadn't told his wife about it yet, any of it. Not about the affair and not about the fight. He didn't have the balls. Pete wanted to show his face to bait James, make him nervous. Or better yet, make him scared.

Pete waited while Andrea whipped up a quick snack for the two of them. James was still asleep and Andrea thought she should let him rest a little longer. It was one of the first times James had slept peacefully in weeks. She didn't want to disturb him. Pete had no problem with that. Andrea also told him that she wanted to talk with him about something. *Anything you want, baby.*

Andrea wore a casual extra-large t-shirt over old sweatpants. Flip-flops that had seen better days adorned her feet. He gazed at her small, pedicured toes and smiled. She was so dainty, so perfect. She worked with her back to him, pulling out plates from the cabinet, putting on another pot of coffee. She was talking about James' nightmares, asking Pete if he had any ideas on how to help him shake them.

"They're real zingers, Pete. Not just little kid stuff, things that go bump in the night. These dreams would make the hair on your neck stand up. And those are just the ones he's told me about," she said as she walked into the kitchen nook. He nodded, looking appropriately concerned, not wanting to let on that he couldn't care less about James and his screwed-up dreams. "Dreams are mirrors that show what's inside us," someone had told him once. "If you have fucked up dreams, then you are a fucked-up person." It was as simple as that. And James, Pete had learned, was a fucked-up person if anyone was.

Andrea hesitated at the counter, turning and stealing a glance at Pete as he sipped his coffee. She wanted to know what happened the night before between he and James. She wanted to know why friends would punch each other. Pete looked up and caught her eye. He didn't smile so much as he smirked at her. Something about the look stopped her cold. Andrea abandoned the questions forming in her mind, thinking better of asking about the fight. She figured it couldn't have been that bad, or Pete wouldn't have come by. Andrea served him a bagel before going to the bedroom to wake James.

James stood in the shower staring at the drain as the hot water beat his neck and shoulders. He watched as the water circled the drain, trying not to fall in, and equated it with the way his life had been for the past couple of months. His nighttime horrors had slipped into his daytime reality and it scared him. He didn't know what was real anymore. He felt as if he was spiraling downward, just like the water, into the dark abyss of the drain, unaware of what awaited him as soon as he fell in. But he did know, he thought suddenly, as water dripped off his face, falling into the emptiness beyond the drain. He did know what awaited him when the lights went down. What waited patiently during the light of day, only coming out long enough to feel the temperature, to gauge just how much longer it would have to remain hidden. He knew. Karen waited for him. His father waited for him. Death was waiting.

He turned his face upward into the stream of water, letting it splatter over his forehead. As he closed his eyes against the flow, he saw them - his father and Karen - on the inside of his eyelids, the great movie screen in his head. They stood, bloodied and battered, looking at him. *Why are you here?* he asked them silently. He had never done anything to his father, yet he had tormented James' mind since the day he died. *Why can't you leave me alone?* he asked futilely.

James stared at the apparitions manifesting themselves in his head, his heart racing. He could see his father's face as though he was standing in front of him. Ghostly, but still the man he knew. The man he loved. The man he detested.

"Why are you doing this to me?" he asked aloud.

The sweetest voice spoke softly, almost in a whisper,

"You know why, Jimmie. You know."

James let the melody of the voice shower over him. It caressed his ears and made his heart flutter. It was the voice of his beloved Susan. On the mornings when they would leave their bed and breakfast in Nyack to go back to their spouses and resume normal life, they would share a leisurely shower that usually lead to more lovemaking, just one last quickie before going home. Susan always slipped into the shower after James and ran her hands down his back. She would whisper in his ear, the sound resembling the beautiful cooing of a cockatoo, as she soaped his body. James imagined Susan moving in front of him, her hair wet and slicked back as the water saturated it. He saw her kissing his neck, slowly moving down his chest, pausing to give attention to both nipples. He felt her hands encircling his stiffened member, caressing it, placating it until she could greet it with her lips. His own hand stroked his member as he succumbed to the fantasy, envisioning her hand instead of his in rhythmic, tantalizing motion. It was her voice he heard as he stood under the gentle flow of hot water from the showerhead, his mind allowing him the moment to indulge in the memory of his lost love.

A draft swirled the faint mist that was accumulating in the opaque glassed shower stall, raising goose bumps on his back. As the air cooled the water on his skin, James was pulled away from Susan and pushed forward into the darkened corners of his mind. He heard the voice for what it was then. It was Susan's voice on the surface, yes, but with a mucusy, wet undertone. The voice seemed to crawl over his skin, filling his open pores with its greasy discharge. He forced his eyes open and recoiled from the direction of the draft, vaguely acknowledging that there was no window in the bathroom.

The face that stared back at him from the other side of the shower stall, masked in the steam, was his own. James recognized the man instantly, his stomach dropping like he had just survived the first drop of an amusement park roller coaster. The man was standing in front of the side panel next to Andrea's showerhead, within arm's reach. Only two steps stood between James and a killer. He felt the muscles in his legs tighten.

The man smiled at him. It was an endearing, almost loving smile that would have melted any woman's heart. It chilled James to the base of his spine. The all-too-familiar feeling of paralysis crept up his legs, through his torso, and down his arms before he was able to blink. On some level of his consciousness, James was aware of a stream of warm liquid running down his leg, far warmer than the water that beat his back incessantly.

The man looked at James' penis and shook his head in pity. Its erect form had gone limp, succumbing to the fear that had gripped him. A knowing, sickening smirk crossed the man's face, and James feared that he might touch him.

James stared at the man, unable to believe the similarities between the stranger and himself. Not only did he look like James, but his mannerisms, facial expressions, hell, the way he moved all reminded James of himself. It was as if he were watching a videotape of himself in motion. It was unsettling.

Somehow James forced himself to speak, "How did you get in here?" he asked in a raspy, choked voice that he barely recognized as his own.

The man's smile widened as James floundered. The shower spray had turned cold, James realized distractedly. The man looked up at the showerhead after James completed the thought, as though he had heard the sentiment voiced in James' mind. James' eyes widened as his mind, fraught with horror, thought, *Can he read my mind?*

The man laughed heartily. The sound, though not all together unpleasant, had an edge to it. One that was as sharp as a knife. It did not echo off the glass doors of the shower. In fact, the sound seemed to emanate from James' head. The deafening effect was almost unbearable.

"Who are you? What are you doing here?" James asked, his pulse quickening. The fear mounted steadily within him, constricting his throat as he pled desperately for an answer. He needed to know who the man was. He wondered if he would be the man's next victim.

The man stepped closer to him, his shirt dampening from the water bouncing off James' shoulders. Without hesitation, the man said, "You know Jimmie. You know."

The man smelled of leaves and dirt wet from a summer storm.

He lingered in front of James for a moment before turning and walking toward the glass panel where he stood before.

James found his strength and swung at the man with everything he had. His foot slipped on the combination of water, soap, and the slick ceramic floor. James went crashing down to the floor of the shower without his hands out in front of him to break the fall. He hit his head hard on the ceramic tile, opening a deep gash over his eye. As the blood dripped to the floor, James looked up through blurry eyes and saw the man standing over him. His expression was one that depicted both God and Satan at the same time. Love and hate. Benevolence and punishment.

CHAPTER 19

Andrea opened the bedroom door and saw that the bed was empty. She could hear the shower running through the closed bathroom door, the spray smacking against James' back as he rinsed. Andrea walked through their bedroom to the bathroom door on the opposite side of the bed and stopped, her hand hovering above the doorknob.

She heard James' voice on the other side.

Andrea couldn't quite make out what James was saying, but he seemed to be having a conversation.

She stood in the bedroom, her ear pressed to the bathroom door. She didn't know what to do. With the nightmares James had been having, Andrea wasn't sure if she should enter the room and help him or let James sort out his thoughts in peace. She sighed as she thought, tossed between the two options. Finally, Andrea decided to leave James alone with his thoughts.

Andrea was about to turn away, to write a note telling him that Pete was downstairs and return to her company when she heard a loud thump. She raced into the room and found James lying on the floor of the shower stall, bleeding from the head.

CHAPTER 20

James stared at the demigod standing before him, certain that his life would be drawing to a close that day. That minute. But the deathblow didn't come. The man merely looked at him hatefully, pitifully, lovingly all at the same time. James spoke, breathing so heavily his words came out in a whisper,

"Go on then. Just do it."

The man revealed a smile that resembled a grimace. It was full of fangs and jagged teeth. James cried out, hating himself for that final show of weakness in the face of unsightly evil.

The door to the bathroom flung open and James could hear Andrea's feet padding frantically on the tiled floor.

"James? James, can you hear me?"

James, realizing that Andrea was in imminent danger, lifted himself up, supporting his upper body with his elbow. The shift took tremendous effort. James couldn't suppress the moan that escaped his lips.

"No! Andrea, stay back! Get out of here!" he yelled frantically from the shower stall, the sound reverberating off the walls. He begged her to leave. Whatever was happening was between him and the man, not her.

"James, what happened? Are you hurt?" Andrea asked as she approached the door to the shower stall.

James watched the man, trying to gauge his movements. If he had to tackle the man before he could get to Andrea, he would do it. James vowed not to let anything happen to Andrea, not to another person. He could stop the man this time. He could stop him. The thought grew strong in his mind, running side by side with the notion that he was a dead man.

The man looked at James one last time before turning away. The door to the shower stall opened abruptly, kicking chilly water onto James as he lay in a puddle that was quickly becoming more blood than water.

"James! Oh my God, honey. Are you all right?"

Andrea reached into the shower stall to help James stand. Panicking, James pulled away and yelled, "Andrea, get out of here!"

James turned back to look at the man, hoping that he hadn't advanced while James was distracted. The spot where he had stood was empty. The man was gone.

Disbelief clouded James' vision as he stared at the fogged glass of the shower stall behind where he last saw his nemesis. His head was throbbing; the pain from the deep gash penetrated his thoughts and pushed them aside, vying for attention.

Andrea entered the shower, her sweatpants darkening from the cool water raining down from the showerhead.

"James let's get you out of the shower. Come on, baby."

James got to his feet with Andrea's help. He glanced back and forth between her and the shower stall, still trying to understand what happened.

Andrea laid him down on the bed, wet a hand towel, and pressed it against the ugly gash just above his eye.

"James, this may need stitches."

Andrea sounded like she was speaking from the bottom of a

funnel, slowly spiraling away from him. He turned to her and tried to focus.

"Did you hear me?" Andrea asked. "I think we need to go to the hospital to have this looked at. It's a really bad cut."

"No, no," James protested. "I'll be okay. It's not as bad as it looks."

"How would you know, James? You haven't been able to pull your eyes away from the shower stall long enough to see it."

It was then that James realized that he had once again turned away from Andrea to look into the bathroom, even though the shower stall was barely visible from where he sat.

"What are you looking for, honey? What's in there?"

Part of him knew that Andrea had called him *honey*, but his rational mind lost the fight to the irrational side, the one that told him that she called him *Jimmie*. Before he could stop himself, he shoved Andrea away from him, causing her to bump into the chaise lounge and fall onto its cushion.

"Get out! Get out!" James shouted at the top of his lungs, suddenly furious.

Andrea sat up on the chaise and looked at James in shock. Before she could react, James stood up, readying himself to advance. He looked frenzied, the blood dripping onto his cheek from the gash above his eye adding to the ominous demeanor his body had created. Andrea realized in horror that the man standing in front of their bed was not the man she had married. All at once it seemed the man she loved went through some kind of metamorphosis, both emotional and physical. The physical changes were subtle, almost imperceptible if you weren't looking for them. But Andrea saw them. James' shoulders slumped with the weight of anger and malevolence. His hands were balled into tight fists. His thigh muscles were tensed, his legs ready to spring. His face was a violent visage that she barely recognized. She was terrified.

Andrea got up from the chaise quickly and rushed to the door. She looked at James once more through tear-filled eyes. He had turned away from her again and was staring into the bathroom, oblivious to Andrea's cutting stare. Andrea slammed the door with all the force she could muster.

James peered into bathroom again, looking for something—anything—that would prove that the man had actually been there, in the shower stall, with him. The shower, its water turned off, was empty. The fog on the opaque glass dissipated and revealed nothing.

CHAPTER 21

Andrea walked into the family room with tears streaming down her face. Pete, who was engrossed in a basketball game on television, didn't see her come in. When she sat down next to him, tissue in hand and tears streaking her face, he embraced her without question.

"Andrea, what's wrong?"

Andrea sobbed into Pete's chest, not answering him for several minutes. When she finally got her breathing under control she whispered, "It's James. I don't know what's happening to him, Pete."

"What do you mean? What happened when you went upstairs?"

Pete wondered if James had heard his car when he drove up to their house. The purr of his 1957 Mustang was unmistakable. He fought to suppress the smile teasing his lips.

"He was in the shower and I could hear him talking."

"Talking?" Pete asked, his interest piqued more and more.

Andrea sat up so that she could look into Pete's eyes when she told him what she had witnessed in the bathroom.

"It was like he was having a conversation with someone, but he's alone up there.

There's no one else in the house except you and me." Andrea sighed and sank into Pete's arms as she recounted the details.

"At first I thought he was just talking out loud," she continued, "trying to reconcile his dreams. I started to walk away to let him deal with whatever it was by himself. I was going to give him some privacy. Before I could turn away from the bathroom door, I heard a loud thump. When I opened it, I saw James sprawled out on the shower floor. He had banged his head so badly there was blood all over the floor of the stall. I think he's going to need stitches."

"We need to get him to the hospital," Pete cut in, pushing off the sofa and standing quickly. He was eager to get upstairs and see James. He wanted to taunt him, to rub it in. He was almost giddy with excitement.

Pete was about to walk up the steps that led to James and Andrea's bedroom when Andrea grabbed his arm and continued,

"Pete, James kicked me out of the room. He shoved me—." Her voice broke, and she folded her arms tightly across her chest, trying to keep in the sob that threatened to rise from her diaphragm.

"He what?" Pete sat back down and put his arm around Andrea's shoulders. "Are you all right? Did he hurt you?"

"No, no. He startled me more than anything. But it wasn't him, Pete." Andrea paused, hoping that what she had said would sink in, would make sense somehow. She didn't want to have to explain what she meant because she didn't know how to. James just seemed... different.

"What do you mean it wasn't him?"

"It just didn't seem like him. He was different. His posture, his eyes. I felt like I had never seen him before. Maybe it was because he was so angry."

"With you? How could he be angry with you? You didn't do anything but try to help him." Pete's face showed anger. His brow was furrowed and his forehead was creased. Inside though, his mind laughed heartily. *What's the matter, Jim?* Pete thought to himself. *Can't take the pressure?* Pete maintained his facial expression, every feature appearing full of concern.

"No, he wasn't mad at me. At least I don't think so," Andrea started. "There was something else. I don't think he focused on me the whole time I was in the room with him. I'd be surprised if he even knew I was there, or that it was me that was with him."

Pete's face frowned in confusion.

"I know. It sounds strange, but I'm not sure he knew it was me that he was talking to." Andrea's arms remained wrapped around her body, the touch comforting her somehow.

"There was something more than anger in his expression," she continued. "I could swear that James was afraid of something in that bathroom. He was staring through the door at whatever it was when he threw me out."

CHAPTER 22

Pete left Andrea in the family room to recover from her ordeal with James, her body sinking dejectedly into the plush sofa. He walked up the stairs to James and Andrea's bedroom. As he walked up the steps, he looked at the pictures that hung on the wall. They captured special moments when James and Andrea were dating up through marriage. As he looked at them, each in varying sizes but always showing the same jovial smiles, emitting the same warmth, Pete was struck with weighty jealousy. James betrayed him with his wife, yet he still lived the life of a happily married man. He had a nice house in a nice neighborhood with a beautiful wife who adored him. How was that justice?

He mounted the top stair and turned to walk down the hallway towards the bedroom, tingling with expectancy. A sardonic smile spread across Pete's face as he approached the bedroom door. He fought the urge to laugh as the reality of the situation became clear in his mind. This was the beginning of the end.

James was cracking up; losing it. His guilt was tormenting him, eating away at him in the night, terrorizing him with demons and ghosts in his dreams. He was faltering under the weight. *Good for him,* Pete thought as he put his hand on the doorknob. James was right where Pete wanted him to be. He glanced down at the damp spot on his shirt where Andrea's tears had soaked through and smiled.

"Don't worry," he said aloud in the empty hallway, "I'll be there to pick up the pieces."

CHAPTER 23

James stood next to his bed for a long time, looking into the bathroom, trying to find some shard of evidence that the man had actually been there. Fear kept him paralyzed by the bed, the open shower door daring him to venture closer. His forehead felt numb where he had banged it against the ceramic floor of the shower stall. The pain was dull but persistent. He touched his head and felt the blood that had been streaming steadily from the gash, realizing that he was bleeding too much and needed medical attention. Yet he couldn't stop looking into the bathroom.

James had been willing to dismiss that woman's horrible murder as a daydream, a terrifying vision brought on by the stress over the affair with Susan and her tragic death. He wanted to believe that—had to, to keep his sanity. But the dream—if that's what it was—was so realistic. James sat staring into the bathroom recalling the coolness of his skin as he stood in his foyer; the crosswinds on the rooftop chilling him even then. He could feel the tension in his forearm, the muscles throbbing from being flexed in vain. All those things were real to James, tangible after the fact. But he told himself it was a daydream. Had to be.

There was no woman (the memory of her face smiling at him just before plummeting to her death still haunted him). There was no mysterious man, twin to him or otherwise. It was all just a figment of his imagination. James had almost made himself believe it, despite the inordinate time loss he experienced during the daydream—could he have really been in the foyer for an hour and ten minutes? Maybe, but he doubted it. And what about the keys? He remembered bending to pick them up but didn't remember actually touching the metal ring. The questions nagged at him incessantly, lingering in his mind, teasing him with their validity, dodging the sweeping hand as it arched to nudge them out of the way. They had bothered him during his talk with Andrea as they awoke sleeping ghosts. He tried to dismiss them but couldn't. Not completely.

It was ridiculous, wasn't it? James' rational mind tried to rally that morning before his shower. If he hadn't been standing in the foyer for an hour and ten minutes, where had he been? Had he walked through the wall where that strange shadow had marked a circle into another world? Into that woman's apartment? No. Had he stood on the roof of a building in a neighborhood he had never been to while a woman he had never met was thrown over the edge, tossed away like a rag doll, by a man who looked frighteningly like himself? This, only after he watched her being stabbed in the throat while she lay sleeping in her bed? No. It wasn't possible.

Yet the possibility nagged at him. No matter how irrational the whole thing seemed he couldn't obliterate the chance from his mind. The possibility of truth, the sliver of its validation, terrified him. He raised objects against it, like concrete walls around the inkling, but still it sat, resilient and compelling. In that reality, the man was real. In that reality, the man is him. The weight of those thoughts made his skin perspire and caused his hands to shake.

It couldn't be, he challenged. *I watched it happen. I didn't partici-*

pate at all. The silence in his mind at that assertion was more accusatory than spoken words.

James blinked painfully, the pressure of his wound creeping into his eyes. The blink washed away the thoughts bouncing around in his head and cleared his ever-blurring vision. Some of his blood had splattered on the cream carpet, the contrast so striking James couldn't pull his eyes away from the staggered droplets. It was as if he relived the episode with the sighting of every drop; a red dot of himself sinking into the carpet fibers, embedding in the padding forever. The gash above his eye beat steadily like a metronome keeping time.

The door to the bedroom opened abruptly, jarring James out of his hypnotic trance cast by the horrors in the bathroom. James turned to see Pete walking into the room, a look of concern darkening his face.

"James, what's up man?" Pete asked lightly as he closed the door behind him. He walked over to the foot of the bed and looked at James meaningfully.

James looked at Pete in shock, questioning his presence. "What are you doing here?"

"I was downstairs when you and Andrea had your... whatever just happened between you two. She wanted me to come up and talk to you."

James, suddenly aware of his nakedness, sat down on the bed and covered himself.

"I'm okay, man. I just had a fall."

Pete laughed humorlessly and said, "I think you had more than just a fall, James. Have you seen your head?"

Pete walked over to James and turned his body towards the mirror. It reflected a disconcerted man with most of the skin on his head and chest painted red with blood. The gash was still oozing blood that streamed steadily down his cheek.

"Oh God, I need to go to the hospital."

James stood and tried to walk toward the dresser to get some underwear. As he took his first step, he felt wary of turning his back on Pete, given their interaction the day before.

Before James could take a second step, he stumbled. Pete caught him under the arms and laid him back down on the bed.

"Easy Jimmie, easy. Let's take this slow. I'll get you some clothes."

Pete walked toward the dresser, and after trying several drawers—after lingering longingly at Andrea's undergarment drawer—took out underwear for James to put on. James stared at Pete as he moved languidly across the room to the closet, taking out jeans and a shirt. Did he hear Pete correctly? Did Pete just call him Jimmie?

Pete came back to the bed and dropped the clothes to James' right side.

"Can you do this yourself?" Pete asked.

"Yeah, I got it," James replied distractedly. "Hey," James started as he pulled on his underwear, "Why'd you call me Jimmie?"

Pete, who had gone back to the closet to get James' tennis shoes, smiled into the darkened closet while his back faced the room. He had slipped the nickname in, debating whether or not to do it up until the last second. He was unsure of what James' reaction would be. Pete had already prepared a story for Andrea if James had attacked him. It would be easy to say that James had lost control of himself, all the while giving her the most mournful face he could. Given his antics that morning, the story would have gone over easily. But he didn't have to use it after all. Pete's smile widened as he made James wait.

When Pete turned to face James, his expression was one of confusion.

"What do you mean?" Pete asked as he brought the shoes over to James and sat in the chair opposite the bed.

"Jimmie. You called me Jimmie, Pete. Why?"

"I guess—I don't know, man. It just came out."

"You've never called me Jimmie before. No one ever calls me Jimmie."

"What's the big deal? Jim, Jimmie, James. Who cares?"

James paused at this. Pete seemed taken aback, like he really didn't know what the problem was. Didn't he remember the story James had told him that night in the dorm when they were drunker than they should have been? James had told Pete about the suicide and his father's mysterious illness. He told Pete about the potential heredity of whatever had plagued his Dad, and how frightened he was that it might have transferred to him. James had even told Pete about his grandmother, and how his father had distanced himself from her as soon as he became an adult. James' father never said exactly why he didn't talk to his mother, just that she wasn't healthy, and that he didn't want her poison to make him sick.

James never understood what his father meant when he said that, but he had never forgotten it. All of his life, before the suicide, James wanted to be close to his Dad, wanted to grow up to be just like him. After the suicide, he wanted to forget everything about him that he could. James wanted to escape, to run away from the memories. They seemed to haunt him since his father's death. Pete knew that. Drunk or not, Pete had listened that day. James knew he remembered every word. Pete could cram for a test while drinking rum all night and ace it the next day. Pete knew James' issue with the name Jimmie. So why did he call him by it?

When James bent over to put his foot into his pants leg, the floor rushed up at him and he collapsed, his head spinning dizzily. Pete joined James on the floor, kneeling beside him. James' eyes were glazed; he was close to passing out.

"It's okay, buddy. I can hold the police off for a little while."

"What? What are you talking about?" James mumbled, barely coherent.

"The police. They called and said they wanted to talk to you about Susan's death. I'm sure they can wait until you feel better."

Images of Susan rushed into James' mind. Her car burning. Her smiling face upturned to him as they walked along the sidewalk in Nyack. Her face, upturned to the crack in the window, just barely open, blocked now by the melted plastic that pressed against it, her eyes wild, and her lips gasping for air...

CHAPTER 24

The whirlwind of waking up in the ambulance on the way to the hospital, getting six stitches to close the gaping wound above his eye, and going home ten hours later was a blur to James. Andrea sat with him for an hour in their bedroom where she insisted, he remain for the rest of the night. She gave him Chamomile tea to bring him down from the day's activities. She played soothing music and kept the lights dim. Under different circumstances, the relaxed mood set in the room would have sparked romance between the two of them. Instead, Andrea worried about James and the demons he fought in his head and James tried desperately to remember what happened before he passed out.

For James, his head in Andrea's lap, the memory of the man in the bathroom was vivid. Remembering the incident made his skin crawl and caused goose bumps to surface on his forearms. He remembered being distracted after the fall and telling Andrea to leave. Is that all that happened? He remembered her face, frightened and bewildered, staring back at him from the chaise lounge. Had she seen the man also?

James opened his mouth to ask her what she saw but thought better of it and snuggled closer to her thigh. When Andrea came into the bathroom, the man was still there. James could still see his ominous black clad figure angelically silhouetted by the rising steam created by the shower spray. Andrea, James, and the man were in the same space at the same time yet she didn't see him. Surely, she would have said something if she had. The striking resemblance between the two of them would have been enough for her to question. His presence in the house without her knowledge, and in the shower with him would have raised a question from anyone.

Andrea hadn't seen him.

Only he had. Hadn't he, in his mind, referred to the man as an apparition? Some part of his psyche knew that he wasn't tangible, yet his eyes told him that he was real. His conscious mind rejected the thought time and time again. Something was pressing him, making him see. *How could the man be anything but real?* his mind questioned. *That would make me—*

"Crazy," James said aloud.

"Honey, what did you say?"

"I feel like I'm going insane, Andrea," James confessed. Tears welled in his eyes as what had been lurking in his subconscious for days was given voice. If the man wasn't real, and if he was a figment of his imagination, a projection of sorts, why was he seeing him now, in his waking world? In the light of day? Why did the man provoke him? And why, why did the man look so much like himself?

The prospect that the man and James were one in the same continued to play at the corners of his mind, barely uttered, but unquestionably there. James pushed it out every time it advanced. He had witnessed the man brutally murder a woman—a woman that he had never laid eyes on—while she slept. James saw the man throw that same woman off a building and had himself felt arousal at her demise.

The thought made bile rise in his throat and he sat up from Andrea's lap, preparing to run into the bathroom.

"James, what's going on?"

James looked at her and saw the hurt in her eyes. Had he done something to her while dealing with the man that had invaded his thoughts? He couldn't remember. Her tentative touch when they returned home gave James some indication that he had. It was as if she felt uncomfortable alone with him, without the protection that Pete had provided earlier that day. The guarded veil he saw in her eyes shamed him deeply.

James looked back at the bathroom door, the opening that haunted his morning and beguiled him now, searching for answers. His breathing increased; it panted out of his mouth as the day swirled before his eyes at a dizzying pace.

Is all of this in my head?' he asked himself, pleading for some answer whispered in the catacombs of his mind. *Am I going insane?*

CHAPTER 25

Andrea fell into a restless sleep next to James' rigid body hours after they returned home from the hospital. As soon as he could hear her rhythmic breathing, James slipped out of bed, threw on some old shorts, and ventured out to his office. The lights illuminated the paneled room, and James cast his eyes around it as if for the first time. It resembled his father's office so closely, it was eerie. What at one time was a testament to the memory of his father, the only one that he would allow himself, now seemed oddly macabre. He shivered unconsciously as he entered the room.

James opened the closet door at the far end of the room, the one that held the keepsakes he took from his mother's home. There wasn't much of anything left when James' mother died. Just some old, faded pictures, insurance policies, and $5,000 stuffed inside the mattress that witnessed his mother's death.

James pulled out the heavy trunk that contained all the memories of his youth and dragged it over to the sofa. He jumped at the disconcerting creak that the hinges made as he opened the trunk. The sound reverberated off the walls, distorting it so that it sounded as if it had come from behind him instead of from right in front of him. He shrugged off his edginess, conceding that he had been through a lot, telling himself that it was perfectly normal to be a little tense, given the circumstances. A mysterious man appearing in his shower and giving him something to remember him by, in the way of six stitches hadn't helped matters. But that wasn't the only thing, was it?

The jumbled mass of loose papers, framed pictures, and sports apparel cluttered the trunk. James dug through it to find a box all the way at the bottom labeled 'Jimmie's Junk'.

Apprehension slowed him as he regarded the box. Worn, stretched leather covered the box top and encased a velvet-lined cardboard box. James remembered how the velvet looked, its maroon color as vivid as the day it had been glued to the sides. He felt it waiting there, its luscious color giving way to the darkness of the box. The outside of the box was the worse for wear, its rich brown shine replaced by nicks and scratches. James ran his hand lovingly across the lid. This was his father's box. James felt a kinship with him as he caressed the box, preparing to open it for the first time.

James opened the box. His father's wallet sat on top, bent, worn, and ragged, the way a good wallet was supposed to be. James laid the box on the floor in front of him and opened the wallet. The contents were the same as they had been the day he died: his license, business cards, a picture of James when he was eight years old, and a ten-dollar bill. The old man never carried a whole lot of stuff around with him, but the picture of James had been a staple. James had forgotten that his father carried a picture of him as a kid. He stared at his young countenance, amused. He never changed it; it had always been the same one. It was almost like he was trying to recapture James' innocence, even if only through a photograph. Maybe he kept it to remind himself of what innocence looked like.

James tossed aside the coin collection, fountain pen, and

miscellaneous ties in search of one thing. About halfway through the clutter, James found his father's photo collection.

Jimmie loved to take pictures, that was one thing James remembered about his father. He loved to take pictures, collect pictures, and develop pictures. Anything at all that had to do with pictures, Jimmie was into it. When James was a kid, he remembered a camera always being stuck in his face. "Cheese!" James would yell, grinning fiercely for the camera. The flash would go off, temporarily blinding him with its brightness. After a couple of seconds of brilliant white, James' vision would clear and rest on his father's smiling face. That smile was always accompanied by a hearty clap on the back. Those were the days.

Some of the pictures were loose, and after thumbing through a couple of them, James knew that what he was looking for would not be in that stack. He pulled out the black scrapbook at the bottom of the picture pile. It looked ancient; some of the black edges were ragged and torn, jutting outside of the black cardboard cover. The binding was a single strand of yarn woven through the front and back covers.

James opened the book gingerly, concerned that the pages would be so delicate they would rip easily. The first picture, a sepia-toned relic printed on heavy processing paper, was of a young woman sitting on the ground, stern-faced, with her eyes squinting against the sun. She had on a swimming cap and a tank top, bikini bottomed bathing suit. Her arms were folded around her drawn up knees. Her feet were covered with a style of beach shoes, the precursor to modern day sand shoes, providing protection against the rocks and shells on the shore. The label beneath it read, "Clara Elizabeth, Aunt."

James had seen that photograph before, when his father sat with him and flipped through the photo album. His Dad had been very forthcoming that day, sharing family pictures and even some stories about his life before he married James' mother. He talked about when he and his mother lived in Maryland, describing his street, and even telling him a little bit about the house he grew up in. James remembered that his father had also talked about his favorite aunt, Aunt Clara, who came to visit them every once in a while in a grand car. "When she walked into a room, you took notice," he would say on the rare occasion when he talked about the past. Then his face would cloud over and he'd dismiss the happiness of the memory curtly saying, "But that was then. She's dead now."

James' father didn't talk much about his family, never did. The few times that Jimmie sat with his son and showed him the pictures in the photo album, he usually flipped past the second photograph. When James would ask what was on the page, he would ignore the question and begin to discuss the next picture. Feeling it was off limits, James never pushed hard about it. He never snuck into the office to take a peek at the image on the second page. He didn't want to upset his father.

For a little while, when he was about ten or eleven, James was afraid of the image on the second page. Afraid that it would have some picture of some sort of gruesome visage. Maybe it was a picture of a body in a coffin at a funeral. Or maybe it was a picture of a person on their deathbed, their eyes fixed on some object that only they can see. Both possibilities terrified James. His mother used to tell him that death was a part of life, and that he had to learn to accept that fact. James understood. He didn't want to see it in a picture. So, even though his imagination provided him with alternative images that could have been on the second page, like a picture of his father's first girlfriend topless, or even better, naked —that seemed to be his favorite option—the possibility of a death photo glued to the page, carefully framed on all four corners with black decorative edge covers squelched his curiosity. The idea that it could have been an old death photo of a person who did not benefit from the wonders of mortuary science and was displayed 'as is', as it were; mouth slack, eyes open—that would be unbearable. When his father died, the contents of the second page couldn't have been further from his mind, even though he made certain that he retrieved the photo album from the office before his mother could toss it in with the rest of the junk in the cluttered house. James packed the album away and forgot about it.

James took a deep breath and flipped the page for the first time. The familiar dread seized him as the page turned, sending vivid images of death and dying in front of his mind's eye. His fingers caught the page before it revealed the image. The scrapbook page stood perpendicular to the heirloom album. James held the page there for a moment, the shaking of his hand mimicked by the old paper. Shutting his eyes, James admonished himself to continue. *This is silly*, he told himself. *It's nothing but a picture.* The tips of his fingers began to sweat as he made up his mind. He turned the page, his eyes squinting against the image unconsciously.

The sepia image of a woman standing in a side yard was glued to the page. There were houses lining the street behind her, and James could see the corner of an upstairs window and the side panels of a house on the right side of the frame. Part of a rose bush could be seen on the edge of the frame, it's lush roses peeking into view. The woman was dressed in a loose-fitting housedress with a short white apron on top of it. The wind had blown her hair and skirt slightly to the left. The picture caught her raising a hand to push errant strands of hair out of her eyes.

The woman was young, although her face showed the wear of life on it, creating premature crow's feet and laugh lines on youthful dermis. She seemed uncomfortable under the scrutiny of the camera lens. Her mouth held a small frown, one more of impatience than of aggravation. Her body language was aggressive. James imagined that, no sooner than the blinding flash went off, the woman took a step forward and told the photographer that one picture was enough. But her eyes danced. They were probably the most interesting and disturbing aspects of the photograph.

The woman's eyes, their hue lost in the sepia tone, seemed

playful and excited. They were in direct contrast to the woman's face, whose image disclosed burdens and hard times. They were piercing eyes, direct and steady. James could feel their pressure through the photograph. The eyes were disquieting yet compelling. James averted his eyes from hers with effort.

James read the caption beneath the picture 'Lillian Sarah Boone, Mother.' The name resonated in his head, bouncing off the sides, reconstructing its pitch from soprano to baritone; lingering.

Boone, James thought. *But our last name is Adams.* Where did Boone come from? Suddenly James had to solve the mystery.

He carefully put the photo album aside, noticing offhandedly that Lillian's eyes, his grandmother's eyes, were watching him as he moved. James dug through the box, pulling things out, strewing the contents around the room. When the box was empty, James went through all of the stuff on the floor. *Maybe it's stuck between the pages of a book,* he thought, keeping himself hopeful. But after two hours of sifting through all of the pages of every one of his father's books, unfolding and folding the kept sweaters, sorting the loose papers in the box and in the rest of the trunk, he hadn't found it.

James looked around the room feeling defeated. "Some secrets are meant to be kept," his father had been fond of saying towards the end. This secret seemed to be one that he'd planned on keeping forever. James picked up some of the stuff he had dumped and started to reload the box when he saw them. Two neatly folded pieces of paper were crammed into the sides of the box. They were folded so tightly, to about an inch in length and width, his eyes almost disregarded them as trash, some remnant of his father's past crumbled at the bottom of the cardboard box. James reached in and grabbed one of the pieces of paper. He worked the folds open gently, afraid of tearing it.

He had found it.

With both documents open, James couldn't understand why his father had kept them, why he hadn't burned them in the fireplace that heated his office. For a man who had gone to such lengths to conceal his family—his history—one would think that simple things like a birth and death certificate would have been easy to make disappear. Maybe, James pondered, saying goodbye to the past wasn't always a decision we could make.

James looked at his father's birth certificate, reading clearly the name James Adams written on the line next to the header *Name of Child*. Written on the line next to the header *Mother's Name* was Lillian Boone. Adams was written next to *Father's Name*. No first name was given. The certificate went on to list all of the other vital information: date of birth, weight, gender. The checkbox labeled *Legitimate?* was left blank.

James sat back on the sofa and studied the birth certificate. His father had been illegitimate. Was that his reason for hiding his past? Sadly, illegitimate children were more commonplace than oddity in James' time, so the news did not affect him as much as it may have affected his father. James felt sorrow for his father for the first time in years.

James put the birth certificate down on top of the opened photo album, covering his grandmother's surly face, and looked at the death certificate. *Name of Decedent:* Lillian Boone. *Date of Death:* July 3, 1981. James scoured the death certificate, taking in all the information that it held. He went to his desk and copied down the address under *Location of Death*, knowing somehow that he would need it.

James put his father's belongings back into the box, leaving the photo album for last. As he stood over the album, opened to his grandmother's picture, he noticed something odd. The birth certificate that he had placed on top of the photo album was now moved to the side, showing his grandmother's face in full. The picture seemed different. Instead of showing a full body shot as it had before, the picture was zoomed in closer, obliterating the view of her lower legs and feet. Her face was clearer and her expression easier to ascertain. Where before Lillian looked as though she was irritated at the idea of taking a picture, this new vantage point showed her smiling coyly into the camera lens, endearing it to her. James stared at the picture, his eyes unmoving, disbelieving what he was seeing. He was afraid that if he averted his eyes he would look back and see some new image nestled in the album. James' mind shouted commands to his eyes. *Blink!* But they didn't obey. Amoeba-shaped floaters danced in front of his irises, blurring his view of the picture further, yet his eyes remained trained on the image. James suddenly felt cold. A terrific thought occurred to him: if he continued to look at the photograph, he might witness the next metamorphosis. That was more than James could bear. He tore his eyes away from the picture and raced out of the office without closing the book or returning the trunk to the closet.

CHAPTER 26

He didn't remember getting into the car. James sat behind the wheel of the moving vehicle, already an hour and a half away from his home and realized that he didn't know how he had gotten there.

Or where he was going.

James passed a sign marking Exit 7A on the New Jersey Turnpike and loosely assessed that he was making good time. If he had entered the turnpike at Exit 13 after driving over a half an hour to reach it, to be at Exit 7A in an hour was unheard of. This logic was calculated casually, as if he were assessing drive time for a leisurely day trip. A sickening feeling plagued his stomach. Where was he going?

James looked down at his clothes, unsure of when he had made his way back up to the bedroom and put them on. The only thing he remembered was the sight of his grandmother's face, changed somehow in the old picture. Looking back at him. Beckoning him.

He drove in the dead of night; no one was on the road at the unseemly hour of 4:00 a.m. He didn't know what had driven him out of the house and into the car in the middle of the night. It was as though he had no control over himself after he laid eyes on the picture that seared itself in his mind, changes and all. Perhaps, particularly the changes.

As James sped along the darkened highway, caution be damned as he crested eighty miles an hour without regard for police cars meeting their monthly ticket quota, thoughts of Susan crucified him with their clarity. That night, though, his thoughts did not teeter on the sensual memories of Susan's body, tense and glistening with sweat, her back arching at his touch. His thoughts loomed over the burning car, seeing her inside, suffering. He sensed another soul suffering with hers; an unborn child trapped within her dying body, consuming the same smoke as its mother. The child that was probably his. James had not thought of the pregnancy since Susan's death, had not allowed himself to. Mercifully, his mind didn't bring that horrible truth to the forefront of his thoughts during the waking hours. Rarely did the death of the child enter his dreams, sparing him the unbearable anguish. But then, as he sped to nowhere, the pregnancy seemed to torment him as his mind rehashed the terrible memory, projecting the image in full color.

For a moment everything was normal. It was a clear day with a brilliant blue sky; it was picturesque Nyack at its finest. Susan was on her way to Manhattan to meet with friends, leaving Nyack. James saw her behind the wheel of her little two-seater, a relic from a decade before that she was unwilling to part with. She made a stop, probably to pick up one last knickknack before lunch. James could see her turning off the main drag to find parking. Before she put the car in reverse to parallel park, a strange odor permeated the air. Susan wrinkled her nose and leaned down toward the air vents, since the smell seemed to be coming from there. James was aware, though distantly, that his face was wet and hot with tears. James didn't want to see what came next. He pled from the one vestige of his mind that he was still able to control, for his imagination not to piece together

Susan's last moments. From deep inside a voice whispered, "You know."

Startled into silence, James' mind once again quieted and settled in to watch the dream play out. He could see her swollen stomach protruding from her, far bigger in the daydream than it had been in life. It almost touched the steering wheel as she leaned in to smell the air coming from the vents. She struggled against her belly, the pregnancy seeming to advance to the final trimester. As she descended closer to the vents everything slowed to a crawl. It was as if James saw the events one frame at a time, in slow motion.

Susan closed her eyes when she smelled the air coming from the vents. She didn't see the sparks shining just behind the plastic vent covering. The flames licked out at her prone face instantly, burning her skin, and racing up her nostrils and down her throat to scorch her lungs.

Susan recoiled, raising her hands to her face instinctively. The fire spread to her hair before she was able to move. Fire continued to pour out of the vents like water, melting the dashboard and engulfing the cloth seats.

Susan was screaming, the sound inaudible now as the fire had destroyed her lungs and larynx. In her last moments, she laid her burning hands on her stomach, the last comfort she could give to her dying child.

James jerked himself out of the daydream. Sweat coated his face and dampened his shirt collar. His hands were gripping the steering wheel so tightly that his knuckles had turned white. He took two deep breaths, trying to suppress the sob that was rising in his throat.

"Why Susan? Why her?" he asked aloud to the empty car, finally able to give voice to the pain he felt inside at losing her.

Suddenly the car filled with voices; deep, high-pitched, adult, juvenile. They spoke separately at first, their words incoherent and jumbled, overlapping each other. James looked around the car frantically, searching for the source of the voices, knowing that he would not find it. The chaotic sound continued for minutes; voices of varying pitches and intensity shouting, speaking, mumbling, whispering. Then, with paralyzing clarity, the voices spoke as one. The words they spoke cut into James' mind like a knife. He was unable to hold in the cry that escaped his lips nor still the shaking of his limbs as the disembodied voices said in unison, "You know."

CHAPTER 27

James thought he was still screaming. His throat was raw and scratchy. He opened his eyes, thinking that he would stop at the nearest service area to get a cup of coffee before turning around and making his way back home. His mind had sent him on a wild goose chase that was designed to make him do nothing more than think about Susan's horrible death. His mind had worked to torture him with the details, this time providing an imaginative ending to her life. James hadn't seen Susan die. He wasn't on the same block where the car blew up. But his mind wanted him to see. It wanted him to see what he had done to her. James was awake then, though. His mind had held him hostage long enough. He was going to put an end to the dreams, an end to the torture.

James' eyes opened to a neighborhood street lined with old, detached houses. He blinked rapidly, trying to focus. He was parked in front of a house on a deserted street. Panic swept over him as he tried to piece together the past couple of hours. The last thing he remembered was being on the turnpike. The roadway was empty except for his car and a scattering of eighteen-wheelers.

James didn't know how he had gotten to the house. He didn't know where he was.

The clock on the dashboard read 7:45 a.m. James ran his hand over his forehead, rubbing it, trying to make sense of what was happening. He looked over at the dilapidated house as if in a daze. The windows were boarded up, layman's work if ever there had been. The old porch had a lone wicker chair sitting on it, facing the street.

James looked around the street and saw that similar structures had been erected, their lawns bordered by a continuous concrete walkway. The houses were at least forty years old, one house resembling the next. The house that he was parked in front of was no different, except that it sat on a slightly larger patch of land than the others. The property had long ago been overtaken by weeds and overgrown bushes.

James got out of the car and walked towards the house. The local kids had found it an ample canvas for their tags and cartoonish drawings. Spray paint covered the boards that locked trespassers out yet none had touched the original structure. As James approached the steps, a sense of déjà vu filled him with insuppressible dread. He backed away from the steps to look at the house again. It looked familiar to him. Disturbingly so.

James fought the urge to turn around and run back to the car, drive away from wherever he was and head back home where it was safe. Some part of James' mind knew that he wouldn't be able to leave even if he tried. He continued up the stairs to the front door. It was as if some force had brought him there. He didn't remember the ride to the abandoned house, didn't remember what turns he took after he got off the highway. Yet he was there. Something was calling to him, beckoning him to come. James had felt it all along, underlying his dreams, whispering in his ear while he was awake. He was supposed to be there. The thought terrified him, but he knew that he was helpless against it. The house wanted James there. And he had to oblige.

As James got closer to the house, he noticed just how haphazardly the boards were put up on the windows and the door. Much of the glass was visible, the boards mounted so lopsidedly that it did nothing to obstruct the windows from view. James got close, so close that his nose almost touched the board, and peered into the dirt-caked window sitting next to the front door.

A dim light was on in the house. James moved even closer, trying to remember if he had noticed the light behind the board when he first approached the house. As his eyes adjusted to the contrast of morning sunlight shining outside and the dim light of the light on the inside, his eyes passed over something. There was something lying on the floor between the living room and dining room.

James knew what it was before he was ready to accept what he saw. There was a body on the floor. James squinted through the dirty glass, pressing his hands to the sides of the window frame, trying to inch closer. He could see an old woman with pale, lifeless skin. Her face was turned toward the window, her mouth agape. Her left nostril was caked with dried blood that had pooled in the crevices of her lips.

James pushed away from the window with such force that he almost fell down the porch steps behind him. His heart raced as his mind reeled. James was standing there, looking at the paint-chipped planks that made up the porch, as his breath moved in and out of his lungs in deep gasps. A light film of sweat formed on his forehead, chilling quickly in the morning air.

A terrible shaking sped through his body, from limb to limb, across his chest and down to his stomach when he heard a woman's voice say, "Well, what the hell took you so long, Jimmie?"

CHAPTER 28

James turned his head to the voice like he was in a trance, his vision trailing behind his motion as though inebriated by the voice alone. The porch seemed to regain some of the luster it had lost over the years of people walking back and forth on it, the paint rejuvenated, filling its cracks. Before his eyes, the porch planks that had warped from water damage and inattention righted themselves and became straight. The house had also changed. The boards that had blocked the front door and windows were gone. The shingles that clanked against the house with the wind were secured to the sides with decorative iron pins. James could see cream drapes framing the window, licking out with the breeze that carried them.

James turned to face the owner of the voice; his mind unable to conceive the nightmare that had somehow made its way into his real life.

The woman was middle aged and looked vaguely familiar. She wore a steel blue housedress with snaps centered in the front. A cream apron was tied around her waist from behind. It was clean, except for a couple of dark splatters on the right side and a stain at the bottom, a stain that ran from the bottom of the apron onto the housedress. She had on black soft-soled shoes that were soundless as she moved toward him on the porch. As she drew nearer, he took note of her face. Her skin was smooth and lively even while distorted by the scowl that darkened her face. She didn't wear makeup, at least not that day. Her hair was pulled back in a matronly bun, wisps loosened by a morning of work. At least two of her teeth were capped in gold, he could see as she approached him with her mouth fixed in an angry grit. Her eyes were the most upsetting. They were ordinary brown, as many people's eyes were. But the irises were abnormally sized, larger than normal. They widened as he watched, the brown overtaking the whites of her eyes by the second until only the corners of her eyes showed white. The color of the eyes themselves changed from a rich brown to an iniquitous black, insect-like and dead. Her eyes were empty to their core, yet still they stared at him.

James couldn't look away from her, even though the sight of her eyes frightened him more than he ever imagined he could be. He was drawn to them, falling through the hole they opened up and tumbling in the infinite expanse that was their hell. His mind was imbued by their depth, thinking nothing more than the blackness therein. A tear fell from James' eye as he surrendered to hers.

The woman stopped in front of James and looked at him for a while, her facial expression changing from anger to resolution. She regarded James as he stood before her, entranced, casting her eyes over every inch of him. A smirk formed at the corners of her lips and she let it spread across her mouth slowly. Finally, she said, as she turned to walk behind the house,

"Well, come on then. We'd better get started before it gets late."

The woman disappeared around the corner of the house.

And James followed her.

CHAPTER 29

As James rounded the corner following the mysteriously familiar woman a bright light, so bright he was sure his eyesight would never return, accosted him. He held his forearm in front of his eyes for what seemed like forever, trying to block the light. When it finally subsided, everything was colored in black and white. James blinked his eyes repeatedly, trying to get them back to normal, but nothing changed. The world seemed to have been colored in grayscale, the vibrant greens of the grass and trees surrounding the house reduced to a light gray hue.

James saw a large rose bush blooming its beautifully delicate roses. The velvety red petals looked dark gray, almost black; their hue diminished from vibrant to flat.

The woman had climbed a set of stairs and was opening the back door of the house when James caught up with her. The wooden door creaked on its hinges as she muscled it open.

"I told you to fix this too, Jimmie. You probably should get to that after you finish up in here," she said offhandedly as she walked into the kitchen.

James mounted the steps tenuously, realizing that he had no

choice but to go inside, even though his soul beseeched him to turn around and run. When James stepped into the kitchen, a vision overcame him, spinning his sight and almost driving him to the floor. A boy was standing in the same room, but on the other side, entering the kitchen from the living room. The boy looked as James had in his youth. He was chubby, but not displeasingly so. Basketball and football would take care of that in a couple of years. James smirked incredulously at the thought that flew into his head from out of nowhere. *That's Dad.* He tried to dismiss the thought but couldn't. James looked closer at him. The chubby young boy stood in the door jamb of the kitchen, his body half in and half out of the room. He was on the cusp of puberty, his face still soft and indistinct. Understanding descended upon James as he realized that the boy really was his father. He was Jimmie.

The color had returned to the world. James saw the mustard yellow of the refrigerator door and kitchen table spread. The linoleum tiling was yellow and brown. The dark brown wood of the cabinets contrasted with the shiny metal handles to open them. The kitchen table and chair legs were metal. The chairs had white vinyl seats. Most of the cushions were sprinkled with drops of paint and stained with print that had bled off newspapers that had been stacked on top of them in the sticky summer heat. The curtains in the window above the sink flowed in the breeze, the country design brightening the room. A haze of cigarette smoke and dust particles hung in the air.

Jimmie seemed nervous. He fidgeted, shifting his feet absently. He looked afraid. He looked like he wanted to escape.

The woman was there too, sitting at the kitchen table smoking a cigarette and nursing a glass of rum on the rocks. She was dressed in the same housedress she wore when James met her on the porch - the same apron, the same black shoes. But something was different. Her eyes looked normal; the irises didn't overtake the whites and they didn't seem to look right into his soul. She looked different, calmer than she had when she approached him outside, less harried. Her face showed mild aggravation, the kind you might see on a mother's face when her child has flooded the toilet for the second time in an evening. Still James could see something brewing. It sat just underneath her skin, moving around as if restless.

The bottle of rum sat on the table, three quarters full, waiting to be uncapped and poured again. She was reading the newspaper, or looking at it, anyway, when another woman entered the room. She was tall and slender, clad in a flowered dress and high-heeled, open-toed, sling-back sandals. Her hair was curled tightly, its length allowed to hang loosely only in the back with bangs framing her face. She carried a sophisticated air about her, it emanated from her like the fancy perfume she wore that sweetened the air.

The sophisticated woman walked into the room; her jaw set to discuss pressing matters.

"We're leaving now, Lillian. I'll have someone come for Jimmie's things."

Lillian, who was in the middle of taking a swig of rum from her glass, looked over at the woman slowly. She put the glass down on the table, its base fitting snugly in the indent it had made earlier on the yellow plastic table covering.

"No, you're not."

The sophisticated woman sighed irritably, but her face didn't waver. She had expected that response.

"We are. Please don't make a scene, Lillian. It's not healthy for anyone involved."

Lillian regarded the woman standing next to her child, the boy she had raised by herself in that very house. It was Lillian who had clothed and fed him. She alone had taken care of him when he couldn't do anything for himself. Never once had she asked for help. How dare anyone try to take him from her? Jimmie was all she had left, for God's sake. Shouldn't she be left with something after all she'd been through?

Lillian looked at her son. Jimmie. Poor old Jimmie. Jimmie, who from the moment he was born, so resembled his father that Lillian was unable to nurture him, to love him the way a mother should love a child. Jimmie's father didn't allow it, so Lillian got tired of giving it. To anyone. Including her son. Her only child.

Jimmie stood in the doorjamb looking down at his feet. The sight disgusted Lillian. He was more like his father than he knew, she had told herself over the years. *He's worthless, but he's mine,* Lillian often said before her first drink of the evening, the phrase becoming a toast of sorts. She ignored the anguish that showed in his face when she spat those words and turned her glass up to her mouth. Jimmie's face was soft, the tightness of testosterone barely visible in him. He was just a child.

During lucid moments Lillian realized that she was projecting all of her anger at Ben—at wretched life—onto Jimmie. She could see that he was a child, just a boy who wanted to please his mother. Lillian knew she should not have denied him the life that she had lived, one of opulence and wealth; the sense of comfort that she had grown up with in New York. She had traded that life in years ago for a dream that never came true. Should she punish her child because she didn't live happily ever after? Clarity of thought was not something Lillian dealt in those days, not since Ben had left. She washed her loneliness and frustrations down with vodka, rum, or bourbon. The drink made trading in cashmere and silk for polyester a righteous decision. And so went her life. And so should Jimmie's be.

Jimmie raised his eyes to his mother slowly, aware that he was being watched. She frowned at him and he looked away quickly. *How dare you accept this invitation?* her eyes asked. *Your home is with me. I am your mother. I gave you life, you ungrateful bastard.* Jimmie's bottom lip quivered as he looked at the floor. He knew the words she wanted to speak all too well. The heat of his mother's eyes on him was unbearable.

"Jimmie, you ungrateful—."

The sophisticated woman cut in, stopping the barrage before it started.

"This is between you and me, Lillian. I've made this decision. Jimmie is a child. I can't let you ruin him the way you have ruined yourself."

Lillian rose from her chair slowly, her hands resting on the table. Her eyes fixed on the sophisticated woman with rage.

"You're not taking him, Clara."

"The boy needs a home. He needs a mother."

"I'm his mother. This is his home."

"Lillian, you're in the bottle most of the time. You don't know him. You don't care to know him. You barely know he exists."

Clara walked over to the country wall unit and fondled one of vases on the middle shelf. A film of dust lifted off it and onto her hand. She sucked her teeth and mumbled something under her breath before she continued,

"Lillian, you don't care what goes on in this house, you don't care what happens to yourself, and you don't care what happens to Jimmie. All you care about is that damned bottle."

Jimmie stood in the door jamb; his eyes still fixated on the floor. Lillian looked at her sister Clara with eyes that showed anger but masked her shame. Clara had chosen to stay in New York and live the life within which they had both been raised. She went to fancy restaurants and attended the opera and ballet. She went through the motions that defined the elite. Everything about Clara —her appearance, her demeanor—oozed sophistication. *When did I come to think of it that way*, Lillian thought.

Clara was the only one who remained in contact with Lillian after she left New York and ran to Washington DC behind Ben Adams. When Lillian refused to go back home, turned down the marriage proposal from the son of one of her father's business associates, and shacked up with Ben, a man without a job to speak of and a slick coating on his voice, Clara stopped talking to her also. She was trying to make Lillian feel the pain of total alienation, but when Lillian and Ben broke up and Lillian found out that she was pregnant with a bastard child, Clara couldn't stay away from her sister. She worked on the family and got them to allow Lillian to come home and deal with the situation. But only if Lillian asked to come. Lillian remembered that she got angry, said some horrible things to her mother, told her father where he could go, and slammed the phone down onto its carriage. Lillian never went home to introduce the baby to his grandparents. She never told her family about what happened with Ben, and never asked for money or help. Lillian divorced herself from the family and the life she had in New York to start anew in Maryland. Just her and her infant son. When her parents died together in a car accident years later, she didn't even attend the funeral.

Clara came by every once in a while, to visit Lillian and Jimmie. She would tell Lillian about New York and what people were doing, what people were saying, if anyone was still talking about Lillian Boone. Both sisters enjoyed the visits. They felt the closeness that had been a part of their lives since they had been young girls growing up in New York's jet set. Clara would try to get Lillian to let go of her anger and return home, if only for a couple of days. But she never did. That type of conversation—surface and teased with gossip and the occasional moral nudge— lasted for about ten years until Lillian's drinking got worse. Then Clara would only talk about Lillian's drinking and the affect it was having on Jimmie. The sisters tired quickly of each other then. Clara would leave soon after she had come, to Jimmie's dismay, the visits becoming shorter and shorter as the years went by.

To Jimmie, his Aunt Clara was different than any of the women he met in his neighborhood. She was classy. She dressed in the newest fashions, with every detail of her look in place. Jimmie thought she looked like the women on television, all class and style. Her movements were fluid, her self-assuredness emanated from her pores. She was the first person Jimmie ever considered truly beautiful.

Clara's hair was always styled perfectly, even when it had been tousled by the wind. Jimmie found the wayward strands adorable, the perfect accent to her girlish smile. Her eyes were oval, shapely, and pretty underneath thick, lush, ebony eyelashes. They danced when she spoke, absolutely shined when she laughed; their brilliance was so blinding Jimmie could barely look at them. The light caught them at just the right angle every time, making them glint like jewels. He liked to fancy that her eyes only smiled for him, that he was the only one who could make her eyes do that. His mother certainly couldn't, so it was an easy fantasy to believe.

Jimmie had a terrible crush on his Aunt Clara.

Her legs, the sway of her dress when she walked, captivated him. The image of her walking away from the house and toward her nifty car was engraved in his mind. No, that's not being honest. It was the sway of her hips that really got him going. Jimmie called that image up often, relishing it, taking it all in over and over.

Sometimes Jimmie was ashamed of his attraction to his aunt. He knew it was wrong to fantasize about her. He tried to like other girls, girls on television or girls that he knew from school. None of them measured up. So, when he was alone in his room and his mother was asleep down the hall, he thought of her. She wasn't his Aunt Clara in the dark in his bedroom during those secretive interludes. She was a sophisticated, sexy, worldly woman. She was his Clara. His Clara Belle.

Clara drove a late model convertible top car. She was the only person Jimmie knew who owned a convertible. She was 'it' to Jimmie, personifying everything that he thought was new and hip; everything he wanted to be. When the time between visits became longer and Clara stayed less time when she did come, Jimmie missed her terribly. But he suffered in silence. If he mentioned her name to his mother, he would get a tongue-lashing and might have gotten belted for it, so he kept it to himself. And waited.

This would be her last visit.

Lillian squared her shoulders to Clara and said, "Clara, you can't have him. He's my boy."

"Your boy. You care so much for your boy. Why don't you take care of your boy, Lillian? He gets bad grades in school, if he ever goes. Discipline isn't a knock across the back with your latest bottle and then back to normal."

Clara paused for a moment, a shadow crossing her face.

"You've always let your temper get the best of you. You're no different than Father."

"What would you know about it, Clara?" Lillian retorted angrily.

"I know what I see."

Lillian stared intently at Clara who continued fondling the dusty vase.

"I know what this is about. You're not fooling anybody, Clara. You're just like you've always been. Jealous and greedy."

"What are you talking about?" Clara asked, the sound resonating haughtily on Lillian's ears.

"Oh, don't give me that 'Holier than Thou' act. It may work in those snooty circles you run in, but it won't work with me."

"Snooty circles? Funny, I seem to remember that you were raised in those very same circles, dear sister."

Lillian smiled at Clara. A smile that could have killed a canary's song in its throat.

"You want my boy because you can't have any of your own. Your parts are dried up so you want the fruit of my labor. You jealous witch."

Stricken, Clara retorted, "That's the most terrible thing you have ever said to me, Lillian, and I will not stand here and be insulted by you. I am taking Jimmie back to New York with me where he will be nurtured, where someone will care if he lives or dies. If you choose to stay here and drown your sorrows with liquor, that's your choice. But you will not ruin this child's life. It's not his fault that Ben left you and I won't let you continue to blame him for it."

Clara walked over to Jimmie, put her hands on his shoulders and said,

"Let's go Jimmie."

Clara turned to leave the room. She had intended to walk through the living room and leave the house through the front door. James could hear the click clack of her heels on the hardwood floor that spanned the hallway as she turned towards the door, the sound enhanced and sharp. He wondered if Jimmie had heard it the same way. Jimmie turned slowly to follow his aunt, his eyes never leaving the floor. Lillian, enraged now, grabbed the bottle of rum off the kitchen table and walked soundlessly towards Clara.

Within three steps, just past the doorjamb, Lillian caught up with Clara and Jimmie. She raised the bottle over her head and brought it down hard on the back of Clara's neck, all the while screaming, "You will not take my boy, you bitch! He never left me!"

Clara fell limply to the floor from the first blow, never seeing it coming, never able to defend herself. Lillian descended upon her quickly, hitting her on the back and side of her head and neck with the bottle until it broke and rum mingled with the blood. The mixture dripped onto the knock off Persian runner that was centered on the hallway floor leaving indelible stains. Lillian continued to assault Clara, stabbing her in the face, temple, and in the side of the head with the jagged glass as her ranting diminished to incoherent mumbling.

Jimmie stood to the side of the bloody rampage, watching his mother kill his aunt in silence. Lillian's mumbling grew louder and louder as Jimmie watched, his mouth slack and grimacing. Saliva rolled over his bottom lip, dripping to the carpet in slow motion, breaking midway into two droplets; one falling to the floor and sinking in, the other retracting to Jimmie's open mouth. The mutilation continued as Jimmie lifted his head to look over to where James was standing. His arm rose while his face remained a mask of fright and sadness and pointed at him.

CHAPTER 30

James screamed; it was a high-pitched sound that seemed to come from outside of his body. He was surprised to find himself standing, the visions he saw before had made his knees buckle. James found that he was in the kitchen by himself. He looked over at the kitchen table and saw a glass of rum, half empty, sitting on a light gray table covering. *It's yellow,* his mind told him. Color had abandoned his vision again, leaving cold grays and blacks in its wake. He shuddered at the knowledge swimming in his head.

The kitchen was quiet. The counter was jumbled with drying plates, glasses, pots and pans, and the small sink was still filled with more. James attempted to move, unsure if he would be able to will himself to walk. He took a shaky step forward onto a cracked linoleum tile, colored light and dark gray from his vantage point, but would have been yellow and brown if seen in color. With more confidence this time, James walked towards the kitchen table. The newspaper was open. He looked down at it and his mouth fell open when he read the date: April 23, 1954.

His eyes were glued to the page, the words nothing more than a blur of black on white paper. 1954? He was shaking, his bladder threatened to give way, as he tried to gain composure. A drop of saliva fell from his mouth to the thin newspaper page in slow motion, catching the light as it went; silver cascading off the tear-shaped liquid. It hit the paper with an audible boom. James' senses were acutely aware of the splash, minute droplets splashing up from the paper and back down to settle. He heard other sounds, the time moving at normal speed again like a black and white reel film continuing the movie after a hitch.

There were rustling sounds coming from the hallway. James turned his head, involuntarily, in the direction of the noise. He stood in front of the kitchen table looking into the hallway that separated the kitchen and living room. He was waiting for the sound to draw closer. Like a fade in on a contemporary movie, the scene took shape before his eyes. James saw a woman pacing in front of a lifeless body that was clothed in a dress with a floral pattern that was made lackluster by the grayscale tone in the room. A black stain covered the top of the dress, as well as the back of the woman's head, her hair was matted with it. Blood.

As the pacing woman turned to make her next lap around the body, James caught a glimpse of her. Her face was hard. Her brow was furrowed and her eyes were wild. She was muttering something under her breath that was almost unintelligible. "He didn't leave me. Bet you know that now, don't you?"

She turned to face James, seemingly aware that she was being watched. She stared at him with fresh anger setting in her face. James wanted to recoil, to leave the room and be out of the sight of this woman, but he didn't think he could. He didn't think he would be allowed to leave.

James was looking into the face of the woman who appeared to him on the porch what seemed like hours ago. The face of Lillian Boone. The face of his grandmother.

Her stare was strong and steady. She bore into him with eyes as black as coal, seeing through him. Finally, she said,

"What the hell are you doing, Jimmie? Jerking off? We've got work to do!"

James started to walk toward his grandmother, drawing closer to the body that lay in front of her. He didn't want to see his grand aunt lying there in a pool of her own blood, blood that was seeping into the knock off Persian carpet runner, but he knew he had to. That's why he was here. To see.

A gust of wind whipped by him. It didn't rustle the newspaper on the kitchen table, nor the napkins sitting in the dingy napkin holder behind the salt and pepper shakers. But James felt it on his face. It ruffled his hair as it went by him, leaving the faint scent of dead leaves in its wake. Jimmie appeared in front of James, walking toward his mother as he had been beckoned to do. He was still a young boy of about twelve or thirteen, ambling behind his mother apprehensively, not wanting to get close to the carnage that lay in the hallway.

Lillian turned away from Jimmie and continued her pacing. Jimmie stopped at his aunt's feet with tears streaming down his face.

"Don't ever run away from me again!" Lillian shouted at Jimmie. He had left the room while his mother stabbed at Clara, blind with sadness and fury. He had watched his mother kill his fantasy, his Aunt Clara. His body shook with anger over it and at the same time, trembled with sadness for the loss. The mixture of emotions was driving him crazy.

Lillian stopped pacing and looked at her son in silence. Her face softened slightly before she spoke again.

"All right boy," she said with forced patience, "you have to help your mother now. We have to take care of your Aunt Clara before too long. Let's get her all the way on the runner, now."

Lillian walked over and picked up one of Clara's arms. She looked up at Jimmie who hadn't moved from the spot he was standing in and said,

"Jimmie? Jimmie, come on now. We've got to take care of this."

Jimmie was paralyzed. He stood staring at the back of his aunt's head, the blood congealing now. The tears flowed freely down his cheeks.

"Come on Jimmie," Lillian said, exasperated, "pick up her arm."

Jimmie gasped at the thought and sobbed harder.

"We don't have time for all this foolishness now, boy. Stop all your crying and let's do this now."

"Why'd you do it?" Jimmie asked through his tears.

Lillian released Clara's arm and it hit the floor with a heavy thump. She put her hands on her hips and cocked her leg out to the side.

"Do what, honey?" The sappy sweet inflection she assumed sounded alien coming from her mouth as she stood over the dead body of her sister. The lift of her voice, the stiff, patronizing smile that crossed her lips made reality all the more nightmarish.

"You killed her! How could you kill Aunt Clara?"

Jimmie raised his voice as he asked her, his grief getting the best of him. Lillian rushed over to him, her face changing from forced sensitivity to ferocious anger quickly. And there was something else. Under the anger, under the fear of being found out, under all of that, there was another emotion peeking through. Satisfaction.

Lillian grabbed Jimmie by the arms and said,

"Now you listen to me, Jimmie Adams. Your Aunt Clara hit her head and fell. That's what happened."

Lillian almost went back to work, thinking that her words and tone were strong enough to shut Jimmie up about the whole incident. She stared at him, trying to wear him down, trying to instill fear in him to keep his mouth shut. She quickly realized that more had to be said. His eyes were hot and angry, wet with tears. She felt threatened by the fury they revealed. And it made her angry.

Lillian continued, "Okay. I killed her. I hit her in the head with a bottle of rum and I killed her. Bludgeoned her to death and wasted my good liquor. Is that what you wanted to hear? You don't need me to tell it, you saw it for yourself."

Jimmie's tears stung as they fell from his eyes. He felt their warmth as they melted into his pores. Jimmie cringed at the harshness of her words, at her mention of what happened before his eyes. His aunt was dead and his mother had killed her. She had taken Clara away from him. He hated her for it.

Lillian laughed at him. It was a sharp sound, calloused and rough. It made him sick to his stomach. Jimmie tried to look away from her, too angry to keep her gaze, too frightened to be in the room with her anymore. Her patronizing laughter was ripping him apart.

Lillian gripped Jimmie's chin firmly just as he tried to turn away, her laughter stopping abruptly in her throat. She pulled his face close to hers, daring him to resist.

"Don't try to avoid it now. You're the big boy who wouldn't just let it lie. You were the one who was bold enough to challenge me. You want to act like a man? Maybe it's time for you to grow up and be a man."

Lillian paused, her eyes darkening as she leaned even closer to Jimmie, prohibiting movement by her presence alone.

"How Clara died doesn't matter," she spit. "You got that? It doesn't matter because you're never going to talk about it. Do you understand me? You are never going to talk about what you think you saw today, or about your Aunt Clara. Do you understand?"

Jimmie stood mortified in his mother's tight grip, crying for his aunt and for himself.

"Do you understand me, Jimmie? Do you? You will never utter a word of this to anyone. Ever. If you do, I swear Jimmie if you do, I will kill you myself."

James cringed at the words coming from his grandmother's mouth. Had she just threatened to kill his father?

"Do you hear me, Jimmie? Wise up, boy. You and me, we're just alike. Just like my father, his father, and his father before him. It goes way back, this thing you and I share. You are no different than me, understand? No different at all. You don't believe me? Try me. You saw me kill your aunt. Believe what your eyes showed you, boy. I can kill you just as easily. And I will if you cross me."

Jimmie had stopped crying. He looked at his mother, seeing her as if for the first time. Jimmie imagined overtaking her and choking the life out of her until she fell dead on the floor next to the sister she murdered. He wasn't tall enough to do it, not yet. But he was taller than he had been the first time he had considered it, and stronger. His body was transforming from that of a boy to that of a man. He could do it soon. Soon he could kill her.

James could read his father's thoughts as clearly as if he was having them himself. They frightened him.

Lillian released Jimmie as if sensing what he was thinking. She stepped backwards, putting distance between them.

"You think about that, boy, before you decide to go telling anyone about what happened here today. I can and will kill you just as sure as my father took my mother's life with his that day in the Blue Ridge Mountains."

Jimmie's eyes clouded over.

James' eyes watered. Was there a trend? Some family curse that turned them into murderers? That bore them as such? He felt like his mind was dangling a carrot in front of him, some shred of clarity that he couldn't quite grasp. A question formed in his head, so faintly voiced he almost didn't hear his inner voice utter it. *Did I kill Susan?*

"Oh yes," Lillian continued, "My father killed my mother. His father killed his last child because he was retarded. The list goes on, Jimmie. I killed your Aunt Clara. You'll kill in your time. You probably already want to kill me. I wouldn't be surprised. I wanted to kill my parents when I was your age. There's no point in it, though. You'll soon learn that we take care of ourselves in the long run anyway, Jimmie. That just seems to be the way we check out of here. But you will kill. I can see it in your eyes."

Jimmie was silent. His eyes cut into Lillian like knives cutting into ripe, supple fruit.

Lillian laughed bitterly and said,

"Humph, you may just kill me, Jimmie boy, and break the trend. You wouldn't be the first to try. You're father tried to kill me the day I found him, but he didn't succeed. Maybe you'll do better than he did." Lillian paused pensively, that day rerunning in her mind.

"He knocked me up with you and then left," she continued. "Just like that. Left me in the middle of DC with no idea where to go or how to get there. He'd found a new girl. A little young thing, barely eighteen with tits so perky they'd punch a hole in your eye if you got close enough. But I found them. I found them, Jimmie." Lillian walked back to her sister's side and bent down to retrieve the arm she had so casually dropped before.

"Yeah, I found them in Virginia, living the good life, not that far from where he and I had laid our heads at one time or another."

James was eager for her to go on. Jimmie's face was blank.

"But now he's mine forever. And you can be too, if you don't stick with the plan and keep quiet about Clara."

Lillian picked up the arm and looked back at Jimmie.

"What's it going to be, Jimmie?"

Jimmie stared long and hard at his mother, hatred flashing in his eyes. He looked at his aunt, his precious aunt, lying on the floor, her legs awkwardly spread, the back of her head bloodied. She lay on her stomach with her face turned toward him. Her eyes seemed to be smiling at him. Jimmie stared at his Aunt Clara, her shapely legs prone underneath her flowered dress. His stomach curled at the thoughts that were swimming in his head. He couldn't help but want to get a look under her dress. He was sickened by the thought. And excited.

Jimmie walked over to the other side of his aunt slowly, picked up her other arm and helped his mother lift the dead weight onto the carpet runner.

CHAPTER 31

J ames wasn't sure how long he had been standing there watching his father and grandmother dispose of Clara before the next vision came to him. A glint of sunlight reflected from Clara's diamond ring, the engagement ring her husband Clifton had given her twenty years prior, flashing color to James' eye in brilliant blues, reds, and greens.

The light cut into the room like a lightning bolt, transforming it, colorizing and aging it. As his eyes adjusted to the brightness and the return of color, he began to feel hope rising within him. Had he finally awakened from the dream?

As soon as his eyes adjusted, he realized that he was standing in the living room of his grandmother's house. Panic gripped him as his mind brought the truth to the rest of his senses. He was still in the house. He was still in the dream.

The front door was behind him. A rotting closet door was on his left, the wood looking worn and splintered. Stained wallpaper, once a lively peach and white design, curled at the edges. Earth toned furniture lined the walls, the sofa cushions were moth bitten and ragged. The wood bases of the coffee table and chairs were chipped and dull. A china cabinet with plates and crystal displayed sat in the far corner of the room, its hulking mahogany mass standing in the shadows. The hardwood floor was worn and splintery.

It was dim. The window coverings had all but rotted away, but the natural light was blocked by an outside source, letting in only pockets of light. The furniture in the room, all mahogany and cherry wood, didn't add to the ambiance. They gave the room an old hotel quality, one that held the many secrets of its patrons from times past. An eerie haze hung in the room. A bare, dim bulb dangled from the ceiling, casting a dusty light over the forgotten space. This was the room that James had looked into from outside the house.

Fear rose in James quickly as he realized he was in the room where a body had lain earlier in his dreams. He turned to the front door quickly, averting his eyes from the doorjamb that was in front of him as he went. He grasped the doorknob, turning it quickly to the left. It turned easily, yet the door did not open. He checked the singular lock on the door and found that it was unlocked. He pushed on the door, trying to unstick it, to rip it off its hinges if need be. He had to get out of that house.

"Jimmie."

It was as though four voices called the name at the same time. The sound hung above him; it echoed off the walls and in his head. He stood facing the front door, willing it to open, refusing to turn around to face the room and its phantoms. He caught a glimpse of the room reflected off one of the four dingy squares of glass in the door. A silhouette rose from the floor, slowly, steadying itself on its feet. He knew it was the woman from before, rising from the floor as she had in his dreams. Dried blood crusted around her nose and mouth. Her white nightgown stained with it. James turned around, more afraid of having his back turned to such a creature, one that could rise from death to stand, than facing its horrors with his eyes open. When he turned, the woman took three quick steps toward him, stopping right in front of his face.

There was no breath; the smell of death came solely from the blood that had dried on her face. The woman was his grandmother, he realized as he shrank away from her, the putrefying smell almost unendurable.

She was older, her hair sprinkled with gray. Her face was creased with wrinkles around her eyes and mouth, many more than before. Her mouth was down turned and her cheeks sagged. She was different in many ways, but her eyes, her cold eyes, were unmistakably the same.

She regarded him slowly, languishing in the fear that emanated from his pores. She moved from one leg to the other, trying to get the right angle of view. She was searching his face, seeing the familiar and the different.

When he thought he could no longer take it, Lillian spoke one final word,

"James."

And she laughed.

It was a hideous sound that filled the room, banging roughly against the walls.

While she laughed a rich burley laugh with just the hint of a rattle at its base, she put her hands on the side of James' head and drew him to her. James, rigid with fear, tried to scream, tried to yell, tried to push her off him, but was unable to do anything. He was delirious with fear, but he was impotent against her. James succumbed to her when, inconceivably, she opened her mouth and closed it upon his in a kiss.

CHAPTER 32

James was standing in front of the door, facing the living room. The windows were unobstructed and clean, and the sun shone brightly through them. The bulb, brighter now, hung from the ceiling. A woman dressed in a white, formless nightgown, one that only revealed the semblance of a contour at the curve of her breast, stumbled into the room holding a glass filled halfway with brown liquid in her right hand. She swirled it absently as she walked. Her left hand held a pouch and a bottle of drain cleaner, her finger fondling the label.

She tried to sit on one of the chairs in the room but missed clumsily and landed on the floor with an audible thump. She laughed aloud as she rocked on her hips from the force of the fall.

"Whoa!" she said to the room, empty as far as she was concerned. Putting her drink down on the floor carefully, she uncapped the liquid drain cleaner and poured a healthy dose into the glass.

"That should do it. What do you think, Ben?" she said as she capped the bottle, put it down, and looked at the pouch.

"I think that oughtta do me, don't you?" She picked up the pouch by the drawstring and dangled it in front of her eyes.

"What do you say? You want to come with me? Huh? We can do this together. You and me, the way it was supposed to be." She paused and looked around the room, her eyes watery and her hair wild and stringy. "Yeah," she said, smoothing her white nightgown with her hand, "I think you're gonna come with me. This way you'll be with me forever."

She rambled on about the two of them being together forever as she opened the pouch. She licked her finger and dipped it into the bag. Powder clustered on the top of her finger. She looked at the white, flaky substance for a while before for she put her pinky in her mouth and cleaned it.

After savoring it for a moment, she exclaimed with drunken glee, "Ben, you still taste good to me, baby!"

She erupted into a barrage of laughter, cackling at the top of her lungs at times, and from the pit of her stomach at others. Once she regained control of herself, she became wistful, her eyes clouding over to a melancholy glaze.

"Well, I guess it's time now, "she said to the pouch. She looked around the room with despondent eyes. She lingered on every piece of furniture, every crevice in every floorboard. James could feel the pain, the utter loss he was sure she felt as she looked around her home for the last time. A strange sense of sadness came over him as he recognized the woman as his grandmother, his vision coming full circle.

Lillian sat a second longer before she turned the pouch up, emptying its contents into her mouth. She was careful not to spill anything; she drank all of it. She swallowed with concerted effort; her mouth made pasty from the ashes. Then she picked up her glass, a deadly mix of rum and drain cleaner, filled just under the brim.

With an unsteady hand, Lillian toasted the room, raising her toxic cocktail up, and said, "Down the drain she goes."

The tears that were brimming her eyelids now ran over, wetting her face.

As she tasted her salty tears for the last time, she said, "It's the only way. For all of us."

Lillian brought the glass to her lips and drank the mixture, forcing herself to finish it all. She gagged and dropped the glass to the floor as the poisonous mixture ran through her body, destroying her from the inside out. Barely conscious, she lay down on her stomach and waited for death to come. It wouldn't be long. Blood had already started trailing out of her nose.

CHAPTER 33

James heard himself screaming, his voice cutting into the quiet morning like a fire alarm. He was outside again. The sun was shining on the lawn in front of him and the day had become warm, if not hot. He squinted his eyes, the brightness of the sun too much for him. He let them adjust gradually.

James surveyed his surroundings, swiveling his neck from side to side. He was outside, not trapped inside the house of horrors behind him. He could see colors again, vibrant colors. The blue sky was a welcome vision. He was standing in the same spot he had been when he slipped into some level of a dream, illusion, or vision; he didn't know which. He was out of it now. He was awake.

James took an unsteady step forward and was shocked at how off kilter he felt. He paused to allow himself to regain some sense of stability. He needed to get his feet under him so that he could drive home.

James took another step and was awash in sunlight, out from under the shaded cover of the porch. He enjoyed the warmth of the sun on his face. It made him feel alive and connected to life. He closed his eyes and turned his head up to the sky, allowing the rays to cover his face unobstructed. Still feeling unsteady, James pivoted slightly to keep his balance as he took in the warm afternoon, breathing in air deeply.

James opened his eyes and his breath caught in his throat. He was standing in the front yard of his and Andrea's home. His legs gave out from underneath him and he fell to the ground hard, staring at the house in front of him. He was in New York, at home, not in Maryland in front of his grandmother's abandoned house. The quiet street he had opened his eyes to was his own. A choked gasp escaped his lips as he felt his sanity slip away from him. He pulled his knees to his chest and sobbed, his eyes dry and dazed.

CHAPTER 34

Andrea saw James sitting outside on the front lawn, staring at the house like he had never seen it before. She looked at him from their bedroom window, his skin brightened by the morning sun. She was frightened for him. James had become a different person over the past couple of months, and his demeanor had gotten worse over the last three days. Much worse. The man on the lawn was a haunted shell of her husband. She hated what was happening to him, hated that he couldn't tell her more about what was going on in his head. Andrea couldn't help him. She thought about taking him to a doctor. Just throwing him into a car and taking him to see someone who might be able to help him work it out. Andrea had done some research on dream therapy on the Internet and had even checked out a book on the subject from the library. She found that there was a program that taught skills that could help James minimize his nightmares, or so they promoted. Three sessions for two weeks and he would be cured. Andrea didn't know if she believed it or not, but it might be worth a try.

But James would never seek help from a psychiatrist. The

prospect was close to the top of his 'Off Limits' list, right next to interior decorating for men and poetry readings as a Saturday night date. It would have been a waste of time and energy trying to argue the positive points of a diagnostic program, and nothing she had read convinced her enough to push it. So, she did more research and said nothing, convinced that James wouldn't go no matter what she did anyway.

Andrea watched from the window as her husband sat on the front lawn looking bewildered and petrified at the same time, not knowing if she should hurry to his side or let him work it out on his own. On the one hand, she rationalized that James had to do this by himself. She would only add stress to the situation if she joined him on the lawn, the whole thing a spectacle for all the neighbors to see. At 11:30 on a Tuesday morning, though, there weren't many neighbors out to see it, thank God.

On the other hand, she chastised herself for not running outside the moment she saw him. What else could she do if not comfort him? Andrea felt guilty that she hadn't gone outside to help James. What was worse was the reason why she hadn't gone outside, the reason that kept her peeking out at James from behind their bedroom curtains. Andrea was afraid of him.

Andrea wouldn't have been home either if James hadn't started acting more and more erratic. She had taken the day off to try and find a psychiatrist that would be able to help him, using traditional methods, rather than new age practices. James would still balk at it, but at least Andrea would be able to argue the precedence of the treatment. If it came to that. Andrea had kicked her research up a notch after the call she received from the medical center about her visit the week before. Things had changed for them. Andrea had to do something to help James if he wouldn't help himself. And fast.

Andrea had planned on meeting with several psychiatrists later on that day. She was going to find out more about what they did and what kinds of treatments they could prescribe. She was going to interview them and find out what they thought might be going on with her husband. Maybe they could help Andrea convince James he needed help. She had to help him somehow. This thing had progressed so fast.

Something had triggered in James and it was counting down like a ticking bomb. The changes had been gradual at first, but then they speed up, accelerating faster than either of them had been prepared for. James' nightmares had started a couple of months before. They had gotten progressively worse and now were completely hellish.

The dreams seemed to have kicked into overdrive recently. James was already different than he had been a few days earlier. He was skittish and jumpy. He had drastic mood swings. He didn't sleep well; James' dreams were always plagued with demons. Why was it happening? Was her husband losing his mind?

James told Andrea about his family early in their relationship, what little he had chosen to disclose. He always kept everything very surface and she didn't press him about it. Andrea met his mother before she died but hadn't seen or talked to her often enough to develop a relationship with her. James hadn't visited his mother a lot when she was alive and his mother didn't reach out. They seemed to like it that way. It worked for them. So, Andrea didn't worry about it.

The times that James talked about his father were few and far between. He mentioned that his father was ambitious. Andrea said that James must have gotten that trait from him. She thought the comment would have gotten a smile out of James. It was a compliment, after all. James tried. He offered a thin version of a smile, his lips barely parted, and turned away quickly. Andrea didn't probe. She didn't know what she had said wrong and wasn't willing to make the same mistake again.

The other thing James said about his father was that he had mental problems. James couldn't name the affliction, or even many of the symptoms. He said he didn't know exactly what it was. James knew that his father lost time. Sometimes he couldn't remember where he had been for hours in a day, sometimes whole days. Sometimes he would talk about places he hadn't been in years or people that had died long ago as though he had just gone to them or spoken with them. Andrea remembered a story that James told her about his father just before he died. He had been sitting at the dinner table with his wife and James. It was a typical mealtime in their house. The table was silent, all the small talk exhausted over the first bites of food. James was fidgety, ready to leave the table and return to his comic books.

James was just about to ask to be excused from the table when his father blurted out, "Mother told me that I was just like her again today. I don't know, Mary. I'm starting to believe her."

Mary, James' mother, turned sharply and looked at her husband, her hand still holding the fork up to her mouth. The succotash trembled slightly as it rested on the prongs.

"Jimmie, what are you talking about?"

James still wanted to leave the table but the conversation was getting interesting. He decided to hold off on asking to be excused.

"She said I couldn't hide from it," Jimmie continued like he hadn't heard Mary. "Said it was in my blood. As much a part of me as it was of her."

Mary placed her fork back on her plate shakily, the lima beans and corn spilling onto the tablecloth. Her face looked distraught. James had only seen his mother look like that once or twice before. Her face did that weird sucking in thing, like she had tasted something really sour, only if something was really wrong. When he was a kid, he broke his leg trying a stunt on some dirt mounds near the school. When they got home after his cast was set, she told James how upset she was at him for doing such a stupid thing. She made the same facial expression then. When James saw it, he knew he was going to get punished and he did. He couldn't ride his bike for a month after the cast came off. James wondered what kind of punishment his Dad was about to get.

"Jimmie, did you hear what you said?"

"I told you what mother said to me."

"You couldn't have talked to your mother, Jimmie. She's been dead for years!"

Mary had placed her hands on the sides of her plate, her palms pressing against the table. She raised her voice as she lifted herself out of the chair. That was uncharacteristic behavior for her, especially in front of James. Mary sat down quickly and glanced over at James who was watching them in silent horror. She smiled apologetically and motioned for him to leave the room.

James got up quickly and walked into the kitchen where he rinsed his plate. He was shaken. His father said he had talked to his dead mother! James knew his grandmother was dead, his father had told him that much. But that was about all he would say. Jimmie never told James anything about her, what she liked to do, where she was from. Nothing. James didn't even know where his father was born. All he knew was that his Dad was from Maryland. Well, Maryland is a big state.

James could still hear the conversation going on in the dining room. His father was trying to tell his mother that he *had* talked with his dead mother earlier that day. James' mother kept cutting him off, telling him it wasn't possible. James agreed with her. Living people couldn't talk to the dead, could they?

"Jimmie, what's the matter with you? You can't really think you talked to your mother, can you? You know she's dead, don't you? You can't talk to dead people, Jimmie. You just can't!"

"Mary, I'm telling you what happened. She was sitting right where you are, waiting for me to get up and have my morning cup of coffee. She told me that it wouldn't be long before I would see how much alike we were."

Mary jumped when he pointed in her direction, referencing where his mother had been that morning. It gave her chills, even if it was a figment of Jimmie's imagination.

"She said soon everyone would know," Jimmie continued. "And that I would see her again."

Mary shook her head. Jimmie hadn't so much as visited his mother's grave since she had died over a decade before. Where was this coming from?

"Jimmie, what are you saying? Your mother told you that you'd see her again soon? Jimmie, that's not possible. She's dead. She's been dead for over ten years!"

Mary stopped talking abruptly after her last sentence. Goose bumps sprang up on her arms as the thought popped into her mind.

Jimmie had told her about his family long ago, just after they got married. She tried to calm him down about it, tried to get him not to fret about something that would probably never happen to him. Mary tried to convince him that just because it happened to his mother it didn't have to happen to him. He'd fought her on it, had given her a laundry list of family members who had suffered the same fate. Still, she held her ground, telling him that it didn't have to be. Mary tried to get Jimmie to see a doctor, to find out if there was anything to worry about, but he wouldn't go. He internalized his concerns and stopped talking about it all together after a while. Somewhere along the line, he actually stopped worrying about what might be and lived his life in the present. It never left his mind completely, though. The possibility of it. And now here it was, rearing its ugly head.

Mary rejected it. She shut her eyes and shook her head harder, denying the thought the foothold it sought in her mind. She didn't hear herself saying, "No! No!" over and over again.

"Mary," Jimmie said, grabbing her arm. His voice, low and tense, cracked as he spoke her name. Mary opened her eyes slowly, the fear in his voice breaking her heart in two. She regarded her husband, faintly aware that he was no longer the man she had known for all those years. He was already changing.

Jimmie saw Mary's reaction and his face began to crumble.

"It's happening already, isn't it?" he asked her miserably.

James eavesdropped from the kitchen, rewashing the same

plate over and over, trying to look busy. *What's happening?* he wondered.

Mary nodded imperceptibly and put her hand on Jimmie's cheek. She pressed her forehead to his.

James told Andrea that story with such sadness in his voice that she had never forgotten it. Whenever they talked about the illness, which was almost never, James didn't return to the sensitivity he had displayed that day. Instead, he dismissed it callously, almost completely devoid of feeling,

"Mom said he was crazy, and he was," he would say offhandedly. "He proved her right when he killed himself, didn't he?"

Andrea knew it bothered him. The idea that there was some unnamed illness floating around in his father's head that drove him to murder his lover and to kill himself. It was embarrassing. And frightening. Andrea was sure James wondered if the same illness would affect him. She could see it in his eyes. She didn't bring it up, even though she wanted to know. She figured she would probe deeper when they were ready to start a family. She would find out the symptoms and try to determine exactly what sort of mental illness his father suffered from. Andrea thought she had time before she needed to dig deeper into the sensitive subject. But she had waited too long.

Andrea thought James harbored some anger, some resentment towards his father. He never told her that, but he didn't have to. She had overheard him a couple of months before talking to himself while he was in his office. She rarely went back there, the only rooms in the extension were James' office and the storage room. She was loading the dishwasher when she realized she had run out of detergent, so she went to the storage room to get another container.

It was midafternoon, but the hallway was dim. The only windows in the addition were in the office and in the storage room. The walls of the hallway leading to both rooms were paneled with wood. The office was on the left and the storage room was a little further down on the right. A windowless door to the backyard was situated at the end of the hallway. By the time Andrea realized she wouldn't be able to see her way to the storage room, she had passed the light switch for the ceiling lamp. She felt her way along the wall, her fingers slipping into the grooves that separated the panels. When she approached the first door, the door to the office, the light from the window trickled into the hallway.

Andrea turned towards the door, thinking she would go in and say hello to her husband. A smile formed on her lips when she thought of what else they could do that afternoon in his office. Her nipples hardened as she thought about sitting on top of him while he sat in the broad backed office chair. Andrea thought about how surprised James would be and the way his face would look if she walked in and did an impromptu strip tease for him. He could use the distraction. James had been working a lot for the past year. Late nights, business trips, overnight stays; they had been almost nonstop until a couple of months before. The late nights at the office and weekend trips stopped abruptly after they had become a staple for the past year. Now James spent more time in the home office at night than with her. It was time for a break.

Arousal was quickly replaced by alarm when she saw him. The door was cracked slightly, allowing her a sliver to look through. Andrea could see James with his head in his hands. His fingers were curled downward, his knuckles pressed against his temples. He banged them against his head rhythmically as he chastised himself.

"Why? Why?" she heard him saying. He wasn't talking loudly; his voice was only a little above a whisper. It was the intensity of his voice that chilled Andrea to her bones.

She watched as he sat there, his elbows on the desk, banging hard as he trembled. A strange sound emitted from him. It sounded like a low, guttural moan. It was the most painful thing she had ever heard. Andrea wanted to go in and comfort him, but something made her stay in the hallway behind the shield of the door.

Andrea saw James get up fast, knocking the chair over. It tumbled onto the floor loudly, but he didn't bother to pick it up. James turned his back to the door and stared at the pictures that lined the wall. Photographs of his mother's family from as far back as the late 1800s were framed and hung on the walls. The only image from James' father's side was of James' father himself. It was hung on the right side of the desk, next to one of the two windows in the room. James strolled over to the portrait and looked at it for a long time, his body stiff and motionless in front of it.

Andrea became concerned that he would turn towards the door as he returned to the desk. She couldn't decipher his state of mind, hadn't been able to for a long time. James had been so edgy lately. She never knew what would set him off and what wouldn't. Andrea had no idea how James would react if he saw her peering through the crack in the door, watching him.

James stood looking at his father's portrait for a long time. James' mother had forced his father into sitting for the painting. She said that it was better than a photograph, more artistic. She was right. The rendition was breathtaking. His features translated handsomely to the canvas. Still there was always something disconcerting about it, Andrea thought. His face was expression-less. He stared out at the world with vacant eyes. Maybe it was all the secrecy surrounding his death. Maybe it was because, when he was alive, he never told James anything about his family; he never divulged anything about his past. Andrea didn't know. She only knew that the portrait bothered her. She was glad it hung in the office, where she rarely visited, so she didn't have to see it often.

After a while of standing outside the door and eavesdropping on her husband as he gazed at his father's portrait, Andrea thought it was time for her to leave. Maybe James was remembering his father and the memory saddened him. Whatever it was, James should be able to have the moment to himself. Andrea scolded herself for staying so long, invading his privacy. She started to leave when she heard him speaking again.

It was low at first, nothing more than mumbling. Slowly his voice got louder and louder, until he was almost shouting at the top of his lungs.

"I'm not like you! I'll never be like you!" he screamed. Andrea stood still, taken aback by the outburst.

"There's nothing wrong with me! I didn't do it!"

He went on like that for more than a minute before falling silent. He put his hands on his hips and cast one more glance at the picture, his lips snarled in anger.

Andrea sank into the shadows, trying to fade away from view, just in case James turned in her direction. For one horrible moment, Andrea thought he would sense her presence and confront her. The air felt electric against her skin, she flinched as if shocked.

James turned in the opposite direction, facing the back wall, and walked heavily back to his seat.

"Yes, you are," she heard him say. His voice was different, somehow. Deeper.

"You and he are one and the same. There's no way to avoid it. You know that. You've always known that."

It wasn't the words that bothered her. The sentences themselves were troubling in and of themselves, but that was the least of it. It was the voice that uttered them. She had never heard James use it before. In fact, it almost didn't sound like James at all. But then again, it did. Andrea stood on the other side of the door replaying the voice she'd heard over and over in her head. She confused herself as she thought about it. She knew that the words had come out of James' mouth; there wasn't anyone else in the room who could have spoken them. The voice sounded enough like him to be believable, but different enough to give her pause. It was like talking to identical twins. More often than not, they sounded so much alike that it took concentration to tell them apart. If you listened closely, you could hear the difference. The slight lift in one, the different pitch in the other. The nuances were subtle, but there. But that voice, that eerily similar voice, was coming from James, and not another person. It made her skin crawl.

James fell silent. No more protests, no more outbursts. He just sat in his chair staring at the desk in front of him, his mouth open, his body slouched, his arms dangling limply over the sides of the armrests. He was breathing heavy. He looked spent.

Andrea never mentioned what she saw to James or to anyone else.

As the memory of that day faded to the reality of present day, Andrea watched James sitting on the lawn and felt pity well up inside her. This behavior had come out of nowhere. It had caught her off guard. At first James turned his suffering inward, like he was fighting a battle with the evil side of himself. But recently, just those past couple of days, something had changed. He was different. The dreams were more intense. It was like a character from one of his gruesome dreams was manifesting itself in him, taking him over.

James didn't look at her the way he used to. His reactions to what was happening were more aggressive than passive; he outwardly displayed his rage at the images in his head. Sometimes he looked at her like she was a stranger, other times he regarded her as a threat. She never knew how he was going to behave from one moment to the next. She couldn't help but think that whatever was happening to him, whatever had awakened in his mind, had always been there, lying dormant, waiting for its time to strike. Telling James about the pregnancy might enrage him, send him spiraling downward instead of making him happy. Andrea couldn't bear the thought of that reaction, not to their child. She just didn't know what James would do and it frightened her. Andrea thought again about the portrait of his father on the wall of the office and shivered.

James sat outside, holding himself in a tight ball, staring at the house. She wondered if he saw her standing in the window looking back at him. Could he see the pity on her face? The terror? James was dressed in the same worn sweats he always wore around the house and a t-shirt. No shoes, no socks. It was like he sleepwalked outside and took a seat on the front yard, still embroiled in a dream. She knew he was cold. It couldn't have been more than 45 degrees outside, even though the sun was shining directly on him like a spotlight. Andrea steeled herself. She had to bring James a coat or get him inside before he caught his death of cold.

As she turned to leave the room and go outside, her eyes rested on the digital alarm clock next to the bed. 11:35 a.m. He had only appeared outside a couple of minutes ago, seemingly out of nowhere.

Where had he been all morning?

CHAPTER 35

James saw Andrea watching him from the house, the pain in her eyes evident from outside. He couldn't say anything to her even though he wanted to. He wanted to tell her that he was all right and he'd be inside in a minute. He wanted to tell her that he had taken the day off especially to spend time with her. He wanted to say something that would make sense as to why he was sitting outside on his lawn staring at his house as though he had never seen it before. *Thinking of getting the house repainted? Admiring her remarkable garden?* his mind quipped. *How about this? I don't know why I'm looking at the house. Honestly, I thought I was in front of a different house, one about four hours away from here, in Maryland, where my father and grandmother used to live.*

Something. But James couldn't say any of what he was thinking, neither the lies nor the truth. All he could do was stare at the house, in awe of it being there.

James sat on the lawn until Andrea came outside, trying to make sense of what was going on. The last thing he remembered doing, the last time he remembered having control over his actions, was looking at his grandmother's death certificate. James remembered reading it completely, even reading the name of the certifier who stamped and filed the document. James read it all. He remembered thinking he would go up to bed, maybe take the next day off from work, and drive out to the address on the death certificate. Part of him knew that going there would answer some questions for him. James didn't know how he knew that. He just did.

The part of his mind that knew he would go to the house eventually tried to muscle out the disjointed memory of a woman—his grandmother—rising from the floor, her straight white nightgown swaying at the sides when she approached the window quickly. Too quickly. Confused images crowded James' thoughts. The same woman, younger now, shouting instructions at a young boy, a woman's body on the floor, lifeless, a faceless woman laying broken in front of an apartment building wearing a white nightgown that was stained with blood. The images ran together in his head, one after the other, zooming in and out, like a horrific collage. There was an underlying current to all of the images, one that he wanted to close himself to, but couldn't. He wasn't supposed to, James understood now. Finally. "You know," a gravelly voice repeated over and over like a chant. "You know."

Andrea ran to her husband, at first to bring him inside to get him warm, but that changed almost as soon as she opened the door. As she raced to him, the coat she held in her hands a second before abandoned, she heard him yelling, "Stop it! Stop it! Stop it!" Over and over, he repeated the line as loud as he could. His hands pressed against the sides of his head to cover his ears so tightly the tips of his fingers were white. James rocked back and forth on his tailbone, his legs bent in front of him, his heels digging into the hard ground.

Andrea dropped to her knees next to him, tears falling from her eyes and landing on his shoulder. She hugged him and held firm, trying to stop his rocking, trying to stop his yelling. She pressed his face into her shoulder trying to bury the sound. Finally, he grew still.

James stopped shouting and rocking just as quickly as he had started. She pulled away from him slightly, just far enough to see his face, but close enough to grab him if he started yelling again. James made eye contact with Andrea. His face was serene, calm even, as he looked back at his wife. He didn't have the manic eyes she'd seen a minute before when he was in the middle of his episode. What replaced the delirium was resignation. The look of it chilled Andrea more than the brisk air circling them.

"James," she said sweetly, not wanting to provoke another eruption. "Why don't we go inside and get warm. It's freezing out here. Whatever it is, we can talk about it inside."

Andrea tried to get up, to get James to follow her lead and go into the house, but he grabbed her elbow, holding her firmly in place. She didn't say anything as he stared into her eyes. James was looking through her like he never had before. It was an uncomfortable feeling, but she did not give in to shifting positions or averting her eyes. She held his gaze. After a long minute, his mouth cracked open slightly to speak. His breath smelled of dirt and grass wet from a storm.

James caressed Andrea's elbow lovingly, almost as an afterthought, but said nothing. He seemed far away. Andrea tried again to stand and this time met no resistance. James gave himself over to her, following her lead into the house, putting some of his weight on her as they walked. Andrea took James upstairs and put him in bed. She didn't ask what happened, where he had been all morning, or what had caused him to scream that way. She wanted to know but didn't think James was capable of answering her. His face looked haunted, vacant. She didn't even know if he was there.

Andrea made James comfortable in bed, gave him some hot tea, and left him in the room. She hoped he would drift into a peaceful sleep, though she was pessimistic about it. She went downstairs and started calling the numbers she'd found when she was researching dream therapy.

CHAPTER 36

James laid awake in bed for an hour, unable to get to sleep. He shed the covers to sit in the chair next to the roll top desk that was cattycornered to the window. The television was on, voices bantered back and forth, but he didn't hear them. Not really. The only story that had kept his interest was the earlier police account of a Spring Valley woman who had been arrested for committing a double homicide, killing her husband and best friend in jealous rage. The two had been having an affair behind her back, sources said. The woman killed her husband first, transported his body to the friend's house, and then killed the friend. James shuddered as his mind superimposed Andrea's face onto the attractive woman being led out of a house James had passed many times in downtown Spring Valley. The house was at the edge of the business district and at the beginning of the residential area on Maple Avenue. The alleged murderer, a tall woman with a shapely body and shoulder length brown hair, looked familiar also.

The woman flashed a smile at the reporters who snapped pictures of her as she was led to the police car. She strolled casually, her hips rolling luxuriously with every step, her shoulders fluid as they adhered to the sway of her gait. Her smile was light and happy as she looked at the reporters, each of them greedily snapping photo after photo of this woman who had just made herself the cover story of all of the small-town newspapers. She looked as if she was going to the theater rather than to jail.

She would be fodder for the town rumor mill. When a town that only had six murders the year before gets two on one day, it's big news. The small village hadn't seen a sensational murder like that one since 1980 when Sheryl Sohn set up a burglary at her parent's home in Blueberry Hill that ended in murder.

The woman already had a fan club. James could see a huddle of women, maybe seven in all, standing close together, watching with admiration as she passed them. They were quiet; no shouts of support escaping their lips, no thumbs pointing toward the sky, unlike the woman's opposers who yelled catcalls and expletives at her that had no effect, much to their chagrin. Her fan club was silent as they watched the woman walk by, their strength joining with hers to pave a clear line to the police car, unobstructed by those who went against her.

There were other types of people sprinkled among the angry and the admiring. James saw a woman dressed in jogging clothes looking on in hushed disbelief. A man holding a rake stood on his lawn at the top of the shot, the angle just wide enough to find him watching the spectacle in his neighborhood, the surprise evident on his face. People that knew her, that had socialized with her for years, were confused at the accusation. And frightened. Terribly frightened.

This woman, this Christine Mason, would live in infamy on the lips of the villagers and she looked like she knew it. Her self-assuredness gave voice to it. She ate up the attention.

As the news moved on to another segment James lamented about Andrea. He wanted to talk to her, to try and explain his behavior. He knew she was confused and scared for him, and probably for herself. James wanted to try and explain why he had been acting so strangely, but he didn't know how to. He didn't know how to explain that he thought he saw his grandmother kill her sister then kill herself, both acts happening over a decade apart, decades before that day. He didn't have answers for her. At least, not ones he could tell her. He needed to understand more about what was happening to him before he could explain anything to Andrea. James needed to get to the bottom of what was going on. For him and for her.

Andrea had left James alone in the bedroom for about an hour before she checked in on him. She found that he was awake and started to ask questions about what he had been dreaming. The questions were light and surface, questions designed to get him talking about what was happening to him. James didn't even acknowledge her. He mumbled that he was sleepy and rolled over in bed, turning his back to her. Andrea put her hand on James' back and let out a sigh that broke his heart. She left the room, leaving him to stare at the wall.

Not long after that, Andrea left the house. James thought Andrea might have gone to run some errands, but he knew better. She needed a break from the chaos happening in her house. He didn't blame her. If he were in her shoes, he would need a break too.

James hadn't left the room since he walked in the front door supported by Andrea, his fingers and toes numb from the cold. He jumped in the shower hoping the warm water would make him drowsy. On top of everything else that was going on, there was a dull pain in his head from the gash he had gotten the day before.

James tried to sleep. He pulled the covers up to his chest, snuggled down into the warmth of the bed, and closed his eyes, beckoning it. None came. It was probably for the best, he surmised. He needed a few hours to think things through.

As he sat in front of the television screen, the sounds of wise guys mouthing off in a bar blaring from the screen, he recounted the day. One of the last things he remembered was going to his office and pulling out his father's photo album. He saw the picture of his father's mother, Lillian Boone. A woman whose name had never once been uttered in his presence. A woman whose face he had never laid eyes upon before that day.

James remembered looking at the picture, trying to find similarities between her and his father. Between her and himself. James recalled that he thought she was beautiful, although not in the conventional way that the world judged beauty. There was a rugged edge to her face. Her features were delicate but weathered. Her frame was small but strong. Her eyes stuck in his head. They were hauntingly cold. He felt like they were looking back at him, seeing beyond his flesh, to his soul.

Everything from that point on existed in a haze. It seemed surreal; him ending up in Maryland in front of a house that he had never seen before, except in his dreams, not remembering how he had gotten there. James remembered walking toward the house through no volition of his own, almost as if some unseen force was leading him there. The feeling of being led stayed with him, filling him as he thought back in earnest to that morning. James strained to remember, working the pulsating throb from his wound into a headache above his eye, but nothing more surfaced. That was all he could remember. Everything else was jumbled up into a mass of clouded images, shouting and angry, and coated in blood.

James touched his bandage and cringed from the pain. His hand hovered around the wound, touching it lightly trying to sooth the pulsing that beat underneath the bandage. James tried to remember clearer images. Nothing past approaching the house broke through. His conscious mind wanted desperately to know everything that happened to him. Wanted to know where he was, what he was doing, and what he saw in the hours that he lost. It struggled against itself as though running in water, trying to zoom in on the blurred images that stood just beyond his view, hanging on the fringes of his mind. His subconscious, however, didn't struggle at all. It knew all it needed to know. It understood.

The voices carrying on conversation on the television screen spoke in hushed tones, whispering conspiratorially to one another. The sound, the tone of their voices camouflaged in an airy lilt, had a soporific effect on James. The room became blurry as his eyelids drooped, sleep coming when he least expected it.

James drifted off thinking distantly of a woman in a white nightgown laughing at him.

CHAPTER 37

The rest was fitful and short, full of quick flashes and disjointed scenes that were out of sequence if they even belonged to the same situation at all. James was walking down a dimly lit street. It was familiar but he couldn't put his finger on what town he was in. Cars lined both sides of the street. It was late, close to midnight, he thought, and the streets were empty. A cool wind whipped around his head as he turned the corner. A crowd was gathered at the far end of the block. Police cars blocked vehicle traffic into and out of the street. James walked faster towards the site, intrigued now.

The crowd talked among themselves, pointing and looking, shaking their heads. James got closer. Crime scene tape was tied to the trees and lampposts that surrounded the victim, forming a rough perimeter. James pushed through the crowd until he was standing directly behind the tape. A woman lay motionless on the ground. Police officers and detectives milled around the body, some kneeling over her, some standing, waiting for the ambulance to arrive. A mass of legs blocked his view but he could see the blood that trailed from her broken body, staining the concrete.

As he peered through the confusion surrounding her, his vantage point changed. He seemed to be lifted above the scene, looking down at it, his body feeling as light as the air he was suspended in. He could see the woman clearly now. Her body was lying on the ground, blood framing her like velvet matting. The woman was beautiful, even in death. Her eyes were open. She watched him float above her. A smile played at the corners of her bloody lips.

The next image superimposed itself on the last. He was standing alone in a bathroom. The bathroom itself was normal. A commode sat to the left of the sink. A mirror was hung on the wall above the sink, and a medicine cabinet with a mirror framed in wood was mounted on the wall to the right.

James looked at the reflection of himself. He was dressed in bummy sweatpants and a t-shirt—the same outfit he'd had on that morning on the lawn. His bandage was red with blood; it was soaked through. He opened the medicine cabinet door, positioning the mirror so that he could see the side of the bandage without moving his head. As James looked at the bandage, pulling one edge up gingerly to see his cut, his eyes wandered to the reflected images of himself in the mirrors. The medicine cabinet mirror reflected the profile of the right side of his face, as well as a part of the image reflected from the larger bathroom mirror. The larger bathroom mirror showed more of his face; the angle of his left profile was less pronounced. Both mirrors combined to show both sides of his face, from different angles.

James' hands fell away from the bandage and his jaw dropped when he saw his reflections in the mirrors. The reflection in the larger bathroom mirror was recognizably his, but distinctly differ-ent. The eyebrows were furrowed and the forehead was creased. His lips had been pulled back to reveal razor sharp teeth that looked like they had been filed into points. There was a coldness in the eye that was visible in the reflection that made James' blood cool.

The medicine cabinet mirror reflected the right side of his face. But this side didn't resemble him at all. A decidedly feminine profile was reflected, one with shoulder length brown hair. Her mouth was drawn into an evil smirk that widened into a smile while he watched. Her eye was also as cold as ice.

Rows of duplicate images cascaded behind the two reflections, each mirroring the other, every profile the horrifying same. They seemed to stare at each other, one acknowledging the other with icy glares.

While James looked at the two profiles in horror, they both turned toward him, revealing their entire faces. James could see the resemblance—the three of them looked as if they were siblings. They had the same eyes and the same hair color. They shared the same facial structure. They were the same person, yet different.

James backed away from the mirrors, shaking his head imperceptibly at first, and then ferociously as the images appeared amused with him. His reflections watched him as he backed away until he bumped into the closed door behind him. He pawed at the doorknob, trying to turn it without taking his eyes off the mirrors. It wouldn't move; it was locked from the outside. The sweat that dropped from his forehead mingled with the tears on his cheeks that he didn't know he had shed. They looked at him and laughed.

CHAPTER 38

James woke up abruptly, his heart racing with fear. He could still feel the doorknob pressing into the small of his back as he tried to shrink away from the reflections in the mirror, their faces so cold, so sadistically satisfied. So much like his own. He shivered against his will at the memory that hung in his mind.

The sun had already set. James turned to look at the clock. 5:15 p.m. He had slept longer than he thought he would. The house was quiet. Andrea had not yet returned. James hoped that she was talking with a friend. Even if Andrea was telling Samantha, Ann, or any of her other friends about what was going on with him, as embarrassing as the truth may be, he didn't mind. At least she would be getting it off her chest. She would be releasing herself from her own nightmare the way he wished he could.

James stood up, splitting the funnel of light projected by the television screen. An '80s vampire movie was on now, all fangs, punk hair, and pop music. He walked over to the dresser and took out a change of clothes—a pair of slacks and a sweater—aware that he was avoiding a glance into the mirror. After a minute of this, dressing with his eyes focused on the bed without looking toward the mirror to his left, afraid of catching a glimpse of someone else in the reflection, he decided to confront the monster head on. As he buttoned his slacks he walked over to the mirror, watching his reflection inch closer and closer. It was him. It was the face he had been living with for thirty-four years. A sigh of relief escaped his lips before he realized it.

James walked downstairs determinedly. He knew where he had to go to make sense of what was going on in his head, or at least some of it. James recognized the location of his last dream. He had been there before. He needed to go back there to bring the rest of the memory forward. James was sure he would confront much more before all was said and done.

James locked the front door and walked down the driveway to his car. As he was backing out, a car pulled in the driveway behind him.

CHAPTER 39

Pete drove to James' house right after work. Andrea had called him at the office, telling him that James was getting worse. She also told him that she was pregnant. The news hit Pete like a shotgun blast. A baby. James' baby. At first, he thought the pregnancy would ruin his chances. His mood was shot right after the phone call. He felt like he was mourning the loss of Susan all over again. And then it hit him. He could use this to his advantage. James was already on his way out, wasn't he? It was just a matter of time before he cracked up like his father had. When James was finally gone, it would be just Pete and Andrea. They would come together during the pregnancy. Pete would help her through Lamaze classes and through the delivery. He would bond with the baby. Andrea would depend upon him for support and that would grow into love. He couldn't have picked a better angle.

Andrea also told Pete that she was going out to talk to some doctors who might be able to help James. Pete agreed with her, playing the game, telling her that she was doing the best thing.

"He'll be furious, Pete. That's why I wanted you to come over. I want you to be there when I talk to him about it tonight."

Pete agreed, of course. He was never one to turn down a dinner invitation from Andrea. She said she would see the last doctor at 5:30 p.m. then go home to make dinner. She asked him to come by at 7:30 p.m.

Pete planned his meeting with James for the rest of the afternoon. He was close now, but not too far over the edge to notice if Pete made a mistake. In some ways, Pete felt sorry for James. Whatever was happening in his head, whatever demons were revealing themselves to him, their insurgence was inevitable. James might be afraid to lift the sheet off the ghost and see who it was, but Pete wasn't. Whatever its name, whatever its reason, it had come to do its job and was doing it well.

Things were happening faster than Pete expected them to. He was going along for the ride like everyone else. James' mind was eating him inside out. He was so skittish that Pete thought James might do something to get the police on his trail. Anything that Pete might add in would just be icing on the cake. As long as he didn't make a mistake.

Pete remembered how James would seem fine most days when they were in college. He'd be a normal guy going to class and hanging out with friends just like the rest of them. But some days he would be despondent and withdrawn. Some days, he didn't come out of his room at all. It was happening even then, but no one knew it. Not even James. You had to feel sorry for someone whose fate was mental illness, written in their genetic code, almost timed, just waiting to come out and play.

Pete couldn't help but see it as a golden opportunity. He had already planted the seed, karma had watered it, and fate would make it grow like a weed.

Pete chuckled at the turn of events. In school, Pete had always been the insecure one. He hid it from his friends well, he thought. He went to all the games, talked to all the girls, and drank all the beer that his friends did, only he did it always feeling like he would fail. Like he was being laughed at. Pete was pleasantly surprised when he was proven wrong time and time again. He was cool, contrary to what he thought about himself. He was part of a popular group of guys on campus and, through osmosis, got with some of the popular girls on campus. Pete lived college life in a dream, amazed that he didn't hear laughter trailing behind him every time he left a room. It took him a while, but Pete got comfortable, became confident. He was just a normal guy living life like everybody else. Nobody was laughing anymore.

Pete hadn't been laughed at since he was a kid in middle school. He had been the shortest boy in the class and the weakest basketball player in Phys. Ed. Even girls scored on him, fouling him hard as they charged the basket. Pete would hear the laughter even before his behind hit the parquet gym floor. It echoed, bouncing off the gym walls, tormenting him. Pete heard that sound in his sleep until the end of college. He winced, realizing that the sound of laughter was the only remnant he could recall from a dream the night before.

But that doesn't happen anymore, he reminded himself. *Nobody's laughing now.*

"James and Susan laughed at me," he corrected himself, speaking the words aloud in the car as he made his way to James and Andrea's house, two hours earlier than he was supposed to be there. Pete thought about his wife's upturned face as she looked at his best friend when he saw them embracing in a park in Nyack. *In the middle of the goddamned street,* his mind shouted. Anger welled in him again, as it always did when he thought about how they betrayed him. His face felt warm all of a sudden, a sweat breaking out over his brow.

"You fucking bastards!" he shouted to the empty car, the steering wheel sliding within his grasp from the moisture on his palms. They carried on behind his back, having a relationship. It had been more than just sex. Susan had been in love with James.

She said as much right before she died. It made Pete sick to his stomach when he heard it, much like it did now. She had laughed and spit in his face at the same time.

But no one was laughing then. Susan certainly wasn't laughing anymore. And Pete had a feeling that soon James wouldn't be laughing either.

CHAPTER 40

Pete got out of the car and walked quickly to James' window.

"Hey man. Where are you heading?" The levity in his voice was betrayed by the urgency on his face.

"Pete, what are you doing here?"

James found it odd that, twice now, Pete had come to the house and seemed, well, friendly to him. It was only a couple of days ago when Pete had punched him in the face, and rightfully so, for sleeping with his wife. How could he have forgiven James so easily? He wanted to ask, but his mind was cluttered with issues that pressed against each other, against the very walls of his psyche, demanding attention.

"I was just coming by to see how your head was doing," Pete said with obviously feigned sincerity. He wanted James to probe.

James stared at Pete. He could see that Pete was uncomfortable. He pressed,

"My head is better. Pete, what's really going on here?" It only took a second for the reason for the visit to come to him. "Andrea told you about this morning, didn't she?"

Pete hesitated and finally decided to lie. "Yeah, she did. What's happening to you, James? What's going on?"

James' face contorted, breaking down at the realization that something really was happening to him. He straightened his face self-consciously, returning it to its natural countenance under the gaze of his friend.

"I don't know, man. That's what I'm trying to figure out."

Pete nodded at James, drawing the silence out, his face clouding as he stood silent.

"What is it, Pete?" James asked. "If it's about what happened the other day—what happened between Susan and me—."

Pete's face flashed with anger but he controlled it quickly. "No, it's not that. It's just that," he leaned closer, resting his arm on the car door, "I got another call from the police about Susan's murder."

James recoiled, shocked by his choice of words.

"Murder? What do you mean murder? Her death was ruled an accident," he said a little too loudly. He turned his head both ways, looking up and down his street to see if anyone was outside who might have heard his outburst. The street was empty except for Mrs. Jacobson. She was strolling up her driveway, the day's mail in her hand, like she was in a trance. Her legs moved mechanically, as if by rote. Her eyes were vacant; they had been ever since her only son, retarded since birth, disappeared one day without a trace. If she had heard what James said, she didn't let on. James doubted she cared about much of anything anymore.

"I know, but the police are calling it a murder now," Pete said, calling James' attention back to the conversation. "They've reopened the case." Pete paused to look into James' eyes. He could see the confusion in them as clear as day.

"What?" James asked incredulously. "Why would they reopen the case?"

"I don't know," Pete said, shrugging his shoulders. "Some overzealous intern took a look at the evidence again and found something."

"What did they find?"

"I don't know, James. They didn't give me all the details." Pete paused, hanging his head.

"I don't know, maybe I wasn't ready to hear all the details when they called me about it. I'm trying to heal. I'm just getting to the point where I can get up in the morning and not put my hand on her side, expecting her to be there, you know?"

James nodded and looked away from Pete. It would be inappropriate to show how he truly felt about losing Susan with Pete. With anyone.

"They don't think the fire was an accident," Pete said flatly.

"I thought they said it was caused by a leaking gas line that deposited gas on the engine manifold."

"That's what they thought then, and the basis of it is the same. Gas leaked in the engine and it caught fire. The only difference is that now they think the leak didn't happen by accident. The car was old, but not old enough for the gas line to crack. They think the car was tampered with. They think the gas line might have been cut."

James looked back at Pete's face in disbelief. He tried to block his thoughts from coming in, tried to keep them from getting a clear shot at his attention, but he failed. *There's evidence now,* the voice in his head said. *Now everyone will know what happened.*

Pete continued, "I can't believe it, man. Who would want to kill Susan? She didn't have an enemy in the world. All I know is that if this was murder, I want the bastard who did this to pay."

James hoped his face didn't betray how frightened he was. He had to get out of there.

"Pete, let's talk about this later. I have to go somewhere, but I'll be back later tonight. Maybe we can talk then."

James put the car in gear, keeping his foot on the brake, hoping that Pete caught the hint. He knew he should stay and talk to his friend. He should try to be there for him through this, to be the friend he should have been all along. James just didn't know if he had the right to stand by Pete when he was probably the one who was to blame for it all.

After a long pause, Pete said, "Okay, man. We'll talk about this later." He appeared to be trying to pull himself together as he spoke. "I just wanted to give you a heads up about this before the police called you."

James' eyes widened. "They want to talk to me? Why?"

Pete hung his head for a moment, kicking the grass framing the driveway. Raw emotion stood in his eyes like high water. "The ATF wanted to know everything. They asked me to tell them about our marriage, about Susan's outside interests."

Pete paused, anger threatening to take him over. His gaze pierced James.

"The police made me give them her phone book, the names of her regular hang outs, you know, the places she went shopping, where she liked to eat, things like that," Pete continued. "I got angry. I asked them what it was all about. 'Susan's death was supposed to be an accident,' I said. God, I was so pissed. I didn't want them probing into our life, asking personal questions, digging around all over again. I knew where they would eventually end up. I didn't want them to find out about the two of you. For my sake as much as hers.

"That's when they told me they were going to look at the gas line more closely this time, to see if anything turned up. They had an agent from the Justice Department on the line with them. He was part of the Alcohol, Tobacco, and Firearms division. They said he was going to take over the case and look into the prospect of wrongful death."

The words sounded like they were coming from far away to James. He couldn't believe what he was hearing.

"They asked me if she had a lover," Pete said.

James closed his eyes, squeezing his lids together.

Pete watched James as he sat in the car, the gravity of the situation seeping into his pores. James' reaction disgusted Pete. He could barely stop himself from reaching into the car and choking the life out of him.

"I had to give them your name. They would have found out anyway. I'm sure Susan told her friends about your... the affair." The words left a sour taste in his mouth.

After a pause, Pete added, "They asked if there was anything else. I told them that Susan and I had talked about the affair and that we had worked it out. I told them how happy we were that we were expecting a child." His voice hitched.

James turned to look at Pete, the sky growing increasingly darker as the sun disappeared beyond the treetops. Pete had known about the affair. James had stressed about telling him about the affair for a long time, worried about what would happen to the friendship they had. Pete had been stringing him along the whole time, waiting to see if James had the guts to own up to it, or if he would hide behind Susan's death, counting it as a blessing. James was angry, even though he realized how ridiculous that was. Susan had lied to him that day. He felt like a fool.

"Everything was going to be all right between us," Pete continued. "She was going to break it off with you and we were going to start over. Be a family again. I told them that Susan was supposed to be meeting with you that day to end the relationship."

James slumped in the seat and laid his head in his hands. He had been in Nyack that day. Susan called him and asked him to meet her in Nyack at their secret place. She sounded upset so James quickly cleared his schedule to meet her. Luckily, Andrea was in the city visiting her parents at the time, so he didn't have to come up with an appropriate lie to get out.

James got there first and parked around the corner on a side street. It was a clear day, he remembered, and he got out of the car to wait for Susan to arrive. When she got there, she looked haggard, like she'd had a long night. Susan got out of the car slowly, deliberately. She didn't meet his eyes when she walked toward him like she usually did. The happiness that was usually present didn't radiate from her face that day, and he noticed it. They usually enjoyed their secret getaways together, relishing every second from the moment they saw each other to the moment they left to go home. James saw the difference in her behavior immediately but chose to ignore it.

Susan stopped about three steps away from James, her body tense. She was just beyond his reach; he would have had to take a step forward to touch her. That was different. They usually stood so close to each other, they couldn't tell where one stopped and the other began. Her distance concerned him. Something was wrong.

He moved to her tentatively. She didn't refuse him but didn't encourage him either. He leaned down to kiss her lips, but she turned her head. His lips grazed her cheek lightly as she turned away and took a step backwards.

"Susan, what's wrong?" James asked. She had never behaved like that with him before. The last few months had been incredible for them. They met often, sharing time with each other in their special town. They felt safe there. Pete and Andrea were strangers to Nyack. The threat of being caught was slim to none and they exploited the opportunity to be free. James and Susan had been happy. All of a sudden that had changed.

"I can't do this anymore, James," Susan started slowly. Her eyes brimmed with tears already, her face saddened by her statement.

"We can't do this."

James tried to hug her, but she recoiled. His arms dropped to his sides as he let her words sink in. He knew their relationship would have to change at some point. Either they both had to leave their spouses or they would have to end it, sooner or later. An affair can never last. Even those that went on for decades. There had to be an end; they couldn't just continue on in limbo, the participants sneaking out to meet like thieves in the night. It was a fantasy, make believe. James knew it and Susan knew it. They had never talked about the end, what their decision would be. He knew that when he was faced with the moment of truth, when it was time for

Susan and him to make a decision about whether or not the relationship had a future, that he would never leave his wife. That knowledge was his security blanket. It satisfied him, somehow, that he knew what lay ahead. But now, on that clear day in their secret little town, James realized he wasn't ready for it to be over. Not yet.

"Susan, okay. Let's slow down a minute. Let's talk this through."

She shook her head and put up her hand, stopping him mid-sentence.

"There's nothing to talk about, James. We can't go on like this, sneaking around behind people's backs, carrying on this charade."

The words stung James. His eyes pleaded with her to reconsider, to make everything go back to the way it was.

"What happened? When we saw each other yesterday things weren't like this. We were still having fun. What changed?" James hated himself for sounding so whiny, but he couldn't help but think that his world was turning upside down. He wanted things back the way they were. He wanted Susan back.

"James, I—," she started. A lump formed in her throat and tears threatened to spill over her eyelids. She swallowed hard, trying to regain her composure.

"I'm sorry, James."

Susan tried to get back in the car. James chased after her, covering the space between them in two quick strides. He grabbed her elbow, holding it with just enough pressure to stop her. She turned to him, new tears glistening in the sun as they cascaded down her cheeks. He marveled in despair at how gorgeous she was.

"Susan, wait. You have to tell me why. Why now?"

Susan faced him squarely, suddenly angry.

"You knew we couldn't continue this relationship if that's what you want to call it. We're married, for God's sake! How much longer did you think this could go on before one of them found out?"

James' stomach dropped, he remembered, at the prospect of either Andrea or Pete finding out about the affair. He knew it was a possibility, but he had put it out of his mind. James had lived in ignorant bliss for the past couple of months. His happiness with Susan seemed beyond consequence. Now, standing on a quiet street, witnessing the end of his sordid relationship with his best friend's wife, he felt exposed.

"Did Pete find out? Is that what happened?"

Susan looked away again, shielding her face from his scrutiny.

"How did he find out? We were being so careful."

"Careful!" she exclaimed. "You call this careful? We're standing on a sidewalk arguing over our affair without regard to who may be listening on the corner or from their bedroom window. I don't know everyone that Pete knows and I'm sure you don't know everyone that Andrea knows. One of Pete's colleagues might come into Nyack on the weekends. Or one of Andrea's high school friends. Anyone could have seen us at one of the restaurants on Main Street or at the park."

Susan's face betrayed her. She wanted to be angry. She wanted to break the relationship off and drive away. But it wasn't that easy. She and James had a bond that she didn't share with Pete. She didn't want to break up with him, but she didn't want to leave her husband either. If the two men were combined, they would make the perfect man, she had thought on more than one occasion.

But now, with the baby coming, she knew she had to end the relationship. The baby was Pete's. She had to believe that if she wanted her marriage to work.

"We haven't been careful. We've been lucky," she continued. "But now it's over, James. It has to be."

"Did he threaten you?" Fury rose in James quickly at the thought of Pete putting his hands on Susan. He inadvertently tightened his grip on Susan's arm as he thought of it.

"No, nothing like that. He didn't find out about us, James," she lied. She knew she would when she was driving there to meet him. Pete confronted her the night before. He was in Nyack that day, coming from a client visit when he saw them on the street. She could only imagine how he felt. The thought that she had engaged in a sexual relationship with her husband's best friend made her sick to her stomach, no matter how she may feel for James. What kind of woman was she? How could she do that to Pete, who had treated her with nothing but kindness since they first met? She loved him, she never questioned that. Pete was everything Susan wanted in a man. He was attractive, successful, well rounded, had a great sense of humor; he was the perfect catch. How could she toss the whole relationship away because of one thing?

Pete was not what she wanted in bed. He was attentive and he was more than enough for her, but he didn't arouse her. Susan knew that before she married him but thought she could get over it. She thought she had, until she saw James that day at the pier. The attraction was instant and Susan couldn't help herself. She gave in to it.

Now that all was said and done, and Susan realized what she almost lost, she was shaken. She saw Pete in a whole new light, his shortcomings seeming less and less important. She was so grateful when he said he would deal with the pain as long as she ended the relationship with James. He said he wouldn't bring it up again, not to her or to anyone else, if she broke it off. If they didn't end it, Pete said he would tell Andrea about the affair and file for divorce. She knew he would do it. Pete wanted to forgive her and move on with their lives. He was willing to let it go. He wanted their life to go back to normal, like this had never happened. All she had to do was end it.

Susan remembered her shock, the feeling of utter amazement when, after two hours of talking, yelling, cursing, and slamming doors, Pete came back to the bedroom and embraced her. He held her with such tenderness that she cried, burying her head in his chest. It was then that he whispered the ultimatum softly into her ear, like a lover whispering sweet nothings to another. His face was cluttered with emotions, sadness, anger, and resignation commingling. His eyes showed the pain that he was going through and it tore her apart. She knew that if Pete was willing to forgive her and go on with their marriage, she wanted to do everything she could to make it work. If James didn't know that Pete knew about them, he wouldn't confess to Andrea. Surely, he didn't want his marriage to end. As long as he kept his mouth shut, maybe everything would go back to normal. For both of them.

Susan could have told James about the night before, about the deal that she and Pete struck, but those were more words than she wanted to say. This was hard enough already and she didn't want to talk about it any longer than she had to.

They had made a mistake. They both knew it, but neither one of them was ready to return to reality, unwilling to give up the thrill and return to normalcy. But they had to. It didn't matter what either one of them wanted anymore. The relationship had to end.

"Then why, Susan? Why change what we have?"

Susan thought long and hard before she answered him. She couldn't hide it, he would find out sooner or later about the baby and wonder if it was his. She decided it would be better if she told him herself, rather than letting him hear about it from Pete. Who knew what kind of spin he would put on it. She didn't want to take the chance at finding out.

"James, I'm pregnant." She didn't mean to pause there, but she did. James' face went through several emotions instantaneously, one right after the other. Shock, fear, happiness, apprehension.

"You're pregnant? Oh my God, what—." He let go of her arm as the news sank in.

"It's Pete's child," Susan cut in, not letting him finish.

"How do you know that, Susan? It could be mine. You can't be sure—." James hadn't realized he had raised his voice.

"Yes, I can. It's Pete's child, James. I was still sleeping with my husband while we were together. The timing.... It's Pete's child. Believe me."

James stood there in shock. Deep down, he knew that Susan was still sleeping with Pete. They were a married couple, what else did he expect? He hadn't stopped sleeping with Andrea. But, somehow, hearing it seemed obscene. He felt like she had been cheating on him.

"I know, but Susan, you can't be sure," James continued.

As they stood on the street talking about the fate of their relationship, Carmen walked on the sidewalk opposite them, towards her apartment. She heard the voices carrying from the other side of the street and looked over out of curiosity. She saw a woman and man standing closely. They were obviously having an argument. She could tell by their aggressive body language and from the snippets of conversation she could hear. She thought she recognized the woman. She didn't know that many people in New York, so it wasn't as if she had a long list to pull from.

Carmen stopped walking and looked over at the couple, trying to place the woman's face. Susan. The woman's name was Susan. She had come into Carmen's shop to get a reading. She wanted to know what was going to happen with the relationship she was in. Carmen told her that it wouldn't last, that there was someone else out there that she belonged to and he would soon claim her as such. It looked like the reading she had given was on the right track.

Susan seemed agitated. She didn't look afraid, she just looked like she wanted to leave. The man's voice was elevated. He wasn't shouting, just speaking a little louder than he should have been. For some reason the hairs on the back of Carmen's neck stood up.

"Susan," she called out from across the street, startling Susan and the man she was with. "Are you okay?"

Susan looked at the woman, not recognizing her at first. The woman was younger than she was, casually dressed in a kind of '70s hippie throwback outfit. She was wearing a peasant top, hip hugger bell-bottom jeans and thick-soled clogs. Susan looked closer at the woman, her face becoming familiar. It finally dawned on her. She was the psychic she had gone to visit while waiting for James to meet her one weekend. Susan did it on a whim. She spent twenty dollars on a reading and forgot about it. It was the kind of thing you did without thinking. Susan never thought she'd see the woman again—didn't think twice about her—but there she was, a witness to a secret relationship breaking up on a nameless side street in a small, forgotten town.

"It's Carmen, Susan. Don't you remember me? I gave you a reading," Carmen said when Susan didn't respond. The man she was with seemed familiar. It wasn't his face as much as it was his being, his aura. He made her uneasy.

"Carmen, I'm fine. Really, I am. Thank you for stopping."

"Are you sure?" Carmen asked. Something about the man just wasn't right, but she couldn't put her finger on it.

"Really, I'm fine. Thanks."

James remembered looking at the woman as she nodded and continued walking towards the apartment building at the end of the street. She looked back once, catching him as he watched her. She turned away quickly.

"I think we've caused enough of a scene, don't you?" Susan said, putting her hand on the car door handle.

"It's over, James. Please accept that. You have to. I have to. What we had was... incredible. But it's over now."

James stared at her, not knowing what to say. They lingered there for a moment before she got into her car and drove away from him. Forever. Susan wasn't more than two blocks away when the she died.

The familiar pain pierced James, his guilt rising from its temporary slumber to torment him again. He felt short of breath and winded, the way he always did when he thought about Susan's death. He wiped the light film that had formed on his brow. *If only she hadn't been in the car that day, she wouldn't have died,* his mind chided. *Susan is dead because of you.*

James' mind filled with the what ifs that had haunted him since the day Susan died, *What if we hadn't met in Nyack that day? If I had joined Andrea in the city, we would have met the next week and this wouldn't have happened.* Invariably, the diatribe ended up with the only what if that ever mattered, *What if we had never started the affair?*

James looked at Pete and sighed. There were no more words to say. Pete took a deep breath and saluted James, his jawbone set.

"Okay then, go do what you've got to do," Pete said, his voice purposefully transparent, covering false dejection. "I'll see you later, James."

As Pete backed away from James' car and walked towards his own, James caught a glimpse of his face. His mouth had contorted into an impish, oddly beatific smile that sprung goose bumps on James' forearms.

CHAPTER 41

James took a different route out of his neighborhood that night. He didn't want to run the risk of seeing Andrea as he left. He had to make the trip. He was sure he would find the answers to some of his questions there. James didn't want to be distracted by Andrea, didn't want to look into her eyes and see her confusion all over again. His mind had to be clear. He had to be focused.

James knew where he was going almost from the moment he woke up. Nyack. It's where everything started. He kept seeing the images in his mind, a building, a faceless woman, blood sinking into the concrete, staining it. Somehow, he knew those visions were different than the other ones that had been replaying in his mind. He knew he could touch these dreams, could get close to them. Nyack had something to do with it, he could feel it. He had to know what it all meant.

James drove quickly, eager at the idea that getting there might actually stop the nightmares from coming. He had read somewhere that confronting the monster took away its power. He wanted to look his demons in the face and watch them disinte-grate before his eyes.

Apprehension washed over him as he drove into the sleepy town. The comfortable feeling, the mounting anticipation it had once held for him, was gone.

As he turned onto the street where he and Susan broke up, apprehension was replaced by anxiety. He parked in front of the spot where they had argued and looked at the lawn that lay beyond the sidewalk. He could almost see them, the way they must have looked to a passerby. A couple arguing on the side of the street would hardly have been noticed on the busy streets of Manhattan, but here in the quiet little river town, it was an oddity. James remembered that a woman called out to them from the other side of the street. She knew Susan's name. He remembered looking at her and having the most incredible feeling of déjà vu, so much so that he couldn't look away. It chilled him now, to think of it. It had been more than déjà vu. It was eventuality.

James got out of the car and walked over to the spot where the woman had stood. Looking over at the sidewalk, just past his car, he could see the street from the woman's vantage point. Susan's face would have been visible from where the woman had stood, her expressions readable and clear. He remembered that Susan was distraught. She wanted to leave. She wanted the ugly episode to end. No wonder the woman called out to make sure she was all right.

Wind whipped off the water at the end of the street. He lifted the collar of his coat and tightened the belt around his waist, trying to insulate himself. James glanced in the direction of the wind, taking its force head on, and saw an apartment building up ahead, a runway of streetlamps lighting the way to the entrance. He started walking towards it. He didn't feel his feet touching the concrete, didn't hear his footfalls as he made his way to the build-ing. It was as if a dolly propelled him to the building's concrete courtyard.

Chest high metal fences adorned both sides of the building, stopping children from trampling the bushes. Benches sat in front of the fences. A walkway paved between them. It was a small town's version of a high rise, ascending twelve floors up from where he stood. It loomed over him like a stone giant. He felt dizzy looking up at it.

A rosy splatter covered a large area of the concrete in front of the building. It bit James' stomach to see it there, so bright, even in the dark of night. It made him uncomfortable. He could almost smell the blood.

James looked up again. None of the dizziness that had plagued him earlier returned. He had that feeling again, the one that nagged at him, the one that told him the place was familiar. Too familiar.

James looked back at the spot on the concrete, memory taking over his mind, filling every crevice of it, threatening to break it open. He knew. His hand flew up to cover his mouth, cutting off the sound that was emanating from his lips. The words died on the inside of his palm. Words he didn't think he would ever utter.

Carmen, his mind moaned.

His head spun. He felt the cold wind moving around him, as if in step with the motion in his mind. He was shaky, off balance. He felt as if he would vomit.

The images from James' dream came flooding in then, as he stood in front of the apartment building. The woman lay on her back, her face unharmed, except for the blood that trickled out of her eyes, nose, and mouth. Her eyes were open, unseeing and cold, looking up at the sky.

James breathed deeply as his mind replayed her standing across the street from where he and Susan were arguing, checking to see if Susan was all right. James didn't remember how they knew each other. He remembered being irritated at the interruption, at the fact that someone was eavesdropping on their conversation. He remembered looking at the woman, a warning etched on his face telling her to leave, to go now, and let them finish their business. For a moment, their eyes locked. He saw the recognition in hers and the fear it roused.

Carmen.

She turned from them quickly after that, only casting one more glance over her shoulder as she walked towards her apartment building. Carmen met his eyes again as he watched her leave.

"Oh God," James mumbled into his hand which still clasped his mouth shut.

He saw himself walking up the stairs and entering an apartment. He broke into her apartment. James had never done anything like that before. He was horrified at the image of himself jimmying the lock and entering the apartment with relative ease. James wanted to dismiss the image as a product of his overactive imagination. He had been hypersensitive to things the past couple of days, and the images running rampant in his head were the product of stress. Even as he spun the trail of justifications for his denial, he dismissed the points one by one, whittling down to the undeniable truth. What he was seeing was a memory, pure and simple. Not a mind movie, entertainment for his consumption alone. Not a dream. What he was seeing, good or bad, had happened.

James saw himself shut the door silently, locking it again from the inside. He found a hiding place behind the sofa and waited. It wasn't long before Carmen entered the room, groceries in hand. She sensed something different but couldn't put her finger on it. Dismissing the feeling, she sat down on the bed and was soon asleep. James waited behind the sofa, listening to the sound of her breathing, for a long time.

James watched in horror as the memory unraveled before his eyes while he stood in front of the apartment building. Evening turned into night as he stood motionless, staring up at the high rise in front of him, the sky above him darkening to a midnight blue.

James saw himself rise from behind the sofa and walk toward Carmen as she laid sleeping on the bed. His posture was different somehow, but the face was unmistakably his. James saw himself standing over her, admiring her beauty. Anticipation was driving James mad as he watched the scene, like a spectator in a movie theater. He saw himself becoming aroused in Carmen's apartment, felt himself rising even then, despite the cold wind that whipped the bottom of his coat around with its force. It sickened him. He kept watching, the darkened sky and the darkness of the room in his memory one and the same.

James stood over Carmen for a long while, enjoying his excitement at her vulnerability. She was there for him to do with what he wanted and he knew it. He didn't rush. He wanted to enjoy the moment.

James watched her sleep for longer than he had intended to. He was enraptured by her serenity and the irony that surrounded the moment. He took out a blade and held it over Carmen, lining it up with the hollow of her neck. James, watching the past in his mind play out in real time, felt himself shaking violently, terrified of what he knew would happen next.

James watched as he slammed the blade into Carmen's throat while she lay sleeping, unaware that she was breathing her last breaths. He watched as her eyes fluttered open and looked at him, pain and horror dancing wildly in them. James remembered the smell of her blood filling his nostrils, sweet and tangy. Hot. He felt his loins stir at the thought of it. Adrenaline filled his body as he remembered picking Carmen up and taking her up to the roof. He'd used the back stairs to avoid detection. He didn't have to. The building was full of older, ailing people. Not many of them were awake at that time of night, let alone using the stairwells. He was alone with Carmen as she bled.

James opened the metal door and walked out onto the roof of the building. Carmen hung limply in his arms, but she was still alive. She would have bled to death in a couple of minutes anyway.

All he had to do was leave her in her bed to die. But that wasn't enough for him. James wanted more of a thrill, more of a grand finale.

He walked to the edge and laid Carmen down on the gravel next to him. He looked down at the sleepy town, its occupants oblivious to what was happening. But soon they would be awakened. Soon they would know.

After some time, James picked Carmen up again. She was almost gone now; her eyes were fixed and rigid, staring at him. He was amused that the last thing she would ever see would be him. It flattered him, aroused him.

James looked down at her angelic face, the color draining from it as she bled out. He couldn't resist himself. He kissed her gently, so softly. James could taste the blood on his lips as he recounted the horrible night in his head.

Carmen didn't stir. James smiled as he looked into her dying eyes. He felt the cold air on his face. He felt more alive on the cusp of murder than he ever had.

Then he dropped her.

James could hear the wind whistling around him acutely. For a couple of seconds, it was the only sound he heard. He didn't hear the old man coming up to him from behind, walking toward the building, his cane clanking against the pebbles caught in the concrete walkway.

"It's a sad thing, isn't it?" the man said, shaking his head. He had taken a position next to James in front of the odd rosy stain on the concrete.

James almost jumped out of his skin at the sound of the man's voice.

"The firemen hosed this place down after it happened, but some folks just don't let people heal."

Both men stood looking down at the concrete. It was then that James realized that the rosy blotch wasn't a stain of blood, the last remnants of Carmen soaked into the cement slab. It was a graffiti artist's form of memorial. Red spray paint patterned loosely behind a splash of water was painted on the ground. Morbid curiosity had cause people to come and look at it, to stand in front of it and remember the woman who fell to her death from the top of the roof—their roof. She was nameless to them, her death the only reason they knew her at all. And soon they would forget even that.

"Sick, I think. Painting a thing like that on the ground where she died. People don't want to see anything like that. It's horrible." The man paused again, still looking at the graffiti on the ground.

"They're calling it a murder now, you know."

James turned and looked at him. He wasn't sure what emotion his face portrayed but he knew what he felt. Absolute fear.

"It's been all over the news today. They say someone stabbed her before they threw her off the roof. All along we thought that girl had jumped."

The man shook his head, more pronounced this time.

"I can't understand it. Who would want to kill that girl? She just moved here not too long ago. She couldn't have done anybody wrong yet. It's just terrible."

James stood frozen, staring at the man. He had been silent the whole time he had company. He realized that he'd better say something before the man started to look at him suspiciously.

"Yes, it is terrible," he said in a low voice, just above a whisper.

"She didn't do nothing to nobody. She was such a young girl. And pretty! Boy, she was a looker."

James heard the man talking but didn't respond again. He was too busy thinking about Carmen, her eyes open when she hit the concrete.

"It's a terrible thing," the man continued. "Well, you have a good night, you hear?"

James nodded and the man walked towards the building,

tracing the perimeter of the graffiti memorial. He mounted the steps slowly, favoring his right leg. Before he went into the building, he turned around and said,

"You be careful out here."

The man disappeared into the darkened lobby.

CHAPTER 42

James walked away from the building quickly. The knowledge of what he had done frightened him so badly that he just wanted to get in the car, wanted to get off the street. He was sure people were looking at him, knowing who he was and what terrible acts he had committed. A woman walked out of her building and made a right, walking towards Main Street. James watched her as she walked down the steps of her house to the sidewalk, staring in his direction all the while. Staring at him.

He didn't know himself anymore.

The man he thought he was would never have murdered anyone. Yet he had. He had stabbed that young woman while she lie sleeping in her bed. And for what? Because she had intervened in an argument he was having with his lover? James was disgusted with himself.

He crossed the street and passed by a narrow alleyway. He glanced into it out of habit. It was like putting mail into a mailbox and reopening the lid to make sure the letter didn't get stuck on the way down. It was just something he did.

He stopped walking as soon as his eyes fell upon the bricked roadway in the dimly lit alley. It looked oddly familiar to him. James walked into the alley, tentatively, aware that it was nighttime in New York, suburbs or not.

Litter was strewn around the alley. Garbage bags overflowed and dropped their contents onto the ground. James kept walking, as if drawn by some unseen force. About a quarter of the way in, he stopped and put his hand on the wall. The brick seemed to pulse beneath it. His hand trembled as he felt the building, alive from his touch. His heart pulsed with the movement of the building, the two beating in time. He shut his eyes and succumbed to the memory, forcing its way out.

James remembered standing in the very spot he stood then, watching the crowd gather. He fed off their energy as they drew closer and closer together, vying for position. There was chatter, nervous rambling, even shrieking coming from the huddled mass of people. But no one left the scene. Their morbid curiosity won over their fear and they remained to see all they could see, to hear all they could hear. A woman lay dead in front of them, her body ruined from her fall from the roof. Those that heard it eagerly shared their stories with the crowd. They said her body hitting the ground sounded like gunfire.

James could see them standing behind the crime scene tape, lifted up on their toes and pointing. The slow rumble of their voices excited him as he stood among the garbage and rats, unseen. He could feel his nipples hardening as he watched them mill around, trying to catch a glimpse of the dead woman. They probably stayed for hours, long after he had left, to talk about the woman as if they had known her all of her life. She was memorialized there, on the city street that took her life, by people who knew nothing about her, other than that she was dead; funereal reflection trumped by sensationalism.

James remembered feeling incredibly warm. His body was sensitive to the wind, sensitive to the way the brick felt as he leaned his chest against it. He had leaned closer to let the sensation run over his body.

James sensed something different about himself as he recollected the night he stood in the alley. His body, the way it reacted, the sensations he felt. They were different than anything he had ever experienced. His senses were alert like never before. His mind was attuned to all of them at once, allowing him to follow them through to their full extent. His body was alive.

James would have described the feeling as invigorating. Rejuvenating, even. His mind was titillated by every detail of the scene unfolding before him and every emotion it brought with it. He wanted to study it, to scrutinize every detail and keep it in his memory. He recalled the faces of some of the people who had been there that night, clamoring for a glimpse of the gruesome display there, in the alley where he stood.

James could remember feeling a stickiness in his underwear, but he had no memory of an erection. His mind drifted back to that morning in the bedroom when he had awakened to find clothing strewn all over the floor. As he gathered the clothes, a distinct scent wafted up to him, enticing his nostrils with its familiarity. He remembered pressing his nose to it, wanting to inhale as much of it as he could. It was the smell of sex. The smell of a woman.

James backed away from the wall at once, knocking into a garbage can. The lid crashed to the ground noisily. He stared in horror at the place where he had just stood, reliving the night Carmen died. The memory was so vivid, so real, he knew he had been there, had mingled with the crowd Carmen's mangled body had drawn, wanting to see it as much as they did. But he wasn't there, not physically. He stared at his hands, taking in the lines and grooves as if seeing them for the first time. He couldn't have been there.

"It couldn't be me," he said aloud, knowing at that moment, that it was.

CHAPTER 43

James ran out of the alley and to his car fast, the memories of that fateful night chasing after him. Before James got in, he looked back at the building, his heart racing. The night was dark. All of the streetlights were lit, except for the one that was burned out at the end of the street. The one in front of the building where Carmen died. Somehow the darkness made the building seem more ominous.

James got into the car and locked the doors, something he found ironic as soon as he had done it. *What do I have to be afraid of,* he said to himself. *I'm probably the only murderer on this street tonight.* He chuckled bitterly to himself.

He put the car in gear and drove. Just got on the main drag and pushed the car forward. He didn't know where he was going. He couldn't go home, not knowing what he had done. He couldn't face Andrea. He'd be afraid she'd see something in his eyes. She had always been able to tell when something was wrong with him. James wondered if he could keep this hidden. If he went home, could he trick Andrea into thinking that everything was fine? He knew better than that. She would know. He couldn't tell her the truth. How could James tell her that he'd murdered two women?

The light ahead turned red and he crawled to a stop. His hands were gripping the steering wheel tightly, his knuckles turning white from the pressure. He loosened his grip, feeling the indent of the wheel grooves on his fingers. He flexed his hands in front of him, trying to circulate the blood again.

The road ahead was empty and the sidewalks were bare; it was a typical Nyack night. The memory of Carmen's face was like a watermark on his windshield; so transparent he almost wondered if it was there at all. It hung in front of him, the curves of her face just prominent enough to lend credence to its presence. His breath quickened as he stared at her, spilt blood on his hands.

James let his eyes roam to the bookstore on the corner of the block ahead. He could see inside its doors, could see books of every color lined up on the wooden shelves, colorful covers and embossed spines. A woman stood in the aisle closest to the door with a book open in her hands. She was facing the doorway, angled only slightly towards the rack next to her. Her face was pleasant; the hint of a smile adorned her lips as she read. She had on a long crimson coat that fell mid shin on her short frame. A fashionable dress scarf topped it, adding a fuchsia, cobalt, and mustard design to the bright red. Her hair rested on the collar of her coat, some strands pulling to the nape of her neck. James could see her delicate fingers as she turned the page.

He was happy for the diversion; the woman occupied his mind, at least for a moment. He watched her for the better part of a minute as she stood alone in the aisle, reading the first chapter of a book. James looked closer, trying to make out the title of the book on the back panel, as it was tilted toward the door. The cover was elaborately colored with golds and reds splotching the jacket in an abstract design. He couldn't make out the black lettering at the top; he was too far away. James stared a little longer, something catching his eye, some tiny flicker, some minute movement. He looked closer, sitting absolutely still, trying to figure out what had run across his line of vision. That's when he noticed that the book was upside down in the woman's hands. The black lettering that topped the bright abstract became clear to him, horribly so. James said the letters in his mind as they appeared on the book:

E I M M I J.

Jimmie. His mouth opened in slow motion as the hand that he thought was delicate curled around the spine of the book. The fingers were gnarled and bent painfully in opposite directions. Thick, yellow nails crested their fingers, jagged and unkempt. James looked at the woman's face as the air around him thinned. Her skin had wrinkled and dulled to pallid from her rich sun kissed brown. Her black eyes seemed to glow in the night like polished onyx, as they reached out to his car and stopped his heart. She saw him and smiled.

James recoiled into the seat. He gasped for air, sucking it into his lungs in great gulps. He shut his eyes against the woman and tried to regulate his breathing, tried to calm down. Her eyes were all knowing; she knew who he was. They sent a panic through him that was so strong he thought he would swerve out of traffic and race away to anywhere as long as it was away, into the night. Her eyes accused him, condemned him. He felt their scrutinizing gaze perusing his soul.

James opened his eyes hesitantly, venturing another look at the woman in the bookstore. The aisle was empty. James squeezed his eyes shut again and pressed his head against the headrest. The visions were taking everything he had out of him. He was fatigued.

James opened his eyes and started to stretch his neck, rolling his head to the left as he did it. His eyes passed over the woman in red as she stood in the window of the bookstore, looking out at him, but it didn't register in his mind. His eyes focused on the people in the car next to him.

Both the passenger and the driver were staring at him with the blackest eyes.

CHAPTER 44

Pete and Andrea sat around the dinner table, their plates empty, with dinner warming in the oven. It was already 8:00 p.m. and James hadn't gotten back home yet.

Andrea's day hadn't been productive. She felt like she had been spinning her wheels as doctor after doctor talked about their experience, their degrees, and their specializations. She tried to find out what might be causing James' behavior, but no one could speculate without talking with him. James had to go in for a session himself.

Pete sat across the table from Andrea and tried to look concerned. He didn't tell her that he had come by earlier that evening and had a talk with James. He didn't want to run the risk of making her suspicious. He had to be careful. He was too far into the game to get out and he didn't want to screw up now.

Andrea wasn't much for conversation that night. Worry was etched on her face as she sat at the table, drinking her second glass of soda.

"I'm sorry, Pete," she said, "I just don't know where he could be. When I left, he was upstairs in the bedroom trying to get some sleep. I thought he would sleep until dinner. He didn't leave a note, and his cell phone is upstairs on the dresser. I—I don't know where he is."

Pete looked at her for a second, saying nothing. He looked down at his empty plate and traced it with his finger.

"It's okay, Andrea."

"No, it's not. I asked you over here for dinner and I haven't fed you anything."

Andrea pushed her chair away from the table and reached for Pete's plate. Pete put his hand on Andrea's arm to stop her. He was so tempted to caress it; he had to swallow before speaking.

"Andrea, really. I can wait."

His hand lingered on her arm for a moment longer before he let it cascade down to her hand. He patted it gently and then put his hand back on the table. He couldn't resist touching her.

Andrea sighed, un-phased by Pete's fondling. She plopped back into her seat and continued,

"This has just happened so fast. I mean, I don't even know what it is. The whole thing must be so frightening for him."

Pete nodded on cue, trying to seem understanding and sympathetic. He thought about his encounter with James that afternoon, trying to remember if he had mentioned where he was going. James seemed anxious, especially after hearing that the police were reopening Susan's case. A chuckle rose in his throat, but he suppressed it, not wanting to ruin the moment with Andrea. She was staring at him with her beautiful eyes, wishing he had answers that could help her understand. He felt a stir in his loins as he thought about her looking up at him with lust in those beautiful eyes. The skin on the back of his neck warmed as he imagined it. He bounced his knee to distract himself from the daydream. Pete cleared his throat and tried to get his thoughts back on James.

"Maybe he's just trying to get some fresh air. You know, trying to sort this thing out by himself. I'm sure he knows the strain it's been putting on you."

Andrea smiled thinly, contemplating the past couple of days.

"I just wish I could help him through this. Pete, I honestly don't know what to do."

Pete got up and circled the table to Andrea's chair. He kneeled beside her and hugged her. As she laid her head into his shoulder and cried softly, he stroked her hair, savoring the moment. Her hot breath penetrated his shirt as she sobbed. He shut his eyes and imagined the two of them in a lover's embrace, her head buried in his chest, her breath hot on his skin, as his hands caressed her body laying underneath his. He wanted to tilt her neck and turn her face up to his. He wanted to kiss her hotly, unabashedly right there in the kitchen. The feeling was strong, impassioned. Pete could see himself doing it. She would move her arms from him quickly, he thought, confused by what was going on. She would want to stop at first, trying to pull away. The delicate sounds of protest he heard in his daydream excited him all the more.

He would keep kissing her while she fought and soon, he would win her over. She would hold him then, gently at first, then tightly, passionately. Pete saw himself running his hands down her back as she pressed her hips closer to him, her nipples jutting through the fabric of her bra and t-shirt. He would cup her ass in his right hand and hold her close with his left. He emitted an airy moan at the thought of it.

Pete saw himself laying Andrea on the floor of the kitchen and getting on top of her. Her chest would heave in anticipation when he lifted her shirt over her head and unhooked her bra. He saw her breasts sitting pertly on her chest, the nipples erect and hard to the touch. She would quiver when he closed his mouth around them, one by one, engulfing them in his warmth and teasing them with his tongue.

He would run his tongue down her stomach. Her back would arch when he circled her navel. He would open the button of her jeans and unzip them as she laid on her back, her eyes closed, enjoying it. His tongue would languish over the lip of her underwear, licking from hip to hip, as she moaned. He—.

Andrea sniffled loudly against his chest, waking Pete from his daydream. Instinctively, he rolled his hips outward, trying to put more space between the two of them so that Andrea wouldn't notice his erection.

"What happened to him, Pete?" Andrea cried, muffled against his shoulder.

"I don't know," Pete said quietly, as he inhaled the sweet smell of Andrea's hair.

CHAPTER 45

James turned onto his street and passed his house slowly. The light was on out front. Pete's car stood in the driveway. James glanced at the time. 8:52 p.m. They were still waiting for him to come home for dinner.

James sighed as he drove past the house. He couldn't go in. He couldn't face them. He had killed an innocent woman. He had killed his best friend's wife. He was convinced of that now. Even though he didn't remember tampering with her car, he was sure he had. Murder was a part of him. He knew that now. It was in his blood. He had killed her. It made sense. Who better to kill than the lover who was about to leave him?

James' mind sagged as though he had been struck, the weight of the truth pressing against the hollow of his chest. It colored the rest of his thoughts, insidiously tainting them with images of blood and the horrors of death. It ripped at his mind, eating it away layer by layer. He was devastated, disgusted with himself. How could he be capable of such evil?

James turned the corner and parked just beyond the trees that framed his backyard. As he turned the key in his ignition, shutting off the engine of the car, James wondered what he was going to do. He felt drained, mentally and physically fatigued. His thoughts were muddled; he was unable to see anything clearly except the color red. It didn't flash in his mind. It flowed like the waves of the ocean against a white backdrop, the contrast almost blinding.

I should go to the police and turn myself in, he thought. His mind bounced the thought back and forth, turning it over in his mind. He thought of himself behind bars. Confined. *I deserve it*, he thought dryly. But could he do it?

James dismissed the option quickly, almost as soon as it entered his mind. Incarceration wouldn't solve anything for him. He would still be alone with his dreams, the horrific phantoms dancing in his head, torturing him. They would never go away. He knew that now. It wasn't just Susan's death that had brought them on, whether he had anything to do with it or not. Nor Carmen's murder, a woman unknown to him except for one fateful moment when their eyes met across a nameless street. It was his destiny. His fate.

There was no coincidence that he was seeing things that he couldn't explain, things more horrible than any dream could ever be. The same thing happened to his father. James remembered bits and pieces of conversations he had overheard between his parents. His mother tried to dismiss the dreams as figments of Jimmie's imagination.

"You're just tired, Jimmie," she would say. "Your mind is playing tricks on you."

"It's not a trick, Mary. My mother was there. She told me this would happen."

Now James knew what his father meant. People talked to him, sometimes whispering, sometimes shouting, in his head. He recognized the voice of his father among the countless others to which he couldn't place a name. Other voices had chimed in to tell him about what he had done to Susan, he just hadn't understood what they meant. He had known all along, just like they had said.

James looked toward the house, his heart heavy. Andrea had started a pond in the back yard with a nightlight and goldfish. With all the things that had happened to him the past few months finally coming to a head a couple of days before, James had forgotten to take the goldfish out of the pond before it got too cold for them. He imagined them frozen in the block of ice that filled the molded pond, still and cold.

A vision accosted him suddenly, making him stare at the house timorously, alarmed at how vivid it was. He shut his eyes to it but that didn't help. He cringed at how real the daydream was. It frightened him.

James saw himself standing in the shadows of his bedroom. The door was closed. Even though they didn't have children yet, they were trying to get into the habit of shutting the door when they entered their bedroom. They were used to walking around the house naked or close to it, any time of the day and on any floor. Dressing for bed, donning clothes when getting a glass of water after sex, these things were going to be a huge adjustment for them, so they started training themselves early.

The lights were off and James was dressed in black from head to toe. He stood in the shadows, hiding in the door swing, so someone entering the room wouldn't see him. His breathing was shallow, undetectable.

Andrea opened the bedroom door and walked in. She was brushing her hair as she walked; the muted *thwok* of the plastic base against the prongs as they combed through her hair was the only sound he could hear.

James watched her from behind the door as she tossed the brush on the bed and took off her robe. Her naked body was kissed by the moonlight streaming in from the window behind the chaise lounge. He licked his lips as she walked across the floor to the dresser, opening her underwear drawer. He enjoyed seeing the curve of her back in front of him as she leaned into the dresser, and the bounce of her breasts reflected by the mirror as she sifted through her undergarments for something comfortable.

He emerged slowly, his footfalls silenced by the carpet, and walked toward her. Andrea looked up from the open dresser drawer and was startled to find James right behind her.

"Honey," she said with a self-conscious giggle, "I didn't hear you come in."

"That's because you didn't close the door."

He stood behind her, staring at her in the mirror, his mouth forming a crooked smile.

"True. But I didn't even hear you come up the stairs," she said as she fished underwear out of the cluttered drawer. James draped his arm over her right shoulder and caressed the flat skin of her chest, just above her left breast, in silence.

"Ah, so now I see why you snuck up on me."

She leaned back into him, rubbing herself against him as he caressed her. James enjoyed watching her as she shut her eyes, enjoying his hands on her. He felt himself stiffening as her nipples hardened from his touch.

As she was about to turn around and face him, he clamped his arm down on her shoulder, keeping her in place.

"Baby," Andrea cooed seductively, "I want to kiss you."

She tried to turn to him again, but he didn't let her move. He braced her arm with more pressure this time, pinning Andrea's back to his chest tightly.

Andrea opened her eyes and looked at James in the mirror, confused at the sudden use of force.

James' face had contorted into a wicked smile. He brought his left hand up fast and clamped the back of her head as his right arm looped around her neck.

Andrea didn't have a second to protest.

James squeezed her neck firmly, increasing the pressure incrementally as she struggled. She kicked backwards, trying to kick him in the shins, but he had spread his legs widely, anticipating her defense. Andrea clawed at his arms, digging in and drawing blood, but he was undeterred.

James flung her to his left and slammed her hard on the floor. He landed on top of her, pressing all of his weight on her small frame, pining her arms under both of their bodies. He could feel the frantic beating of her heart, could imagine her terror as she gasped for air. He heard her choking, saliva flowing out of the corners of her mouth as her tongue worked futilely.

And then, she was still.

A sob escaped his lips as he pulled himself out of the daydream. Sweat had formed on his forehead and he was breathing heavily. He looked at the clock again, terrified at what it might mean if he had lost time like he had done before. It was 8:56 p.m. Hardly long enough for him to have gone inside and killed his wife. He breathed a sigh of relief as he looked at the house again. Sadness surrounded him as he realized that his ghastly vision could easily be turned into reality. The mere thought of it, the simple suggestion to his psyche could make it a reality. He was like his father in every way. If he had learned anything in the past couple of days, James had learned that much. He couldn't let it happen. Again.

James knew what he had to do. He wasn't going to jail, he'd surely go mad being locked in with no diversion, no escape from the demons in his head. And he couldn't stay free and run the risk of killing again, of killing Andrea. There was only one thing he could do.

Resigned, James got out of the car and walked towards the back door of his house.

CHAPTER 46

Pete decided to call it a night at 9:00 p.m. It didn't look like James was going to show up any time soon, and he couldn't stand being around Andrea without being able to act on what he was feeling.

Andrea was growing more upset by the minute, wondering where James might have gone.

"Do you think I should call the police?" she asked at one point in the evening.

"They won't do anything with this until James has been missing for twenty-four hours. Let's just give him some time. I bet he's muddling through this thing while we speak. It's not like he knew he had a dinner party to go to tonight, so he doesn't realize he's standing us up, right?"

Andrea nodded reluctantly, but added, "Still, he should have called to let me know where he is. He knew I'd be worried about him, especially now."

Pete breathed loudly through his nose and shook his head. She reiterated the sentiment as he was about to leave.

"I don't understand why he doesn't just call. Just to let me know he's okay." She shook her head in confusion. "It's just not like him, Pete."

He sighed and put his arm around her shoulder.

"C'mon, walk me to the door."

Pete and Andrea strolled to the door. Andrea was contemplating James' whereabouts while Pete wished he was walking Andrea upstairs to the bedroom.

"Try not to worry about him, Andrea," Pete said when they reached the door. "He's probably on his way home right now."

Andrea didn't look convinced.

"What if he's hurt? He could have had one of those blackouts he's been having recently."

"Blackouts?" James hadn't told him about the blackouts. Then again, James hadn't said much that made any sense for a couple of days.

"He doesn't know I know about them," Andrea said. "He's been losing time, missing hours in his day. He blacked out once a long time ago, right after Susan—."

Andrea stopped, feeling terrible that she brought Susan up, reopening the wound. She started to apologize, but Pete stopped her.

"Andrea, it's okay. I'm much better now."

Andrea smiled sympathetically and looked away from him self-consciously. She continued, "Well, he had another one this morning. I'm sure of it. I thought he had left for work. I started doing some research on doctors in the area that might be able to help him. I came upstairs a couple of hours later, just before noon, and saw James sitting outside on the lawn staring at the house."

"What?"

"He was wearing what he had worn to bed. It was freezing outside, but it was like he didn't feel it. He was rocking back and forth and his face looked like he was scared of something. I let him sit out there for a while, rocking like that. I was afraid to go out there. God, I'm so ashamed to say that, but I was!"

Tears tthreatened to fall from her eyes again. Pete touched her arm and said, "Andrea, c'mon, don't be ashamed. Something really scary is happening to James. It's natural to be afraid for him."

"No Pete, you don't understand. I was afraid *of* him. I was afraid of my own husband."

Pete let the silence sit between them for a while before he said, "Andrea, you know James would never hurt you."

"I know," she said, wiping a tear from her eye absently. "It wasn't that I was afraid he would knowingly do something to hurt me. It was just—I just felt like it wasn't him out there. I felt like it wasn't James. I guess I was afraid of who it might be."

Pete opened the door and turned back to face Andrea. Her face was beautiful, dreamy from the way the moonlight illuminated it. He wanted to kiss her so badly his lips quivered.

"Don't worry," Pete said, inhaling deeply, "Whatever this is, I'm sure it will be over soon. We have to get him to a doctor and figure out what this is. No matter how much he fights, we'll get him there. I'll make sure of that."

Andrea gave him a grateful smile and kissed him on the cheek. How he wished her lips would linger longer.

"Give me a call when he comes in," Pete continued. "Or any time you want to, Andrea. It doesn't matter how late."

Andrea gave him a hug and said, "You are such a wonderful friend, Pete." She smiled sheepishly. "I don't know what I'd do without you."

Pete held her tightly, rubbing her back as she hugged him, his hand stopping just below the top of her jeans.

"I love you guys, you know that."

Andrea pulled away from him and stared into his eyes. She looked like she wanted to say something but didn't quite know how to phrase it. Pete saw the question forming on her lips when he turned and walked to his car in the driveway.

CHAPTER 47

James skulked in the shadows, making his way to the house as quietly as he could. He unlocked the door and opened it, stepping up into the dark hallway. The door creaked a little. James stood still, waiting for the door to settle on its hinges and close gently. He didn't know where Andrea and Pete were in the house, and he didn't want to alert them. He didn't waste ten minutes sneaking around in his own backyard to get caught one step into the house.

James waited a full minute before he continued cautiously down the hall. He was apprehensive. He didn't think Andrea would catch him; she rarely walked down to the extension unless she needed something from the storage room. He doubted that she would be in there that late. The feeling that something was there, waiting for him at the end of the hall, maybe even right outside the office door, waiting to pull him into another demented phantasm, hung in the air, electrifying it. He was almost afraid to keep going, like he could be sucked up in the darkness.

James made his way to the door of his office and slid in. He didn't turn the light on, in case Andrea was upstairs. She might see the glow on the grass beneath the window. He felt his way to the desk and sat down in his chair, waiting for his eyes to adjust.

He pulled out a pad and uncapped the pen he held in his right hand. He tried to think of appropriate words to write down, words that would make sense to Andrea. Words that would help her adjust.

Every false start made James realize that there were no words to explain what was going on in his mind. None that would make her feel better about it after she read them. There wasn't anything he could say that would make sense to her, now or later. Yet he knew he had to say something to her. He couldn't just leave her without a word. James ripped a page from the pad, folded it, and put it in his pocket clipped under a pen, hoping he'd be able to write appropriate words to his wife later.

James got up from the chair, exasperated by his impotence. He walked over to the sofa on the other side of the office and noticed his father's photo album, still open to his grandmother's picture. The death certificate still sat off to the side, half on the photo album and half on the sofa cushion, as he'd left it. The album caught his eye. He walked towards it, almost tripping over the boxes that were strewn on the floor, still left out from his rummage in the closet.

His grandmother's face stared back at him, her head almost filling the frame. The westward wind blew hair in her face, and she had raised her hand to brush it away. Her eyes were squinted against the sun. Her eyes still had the coldness to them, boring holes into him as he looked. Her lips, however, held a mischievous smile.

James looked at the picture in horror, his memory of the photograph not exactly the same as the image mounted in the old album. The picture he remembered was further away, a full shot of his grandmother standing on the side of a house. You could see the row of houses behind her, across the street from where she was standing. The side of the house had been visible on the edge of the frame.

There were other differences. The wind didn't seem to be blowing as hard when the first picture was taken. Only wisps of her hair had been blown into her face, not the thick lengths that were shown in the new rendition. Her eyes weren't squinted in the first picture, not as tightly as in this one. But the coldness in them had never changed.

James couldn't take his eyes off the picture. It was coming alive in front of him. At first, he thought his eyes were playing tricks on him the way they can if you stare at something for a long time without blinking. His eyes felt warm around the edges, drying up from the prolonged exposure to the air. But he didn't blink. He couldn't blink.

The picture was changing. As he watched, his grandmother batted at the hair flowing into her face. Her smile faded into a look of satisfaction and contentment. She stopped squinting and seemed to regard him. A grandmother looking at her grandson.

James inhaled sharply, throwing the album off his lap and standing up. He peered back at the book incredulously as his grandmother continued to stare up at him. He stood that way for a while, unmoving, waiting to see what transformation the picture would take next. After a couple of minutes, James started to believe that he had been seeing things, that the picture had always been a close-up shot of his grandmother, and that her eyes had never been squinted against the sun the way he had first thought. He had almost convinced himself when the image of his grandmother spoke to him.

"Well Jimmie, what are you waiting for?" she said condescendingly, goading him. Then she sounded a shrill, maniacal laugh that made his hair stand on end.

James shrank backwards, trepidation filling him like never

before. He stumbled over the trunk behind him, jumping away from it as soon as his heel touched its base. He ran out of the room, down the hall, and out of the house without looking back.

CHAPTER 48

Pete drove home with the feel of Andrea's body against his still fresh in his mind. He knew what Andrea had wanted to ask. She wanted to know about the fight he and James had days earlier, about what James had done to deserve a punch. He didn't want to talk about it yet, if ever. Telling Andrea about the affair would complicate things. He wanted to leave that task to James. She would be thrown for a loop, like he was when he saw them together. She would be angry, depressed, and maybe even mad at him for not telling her sooner. That couldn't happen. He had to make sure that, whatever happened, Andrea didn't get upset with him for any reason. It would lessen his chances of getting her in bed.

Pete had to be careful not to let Andrea know anything. Not about the affair, not about what was happening between him and Susan before she died, not about the circumstances surrounding Susan's death. Nobody knew about that. And it had to stay that way.

As Pete drove home, he thought back to that clear day in Nyack. He had stopped at a coffee shop on the main drag and sipped a café latte while reading the newspaper. Nyack was a peaceful place if nothing else. He felt serene, calm sitting among the weekend crowd as they worked hard at suburban hip.

The coffee shop was situated on the corner of an intersection with a side street that only allowed one-way traffic. There were a lot of cars out, people perusing the shops as they crept along with traffic. The sidewalks were littered with shoppers looking for contemporary art finds or antiquing. Nyack was an interesting town in that way. If you wanted to be seen, it could provide that bit of cosmopolitan tempo for you. If you wanted to go unnoticed, you could do that too. Anything you wanted was at your disposal. All you had to do was turn the corner and take your pick.

Pete was close enough to hear the explosion ring into the air. He and ten others in the coffee shop looked up from their newspapers to peer out of the picture window, trying to see what was going on. People on the street had stopped walking. They were staring across the street at the billowing cloud of black smoke rising from something hidden from their view. Some ran to the scene, others hung back and watched from afar. The coffee shop cleared out, except for two people, sitting separately, engrossed in their books and completely disinterested in what might have been happening outside.

Pete went outside too, even though he knew what had happened. He didn't want to appear suspicious if anyone in the coffee shop was questioned later on. He stayed with the group that watched from Main Street, wanting to know what happened but afraid to get too close to the fire.

A woman dressed in a navy pants suit with navy high heels ran back from the side street, her face streaked with mascara-blackened tears. She crossed the street without regard for oncoming traffic and would have been hit had the traffic not stopped when the blast rang out. She hadn't even bothered to look. Her purse hung limply in her hand; the strap wrapped around her wrist. Her heel had broken to the base by the time she reached them, but it hadn't slowed her down. She was frightened. A man in the front of their little group grabbed her and hugged her to him. The woman was obviously in shock.

"What happened?" he asked her.

"A woman—," she started, out of breath. "There was a woman in the car!"

She started crying again, tortured sounds coming up from her diaphragm as her chest heaved. The man let her cry into his shirt.

"The car blew up," she sobbed. "I saw her face just before it happened. Oh my God! A woman died right in front of my eyes!"

People bombarded her with questions.

"How close were you?"

"Are you hurt?"

The woman didn't answer any of them. She was far too distraught. Pete didn't need to ask any questions. He had already gotten all the answers he needed.

Pete had been careful thus far. He had to keep it up. His future with Andrea depended on it.

CHAPTER 49

When James drove away from his street, he knew he would never see it again. He didn't turn back, didn't watch it grow smaller and smaller in his rearview mirror until it faded completely out of sight. He just left.

He didn't feel the sadness one would expect to feel knowing that they would never return to their home. He didn't feel anything. There was nothing in his mind except the obscure abandoned house he had dreamt about. The one he was sure he had been in when he was supposed to be at home sleeping.

His grandmother's house.

James didn't believe that the surreal vision was any more a dream than was his fight with Pete. It happened. He stood on the porch of that house just as sure as Pete had punched him in the jaw.

James' mind was filled with images of the house. They replaced thoughts of Andrea and the life he was leaving behind; the kitchen, the living room, the boards covering the windows. He was intrigued by it, the mystery that surrounded it. He felt the house calling to him, a haunting moan in his mind that never ceased. The windows, like eyes, seemed to look back at him from the rearview mirror, glowering, beckoning. Half of him wanted to resist, to ignore the call, but the other half of him wanted to answer it, to succumb to it.

He could hear his grandmother beckoning him as well, her voice rattling in her throat with every word. She wanted him there with her. She wanted to tell him the things he had always wanted to know, show him the things he had always wanted to see. She wanted him close to her, closer than he could ever have imagined possible. Closer still, through the skin. On some level, James thought, he wanted to be with her too.

As he pulled the address out of his pocket and headed towards the turnpike, his fear was met with equal intrigue.

CHAPTER 50

Andrea walked around the house looking for clues. It was 11:00 p.m. and James still hadn't gotten home. She had called the local hospitals and given them a description of James, but no patients had been brought in that matched it. She called the police despite Pete's position and was told to wait until James had been gone a full twenty-four hours. There was no sign of James anywhere. Andrea was sick with worry.

After she had searched all the other rooms in the house, Andrea ventured into the office. She chose to look there last for reasons she couldn't put her finger on. It wasn't the darkness. One flick of the light switch would fix that. It was the feeling down there. Her skin crawled every time she ventured down that hallway. It was cooler there, a distinct difference in the temperature. The silence contained in the walls was eerie, as if no sound could penetrate through. She hated it.

Andrea turned on the light in the hallway and walked down the hall to the office, quickening her pace as she went. She flipped on the light switch in the office and was immediately met by the portrait of James' father on the other side of the desk. The likeness stared down at her, watching her as she walked into the room. The haunting look in his eyes was unwavering.

Andrea was surprised at the disarray in which the room had been left. Boxes sat open on the floor near the sofa. Some of them were knocked over, their contents spilled on the rug beneath the coffee table. She noticed that some of the papers on the floor were creased, as though they had been crushed underfoot. Andrea kneeled and picked up one of them, tracing her finger along the creases.

She had never seen the contents of the boxes before: James' coloring books, elementary school report cards, baby pictures. James had never pulled any of them out to show her. She had never asked to see them either, she realized, a flash of embarrassment warming her neck. After his mother died, they had just packed everything up and pushed it all in a closet. Out of sight, out of mind, at least for her. As Andrea cast her eyes over the details of her husband's life, she felt hollow, empty. She couldn't help but wonder when they had become so distant. When had they stopped caring about the little details that made each of them who they were? Wasn't that what love was all about?

Andrea sighed heavily as she looked through the papers. Something had made James pull them out. Maybe if she could find out what triggered the trip down memory lane, she could find him. Andrea propped herself on her knees and started looking.

She looked through the trunk and found a box labeled 'Jimmie's Junk'. She lifted it out of the trunk carefully and placed it on her lap. She had never seen it before. She was intimidated by it, afraid to open it. She didn't want to intrude on James' memories of his father.

While Andrea contemplated opening the box, she let her eyes roam around the room. The dark décor had never appealed to her. Its colors depressed her. The room always seemed to be in a state of mourning. The fireplace, intended to bring warmth to body and soul, was always empty, bare of fire logs, and cold. The greens and maroons that colored the furniture and walls would normally bring forth images of fall and transition to Andrea's mind. Instead, they brought loss and death, rich and full-bodied when her eyes laid upon them. She shivered unconsciously as the room seemed to close in around her.

Andrea saw the old photo album sitting open on the sofa. She put the box down and crawled over to it, still on her knees.

The book was open to a picture of a woman standing outside. It was old; the sepia color was fading around the edges. The woman was standing next to a house. Andrea could see roses peeking in to view on the side of the picture. The woman's face was hard, weathered. It was the face of a woman who had seen the misery of a life not gone as planned. But it was her eyes that stood out the most. They seemed to stare back at her.

Andrea read the caption, 'Lillian Sarah Boone, Mother.' She searched her mind, trying to remember if she'd ever heard that name. It wasn't familiar. She was sure the woman hadn't been talked about in her presence. All of a sudden it came to her.

Her eyes widened as she realized that she was looking at James' grandmother. It had to be her. Andrea had met most of James' mother's side of the family and this woman was not among them. This had to be Jimmie's mother. The one that no one ever talked about.

"This is what he was looking at before he left," she said aloud to the empty room, a question playing on her words.

Andrea looked at the picture one last time before she stood. She was going to call Pete to see what he knew about James' grandmother. Maybe he could figure out why James was looking at the picture before he left, maybe they could come up with ideas about where he'd gone based upon what she had found. She turned to leave the room, but her eyes fell on a white piece of paper laying haphazardly on the sofa.

Andrea picked it up. She was looking at James' grandmother's death certificate.

CHAPTER 51

James pulled up to the house at 1:00 a.m. Something made him keep driving, going past the house and around the corner to park. He walked the block to the house with the gait of a zombie, slow and unsteady in his step. He ignored the dread mounting within him as he walked up the steps to the porch. Everything about the place was familiar. He had been there before, if only in his dreams.

James looked at the door and smiled bitterly. In his dreams, the door had a board nailed across it, blocking trespassers out. Now the board was lying face up, its rusted nails jutting upward, the obstruction discarded. There was no need for a barricade any longer, not for him. He was home.

James looked into the window and saw that the bare light that hung in the middle of the room was still on, its dull rays casting a brownish tint on everything it touched. No one laid waiting for him on the floor between the living room and dining room. They didn't have to. He knew they were there. All of them. Waiting for him.

James was ready to join them.

CHAPTER 52

Andrea and Pete got into the car, following their instincts, to find James. Andrea called Pete after she found the office left in such a state. Pete came back over and sat with her, trying to figure out where James might have gone.

Andrea took Pete down to the office so that he could see the disarray for himself.

"It's like he pulled this stuff out in a frenzy. Look, some of the papers have been stepped on."

"He was careless," Pete added.

"He must have been planning to come back to look at this stuff. Why else would he have left it out like this? If he was done with it, he would have packed it back in the trunk and put it away, right?"

"Maybe something spooked him. It looks like he left in a hurry."

Andrea walked over to the sofa. She glanced down at the picture of James' grandmother. The woman seemed to stare back at her from the page. Andrea averted her eyes quickly, the beginnings of fear mounting in her body, like icy fingers stroking her spine. She picked up the death certificate.

"I found this too. It was sitting on the end of the sofa."

Pete looked at the death certificate. Lillian Boone. He didn't know the name. He read the address aloud.

"Silver Spring, Maryland."

Andrea watched as Pete tried to figure out who the woman was. She gathered the photo album reluctantly, as she waited for Pete to speak. She didn't want to touch the album and run the risk of looking at the picture again, but she needed something to do with her hands. She was fidgety, antsy. Not knowing where James had gone was driving her crazy.

Andrea glanced at the picture of the woman again, her eyes unable to stay away from the photograph for long. Something about the woman frightened her. It was as if the picture was alive, watching the activity going on in the world from within the photo album. Andrea looked closer, paying attention to the detail of the picture. She regarded the house and its porch barely visible from the angle it was shot. She saw the white picket fence that was set around the perimeter of the house off in the distance. She saw the 1960s vintage Ford parked further down the street, almost out of view. She saw all of those things but still her eyes returned to the woman's. To Lillian's. She allowed no diversion.

Andrea felt pulled into Lillian's eyes, sucked down into the depths of their blackness. And it was dark there. So very dark. And cold. Andrea shook her head rapidly, trying to break the spell. She blinked her eyes and pushed the book aside, her soul shaken.

Andrea breathed deeply before regaining her composure. Her heart rate had gone up in the minute she had looked at the picture, and a light film of sweat had covered her forehead. She cast an uncertain glance at the spine of the album; the photograph was far enough away to hide the eyes from view. She pushed it further still, wary of touching the album itself. She resolved to close the book and put it in the trunk as soon as Pete saw the picture. She'd never see it again, if she could help it.

She nudged Pete to get his attention, all the while pointing to the album in silence.

"Is this her?" he asked before looking. Andrea nodded and sat back on the sofa. Pete looked at the woman, her malevolent eyes penetrating him as they had Andrea. They were unsettling. Before speaking again, he read the caption.

"Lillian Sarah Boone, Mother," he said, holding the book out to Andrea.

"Close it," she said, her voice monotone as she stared at the album extended to her. "I don't ever want to look at that picture again."

"I know what you mean," Pete said, as he closed the book and put it on the floor. "Who is Lillian Boone? I've never heard James mention that name before."

"Neither have I. When James and I were dating, his mother sat me down and showed me a lot of old pictures. I saw a picture of her mother and both of her grandmothers. When I asked if there were pictures of James' father's side, she got angry. She didn't mean for me to see it, but I did. Her face tightened up and her back straightened. She said curtly, 'I've never seen any pictures of Jimmie's family. I don't think any exist.' I wanted to press, but I didn't. She seemed so bothered by it. I didn't want to make matters worse.

"This woman wasn't in any of the pictures Mary showed me. And I didn't meet her at any of James' family functions. The caption says 'Mother'. I think this is Jimmie's mother."

Pete nodded in silent agreement.

"This is what James was looking at before he left, Pete. What do you think it could mean?"

Pete was silent for a while, trying to piece everything together. He looked at the death certificate again. It had obviously been handled. The folds in the paper were deep. It wouldn't lie flat if placed on a table. Pete knew the death certificate had something to do with James' disappearance, he just didn't know what.

Pete looked at the burial information. No location was listed. That ruled out a trip to the cemetery. He scoured the rest of the document trying to find clues. *Place of Death - City, Town, County, Cause of Death, Informant.* They were all hints to the bigger answer. The one he couldn't seem to uncover. He searched the certificate for what seemed like hours, waiting for the answer to jump out at him. His eyes kept coming back to the address of the deceased.

"But that wouldn't make sense," Pete uttered finally, without realizing he had spoken aloud.

"What doesn't?" Andrea asked.

"That he would be going there. To the address on this death certificate."

Andrea leaned toward Pete and looked at the death certificate again.

"Maybe he thinks she has something to do with what's going on in his mind," Pete said, his voice almost a whisper.

The memory of James' father talking to his dead mother flashed in Andrea's mind quickly, leaving a chalky residue, particles suspended in air, like the remnants of spent firecrackers. The image was so chilling, so poignant, as it seared itself in her consciousness. It was visible and intense even when she tried to wash it away with her tears. Andrea started to tremble.

"How could she? He never knew who she was."

Andrea's face crumbled, giving itself over to tears, as the story she'd heard years before about the father rang true for the son. All that he had secretly feared was coming to pass. And she had been powerless to stop it.

Pete didn't see her tears. He merely stared at the certificate beseeching it to tell him more.

"He does now," Andrea said hauntingly. She looked over at the closed photo album lying innocently on the floor and shuddered. She could feel the woman's ominous eyes staring back at her.

CHAPTER 53

James walked around the porch to the side of the house after trying the front door and finding it locked. The columns, once decorative and molded, were weather-beaten, the paint chipping from them in long strips. The boards that made up the porch creaked and whined under his weight. It was late, after midnight, and the moonlight was shining on some other part of town. The sky was almost completely dark. The streetlights were on, but they were too far away to shed any real light on the porch, so James walked slowly, his hands held out in front of him.

His foot touched something. He looked down and saw that it was one of the steps leading to the back door of the house. James walked up the steps slowly. He wasn't hesitating, but he was cautious. He wanted to relish the feeling of the open air on his skin before he entered the stuffy house. Perhaps for the last time.

James turned the knob with some effort. The door was unlocked but jammed from disuse. He twisted the knob right and left rapidly, trying to release it. Finally, it gave. The door squeaked on its hinges, as it swung open slowly.

The air inside smelled stale as it moved like it hadn't in years, swirling, mingling with the fresh air funneling in. James smelled something underneath the musty sourness. It was the smell of rotted wood, and decay. It was the smell of death. James inhaled deeply, letting the stench flow into his lungs. *I am a part of this now,* he thought to himself and stepped inside.

James stood in the kitchen where his father and grandmother had eaten meals together. He could almost see them sitting on either side of the table, silent as they ate, every morning and night. The smell of grease still hung in the air. He didn't know if he was imagining it or if it was really there. It didn't matter. It added to the room, gave it substance.

James cast his eyes around the room, taking it in. An old refrigerator was standing on the far side of the room. It was dingy; the bright yellow color had faded over the years. Tiles lay chipped and broken on the floor. Some were still glued in place while others were lifted from the wood floor underneath. A battle-scarred stove sat opposite the refrigerator; its burners blacked from the flames that licked the bottom of pots for years. Other than that, the room was empty. No table, no chairs, no shelving unit, none of the other things from his dreams. He didn't know whether to be relieved or frightened by it.

He walked through the kitchen and into the dining room, casting a glance at the stairwell at the end of the hallway between the two rooms. No lights were on upstairs, and none of the windows caught any moonlight. It was so dark he couldn't see the outline of the stairs.

James walked into the dining room and noticed that it too was empty. A quick glance into the living room revealed the same. They had all been figments of his imagination. All the things that had taken place in those rooms. There was nothing there to make him believe otherwise. No furniture, no dead woman, nothing. The room was bare, save for the lone dim light that hung from the ceiling in the center of the room. A heavy sigh flowed out of his mouth. He realized at that moment that he'd wanted all of those things to be there. At least it would make what had to be done easier if he could at least think he saw remnants of a past that didn't belong to him. At least then he could fade into the illusion as though he had always been a part of it. This way, with the house bare, the only remnant of his dream being the dim light bulb that hung solitarily in the living room, he couldn't even trick himself into thinking that someone *made* him do it. Neither his father nor his grandmother. Not the spirit of one of his victims. He might even have been inspired to write as much in his note if he had seen all the things that had plagued his dreams. But with the house empty he didn't look psychotic, as he had to have been to do the things, he knew he had done. This way he only looked guilty.

Dejected, James went back into the hall, intrigued by the darkened stairwell. He felt his way along the wall, unsure of his footing and where the steps actually began. His dreams had never taken him to the point of ascending the stairs to the bedrooms. He decided to explore the house before he started writing his note.

CHAPTER 54

James climbed the stairs carefully, placing his feet deliberately on each step. He was amused at the fear that was growing inside him, as if he should have any concern now. The man that he had become shouldn't have been frightened by anything, let alone a dark hallway.

He wondered what Susan had felt when she died, or Carmen just before she was dropped from the roof. How frightened had they been? Did they see their lives passing before their eyes in their last moments, as so many romanticists are prone to have the masses believe? The thought of death being anything more than the end of any form of life, spiritual or otherwise, was beyond popular comprehension. He, himself, had been one of the droning numbers who believed that there was a heaven after life on earth, and that angels of mercy removed a soul from its worthless body at the moment of death so that no pain was felt, no memory of suffering was burned into the subconscious. He believed that people 'passed on', like a Baptist minister would tell a child in Sunday School. He knew differently now. Death wasn't always the end. It was cold, it was painful, and it was terrifying, but not finite for everyone. For most, death was the end of life and the beginning of the great nothingness. He could see that place reflected in Carmen's eyes.

For others, death was the start of a new existence, one lived in shadows and dark corners, sharing the same space as the living. Those who were reborn in the realm, where expiation was no longer possible, coveted the life around them, wanting the life they had experienced before they had awakened in Gehenna. They tortured the living, trying to capture their souls for one last drink of human life, killing them with their thirst. They revealed themselves, their wretched existence for pleasure, punishing the living for simply being alive. James had seen these souls, had heard their voices. He wondered what form of devil he would become in his reincarnation.

James hated himself for their deaths. For Susan, his beloved Susan. His affection had been taboo, and he knew it. He had been a married man, one that hadn't considered sleeping with another woman before, and was judgmental of those who did. He thought he was happy, content. He loved Andrea. Nothing, not even his sordid affair, had diminished that fact. He loved Andrea.

But loving Andrea wasn't enough. He wanted excitement. The fire in Susan's eyes enticed him, made him feel invincible. She worked her way into him, diving so deep that he wasn't sure where she stopped and he began. All of this in the blink of an eye. He was completely and totally enamored with her.

He had wanted her, craved her, needed her as if for sustenance itself. But then she turned away from him, taking her love away as she went, leaving him feeling cold inside; barren and lifeless. And he killed her for it.

He'd been angry, that much he could remember. His body trembled with it when he reached the landing of the second floor in the old, abandoned house, as it had when she turned away from him that day. He stood motionless in the surrounding darkness. Dust particles suspended in the air, hanging together like a blanket of interminable fog. The only sound he could hear was the floor-boards creaking as they struggled to support his weight, having been ignored for so many years. He let the ancient anger well within him, feeling it tumble and turn, boiling as he thought of Susan walking away from him on that side street in Nyack. His fists clenched and unclenched methodically.

He remembered being confused, wondering why it was happening and what it meant that he was so distraught over it. Then he recalled the denial he faced, and finally, the need to possess her. She was his obsession. He hadn't known it until then. He wasn't willing to let the relationship end. Was that the emotion, the final straw that had driven him to kill her?

James stood, his open eyes seeing nothing in the darkness, as he thought of that fateful day, the day when his life changed forever and the beginning of the end began. The day his fate had been sealed.

Susan burned in her car because she had betrayed him. She dismissed their love as nothing more than a cheap thrill. A mistake, as she had so eloquently put it, not mincing words at the end. No, not for him. His face flashed hot as he thought of her callous tone, her unconcealed impatience. She had wanted to wash her hands of him quickly. He remembered feeling love for her even then and he despised himself for it. She thought him cheap; his love, his sex, his sacrifice. And some piece of him couldn't stand for it, wouldn't stand for it. Didn't stand for it.

James ran a clammy hand over his forehead that was now covered with a light film of sweat. He thought of Carmen, the beautiful fortuneteller who was in the wrong place at the wrong time. She was innocent and he knew it. He grieved for her almost as much as he did for Susan. She died a terrible death at his hand because she had looked at him. In her eyes, James saw what he was. In that instant, he knew that it had to be done.

James shut his eyes against the thought, pushing the tears back as he thought of her youth and innocence, her beauty even in death. Her face haunted him as he stood at the top of the steps in the dark, deserted house. It was she he feared most, he had come to realize. Her vengeance, before all others, he deserved.

"You will be vindicated, Carmen," James said to the empty house, thick with memories and ghosts hiding in the shadows.

"I will come to you soon."

CHAPTER 55

Pete and Andrea sat in the car in silence, as they drove along the turnpike. As they peered into the darkness, its omnipresence stifling and intimidating, they both assessed the situation for what it was.

Andrea was more frightened than she had ever been. The raw terror coursing through her made her feel unstable, vulnerable. She wanted to strike out at something, punish it for causing this situation. Was it James she was furious with? She nodded imperceptibly, answering the question ringing in her mind. James was the cause of her fear, her instability. James was at fault.

She winced, feeling tears forming in the corners of her eyes. How could she blame James for this? He was going through something, true, but to think that he brought it on himself? That he was at fault? How inconsiderate could she be? Her own thought process revolted her, she wanted to erase it from her mind, wanted to purge it. But it lingered still, sticking to the walls of her psyche, showing itself in full view. Something kept it there, holding on to it for dear life, shedding her own culpability as it dangled on the edge of her sanity.

She thought about their baby, only a few weeks old. Innocent. Unaware. She wanted its father to be there when he or she was born, free of demons, free of nightmares: sane. But she didn't think that would happen. She hadn't even told James about the baby yet. Something in the back of her mind, some part of her that was soft spoken and distant, wondered if she would ever get the chance to.

All of this was happening because of James. He either created these demons or let them out. She didn't know which. She needed James now more than ever, but he wasn't there for her. She was angry. It was his fault, there was no denying it. He had brought all of this on himself, she thought, as her mind scratched at the cut that had been trying to scab over. She felt her face getting hot as the old familiar pain rushed back in, flooding her senses. She was thinking about James and Susan.

Andrea thought about the day she found out about the affair. On a whim, she had driven out to Nyack one evening after work, taking the advice of one of her coworkers. She had been thinking about remodeling the family room, giving it a more rustic feel. A western antique might be the perfect addition to the room, she thought, so she went to Main Street to do some window-shopping. She walked down to the end of the street, where the road dead ended into the Hudson, and made a right turn. After passing a row of restaurants of varying cuisines—Japanese, Italian, Vietnamese, Chinese, and Caribbean restaurants all living as one on the small street in the quaint little town—the street became more residential. Andrea started to turn around but became mesmerized by the houses that dotted the landscape.

Colonials with tall, arching roofs, and decorative porch pillars done in muted autumn colors were mingled with spectacular contemporary Victorian designs, some with four stories on flat plots, others built into the slope of the hill. Ranch style houses started and ended the development, their basic coloring brought to life by their shutters and trim. The variety she found was different than what she was used to only twenty minutes away in Monsey. On any given street one house looked like the next one, which looked like the next. All of them were built within five years of one another. The builders spruced the houses up with different colored trim—black, blue, maroon, and forest green. There were two types of fronts: brick or wood. Every once in a while, you might happen upon a house that was of identical design but turned opposite all the others on the block. It would have the same architecture as the others, but the bedrooms, living room, dining room, and kitchen would be swapped. That would be considered a different style in Monsey-speak. Andrea appreciated the differences she found in Nyack.

All of the houses were bordered by a cement walkway, Nyack's only semblance to city life. Andrea decided to take a leisurely stroll down the quiet block before she shopped the other side of Main Street.

Andrea strolled the impeccably clean walkway and looked at the well-kept houses, breathing in the brisk air. Being near the water always made her feel calm and serene. She was thinking that maybe she would walk down to the pier and look out over the Hudson on her way back, before she hit the stores again, when she crossed a street that led to the back of a bed and breakfast. She stopped and regarded the modest bed and breakfast, its front veranda-styled gazebo calling to her, telling her to come in and sit a spell under its slatted roof. Its airy Victorian architecture enthralled her. She reveled in the mauve color of the wood paneling that was adorned with white columns. Countless windows stared out at the street, undoubtedly letting a wonderful amount of sunlight shine in each of the rooms. A covered turret stood above her, extended at the end of an open walkway lined with a sculptured white railing. The design reminded Andrea of a gingerbread house.

Mitchell Manor.

Andrea made a mental note of the name of the bed and breakfast. She thought it might be a nice getaway for their anniversary. Smiling to herself at the idea of snuggling up to James under a down comforter and being greeted by the early morning sunlight in Mitchell Manor, she turned and headed back toward Main Street.

A car pulled into the alleyway leading to the back of Mitchell Manor while she had been admiring the building. Andrea could hear voices, male and female, emanating from the back of the building, echoed by the brick walls that enclosed the parking area. She crossed the alleyway to the other side of the street and started to walk, not realizing that she had slowed her gait. The voices sounded familiar.

Andrea slowed to a stop on the other side of the alleyway as the voices approached. As they grew louder, Andrea listened to the male. The cadence, the tone of the laughter, the rich tenor was one she was all too familiar with.

It was James' voice.

A part of her was elated to hear her husband approaching. The part of her mind that thought that it was an incredible coincidence that they would meet in Nyack showed her fantasies of him going into the bed and breakfast to reserve a room for their anniversary, beating her to the punch. That same part of her mind urged her to leave before he saw her so that she wouldn't ruin the surprise. She almost gave in, almost believed the wishful thinking that her optimistic side had shown her. But the other side, the distrustful, pessimistic side, willed her to listen a little longer. The alleyway was the length of the building. A car would have to drive down the narrow alleyway with its lights on, warning oncoming cars of its presence before it made a turn into the parking area that was, undoubtedly, the width of Mitchell Manor. Andrea gave the couple time to reach her. She stood on the other side of the alleyway, opposite Mitchell Manor and listened, a knot rising uncomfortably in her throat.

Andrea heard a woman's voice laughing along with the man she thought was James. The woman sounded uninhibited and happy. She said wistfully,

"I wish we could do this all the time."

"Do what? Go to dinner?" the man asked playfully.

"No," the woman cooed. Andrea imagined the woman nudging the man, leaning her body into him as he curled his arm around her, rubbing her arm lovingly. She cringed as her mind superimposed James' face onto the faceless man in her mind. She blinked the image away, trying to keep her mind clear.

"I mean be here like this. This place—the Manor—it's just perfect. I wish it could be this way all the time."

"Maybe when all is said and done, we'll buy a house here in Nyack. Fill it with a bunch of kids, you know? It would be incredible."

The woman sighed before she spoke, Andrea's throat tightening, hanging on her words. She knew without a doubt that the man was James. She would know his voice anywhere. She tried to hold out hope that it wasn't him, the conversation too personal for him to be having with a woman other than herself. She would wait, she decided, to see what they looked like, instead of leaving before they reached the mouth of the alley, like the part of her that wanted to remain positive begged her to do. Andrea thought she recognized the male voice, but the woman, who was she?

"That sounds like a beautiful dream," the woman said finally. Her voice was much closer now, as they approached the sidewalk. They fell silent as they walked, sharing the tender moment between them. Andrea was in a trance as she listened to their footfalls drawing nearer and nearer—the heels of the woman's shoes clicking against the pavement louder and louder. She snapped out of her dazed state and turned her face toward the building in front of her. A town home sat on the street across the alley from Mitchell Manor; its front yard was the concrete sidewalk she was standing on. A newspaper, still in its plastic bag, lay on the ground near the front door. Andrea hurried over to the door, turning her back to the alleyway, and kneeled to pick up the newspaper. The couple emerged from the alley seconds later, the man's arm over the woman's shoulder as she nuzzled into the crook of his arm. The man's profile faced Andrea's side of the street. Andrea stood carefully, turning just enough to the side to see them out of the corner of her eye. With the newspaper in her hand, she watched them walk on the very sidewalk where she stood, not ten steps away. She couldn't risk being spotted but she had to be sure she was right.

It was James.

The couple turned left towards Mitchell Manor. Andrea stood in silence watching them go as the newspaper slid slowly out of its plastic bag. A few steps later, the couple turned left and walked up the steps onto the front porch of Mitchell Manor. The newspaper came completely out of its bag and fell to the ground with an audible thump, jarring Andrea, clearing the fog that was surrounding her. The couple cast a casual glance in her direction as she bent down to gather up the sections that had spilled out of the fold. Andrea's face disappeared under the mass of her hair, her face burning hot. When she looked up again the couple had disappeared into the bed and breakfast where, minutes before, Andrea had fantasized sharing an evening with her husband. Tears burned trails down her cheeks as she stood, the newspaper forgotten on the ground. Her husband had just gone into a bed and breakfast with another woman, laughing gaily and talking about the future. James was having an affair.

With Susan.

As she sat in the car with Pete, speeding toward Maryland to find James, Andrea remembered the days after she saw them in Nyack. She went home that night and soaked in the tub, trying to make sense of her emotions. She didn't make any calls, didn't enlist her friends and family to help her through it. She wanted to think things out on her own and make her decision without the influence of other people. She cried the first part of the night, the betrayal tearing her apart. She felt like a fool for the rest of the night, first for putting all of her trust in James— 'Never put all your eggs in one basket', her mother used to tell her—and then for crying over him, letting him get the best of her. She sat on the living room floor, paced the hallways, laid awake in bed, and ran the shower while sitting on the covered commode, trying to clear her mind of the hurt, so that she could come up with a solution. She had time to think. James wouldn't be home for two more days. His 'business trip' to Atlanta was supposed to have him home late Sunday night. She felt nauseous at the knowledge of what he was really doing but was thankful for the time alone. She needed the time to think.

When James came home that Sunday night, Andrea was embroiled in a restless sleep, the first of the weekend. She awoke when she heard the front door creak, and thought about confronting him then, but she decided that she needed the sleep. She would deal with the situation the next day. She stiffened, all the pores in her cheek seeming to come alive when James bent down to kiss her. It was all she could do not to slap him.

The next morning James left the house early for work, so she didn't even see him. The rest of the week followed the same pattern. He was early to rise and late to get back in the house. She had hefty requirements at work. She was the acting supervisor while her boss was out of town, so she couldn't afford a late-night confrontation that might last until morning. By Wednesday, after they hadn't had the chance to say more than two words to each other, Andrea decided to have the talk with him on Saturday morning over breakfast. Even though she could barely stand to see him, let alone to sleep next to him, she made the effort not to let on that anything was bothering her until she had time to discuss the issue.

Andrea got up bright and early Saturday morning, made bacon and eggs with coffee, and waited to hear James' feet padding down to the kitchen. As usual, the aroma of breakfast pulled James from his slumber, and he made his way down to the kitchen nook, bleary eyed and groggy. As he took his seat across the table from her, Andrea prepared her opening statement. She bounced between, 'How dare you do this to me, you bastard!' and 'I saw a man that looked just like you Friday night in Nyack, right outside the most beautiful old bed and breakfast. Mitchell Manor, it was called. Have you heard of it?'. She stared at his oblivious face while she thought, her stomach balling in knots as anger filled her to her limit. While she was deciding, the phone rang. She reluctantly went to get it, unable to fight the urge to answer every call that came in. She had been that way ever since her grandmother had a stroke in the wee hours of the morning and her mother called, telling her to come to the hospital at 3:00 a.m. She couldn't shake the habit, always afraid that the time she didn't pick up would be the time she should have answered most. Her mother was on the line, distressed about her father's lethargy. She was considering taking him to the hospital because he had been that way for weeks and the good night's sleep, he had gotten hadn't helped at all. Concerned that it might have been a symptom of his worsening diabetes, Andrea told her mother she would meet her at their house and help. As Andrea spoke, she eyed James eating his breakfast without a care in the world. Her lips curled into a sneer as she watched him slurp his coffee, trying to urge his body to wake up. He should enjoy this last day when everything seems normal, she thought angrily. *Enjoy it while you can,* her mind hissed. Andrea vowed she would talk to him as soon as she got home, regardless of the time.

She took a different route to her parents' house that day. A route that took her near Nyack's only exit to the highway. At first, she thought she might be able to resist the temptation to pull off the highway and drive into town, that she had raised the bar and successfully hurdled it, but that illusion was washed away when she merged into the right lane and joined the line of cars at the exit. She drove down Main Street, looking at the picturesque town lined with trees in front of antique shops, boutiques, and café's. She took the same turn she had taken on the day she learned about the affair and stopped in front of Mitchell Manor. Its stately presence didn't warm her any longer, didn't concoct whimsical fantasies of roaming within its walls anymore. Instead, it left her feeling cold and empty. She made a U-turn and went back the way she came, leaving Mitchell Manor to overlook the Hudson without her.

She left Nyack quietly, never having left her car to walk on its grounds. She stayed only a few minutes, but she had seen everything she wanted to see.

When Andrea got home that evening after spending hours in the hospital emergency room only to confirm that her father was only overly tired and not sick, she found a note on the table telling her that James was over at Pete's and that she should come over when she had the chance. Andrea remembered feeling giddy. Pete must have found out about James and Susan also and he had confronted them both. She raced over to the house, eager to add in her two cents. When she knocked on the door and James answered, Andrea was taken aback. He wasn't bruised or bloodied as she thought he might have been given Pete's temper. He looked at her with eyes that were so sad her heart ached.

"What happened?" she asked before she realized it.

"It's Susan. She's dead."

James' face crumbled as he looked at her. He threw his arms around her to hug her, but Andrea found that it was she who provided the strong shoulder and stiff back he needed to lay his grief. Andrea made her way into the living room to find Pete lying on the sofa crying softly. She knelt on the floor next to him and hugged him gently, letting him lay his head on her shoulder. She smoothed his hair as he let out his grief. She decided then that she would never tell Pete about the affair. No matter what happened between her and James, she would never tell Pete about what his wife had done to him and to her. She was dead and the secret would die with her.

Andrea's eyes brimmed with tears. She found herself crying with Pete, their sobs rising in tandem, their chests heaving together. His tears were for the loss of his companion. Her tears were for the dissolution of her marriage.

Andrea tried to pick her time carefully. She didn't want to infringe upon the time that Pete needed with James to reminisce about Susan, to laugh, to mourn. She didn't want to complicate their talks, preoccupying James' mind with the problems he was having at home. It wasn't that she wanted to make anything easier for James. She knew he was suffering too, having lost his lover. She wanted him to wallow in that and if she could have stacked more grief onto his plate, she would have. But Pete didn't deserve that. He needed James to be there for him. Andrea could wait a little longer for Pete to get his feelings off his chest and heal.

That time never came. After Pete's suffering came James' nightmares and the turmoil they created. Then Andrea found out she was pregnant and it threw a wrench in everything. When she found out about the baby, she felt such joy it all but obliterated her issues with James. She was still angry at him for cheating on her, nothing would take that away, but the burning need to get away from him had dissipated some. She found herself making plans for the baby that included the two of them—building the crib, painting the nursery, deciding on a name. As James tumbled through his nightmares and mood swings, the idea of separating was quickly replaced with trying to help him through whatever was happening to him. It only took a short while for the notion of divorce to disappear from her mind all together. Somewhere along the line she had shelved it in favor of making the relationship work for their baby.

Andrea wondered how James would react to the news that she was pregnant. It wasn't planned—they had been using birth control the whole time they had been married. It just happened.

Would he be happy? Could this be the thing that would pull him out of the horrible state he was in? Or would his concern about the baby, about whether or not it would be normal, push him into depression? She didn't know.

Andrea couldn't help but fear for the baby's sanity also. The thought of her child being plagued with the same illness that its father suffered from—the same illness that its grandfather had suffered from—terrified her.

This was all James' fault.

A sob escaped her lips, mourning the death of her compassion.

Pete stared out at the desolate road ahead and sighed. They didn't know that James was in Maryland for sure. They were just operating on a whim, a gut feeling that they both seemed to have at the same time. The address on the death certificate was where James was going. It had to be. There was no other option that they could see.

As he looked out at the road ahead, almost empty of cars and with only a couple of tractor-trailers sprinkled in the distance, Pete wondered if they were on a wild goose chase. James could be anywhere. He could be holed up in a hotel room, trying to sort things out. He could be on the road going anywhere, fighting with the demons in his head. Hell, he could even be in a bar drowning the bastards in drink. The latter wasn't James' style, at least not anymore. His drinking days had ended as soon as he graduated from college. But the dreams James had been having combined with the little twist of lime Pete had provided could drive anyone to try for the worm at the bottom of the bottle.

Pete snickered to himself. James had murdered Susan. It made perfect sense. A jilted lover upset that his partner was returning to her husband. A crime of passion. Add in the history of mental illness, and it was pay dirt. It was poetic, really. Pete almost believed it himself.

He wasn't surprised that James had taken the bait, just that he had spiraled downward so quickly. Pete hadn't even gotten to the really good stuff. He had been looking forward to spinning yarns about late night phone calls from detectives working on the reopened case, dreams of Susan telling him that she was murdered. His imagination had run wild with stories to share in confidence with James. But he didn't have to. True to form, James was as suggestible as he had always feared he might be. Like father like son.

James had taken the game to a higher level than Pete had expected to go. How far would it go before it was over? Pete expected that he would be handing James over to the boys in blue pretty soon. Who knows? Maybe even the boys in white coats, he mused. It didn't matter to him. He just wanted James out of the way for good.

A calming thought came over him, bringing a smile to his lips. Soon James would confess to killing Susan, succumbing to the food for thought that had been fed to him with a side serving of his own hellish nightmares. It was inevitable. James was too far gone. There would be evidence to substantiate his claim, Pete had made sure of that. And then he would be gone. Out of the picture. Andrea would need comfort and Pete would be there to provide it for her. Soon she would grow to hate James for what he had done. She would pity Pete, the man whose cheating wife was killed by her lover and his best friend. He would drink it up, lapping at it like a dog parched from the summer sun. The baby would grow inside her and she would lean more and more on him for support. And then, yes, then, they would be able to move on to the next chapter of their lives. Together.

This was the beginning of the end, Pete surmised, the thought warming him as it filled his mind. James was teetering on the edge and just needed one final push. Pete would be there. He wanted to be the man left standing on the ledge with his arms held stiffly out in front of him.

Pete let his smile dissolve into a look of pensive concentration. He turned his head to Andrea and saw her facing the window, her body trembling, showing the telltale signs of a person who was trying not to cry out loud. He put his hand on her leg and asked her what was wrong.

She turned to Pete, her face wet with tears. She wanted to tell him what she was feeling, tell him how much she hated James for doing this to her, to them, and yet, in the same breath, tell him how much she loved James. But she couldn't. She couldn't bring herself to form the words of betrayal that danced in her mind. She couldn't announce them to the open air to be judged. She turned away from Pete again, aware that she was being selfish. Her sobs came freely now, no longer muffled by her embarrassment.

A little voice inside her was screaming so loudly it was deafening. It wanted her to speak, wanted her to say out loud what she couldn't believe she was thinking. It wanted her to condemn James for going crazy or being crazy or whatever was happening to him. She would never give life to the malicious truth forming in her mind. She could barely stand the sound of it echoing in her head; the gravity of it, the unbearable weight, was crushing her psyche.

She hated James.

She hated him for ruining their nice, average life. She hated him for locking her out of his suffering, for not trusting her to be able to listen, and be by his side. She hated him for being like his father after all.

She was trembling, her fear enveloping her like a warm blanket against the cold. Where could James be? What was he thinking? What was he doing? She hated him, loved him, and feared for him all at the same time. The combination was dizzying.

Pete cleared his throat nervously. Andrea turned in his direction and saw him swallow hard. He was as concerned as she was. Pete turned to Andrea and offered a weak smile. She didn't return it. Instead, she turned away and looked back out into the blackness that was the night and sighed. No, she decided unwaveringly, she couldn't tell Pete what she was thinking. She was still James' wife and she owed him her allegiance. She owed him that if nothing else.

"We'll find him," Pete said, hoping that he sounded secure and certain. He wasn't sure, though.

Andrea nodded her head at Pete's assertion, her mouth open in a painful grimace, despair and self-loathing coating her lips like so much lipstick. She felt sick. Her stomach twisted and writhed into knots, pulsating, contracting, cramping. Her head rested on the cool glass of the passenger side window, fogging it from the heat of her clammy head. Her emotions were running wild, competing with each other like racehorses. One second she was angry, the next second she was remorseful, in yet another second, she was frightened. All of those emotions were pointed at James. It was all his fault.

She whimpered once and clutched the sides of her head, her eyes shutting tightly. She gave way to fresh tears that stung her eyes as they pushed their way past her eyelids. She couldn't fathom the idea that she could be angry with James for all of this, yet she was. It was undeniable. She blamed him. And she hated herself for it. Andrea sat in the passenger seat crying silent tears as anguish consumed her, berating herself for being a traitor to her husband. A traitor to their love.

Pete watched her cry, watched her fold into herself in the passenger seat until she looked as small and delicate as a child. He couldn't think of the right words to make Andrea feel better. Perhaps there weren't any.

Andrea's pain traveled over to him like a steady stream of smoke emanating from a lit cigarette. He could smell it; it was tinny and dank. He cursed James for doing this to her, for putting her through such pain. He sighed and propped his elbow on the window base. The dark was impenetrable; his headlights barely carved out a sliver of road. *This is bullshit,* he thought irritably.

And then, as if a light turned on in his head, he saw the bright side of the situation. *She'll run into my arms after this,* he thought contentedly. *I may not have to tell her about the affair.*

A cunning smirk spread across his lips as he plodded on into the night toward what they thought was James' hiding place.

Towards Maryland.

CHAPTER 56

J ames stood at the top of the stairs that connected with the dark hallway at the halfway mark. A window at the end of the hallway on the left let in a sliver of light, just enough for him to see the layout of the floor. He looked down his right and then his left, both sides equally dark and daunting. There were two doors down the right side of the hallway, probably the master bedroom and bathroom, he thought. Down the left side were three doors, two on one side and one on the other. He looked in front of himself and saw his image reflected in a large vintage mirror with an ornate frame of brass cherubs and ivy surrounding the dirty glass. The plump figures crested the top of the oval mirror, one with a bow and arrow in its hand, and the other holding a vine of grapes. The ivy draped the sides of the mirror and met at the base. He took a step closer, looking at the round faces, their hair shining from the light that streamed in from the window. Only one side was visible; half of their faces remained drenched in darkness. They smiled down at him from their perch on the top of the mirror, sardonically, scornfully, patronizing him as he stared up at them. The smile that greeted them from his lips was full of the same contempt that they displayed.

James looked at himself through the dirty film that coated the mirror. His eyes were hollow. Dark circles ringed them, and the capillaries in his eyes stood out like bright red lightning bolts. He was unshaven, haggard. He rubbed a hand over the stubble covering his chin. The bandage that covered the skin just above his eye was dirty, at some point the wound had begun to bleed again. He couldn't remember when. He pressed it gently and was met with pain that shot a white light through his eyes. He squeezed them shut and tried to wait it out, to let the pain subside. He stood that way for a while, breathing through his mouth, his hand suspended over the bandage as if guarding it from the very air.

James finally opened his eyes to the blackness of the room, its thickness surrounding him, making him feel claustrophobic. He looked into the mirror at the reflection looking back at him. A man resembling himself looked out from the mirror at James, his face stained with blood. His eyes had the stare of the dead, unseeing and fixed. Their gaze laid on James, the whites turned a sickly yellow. An explosion of broken blood vessels encircled the irises and burst from the corners of the eyes adding dark red to the palette. The skin around the eyes had a purplish hue, almost black in color. James looked closer, hesitantly stepping forward, to look at the lifeless man in the mirror. Dried streaks fell in jagged lines from the man's bottom lid, their pasty white paths leading to the man's nose and mouth. James felt a surge of sadness as he realized that the streaks were spent tears.

The man's chin was downturned, almost pinned to his chest. His face looked uncomfortably bloated. The man's lips were parted slightly. The tip of his tongue was visible, just barely, through the tiny slit his lips made. It looked discolored, almost as dark as the skin around the man's eyes. The lips themselves were dry except for a trail of blood that snaked from the corner of his mouth down to the bottom of his chin. The blood had dried, its flow halted.

James couldn't pull his eyes away from the sight, its resemblance to him too startling to ignore. His heart dropped as he looked at the man, identical to him in size, shape, and clothing. He was looking at his own reflection in some space and time. The reality of it made the pit of his stomach grow cold.

As he watched, a devilish smile formed on the man's lips, cracking them as it spread. The smile revealed jagged, yellowed teeth. His smile both frightened James and affirmed his worst fears.

The man stepped forward, his feet, which were once visible just before the edge of the mirror, met with the ivy frame, disappearing. James stepped back involuntarily, his instincts taking over. The man seemed to loom over him, his ominous grin hideously illuminated by the light. James felt himself cowering under it, as a child would under the gaze of an angry parent. It humiliated him, stripped him of the confidence that had been building within him as he walked up the stairs. It reclaimed the house from him, and James found himself relinquishing it readily, wanting to please the hulking figure on the other side of the mirror.

The smile seemed to disappear from the apparition, changing slowly but steadily, almost melting into a horrifying scowl; a grimace of pleasure in suffering. It was terrifying.

The man's eyes were unfaltering; they stared at James with tremendous pressure. James wanted to turn away but was afraid to. The man's face was expanding, growing. The mirror seemed to shake with the force of it; it rocked on its legs. James took another step backwards, away from the mirror. His heels were dangerously close to the edge of the stairs.

All but the man's face had disappeared. His head took up the entire mirror, filling all sides. And still the man stared at him.

James parted his lips to speak to the ghostly figure, but the words were halted in his throat before he uttered a sound. The reflection had begun to change again. James watched as the face seemed to shrink away, sinking into itself. Orange flames rimmed the sides of the mirror, closing in on the face. The flames slithered along the edges of the mirror, moving inward steadily, blocking his view of the hideous vision completely within seconds. The mirror was moving, or seemed to, as the flames danced over the glass. James felt the heat on his skin as the flames burned away the face of the nameless man.

And then there was nothing.

James stood for a while, looking at the mirror, waiting for another figure to appear. None did. He inched closer, hesitant to get too close, remembering the fire that licked out from the glass. Nothing happened. He looked at his reflection apprehensively, checking the corners of the mirror for any movement behind him, or within the mirror itself. Only his tired face looked back at him.

James turned again, looking down both hallways. The light streaming in from the window had grown bright white in contrast to the blackness engulfing the small hall. White like the moon on a clear night. It shone on the doors, adding shadows that seemed to hide more than just the knobs that opened them. James looked into the hollow, trying to discern a shape, tucked away just beyond his sight. He saw nothing but knew that something was there. He turned to his left and walked as if possessed, making his way down the hallway in measured, rhythmic steps. Something was drawing him closer to the light. He could feel the air around him changing, pushing and pulling him at the same time, while he walked. He was going to it. He had nothing more to lose.

James walked slowly down the hallway in search of his demons.

CHAPTER 57

As James walked down the hallway, the light from the window seemed to only illuminate one door, its ray forming an upside-down V at the base. James approached the door carefully, feeling he had to, as if any sudden movement would disturb the natural order of things and awaken the monsters. He rested his hand on the doorknob, hesitant to turn it. He sighed, his face feeling flush. Even now he was frightened of his destiny.

James stood staring at the closed door. The wood was dilapidated and warped. The rich chestnut luster had faded, leaving an unfinished-looking raw slab separating the rooms. The door itself was harmless. What James feared was what it might hold behind it. He could feel it pulsating on the other side.

The doorknob was warm to the touch compared to the cool climate in the abandoned house. James caressed it, almost tenderly. He took one last deep breath and opened the door.

A gust of stale wind met him, the smell accosting his nostrils. The air smelled dank and heavy. He could almost imagine fungus growing on the splintered floor, a gangrenous spate covering it, waiting to spread to a living host. The thought was so strong that he looked down at the floor expecting to see some green throbbing mass inches above the wood. A sigh of relief escaped him when he found nothing more than old floorboards, split and sunken, beneath him.

James walked into the room, taking it in. A dresser with a foggy mirror stood in the far right corner of the room with two of its drawers missing. A broken lamp laid on the floor next to the dresser. A chair with a moth-bitten cushion sat catty-cornered to the right. Even in its relative decay, it seemed out of place in the room. It was a replacement seat, one that had been removed from some other room in the house and put in here by a squatter or drug addict who wanted to sit upright while he shot up his fix, he thought. It sat innocently, breaking down over time just like everything else in the room, yet it obviously didn't belong. The original chair for the room was broken and discarded behind the imposter. Wooden legs crossed in an X braced by a steel pin lay on their backs in the corner. The hinge that would have supported the director's chair dangled from one leg pitifully. The canvas seat had been stripped away, only a frayed piece of it remained, dangling on the end of the hinge where it had fallen years before.

A bed frame was pushed against the wall on the left side of the room, the mattress and box spring gone. A small desk sat in the far left corner of the room with a small, junior chair tucked underneath the writing panel. The desk was clean of the normal desk litter, holding, instead, food wrappers and empty cans. There was nothing dynamic about the room. Nothing supernatural either, as James had expected when he stood nervously outside. There were no ghosts waiting for him when he opened the door, no gaping black holes pooling in the floor, waiting for him to take a fateful step. There was nothing at all. Except, he still had a strange feeling. The hairs on the back of his neck had still not relaxed. There was something in the room, even if he couldn't see it yet. He had the distinct feeling he was being watched.

James looked self-consciously around himself at the thought. His eyes fell onto the bed frame again. It was basic: wooden with two posts. It was an old-time frame, one that had the horizontal supporting metal slats traversing the open space between four wood slabs that made up the base. The sides were high; a box spring would have lain sunken in the base, nestled in the wood. The exposed slats were rusted. The headboard had deep scratches carved into it at the bottom, closest to where it would meet the mattress. The runners, wooden also, were scuffed and worn. The footboard was low and nondescript.

James approached the bed, seeing only the scratches. They were gashes, deep and jagged, he noticed upon closer inspection. The rest of the room began to fade from his view, paling and distorting off to the sides of his perspective, then blacking out completely until he saw only the cuts in the headboard in front of him. He ran his hand along them. They were even. All in a row, like notches. He counted six sets of five lines and one straggling line all by itself. Whoever marked the headboard didn't draw the fifth line horizontally across the other four to close the set. Instead, they spaced the sets out.

James ran his index finger along each cut individually. It was soothing and hypnotic. He felt his shoulders relaxing as he counted them off in his head. One. Two. Three. Four. Five. Space. Then it started all over again. His eyes felt heavy all of a sudden. He struggled to keep them open. He put his left hand on the headboard making it clank noisily against the wall, as he tried to hold himself up. All he wanted to do was lay down and run his fingers along the grooves in the headboard.

One... Two... Three...

He didn't feel himself fall onto the supporting slats, the rusted mesh awaiting him at the center of the bed frame. His face hit the metal hard, pressing the supple skin of his cheeks inward, splitting it in places and reopening the stitched wound above his eye. His shins banged painfully against the side of the bed frame, toppling him awkwardly as he fell. He felt the bottom of his kneecap hit the top of the wood flush. He could hear the liquid shifting of the cap as it dislocated. His right elbow broke through the supporting slats and hit the floor solidly, shattering under his unimpeded weight. But he didn't feel any of that. James only felt the sensation of his fingers rubbing the carved wood slowly, his finger lingering in the jagged indent, its roughness sensual to him, perversely calming. By the time his hand fell away from the notches and dropped awkwardly to the floor, his elbow rendered useless from the break, James had drifted too far away to feel the pain in his joints.

The room was completely dark now, even the view of the headboard had disappeared, its hypnotic spell broken when his finger lost contact with the alluring grooves. A strange nothingness engulfed him. His senses felt dull, numb. The darkness blinded him to even the tiniest feature. But there was no panic in his mind, no fear. The same calmness that entranced him before worked its magic then. He just drifted away. He felt nothing as he floated in time.

CHAPTER 58

Light crept back into James' field of vision and he blinked against it rapidly, shocked by its suddenness. When his eyes adjusted to the newfound brightness, James found himself in the same bedroom that he had been in when he blacked out. It was different. It had returned to its original luster, traveling back in time to find its rightful place of existence. James found himself standing just inside the door of a teenage boy's room from a time before he was born.

It was a typical boy's room. The walls were covered with paraphernalia: a fading Orioles pennant, a white peace sign painted on black cloth, a black light poster of Jimi Hendricks. The room was set up the way it had been when James entered it. Before James stepped back in time.

The director's chair with its blue canvas seat and back panel intact sat in the corner opposite the bed. Next to it stood a dresser, all of its drawers intact, and a mirror that was somewhat foggy. A lamp with a blue base sat on the side of the dresser. It was turned off.

James looked into the mirror, his eyes picking out the reflected image through the haze. He could see a desk off to the left at the far corner, but now it had a few schoolbooks, pencils, and paper scattered on top of it. A jacket hung on the back of the chair. A nightstand stood next to the bed, the small lamp on it provided the only light in the room. The bulb in it was old; the light was dim. There was a boy sitting on the bed.

James recognized him instantly. He was looking at his father. Jimmie was older than the last time James had visited him in a dream. His chest was bare and James could see patchy hair sprouting on his pecks. He actually had pecks. The baby fat was starting to burn off, revealing some muscle development. James smiled at the thought of his father working out with older high school guys, trying to buff up. He had done the same thing himself when he was fourteen. His mother thought all the weightlifting would stunt his growth. James remembered his Dad's face the day he saw his son posing in front of the mirror in his bedroom. James was standing in his room trying out amateur poses to show off his physique. As he admired himself, he caught a glimpse of his father's reflection standing in the doorway. It startled him. He hadn't heard his father walking in the hallway, hadn't known he was there. James was instantly embarrassed. He turned around to face his father, dropping all of the attitude he had developed while performing for his audience of one, and saw the look of pride on his father's face. James remembered stumbling over his words.

"I was just—you know," he had started, folding his arms self-consciously across his burgeoning chest, "just goofing around."

A smile crossed Jimmie's lips as he nodded. He took in the sight of his young man a second longer before saying, "Keep up the good work, son."

He left the room as quietly as he had come. James hadn't thought about that day in years. It took the edge off the situation he was in for a moment. Until his eyes focused again upon the specter from the past that was his father in his bedroom.

Jimmie was not only shirtless, he was completely naked. His

legs were swung over the side of the bed, his feet planted flat on the floor. His legs were spread apart and he was reclined on his elbows. His head was turned toward the headboard. James tried to focus on his father's head, waiting for it to turn toward him, trying to avoid looking at his father's erect phallus. James felt oddly voyeuristic, peeping-tomish. He tried to shut his eyes, not wanting to intrude on his father's privacy. But he knew he had to. He was powerless to move anyway, his body was paralyzed as it had been several times before, his feet set in place as though cast in stone.

Jimmie was running his left index finger along the very grooves that his son had touched moments before in another dimension. James could see Jimmie's penis throb with every stroke of the headboard.

Jimmie turned to his left while reclined, his member moving stiffly over his pubic hair and abdomen. He picked up the phone on the nightstand and dialed quickly. After a couple of seconds James heard Jimmie's side of the conversation,

"Hi Mrs. Stewart, it's Jimmie. May I speak to Ken?"

Jimmie laid all the way down, flattening his back on the mattress, while he talked with Ken's mother. He was the epitome of courtesy, all of his manners in place, as he made small talk with the woman, all the while stroking himself playfully, letting himself revel in the delicate sweetness of her voice.

When Ken got on the phone Jimmie's hand fell away from his penis and he leaned upon his elbow, propping himself up. He turned again to the headboard and said in a hushed tone,

"Yeah man, I'm getting ready to do it now."

Pause.

"I am! Cool out. Maybe you'll get her tomorrow night."

Pause. James tried to piece together the conversation.

"No, she's here now!"

Another pause. Ken was probably asking how he could have a girl in the house while his mother was home.

"Mom's asleep. She doesn't know about it," Jimmie said, his voice just above a whisper.

Yeah right, Ken might have said, not believing Jimmie's story.

"I'm telling you, she's here with me now. She is so foxy. I wish you could see her now." Jimmie waited a beat, drawing it out. "So," he continued, "how many do you have now?"

Pause. It was a game, then. The notches on the headboard were supposed to tick off sexual encounters. James doubted the tally was supposed to include masturbation, but as he cast his eyes around the room, looking for signs of a female's presence and finding none, he knew his father thought it was fair game. James had counted thirty-one tick marks on the headboard before he fell back in time. He wondered how many of the encounters included a girl.

"Really?"

Another pause. James almost couldn't conceal his laughter.

"Me? I only have thirteen, but that's because I was sick last week. I took a break. You know," he said, chuckling cockily, "I didn't want to get any of my girls sick."

James could almost hear the laughter coming through the receiver.

Jimmie laughed at something that Ken said. He looked down at his penis and noticed that it was losing some of its rigidity. He stroked it slowly, up and down, keeping it primed.

"Okay, I gotta go. I can't keep her waiting too much longer."

Jimmie smiled a toothy grin, said goodbye, and hung up, reaching across his body to place the receiver back on its cradle. His right hand found his penis quickly, even before his left hand had released the phone. It was warming the organ up, preparing it for the show.

Jimmie sat up, his right hand moving up and down the shaft in rhythmic motion. He stayed that way for a while, the sensation rising in him with every stroke. He lifted his head and closed his eyes, allowing his body to enjoy the feeling, the mounting lust. He kept his mind clear, focusing only on the feeling. She would soon come to him when he needed her, he was sure of that. His hips gyrated against his hand as he went, matching the rhythm, dancing within it. His toes pointed and flexed against the hardwood floor.

James stood watching, wanting to turn away but unable to, as his father approached climax. Jimmie was engulfed, swaying off balance as he stroked harder and harder. Then, all of a sudden, he stopped. Jimmie opened his eyes slowly and looked at the door to his bedroom. At James.

James' eyes widened in horror as his father stared right at him. He felt vulnerable, naked standing in the doorway under his scrutinizing eyes. Jimmie watched as the paralysis that had encompassed James, had forced him to stand in the doorway eavesdropping on his father, lifted. James took three awkward steps back from the door, trying to escape his father's stare. He hit the wall behind him hard, stopping him in his tracks. He tried to move, to pull himself away from his father's impossible gaze, but the paralysis had returned. Jimmie watched as James struggled against the wall, but it wasn't James that he saw. James' movements were nothing more than a play of light on the hallway wall as far as Jimmie was concerned. James was invisible to him.

Light poured into the hallway from a room at the other end. A shadow darkened the floor and part of the wall, increasing in size as something approached. Jimmie saw the shadow dancing on the wall outside his door. A smile crossed his lips as he conjured up the image of his woman, the one he had been waiting for. His Clara Belle.

James stood in the hallway with his back pressed against the wall. He noticed the shadow growing on the floor in front of him and turned his head to the light at the end of the hallway.

His grandmother came down the hallway, her footfalls echoing behind her as her weight coaxed a whine from the floorboards. Her light blue nightgown shimmied around her ankles as she moved.

James could see the outline of her body framed and backlit from the light down the hall. There were no breaks in form as her thigh met with her hip or as her hip met with the flare of her waist. She was naked beneath the gown. James' eyes lingered on the shape of her breasts, their roundness distorting the line of her silhouetted body prettily. He was horrified at the feeling stirring in his loins.

Her face was soft and flushed. Wisps of hair fell into her face and out of the barrette that pulled the bulk of her hair up. Her lips were parted and moist. She wore a gloss on them, making her lips appear rosy and lush in the dim light.

Her hips twisted slightly under the gown, her femininity exuding as she glided towards her son's open door. She walked on the balls of her feet, her toes peeking out from beneath the gown with every step. Her approach was slow but purposeful, each footfall in front of the other, moving forward concisely. When she passed him, James could smell a hint of jasmine in the air. He was amazed at the difference in her this night as compared to his other visits. Her face was calm and she looked relaxed. She was radiant and she was aroused.

James watched as his grandmother stopped at the mouth of the door and looked in at her disrobed son. She pressed herself against the doorframe so that only half of her body was visible in the room. She stayed in the shadows while she watched.

Jimmie held his member and stared back at the woman in the doorway, seeing the face of his aunt, the woman who touched him in his dreams, spilling his seed on the sheets of his bed almost every night. She was beautiful, sensual in the satin and lace negligee she wore. It covered her body from breast to ankle, clinging to her curves as she stood. The spaghetti strap on her left shoulder had fallen off, giving him the tantalizing view of her unmarked skin. Her breasts were stimulated; the nipples were erect and pushing points into the satin gown. A split rimmed with white lace, ran from the bottom of the gown up to her hip, revealing the tiniest sliver of skin at the peak. She was nude underneath, Jimmie could see, the knowledge sending tremors through his phallus. He could see the outline of her womanhood teasing him from behind its satin shield.

Jimmie brought himself to climax looking at his Clara Belle standing in the doorway of his bedroom as he would many times after that, even after he was married with a son. When he was spent, he wiped the sweat from his brow and closed his eyes. James stood watching in horror as his grandmother turned and walked back to the light of her bedroom, satisfied. He watched her as she walked down the hallway, leaving as slowly as she had come, the creaking of the floorboards growing fainter. She entered her bedroom and closed the door. Seconds later, her light was turned off.

When James turned back to his father's bedroom, he saw Jimmie's body mounting the bed on his knees. He had gone to the desk and gotten a pocketknife. He used it to cut the next notch in his headboard.

Number fourteen.

CHAPTER 59

James was standing in the hallway staring into the empty bedroom. Sweat coated his face and his hands were pressed against the wall behind him. He blinked, the remnants of the hallucination still standing in his eyes. He tried to get his breathing under control as he looked around. The hallway was dark again and his vision was unable to penetrate the darkness that seemed to reach out to him from the other end. The hallway was like a black hole in front of him, abysmal and ominous. His skin crawled at the thought of what might be lurking there, watching him.

The bedroom was dark as well, only the light from the window in the hallway shone in the room. It was different somehow. Tiny particles seemed to float in the air, like dust. There was tension in the air; he could feel the electricity on his arms as he had before. James blinked, trying to clear his vision, but the granular texture remained, like static on a television screen. It was almost palpable; he could feel the weight of the air on his skin.

James remained pinned to the wall outside his father's bedroom. He was drained, shaken, terrified. He felt like he'd run miles under the hottest of suns without water to drink. He felt winded and tired. A dull pain throbbed in his right elbow and knee. He tried to straighten out his elbow but a sharp pain shot through it, stopping him almost immediately. He held it bent at his side waiting for the needle of pain coursing through his elbow, up to his shoulder and down to his wrist, to subside. He shifted his weight onto his left leg to ease the pressure on his knee. It felt weak, unable to hold his weight. He didn't remember what had happened to him, how he had gotten the injuries. He looked into the bedroom again looking for a clue. For a moment the bedroom was as it was in his vision, the room obviously that of a teenage boy. Jimmie sat on the bed staring at him.

James recoiled wildly, banging his elbow on the unyielding wall. The pain was white, like lightening. James shut his eyes momentarily against it, coddling his arm as it pulsed. He opened his eyes fast, his eyelids fluttering up like wayward shades, and took a blind step to the side on instinct. The darkness seemed thicker, more formidable than before. He noticed as he moved further away from the light that came in from the hallway window. His knee didn't cooperate. It buckled underneath him and he stumbled, almost falling to the floor. James caught himself with his good arm and scrambled forward, trying to move away from the haunted room. He felt as though he were wading in molasses, his limbs were useless to him in the darkness that had taken physical form around him. He couldn't move. He stood with some effort but couldn't move in any direction. It was like an invisible brace had locked him in place.

James looked back into the bedroom, dreading the new horrors that awaited him. He squinted his eyes to temper it. There was nothing there. The room was empty again. Dormant. Innocent almost, denying everything that it had shown him before.

He laughed out loud, the sound echoing off the walls, as his frayed sanity unraveled with every breath of air. He was delusional. Fine. All of it was in his mind. James was willing to accept that.

Once the dreams started, once they really got going, he knew it was the beginning of the end. He knew he was going crazy. He just couldn't accept it. But now it was undeniable. He was too far gone to try to sugarcoat what was happening to him. He was sick. He had to be. Would a sane man have visions of the dead that were so real, he could almost touch them?

James looked back to the room where his father had spent his teenage years. The empty bed frame, the bare desk, the very walls seemed to be laughing at him.

James got angry. The visions had traumatized him. They had been beating him down for the past few months, but he thought it would be over now. He had given in. They had won. No matter how hard he tried to fight it all his life—to cover it with education, a beautiful wife, a successful career—it never went away. He was his father's son. He knew that, had accepted it as truth. James knew what he had done and knew he had to pay for it in blood.

The demons still surrounded him, though. He could feel their presence even then, standing in the darkness, hidden in the shadows. Waiting.

James took a step toward his father's bedroom and then stopped. He turned his head and peered into the darkness. He saw the faintest light coming from the end of the hallway where there hadn't been one before. He was frozen with fear. For the first time since he had left his home in Monsey, he wanted to return. He wanted to run out of that house, drive back home, and go to his wife. Things were different now, he knew, and he could never go back, but he couldn't stop the thought from springing into his mind.

Susan's face, her smile, enchanting him as she lay on top of him, flooded James' mind. In spite of his fear, he felt aroused by the memory of her body as she pressed against him. He squeezed his eyes shut, willing his mind to stop dredging up memories of Susan, wanting to avoid seeing his imagination's image of her face in death. Nothing more came to him. His mind faded the image to black. He opened his eyes and sighed, relieved that he was spared the visage that time.

His thoughts drifted to Andrea. How would she react to all of this? James hoped that she would never find out about Susan. He didn't think Pete would tell her. He wouldn't want to hurt her. She never needed to know about the affair. It would be malicious of Pete to tell her after it was over, just for effect. James cringed, remembering his own confession to Pete. He hadn't known that Pete knew and he confessed just to relieve his own guilt, just to make the dreams stop. His selfishness left him cold. James wondered if he had ever considered how Pete would feel. He didn't know. He could only hope that Pete would decide not to tell Andrea after it was all over, that he would choose to spare her the pain and indignity that he had faced. James didn't doubt that Pete would take care of her in the end, he just didn't know if Pete could keep the affair a secret once James was linked to the murders.

James had tried to think of ways to shield Andrea from the truth. He didn't want her to be traumatized by the knowledge that her husband, the man she trusted with her life, had murdered two women. It would change her, he knew. She would be guarded, jumpy, distant. She wouldn't feel comfortable with people; she'd be unwilling to let her guard down. Andrea would lose faith in her ability to judge character. She wouldn't trust people the way she had in the past. She was such a carefree person, so happy, so trusting, so genuine. James could see all of that changing if she knew that the man with whom she had shared her bed was a murderer.

Andrea would feel betrayed and rightfully so. She'd feel guilty, like she could have saved the women if only she had known what was happening with James. But there was no way she could have known. James didn't know it was happening himself.

Andrea would feel vulnerable. James couldn't allow that to happen. Not because of him.

James was thinking of writing two notes—one to Andrea and one to Pete. He would apologize to Pete for everything he had done to him. He would plead with him to help Andrea through the trying times ahead. He would confess everything in that letter—Susan and Carmen's murders, and the concerns he'd had for the potential of future bloodshed by his hands. He would ask Pete to keep Andrea away from it all, if he could. James knew Pete would do what he could. Pete loved Andrea as a friend, if not more than that. James had always known that too.

Pete had a thing for Andrea. They had never talked about it, of course, and it probably wasn't anything more than Pete enjoying the look of Andrea's body. James had always known there was more than an innocent friendship between them, at least on Pete's side. He wasn't obvious or disrespectful, but James had noticed just the same. Pete's eyes might linger a little longer than they should, especially when he's looking at his best friend's wife, but then again, any man's eyes would. Andrea was a beautiful, sensuous woman without even trying to be. That was part of her charm. She was unaware of how attractive she was, how enticing. It was alluring. James didn't blame Pete for staring at her every once in a while. He took it as a compliment.

It was unreciprocated, at least as much as James could see. Andrea was as oblivious to Pete's roaming eyes as she was to James and Susan's affair. She trusted people to a fault. The thought would never have entered her mind that Pete might be checking her out. She took things at face value. Maybe that's what had made everything so easy.

Pete was harmless in the long run, James thought. He would never have tried anything with Andrea. She was just eye candy to him. And he knew what he had at home. Or thought he had.

Remorse devoured James as his mind chronicled the events that had led up to that point, him standing alone in an abandoned house visiting with the ghosts of his ancestors. His eyes watered as he staggered to the wall. James pressed his shoulder against it and took deep breaths as the memories accosted him. He saw Susan burning in her car, perishing, with his baby, in flames; a demise that he had orchestrated. He saw Carmen, an innocent bystander to his love triangle, but dead, nonetheless, by his hand. He had killed them in cold blood. He was a murderer. No measure of sadness, no matter how many tears he shed for them would bring them back. He could only make a sacrifice for them, spill fresh blood for what they lost.

James' thoughts drifted to his father. They had a sick kinship now, the realization making his stomach turn. James had killed as his father had. Susan and Karen, victims of their lovers' anger, their blood on their lovers' hands. Soon they would share another deed, their hands meshing closer together, bound by blood. What better place to finish it than the house where the evil was nurtured. It would be a fitting end to a depraved legacy.

James took a deep breath then let it out slowly, shutting his eyes as he did so. Karen's misshapen head appeared in his mind, her frightening countenance almost transparent. She beckoned him to come to her. He almost laughed out loud. He had his own ghosts to haunt him now. He didn't need her anymore.

The light was growing stronger at the other end of the hall, the bone beam casting a longer ray along the floor than it had before. She was calling him.

Out of the corner of his eye, James saw his father watching him as he hobbled toward the bedroom at the end of the hallway. A bloody smile radiated from Jimmie's pubescent face.

CHAPTER 60

Pete and Andrea sped down the highway, having crossed the Delaware Memorial Bridge hours before. They were fast approaching Baltimore. Andrea had stopped crying but hadn't been talking much. Pete turned on the radio to give him something to focus on other than the never-ending road.

After hours of silence, Andrea looked at Pete and said,

"Why is this happening, Pete? What is going on with James?"

"I don't know," Pete said, his voice scratchy from disuse.

"Yes, you do. You know something. I know you do."

Pete looked at Andrea quickly and said,

"How could I? He hasn't told me anything. This just came out of nowhere."

"You know something more," Andrea said, her voice thick with sarcasm.

"I don't, Andrea," Pete said reassuringly. "I'm in the same boat you are."

"Really? Then what happened between you two?" she asked, her voice gaining resolve. "A couple of days ago James came home with a swollen jaw. He told me that you did it. What would make you hit him like that?" She stared imploringly at Pete, watching his every move.

Pete measured the question and hesitated before responding, being sure to keep his face emotionless. He knew she would ask at some point. He was hoping that she would forget about it with everything that was going on with James, but he knew better. Pete's lip twitched imperceptibly. He had to answer her carefully, with as much truth and sincerity as he could risk, but saying absolutely nothing that touched on the core of things. This could go downhill quickly.

"He didn't say anything to you?" Pete asked.

"No. Something distracted us and we never got back to it."

Pete sighed, feigning humiliation. He paused, dragging the silence out as long as he could. Andrea's eyes never left his face.

"It's embarrassing. I wish it had never happened," Pete started slowly. "He came by that day while I was mowing the lawn. We went into the house to get something to drink."

He paused for effect.

"He looked like he was hiding something, you know? Like something was bothering him that he didn't want to talk about. I – God, Andrea, I wish this wasn't true. I wish I hadn't felt the way I did."

He looked away from the road for a second and glanced out of the driver's side window, trying to look pensive. He could see Andrea's face illuminated by the neon green light of his dashboard. Her whole body was turned in the seat, her right shoulder leaning forward, like she was preparing to touch him. Within seconds he felt the warmth of her hand on his arm. Her face was full of concern, no longer tainted with accusation and blame, as it had been only moments before. She had taken the bait.

Pete turned his head back to the road. His left elbow was propped up on the door, his hand covering his mouth. Andrea's hand rubbed circles on his shoulder. She nudged him lightly, encouraging him to continue.

"I – I was jealous of him, Andrea," he said through the slits between his fingers. "Here he was, probably about to confide in me about the dreams, and I was too blind with jealousy to listen. I let him down."

Pete's voice broke as he sobbed dryly. He leaned his head to the window and cupped his forehead with his hand.

Andrea inched as close as the seatbelt would allow and put her arm around Pete's shoulder. She knew all too well how Pete was feeling.

"You didn't let him down, Pete. Don't think that way," she said, her voice taking on a soft, comforting tone.

"Yes, I did. You should have seen him, Andrea. He wanted to talk to me, hang out like old times. I know he would have told me what was happening after a while. But I didn't let that happen."

She rubbed his shoulders as he talked.

"What happened?"

"I was upset. Almost from the moment I saw him, I was upset. When I saw that there was something wrong with him, I was enraged. I mean, here's the guy who still has his life intact. His wife is alive. He still gets to wake up every morning next to her, see her smile at him when he comes home from work. It seemed like James didn't know what he had, didn't respect it. I mean, didn't he get it? Everything is different for me because my wife is dead. My wife is dead."

Real tears stung his eyes as he spoke those words. He stole a glance at Andrea. She looked as if she was about to cry also.

"So, I laid into him. I told him to act like a man. To deal with whatever it was, suck it up. I told him he was weak, that he didn't deserve to have everything he had if he couldn't show some backbone. Andrea, he hadn't even said anything to me. We hadn't gotten past 'Hey, how are you doing?'. But that was enough. I was infuriated at the question, the gall he had to even ask it. It set me off. I know it was irrational, but it did.

"I told him to leave," Pete continued. "I told him to go home and fuck his wife—I'm sorry, Andrea. I was just so angry at him."

Andrea nodded her head understandingly. She didn't say a word.

"He was as shocked as anyone would be. He just stood there looking at me, trying to figure out where all the rage was coming from. That burned me up even more. What I saw in his eyes was pity, not confusion. To me, the look in his eyes was invidious, smug even. At that moment, I hated him."

Andrea recoiled slightly, taken aback by his words, amazed that he was vocalizing the same emotion that she dared not say.

"My anger was welling up inside me so fast, I thought I would burst if I didn't do something with it," Pete said. "It was more than I could take."

Pete stopped there, spent. Andrea sat quietly as Pete breathed in deeply. She asked,

"Is that when you hit him?"

Pete nodded. Andrea continued to rub his shoulders as he told her,

"Yeah. He didn't even see it coming. I just swung. I didn't even know I was going to do it until I did it. Everything just happened so fast. I remember seeing him look at me with disbelief in his eyes. He looked hurt, more wounded emotionally than any punch could ever affect him physically. Even then, I wanted to say something, wanted to apologize for being such a jerk. I wanted to tell him how much I was hurting, that I was blind with grief, that I didn't mean any of it. But I didn't. I just stared at him, wanting what he had.

"James didn't say a thing. He didn't hit me back even though I deserved it. He didn't try to apologize. He just stood there. I couldn't stand the look in his eyes, even while I was upset like that. I'm sure I thought it was patronizing, then, but now I know that his eyes only showed his pain. I turned my back on him and walked into the kitchen. I told him to get out. When I came out, he was gone."

Pete took another deep breath and released it slowly. Andrea settled back into her seat and looked out at the road ahead.

"I'm sorry you had to hear that, Andrea. I'm sorry that it happened at all."

"No, Pete. I asked you, remember?"

He nodded.

"I'm so sorry I did that to him. I knew I was wrong when it was happening, but I couldn't stop. I wasn't really mad at him. I wasn't mad at anyone. I just missed Susan. He was only looking for a friend that day and I took out my frustrations on him. I've never hit anyone like that before, you know, unprovoked. I can't believe I did that to him."

"How long was he at your place?" Andrea asked.

"No more than twenty minutes. He got there about noon, I guess."

"He didn't come home until later that night. Like 8:30."

Pete sat silent for a moment letting Andrea stew on the thought. He didn't know where James had gone and didn't care. He was just happy that he was able to pull the story he had just unraveled for Andrea out of the air. It was a masterpiece, if he said so himself. He could barely conceal his amused smile.

"Where could he have been all day?"

"I don't know," Pete said, resuming his dejected tone. "Maybe he just rode around, trying to sort out what had just happened. Along with everything else, I'm sure it threw him for a loop."

Andrea didn't look convinced.

"You know how James is, Andrea. He likes to be alone when things are running around in his head. He likes to sort things out on his own. I'm sure that's what he was doing."

"I guess you're right," Andrea said.

Pete sighed. "God, I wish I had apologized to him. I wanted to. But that was the last time I saw him when he was acting... normal. I was going to do it that Monday we had off, but then he fell..." Pete's voice trailed off and ended in a sigh. "I just feel so goddamned awful about it," he continued. "He's my best friend. He didn't deserve that from me."

Pete almost snickered at his last line, the irony almost comical. *Laying it on thick, aren't you,* his subconscious chirped jokingly. He suppressed the laugh rising in his throat by clearing his voice, his face becoming solemn once again.

"It doesn't look like either one of us have been exactly supportive to James when he needed us," Andrea said, dolefully.

"What are you talking about? You've been there every step of the way, trying to help him through this. You couldn't have done anything more."

"That's where you're wrong, Pete." Andrea turned her head and looked out of the window. "That's where you are wrong."

Her shoulders slouched in the seat and her head lolled against the headrest. She still faced away from him, peering out into the darkness. Pete could tell that Andrea had said all that she planned to say about it. He wondered what she was thinking but decided to leave well enough alone. He had gotten away clean. He decided to let the conversation drop while he still could.

"We're coming up on Silver Spring," Pete said after thirty minutes of silence. "We should be there soon."

Andrea nodded, still looking out of the window, her arm draped protectively over her stomach. She was dealing with some demons of her own.

CHAPTER 61

James approached the bedroom after what seemed like hours of trudging down the hallway, favoring his bad knee. The light was dim but it filled the hallway; shadows of elongated lamps and picture frames created a ghostly scene as he made his way to the door. He hesitated when he reached the break in the wall, the open mouth of the doorway seeming to call to him. He was apprehensive, but knew he had to continue. He had to go inside.

James took a deep breath and looked around the side of the door timidly. The room was cluttered with furniture and papers; seemingly every space on the floor was covered. An old black and white television set sat on a metal stand at the foot of the bed. James stepped in the doorway to get a better view.

The dresser sat off to the right. It was filled with old-fashioned perfume bottles, the colorful bottles half-filled with fragrances, lipstick tubes and compacts. Fake eyelashes protruded from under an ancient issue of *Time* magazine, like the legs of a tarantula.

The drapes that hung on the window opposite the bed were dirty. The cream-colored sheers were turning a grimy shade of yellow, and the pink, mint, and tan floral pattern on the drapes themselves had been faded by the sun. A pile of shoes was stacked up in a corner. Pumps and flats in wine, navy, taupe, and even a pair that were cherry apple red were thrown there without regard to damaging the leather or the heels. Empty pots of long dead flowers propped up by phone books sat on television trays in front of the window. There were enough pots that when all of the plants were alive, they would have blocked out any natural light that could have seeped into the room.

An abstract picture hung lopsidedly on the wall. Bright red, yellow, cobalt, and green formed a jagged star on a midnight blue background. The texture of the painting looked almost like it could have been velvet. A well-worn chair sat between the bed and a closed door. Next to it sat a small bistro table covered with a round lace tablecloth. A small, shaded lamp sat on top of the table, as well as a rotary telephone. The lamp, its shade nothing more than a scalloped bell done in light brown craft paper, mesmerized James. There was nothing special about the base either. Its metal shaft was unadorned before it met with a circular base at the bottom. It was the light itself that intrigued him, its rays seeming to move as it broke through the darkness. They seemed to shimmer, the way the air above hot asphalt does during the hottest days of the summer. The light moved like there was something underneath its calm veneer, hot and anxious, threatening to boil over.

James pulled his eyes away from the light and regarded the newspapers and magazines that littered the floor around the table, keeping the clothes and panty hose that laid on the floor in mounds company. A rug, barely visible under the clutter, covered the hardwood floor around the bed. The sliver that peaked through was a dingy shade of tan.

A nightstand sat alongside the bed, covered with picture frames that were coated with a thin layer of dust. The side of the bed that James could see was spread with a tattered knit covering.

It looked old and handmade. It would have been a precious heirloom had it been taken care of. He was looking at the bed covering when the shadow of a woman spread across it.

The shadow caught him off guard. He jumped when he saw it and tried to take a step backwards, but his knee protested. James looked up slowly at the woman casting the shadow.

His grandmother stood in front of the bed taking off her robe. She faced the television as she did it and let out a cynical chuckle.

"Cheap set. Never has been worth a damn," she said as she walked over to the television. It was only then that James realized he could hear the static from the television. He didn't remember the set being on when he came into the room.

Lillian tapped the television on the side, lightly at first and then harder until the frame that it sat on weaved back and forth. The robe she had been taking off fell in a bunch around her wrists. She let the garment fall to the floor as she yanked the antennas left and right, back and forth. She sucked her teeth in disgust when the television didn't respond to her doctoring. Its monotonous *Shhh-hhhh* was deafening.

Lillian turned to the bed. Her face was frowned in annoyance but it was mild. She was dressed in the same light blue nightgown James saw her in on the other side of the hallway, in front of his father's bedroom. Her hair was loose—it fell just above her shoulders. In the dim light, James could see the beauty she once possessed. Her face was softer, her skin wasn't creased into the frown that she had worn when he first encountered her.

Lillian climbed onto the king-sized bed from its foot and crawled up to her pillows. She nestled into the covers, pulling them up around her stomach. She rolled to the left side of the bed and out of James' view. He took a step into the room to get a better view of his grandmother. He was almost all the way in the room now. The doorframe was a half-step behind him. Lillian was leaning over the side of the bed, her arm reaching underneath it. She giggled when she found what she was looking for. She sat upright in bed. She regarded the half empty bottle of Jack Daniels for a moment before she uncapped it and took a drink. The first gulp was deep and full, followed quickly by three smaller sips. She wasn't pacing herself. She was trying to get drunk.

She finished the bottle off quickly. She held the empty bottle in her right hand, her fingers curled around the neck of the bottle like a child's hand would curl around their parent's finger. She slid off the side of the bed closest to the bedroom door and stood unsteadily, swaying and leaning. James could smell the alcohol on Lillian's breath as she staggered forward towards the dresser. The smell lingered even after she had moved away, sending goose bumps down James' arms.

Lillian put her hands on the top of the dresser hard, knocking some of her perfume bottles to the floor. One of them broke on the rug, the smell of Chanel No.5 wafting into the air. The mixed smells of perfume and alcohol were nauseating.

Lillian saw the broken bottle on the ground and let out a high-pitched laugh, so piercing James wanted to cover his ears. He tried to raise his hands but found that they were pinned to his sides by the same force that had held him outside his father's door, rendering him defenseless to the shrill sound. The laughter went on for a long time, her voice rising to excruciatingly high pitches, using all of the air in her lungs until she was gasping for a fresh breath. And then she started all over again.

After her second outburst, her emotions changed drastically. She began to cry as she looked at the shards of glass scattered on the rug. Her tears were heavy, falling in big drops onto her night-gown. Deep, guttural sounds emitted from her as she sucked in air and let it out in raspy, mournful moans. The sound tugged at James' heart. His grandmother was in immense pain.

Lillian crouched to the floor mumbling incoherently through her sobs. She picked up a couple of the larger slivers of glass, piling them up in her hand. One of the shard's jagged edges caught the skin on the inside of her middle finger, slicing it open. Crimson blood oozed out of the wound, which was, apparently, deeper than it looked. Lillian shrieked and brought her finger to her mouth, trying to soothe the open wound with the warmth of her tongue. It continued to bleed, though, and the sight of her blood on the rug sent her into a rage.

She slammed the shards of glass she was holding to the floor, shattering them against the waxed hardwood. She rose to her feet, putting a hand on the dresser to steady herself. She knocked over more bottles and makeup as she leaned against the cluttered dresser. Lillian stepped over the broken glass as best as she could, clearing most of it in the first leap. A piece of glass splintered her heel, but she walked forward anyway, mashing the shard deeper into her foot.

James watched in horror as his grandmother walked toward him, trying to leave the room. Her face was contorted in a mixture of anger and pain. Sweat beads danced on her forehead, some dripping down into her eyes and cheeks, others pooling together to gain an advantage on the top of her head. Her eyes were cloudy, veiled. Her nostrils flared. Her shoulders were hunched, her relaxed appearance from before was long gone. She gripped the neck of the Jack Daniels bottle tightly as if she planned to brain something or someone with it. An irrational wave of fear cooled his veins like ice as he realized he was standing between her and the doorway. He tried to move to the right, to the left, to back up, but nothing worked. He felt his breathing increase rapidly as Lillian came closer still, the look on her face determined, unfaltering.

A faint sound rose from the bottom of James' throat as he awaited the clash. She couldn't see him, he was sure of that, but he could see her as plain as day. He didn't have time to think about what would happen when his physical body met with what he could only assume was a spiritual manifestation. He didn't have time to wonder what it would feel like, if he would feel anything, when his grandmother bumped into him head on. Before they collided, he could only muse at the oddness of the situation. His grandmother, a woman whom he had never met, was about to crash head first into her grandson in a time that was decades after her death, in a room that, although seemingly filled with furniture and things, was empty.

James braced himself instinctively and shut his eyes. He felt a cool, tingly sensation penetrating the skin of his chest and stomach. Like cool water, the sensation ran from the front of his body to the back fluidly. It was a pleasant feeling. It lulled him as he reveled in the new sensations he felt. He relaxed into them, like laying back into a plush pillow.

For a moment they were one, combined completely.

James could feel her within him, her essence rippling underneath his skin. He wondered distantly what she might be feeling as their bodies were entwined. Could her spirit *feel* him?

He could taste the liquor on her lips, could feel its warmth in the center of his chest, as though he had ingested it himself. He could feel the sweat that dotted Lillian's head on his own, dripping down the sides of his face and wetting his hairline.

James could feel her anger, pure and unfocused. His mind was cluttered with a mingling of her thoughts and his. Hers were incoherent, just little blurbs and pictures that didn't make sense to James. He could make out the face of a woman, dressed in a white blouse and a red and white polka dotted flair skirt. The woman had on red lipstick and wore a red wide-brimmed hat. She was glamorous; the image in Lillian's mind resembling an advertisement of some sort rather than a snapshot of some random occurrence. On top of the image in delicate cursive handwriting was scrawled the word *bitch*. The letters were dark red. They were stretched out across the image, the top of the 't' overlapping the mouth of the woman.

The only other image that James could make out with any clarity was that of a dark room. It was small and empty. The walls were brick and unadorned. There were no windows and there was one light in the room, bare and mounted in the wall closest to the door. The bulb was broken in the socket.

He could feel the cut on Lillian's finger, the trickle of the blood as it ran down to the tip, pooled in the nail, and then dropped to the floor. The glass shard in her heel was nothing more than a tickle to James, but he was aware of it. The feeling in his hand wasn't as painful as it was warm, almost feverish. He could feel heat rising from the cut, mixing with his natural body temperature, changing it. Before long, his own finger became warm; he could feel the heat rising separately from hers. His hand soon followed, then his arm. Her heat—her blood—was becoming a part of him. The warmth climbed through his body rapidly, obliterating the cool that Lillian had brought with her. She was coursing through his body, claiming it.

James stepped forward as the heat ran down his legs and through his chest, frightened by what the feeling might mean. His body moved forward, freed from the force that had bound it before. He felt Lillian detach from him, her face coming out through the back of his head, just as she had entered from the front. The feverish sensation dissipated as she left his body, his temperature stabilizing. James turned to look at her; only one step stood between them now.

An audible crunch sounded as his heel crushed a piece of glass into the floor beneath it.

CHAPTER 62

Lillian was looking at the doorway when the sound of the glass breaking chimed. The crack of the glass was magnified; it drowned out the sound of the snowy television. She stopped walking and stood still, listening.

James lifted his shoe off the floor and looked at the glass beneath it, smashed into tiny pieces, some as fine as grains of sand. He panicked. He had thought it was an illusion, a hallucination that he was watching, not something he was participating in. His mind corrected him quickly. All bets were off now. He was too far gone.

Lillian turned to face James, her countenance fading for a second, and then sharpening into focus. The static was visible on the television screen, but the sound was gone now, as though someone had turned the set's volume down to zero. The house was eerily silent.

James met his grandmother's gaze as evenly as he could, but that was a difficult task. He clinched his teeth, pressing them together in an effort to keep his mouth closed. He fought to make himself keep his head up and face her.

A hellish grin spread across Lillian's face as she regarded her grandson for the second time in her supernatural existence. James had the odd sensation of needing to relieve himself as she looked at him. James fidgeted against his will, his bladder pressing fiercely against his pelvis.

Lillian's eyes took him in and after a moment, she said, "Back again, James?"

James tried to respond, but nothing came out of his mouth. Lillian laughed. This time the sound was filled with contempt.

"How can you see me?" James was finally able to muster. "How can we be talking to each other?"

Lillian laughed again, shaking her head slowly. James stared at her in amazement. He couldn't believe he was participating in his waking dream.

Lillian stopped laughing and looked at James again. His face was full of wonder and confusion, underlined with fear. She snickered sarcastically,

"Give me a break. Wipe that deer in the headlights look off your face. I don't buy it."

James recoiled a little, not knowing what to do. He couldn't believe his ears.

Lillian looked closer this time, stepping forward. James took a step backward, stepping on more of the glass as he retreated from her. He cringed at the sound of it cracking underneath the soles of his shoes.

"You mean you really don't know?" Lillian asked incredulously. "You really don't know what's happening to you? It's been going on long enough. You'd think you would have gotten a clue by now."

She sucked her teeth before turning back to the door.

"God, you're even dumber than your father. Jimmie didn't get it for the longest time either. We had to show him what to do just like we'll have to show you."

"What are you talking about?" James asked, fear beginning to rise within him.

"I thought you had caught on. You sure acted like it when you got here. But now, I'm not so sure you know what you're here to do."

"You saw me come into the house?"

"I felt you in the house. I knew you were coming here before you did. Where else could you go?"

Lillian started walking towards the bedroom door. James felt what little sanity he had left leaving with her.

"Wait a minute. I need to understand what you are talking about. What are you going to do to me?" James asked, feeling desperate.

Lillian stopped walking and turned back to James. She walked back to him, reaching him quicker than she should have been able to, and looked into his eyes. Even though she was close enough for him to smell the liquor on her breath, he smelled nothing. He should have been able to feel the warmth of her breath on his face when she spoke, but he didn't feel that either.

"Don't you know where you are?" Lillian asked, her voice grave and serious. "This is your destiny. This place is where you chose to fulfill it. We're here to make sure that things go the way they are supposed to. None of us ever does it alone, didn't you know that?"

James stood looking at his grandmother in confusion. He wanted to touch her to see what she felt like. To know if she was real or not. *And that's the problem, isn't it?* James thought ruefully to himself. *She's dead, yet I wonder if she's alive in front of me.*

"Don't fret over that, boy," Lillian said as if she had read James' mind. "You're not crazy. None of us ever were. We just see." Lillian allowed a smile to cross her lips before she continued, "Come with me, now. I'll show you what to do."

Lillian walked out of the bedroom and James followed her, helpless to do anything else.

CHAPTER 63

Pete got off at the exit heading towards Silver Spring and pulled onto a side street. He turned on the cabin light and pulled the death certificate from his pocket. He compared it to the directions he had printed out and headed east.

He was speeding, he noticed, as he looked down at the speedometer. He was anxious. He didn't feel like this was a normal disappearance, like James was just trying to sort things out in his head. He didn't believe the things he'd said to placate Andrea, he never had. Something else was going on. What it was, he wasn't sure, but he knew that something had made them take the four-hour drive from New York to Maryland. Something had made them go out in the middle of the night in search of a house that matched an address on the death certificate of a woman none of them had ever met, including James. That death certificate was left for them to find. Even if James didn't consciously mean to do it, he had left Pete and Andrea a clue. He wanted them to come. Pete wondered what they would find when they got there.

Andrea had been quiet since before they got to Baltimore. Pete thought she would drift off to sleep, but she didn't. Her breathing had remained steady as she sat in the passenger seat in silence. She kept staring out of the window.

Pete wanted to talk to her, to hear her voice. Maybe that would calm the jitters he felt in his stomach. The fear confused him. Pete had wanted something to happen to James. That had been the whole idea. Once James was out of the way, Pete would make his move on Andrea. His hands were tied until then. He knew Andrea would never have an affair like James and Susan had. Pete didn't know if he could do it either. All of the secretive meetings, stealing moments here and there, the torture of silence when all of them were together, he didn't think he could pull it off.

Pete wanted James to pay for what he had done. They had been best friends—best friends since college, yet James threw that away to sleep with his wife. In Pete's book, James deserved the tortured dreams, deserved to run scared from the cops. He deserved everything he was getting and more. If his nightmares were going to take over and crush his mental capacity, so be it. There was a padded room waiting for him at the sanitarium. If not, Pete was sure the police would outfit him with a suitable cell so he could rot for killing Susan. Either way James was going away and for a long time. He had to. Pete was banking on it. But something in the pit of his stomach told him that he was about to get more than he expected. Much more than he had bargained for.

Pete tried to keep quiet, tried to pull up to the front of the house in silence the way Andrea seemed to want it. But it was hard. His feelings were pressing on the walls of his mind, screaming at him. Something about this was wrong. Very wrong.

Pete finally broke the silence.

"We're almost there. We should be pulling up in front of the house in about ten minutes."

Andrea merely nodded. Pete pressed,

"Are you ready for this, Andrea?"

"What do you mean?" Andrea asked, turning toward Pete. Her

neck was stiff from looking in the same direction for so long. She ran her hand along it, massaging it.

"I mean, we don't know what we're walking into here. We don't know what state of mind James will be in, if he's even there at all."

Andrea sighed. "I know. I was thinking about that. Pete, what if he is despondent? What if he is so far gone, he doesn't know that we're real, and not part of a dream? What if he doesn't know who we are?"

Pete tapped the steering wheel with his thumbs, thinking.

"I don't know what to expect when we get there," Pete said, finally.

Andrea licked her lips and said excitedly,

"Maybe James won't even be there. I mean, we don't know for sure that he came out here. Why would he, anyway? He never knew his grandmother. His father never visited that house after he moved out. He never even talked about his mother, to James or anyone else. Why would he want to go there? We might just be chasing our tails."

"Maybe. But what if he is there? What could he be doing? What state of mind will he be in? What if he's delusional? What if he's violent or suici—."

"Pete no, not James," Andrea cut in, unwilling to hear the words that would inevitably follow.

"I don't know, Andrea. Are you confident about that?"

Andrea breathed in deeply, letting the question hang in the air. Pete continued,

"Maybe you should stay in the car when we get there."

"What? I didn't come all this way just to sit in the car and wait. If James is in there, he needs me. He needs both of us. We can't let him go through this alone anymore."

"I'm not suggesting that you stay outside the whole time, but maybe I should go in first and make sure things are okay. Then I'll come back out and get you."

Andrea thought about what Pete was saying, leaning more towards his side. There was something that Pete wasn't saying.

"What do you think he could be doing?"

Pete shook his head and said,

"I honestly don't know, but if there is anything going on I'd rather it be me that surprises him and not you."

"Surprise him? What do—."

"Andrea, I don't know, but if he came all the way out here, he did it for a reason. I'm sure he doesn't expect us to walk in and disturb his plans. Whatever they are."

Pete and Andrea both quieted at the end of that thought, both minds settling on the same possibility, the same fear.

CHAPTER 64

J ames followed Lillian through the house slowly, his leg and arm throbbing with every step. She moved at a careful pace allowing him to keep up. As they descended the stairs James saw that the rooms were filled with furniture, as they had been when Lillian died.

Lillian's pace slowed as she crossed the living room and stood on the spot where she had taken her last breath. She lingered there for a moment, looking down at the carpet as though regarding her own body lying prone on the floor, lifeless. James could see the pain on her face. She mourned her body, her life on earth. She missed being alive.

Lillian breathed in deeply and exhaled through her nose. She waved a hand at the floor, dismissing the spot where her body had lain dead decades before.

"It's all a memory, James. All meaningless remnants of the past. It'll do you good to remember that."

James said nothing as Lillian started walking again, turning on lights as she made her way through the house.

CHAPTER 65

Pete and Andrea were stopped at the last light in the Silver Spring business district before reaching the residential area while James followed his grandmother through the living room of her house. Pete had a sense of urgency now, the need to get there, and get there quickly, was stronger than ever before.

Andrea was sitting straight in her seat, as anxious as Pete was to get to the house. Images of James curled into a ball in a corner, sitting among forgotten furniture and nesting bugs haunted her, but also left her encouraged. If that was how they found him, her heart would rest easy. They could get him some help and he could fight the disease. Andrea tried to keep thinking positively, to keep thinking there was a way out of it. She would do better, if given the chance. She would do more to help him instead of shrinking back into a corner, allowing herself to fear the man James was becoming and pitying herself for having married a lunatic.

She tried to think of the things she would do differently, but her mind darkened with images of James lying lifeless in the abandoned house, a needle sticking out of his arm or a gunshot wound congealing on the side of his head. She couldn't shake them, no matter how hard she tried. Andrea was afraid that she would never see her husband alive again. The idea of James' death, although frightening, was real to her. She had felt the cold air of death in his office, had smelled it in the room with her, its stench permeating her very pores. She saw it in the eyes of Lillian Boone.

CHAPTER 66

L illian led James down a cavernous stairwell and into the dark basement. Light streamed in from a cracked window that had been boarded as sloppily as the ones upstairs. They were at eye level with the ground outside, barely above ground enough to see blades of browning grass.

Lillian cut through the darkness, weaving through the maze of tables and chairs, bookcases and trunks that had been stored there. She didn't move around tentatively, didn't feel her way around. She knew the house inside and out. James followed closer than he wanted to, trying not to stumble against the obstacles in their path.

Lillian stopped abruptly in the darkness. Her hand hovered over a doorknob that was invisible to James, the light that had illuminated a patch of space before was far behind them now. She stood in silence.

James looked at the woman in front of him. That's what she was to him now. A real woman, not a spirit. He no longer felt as if he was watching a movie with the plot unfolding in front of his eyes. He was a part of it now. He was the main character in this doomed play.

James could see Lillian's hair moving as she walked, the wisps blowing back from her face in the draft. Before, he had known he was looking at an apparition; a spirit conjured up to manifest itself in front of his eyes. But now, it seemed like his dreams, and the dark corners within them, were his reality. They were no longer the imaginings of a sleeping man, but the matter that made up his daily life. The people in them were real. He could see their features, talk to them, could probably touch them (James hadn't tried that yet. He was too afraid he would touch firm skin and lose his mind completely.). The fact that the dreams no longer seemed like fantasy frightened him, but he pushed it aside. He suspected that whatever was on the other side of the door would be far more terrifying than what he had experienced up to that point, whether awake or asleep. That fear took precedence over all the other flavors that had taken root in his mind. It sat alone, not merging with the others, but pushing itself above them, as if holding court. The dread he harbored was all encompassing. He couldn't even look it squarely in the eye, fearing what might look back at him.

Lillian stood facing the doorway while James stood behind her, waiting. She seemed content to stand there, feeling no compulsion to move forward through the door. James' mind went wild with ideas, adding features to whatever was behind the door. He made it a tangible thing, a creature that crouched low to the ground as it walked. He applied a myriad of faces to the being, ranging from the evil to the angelic; from damnation to salvation. The longer he stood in front of the closed door, the more imaginative he was, painting a picture in his mind that grew more detailed by the second. Finally, when the idea of the thing behind the door had grown larger than life, James asked,

"Are we going in?"

Lillian sniffed loudly and said, "Anxious now, aren't we?"

James didn't reply. He just stood still while his eyes adjusted to the darkness. He was starting to be able to make out the door handle. The knob had been painted black at some point. The paint was chipping off the sides revealing the brass underneath.

Lillian's sigh was unreadable. He fancied that she felt sorry for him. That some place in her, the part that loved him as a grand-mother loves a grandson, felt for him, knew his pain. She gave no indications of it as she stood. In fact, she seemed to relish the mounting fear that rose within him. She could smell it on his skin. The only thing his grandmother felt was anticipation. Lillian turned the doorknob to the right.

"What's done is done, right James?" Lillian asked as she opened the door. What little light was left in the basement illumi-nated the edge of the first step in a long stairwell.

Lillian turned to James and smiled. Her face had taken on a sickly pallor and a trail of blood ran from her mouth down her chin. Her hair was suddenly flat and lackluster. It was streaked with gray where none appeared before. The neck of her nightgown was stained in red.

Her smile was hideous. Her lips were cracked and raw. Her teeth were rotted and gapped; the bottom row was blood stained.

James was looking into the face of the dead woman on the floor between the living room and dining room. The dead woman he had seen in his dreams.

The sight smacked James in the face like a cold splash of water. His eyes widened and he gasped sharply, recoiling away from the image of death in front of him. She laughed again, her maniacal cackle echoing from within his head. James took a step backward, but his bad knee made him hesitate. In that second, Lillian grabbed his forearm and pulled him forward, toward her, with supernatural strength. He flew past her, propelled off his feet. James vaguely noticed the wisps of hair on Lillian's forehead that were jostled in the breeze he created when he careened down the stairs.

James landed in a heap on the sub-basement floor, his head

smacking the concrete with a loud thump. His damaged elbow was bent painfully underneath him. His left foot dangled off the edge of a wooden landing and over the next set of steps he would have to descend to stand on the basement floor. He opened his eyes slowly, seeing a hazy fog in front of him, so dense that he couldn't see his hand in front of his face.

He could hear his grandmother's laughter, patronizing him. He lifted his head from the landing and turned his ear upward, trying to gauge where she might be standing. He still couldn't see anything; his eyes still hadn't adjusted to the blackness of the room. Fear rose within him as he realized that the sound was coming from above him. From the top of the stairs. He was about to call to her when she closed the door and left him alone in the dark.

CHAPTER 67

Pete and Andrea pulled up to the curb in front of the house and turned off the engine. Pete checked the street address with the one typed on the death certificate and it matched. He folded the certificate and put it back in his pocket, all the while looking at the house.

The white Victorian house with black trim sat on a small overgrown lot. It was three levels above ground, the lower windows just barely visible above the grass. A covered wrap around porch split the top two levels. The lawn had gone to rot. The flowers had been overtaken by weeds and the bushes were overgrown; the highest branch touched the base of a window on the top floor.

Pete breathed in deeply. Something about the house bothered him. There was nothing aesthetically dynamic about it—the luster it may have had when it was built had worn away. It didn't look particularly eerie, at least not any more than any other abandoned house he had seen. But there was something about it, its aura, that froze Pete in his seat.

The windows, like vacant eyes, stared out at the street. As Pete looked into them, he had the distinct feeling that they were looking back at him. It was so strong, that the hairs on the back of his neck stood up. The windows seemed to be leaning forward, extending over the roof of the porch, hulking over it. Pete recoiled unconsciously, his back pressing against the door. He stared at the windows as they seemed to grow smaller, depressing themselves into a horrible squint. They emitted a warning to him as he sat shivering inside the car.

"Go away!"

A gasp escaped Pete's lips when he heard the words in his head as clearly as if they had been spoken from within the car. He blinked against the vision rapidly, trying to wash it away and get himself under control. His heart was beating frantically in his chest as his mind registered what he was seeing.

Andrea turned to him, put a hand on his shoulder, and called his name. The sound of her voice crackled in his ear, full of static and unclear. He looked at her and saw her lips moving, but he couldn't make out what she was saying. It was like she was on a different frequency, like a television station that wouldn't quite come in. Her lips formed the words "Are you okay?" He wanted to respond, to tell her, 'No! I'm not okay! The fucking house just told us to go away!' A little voice in the back of his head, the one that always seemed to say the wrong thing at the wrong time, added its two cents. *You're as crazy as James is,* the little voice cooed. *Maybe you'll share a padded room in the looney bin.* Pete started to say something to Andrea about what had just happened, but his eyes were drawn back to the house. It was leaning more now, looming right over the car. Pete could see that the base of the house had detached itself from the ground; the foundation was visible by the light of the moon. The door that had been hidden in the shadows beneath the covered porch was backlit now, a gaping maw inset in a pallid face. The security bars that were added during the decline of the neighborhood in the early 1970s, had transformed into jagged teeth. The house looked hungry.

Pete's eyes widened in fear as the house leaned closer and

closer to the car, wood splintering and ripping away with every stretch. For a moment, Pete met eyes with the beast and the world fell silent. The house looked back at him, sizing him up, smelling his fear and relishing it. A bloodcurdling sound, more of a moan than an exclamation, flowed out of the mouth, the sound full of hunger and torment, the tone so deep the ground beneath the car shook.

Pete screamed as the house lunged forward, its mouth open and ready to swallow the car whole.

Andrea looked over at him with a look that did not match the fear he was feeling in his heart.

"What did you say?" Andrea asked. Her face didn't have the same terror etched in it that he was feeling. Hers was full of apprehension, but not the raw fear he was sure was showing on his face. Or was it? She wasn't looking at him in shared horror the way she would have been if she had seen what he saw. She hadn't seen it. That show was for him alone.

Pete became aware of his posture then. He wasn't pressed against the door like he thought he was, his back straight as a board and his shoulders shrugged up to his chin. He was sitting normally in his seat, looking over at the house. Andrea was looking at him, another question forming on her lips, but it wasn't the one that he expected. She asked him again,

"Pete, what did you just say?"

Pete exhaled, feeling like he had been holding his breath for hours. Surely, she had heard him screaming. She was sitting right next to him! But she didn't ask him what he saw, what had made him yell that way. She only wondered what he had said.

Pete looked back at the house, unable to believe that the vision wasn't real. The hallucination had struck a chord in him, had touched upon a fear in him that he didn't know existed. The house stood as it had when they parked in front of it, its finish the worse for wear, its lawn unruly. It wasn't lifted up from the ground, struggling toward the car. It sat placidly on the quiet suburban street.

Pete chuckled under his breath, disbelieving what had just happened. He had witnessed a house uproot and poise itself to attack. It seemed so real, so vivid was the image as the house loomed over them, ready to strike. And the warning he had heard, clear and unmistakable. The words repeated in his head, this time spoken in his voice instead of the genderless tone that uttered them the first time. *Go away.* But it had all been in his head. His heart was still racing as he shifted in the seat to turn towards Andrea. He was thinking of asking her what he sounded like a moment before but thought better of it. She was agitated, concerned, frightened, all rolled into one. She was all of those things, but she wasn't frightened out of her mind as she would have been if she had seen what he saw. She was completely unaware of what had just happened to him. She hadn't seen it, and she hadn't heard the voice telling them to leave. He decided to leave it at that. It was better that way. He didn't want her to think that what was happening to James was happening to him too.

Pete cleared his throat and said,

"I was just saying that we're here. This is the place. It's a beauty, isn't it?"

"I'm sure it might have been once, a long time ago. But now it's just an old, abandoned house." She paused, turning back to scrutinize the house. "Why would James come here?"

"I don't know. Maybe he thinks he can find some answers here, that he'll be able to sort everything out in this place."

"But why here? He's never been here before, never even laid eyes on the house before. What would make him come here?"

Pete shook his head and looked at his hands. They were still trembling.

"Maybe he's not even here. Maybe this was just a wild goose chase," Pete offered, his voice lacking the conviction it needed to convince Andrea.

She shook her head slowly, her eyes staying on the house.

"No," she said finally. "He's in there. I know it." Andrea shivered against a draft she was sure only she could feel. The cool air chilled her to her bones. "I can feel it."

Andrea fell silent, remembering the haunting picture in the photo album, letting her eyes drift from the windows on the third floor to the shadowy porch. Lillian Boone was the woman's name. James' grandmother. Was it her? Had she lured James there?

Andrea tried to erase the irrational thought from her mind, but it lingered still, pushed backward by rational thought but still very much there. She craned her neck, trying to see the house from a different angle.

"I don't like it," she surmised. "This house is eerie. There's something wrong here."

"What do you mean?" Pete was interested to hear what Andrea thought about the house. He wanted to know that it wasn't just him who felt the strangeness surrounding the place.

Andrea turned to him, her eyes staring through him imploringly, needing him to understand.

"Something about this place is just... wrong. I felt it when we stopped the car. It was like a force field or something. There was a distinct change in the atmosphere when we stopped in front of this house." She paused, shaking her head as she looked at the house. Her eyes cascaded the front, level by level. "It's like something doesn't want us here."

Pete sighed but remained silent. There weren't any reassuring words he could say to her. He didn't believe them himself.

CHAPTER 68

James pulled himself to his feet in the dark room, ignoring the pain that cut sharply through his nerves with every movement. When his eyes adjusted to the darkness, he tried to get his bearings. The room was no bigger than his dorm room had been in college, just enough space to move around, but not enough to really spread out. It was unfinished: the beams and piping visible where a plastered ceiling would normally be. The floor was a simple concrete slab, unadorned by vinyl or carpeting. No furniture cluttered the floor, rimming the room in designer fabrics or lacquered wood, making the space seem bigger, longer. No pictures hung on the walls, no boxes of fluorescent lights littered the floor, there wasn't any extra carpeting rolled up in the corner. Only a folded stepladder stood propped against the wall. Besides him, it was the only other thing in the room.

James turned around slowly, casting his eyes about, studying every nuance of the room. He looked up at the stairwell leading to the main basement. His grandmother had thrown him down the steps, had pulled him with unnatural strength. His dead grandmother. James breathed in deeply and exhaled slowly, trying to make sense of what happened. He told himself that a dead woman couldn't have thrown him down the stairs, that it was yet another thing he dreamed up. But his words sounded hollow in his head.

James made his way up the steps, his elbow and knee smarting with every step. He tried the door and found that it was locked.

"No way," he said aloud.

He jiggled the doorknob softly at first, trying to unstick the lock, and then roughly, frantically. He began to panic as he realized that he was locked in the subbasement. He pounded his fist against the door, the sound echoing off the walls.

"It's no use," a complacent voice said from below. James' fury was quickly replaced with dread. He was sure he was alone in the room and the only door to the space was the one that he had just found to be locked. He stood frozen in place as the voice floated up to him again.

"It's locked, but I'm sure you've found that out by now."

James wanted to stay where he was, to try and pound through the door and get out of the subbasement, leaving whoever or whatever owned the strangely melodic voice by herself, but he knew he couldn't. He wasn't going to break down the door with his hands alone, he realized. It was locked from the other side. The only chance he had was to use the stepladder that was down in the heart of the subbasement. Where the voice had come from.

James took a couple of tentative steps down the stairs.

"Come on down. I won't bite," the woman said, her voice strangely calming.

James walked down the steps and saw a woman kneeling on the floor. The concrete floor was now leveled off dirt from wall to wall. The room smelled moist and dank. James stepped onto the dirt apprehensively.

"You can come closer," the woman said, turning to face him. "I won't hurt you, not that it makes a difference now, anyway."

She was young, she couldn't have been older than thirty-five. She wore a floral dress, done in once bright blues, yellows and oranges. She was kneeling on the ground, the dress bent beneath her. Her hands laid in her lap delicately. Her face was sad, but beautiful. Her eyes looked at him longingly, yet they were resigned at the same time. A dark stain colored the front of the dress.

She covered the scooped neck of her dress in vain, trying to cover the stain.

"I'm sorry, James. I tried to hide that from you, but it didn't work. I'm not as strong as the others. At least you don't have to see my hideous face."

She looked away from him then, self-consciously raising a hand to the side of her head. There was a shadow on the left side of her face, barely visible, but there. She covered it with her hair quickly and turned her other side to him.

"How do you know my name?" James asked, his voice shaking more than he wished. The woman didn't seem to notice.

"I've always known you, James. I knew your father too. Dear, sweet Jimmie."

James looked at the woman, her face full of compassion and understanding. She knew how this played out.

"If only we had gotten out of here that day. Maybe Jimmie wouldn't have done it. Maybe you wouldn't have either."

"What are you talking about?" James asked as he took a step closer.

"I know about Carmen, James. I know what happened to her. I know you never would have done it if they hadn't forced you."

James was standing only inches away from the woman now. She looked real enough, but he knew she wasn't. Her skin was sickly looking, waxy and discolored. What he had mistaken for a shadow earlier looked more like a bruise up close. While he watched, the bruise seemed to spread down the side of her face and onto her neck, purpling painfully. At that moment he knew who she was and it terrified him.

"Don't be afraid of me, James. I'm not the one you should fear. I tried to help you. I shouldn't have, but I did. I knew it wouldn't work, but I had to try anyway. And I was right, because you're still here, aren't you?"

"Aunt Clara—." James started, his breath hitching in his throat.

She closed her eyes and swooned at the sound of her name.

"Ah. I haven't heard my name roll off anyone's lips so gently in decades." She turned to him, smiling softly. "I never thought I would again."

There was a sadness in her that was infectious. Any hope that was within him dissipated as he watched her rock gently back and forth.

"I know what they did to you, James. They did it to your father too. Lillian wasn't the only one. Father, grandfather, throughout the generations, this has come to pass. I tried to stop it, to break the chain, for your father and for you, but it didn't work. I'm so sorry."

James sank to his knees as Clara began to weep.

"What happened? What were you trying to stop from happening?"

Clara looked at him and smiled meekly. "Child, don't you know that you are here to die?"

The words hit him like a rock. He felt as if he had just awakened from a deep sleep; like everything before that moment had been the product of a strange dream. He remembered having morbid fantasies of ending his life, of running from his punishment under the guise of protecting Andrea. His mind spoke the words, coaxing him to finish it, to end it all, but underneath, he was terrified of the finality. Now, as the words were being spoken to him in the subbasement of an abandoned house, by a woman who had been dead for over thirty years, it all came clear to him. He never had a choice.

"My death was swift. I never had a chance to prevent it, to fight it," Clara continued. "I now know that there was nothing that I could do about it, even if I had known it was imminent. I have come to accept that. When Jimmie's time came, I tried to stop it from happening. I tried to stop them from tormenting him so, but they were stronger than me. Your father was such a kind boy. He didn't deserve their evil."

Clara shook her head as she spoke of Jimmie.

"I loved that boy. At the end, he had become so much like his mother, that I was afraid of him. He is with her now." Clara continued to rock back and forth. She mourned Jimmie even then.

"I tried to stop them from hurting you too," she said. "So did your mother. She kept them away from you for as long as she could. But they weakened her, haunted her terribly. She died looking into the face of your grandmother standing next to her bed."

James remembered his mother telling him about the spirits she saw in the house. Tears welled in his eyes as he realized she had been fighting for him all along. The grief he felt for his mother showed on his face as if he had just lost her.

"In death, she is as weak as I am. We've been helpless against them. I broke through tonight, but only for a second. I had hoped you would break Lillian's spell long enough to get your wits about you and run out of here. But the pause wasn't long enough. My interference was nothing more than a blip on her screen. Her strength is indomitable."

Clara looked at her hands for a moment, her fingers wringing each other nervously.

"I've failed you like I failed your father. I am truly sorry."

James' voice was hoarse as he said, "I'm not dead yet. There may still be a way to get out of this."

Clara's face darkened, fresh tears sparkling in her eyes.

"Not for you. It's your fate, as much as it was mine and your father's and will be your daughter's."

James looked squarely at the ghost sitting before him and said, "I don't have any children, Aunt Clara."

Clara's eyelids drooped as though weighted. She reached her hand out and touched his face, the sensation feeling prickly to

James, like the tingling felt in a limb that has fallen asleep. She nodded to him, her eyes shutting, as she cupped his cheek. Something in James' mind collapsed. A child? A sound of protest rose in his throat, but he suppressed it. As he looked in Clara's eyes, he knew she was telling the truth. The sadness they held made it painfully clear.

Andrea was pregnant. The thought filled him with happiness and dread at the same time. He could almost see his daughter, a pretty little girl who had her mother's eyes and his smile. He longed to be there to pick her up when she scraped her knee, or when she was learning how to ride a bicycle. But he knew that wouldn't happen.

She might be happy for a while. He imagined her getting married and having children of her own. She would live life thinking that everything was fine, that she was just like everyone else. She might even forget the stories her mother would tell her about him. But then everything would change.

James started to feel sorry for himself. He would not be there to see her take her first breath, her first step, go on her first date. She wouldn't know him as her father in a real sense. They would never go to the movies together or eat ice cream at the kitchen counter. All she would have to remember him by would be a picture of him in happier days. To her, he would be intangible. He would just be the man who died before she was born. The one who went crazy and killed himself, like his own father had. He knew now that she would succumb to the same illness. Her fate would be the same as his. She would be doomed to die by her own hand. She was predisposed to it. Her fate had been cast before she was even born. James sank his knees deeper in the dirt sobbing loudly as he mourned the fate of his unborn child.

"So, it was you, Clara," Lillian said, her voice thick with venom. She stood behind them dressed in the nightgown that she had died in, the front of it stained with blood. "You couldn't just leave well enough alone."

Clara looked at her sister and said meekly, "I just wanted to save one."

"Haven't you learned? This is his destiny, like those before him and those that will follow. There's nothing you can do to change it."

Clara diverted her eyes, looking away from her sister's cold glare. She glanced at James but wouldn't hold his gaze either. She had been defeated. Again.

"I know, Lillian. I know."

James' face burned with anger. How flippantly they discussed his life! The life of his child and the generations that would follow. Their fate rolled off their tongues like the day's gossip. They were his offspring. His responsibility. He rose to his feet shakily.

"Why?" he asked, anger fueling his words. "Why is this my fate? Why is my child damned this way?"

Lillian took a step forward and said, "It's always been this way, boy. It hasn't changed in centuries since our ancestor, William Boone, took his first life, and the curse laid upon him, and all of his descendants to come, began. This is the lot of our family, like it or not."

"Why you, grandmother? Why are you here to take me and not my father?"

"It will be him that takes your child. And you that takes hers. A generation must pass before you welcome the next in. That is the way it is done. Don't worry. Your father will be here for you when the time comes."

She took another step towards him and reached out her hand.

"Come now, James. It's time."

James began to tremble. He looked around the room trying to find something that would stop her. His eyes laid on his Aunt Clara still seated on the floor near the center of the room.

"What about you?" he asked, beseeching her to look at him. "Why are you here? She murdered you in this very house. Why would you return to this place?"

Clara looked at James with watery eyes.

"I never left. I belong to this house."

Lillian laughed as James stood confused looking at Clara.

"It's a shame that Jimmie didn't share anything with you, James. This might have been easier for you to accept if you knew more," Lillian said.

"What are you talking about?"

"This house. The family. Jimmie should have been proud of his heritage but he never was. He couldn't see past the shame he felt. He abhorred the family and everything about it. He tried to distance himself from us, ignore our existence, much like I did. But, like me, he learned that you can't run. Boone blood flowed through his veins. He couldn't outrun his destiny."

James knew he was going to die. No matter how much he might have thought he wanted death before, he knew that he didn't want it now. Andrea was pregnant with their child. He wanted to experience parenthood with her, to raise a family. But he knew he never would. If he didn't die in the subbasement he would be arrested for Susan's murder—the police were already on to him. Carmen's murder would come to light sooner or later. He stood defeated, wondering which was the lesser of the two evils: die or go to jail for the rest of his life? He wished he could turn back the hands of time to when he hadn't spilled innocent blood, to a time when he wasn't damned.

"This house has been in the family since 1890 and the land longer than that," Lillian continued. "The house that William Boone was born in was built on this land by his grandfather in 1718. The land itself had been in the family for decades before the turn of the eighteenth century. After the house burned to the ground with William inside in 1801, the land lay unused. But we never sold it. My grandfather built this house in 1890 and moved grandmother and father in the same year. After my grandparents died, father moved North and the house stood empty until Jimmie and I moved in some sixty years later."

Lillian raised her head in reverence.

"William Boone's spirit was still here. I felt it the moment we walked in. The rest of the family avoided this place. No one but Clara ever came out here and even she wasn't comfortable in the house. His presence was strong.

"When Clara died here, William welcomed her like he welcomed me. We are one with this house, Clara and I. One with William. Clara and William are always here roaming the hallways of this house. They don't come out often like the rest of us do. They belong to this house. Their bodies lay here."

Clara nodded as Lillian spoke, her left hand rubbing the ground below it.

"The house will remain in the family for generations to come, James. We will always have this place to call home. Your daughter will keep it. She will pass it on to her children and so on. She will be the next one to live here. She'll give it a much-needed face-lift. She will remodel it almost completely except for the wrap around porch. It was William's pride and joy. I loved it also. It will be the only thing she keeps intact, restoring it to its original stateliness with a caring hand. She'll adore it without even knowing why.

"You'll live on in her, James. Take solace in that. You'll be part of this house, as we are. You'll see your grandchildren play in this very room. Their spirits will interact with yours forever."

James shook his head in denial. It was all too much to handle.

Lillian said all that she had intended to say. She paused a moment before finishing, allowing James a minute of understanding. His denial melted away to resignation of the inevitable, his will broken.

"Let's go, James," Lillian said, finally. "It's time."

James backed away from Lillian as she stepped towards him. The back of his leg bumped the stepladder that was now open in the middle of the floor. His eyes searched the room hurriedly, frightened of what he knew was coming. Clara had disappeared, leaving him alone with Lillian.

"Don't be frightened now, James. It must be done. There is no other option."

"I could go to jail," James said defiantly. "Pay for my crimes."

Lillian laughed lightheartedly and said, "But you won't. Who do you think you're kidding? You don't have the wherewithal to handle jail. Neither did your father. You came here to kill yourself, remember? This is the choice you made on your own. This was your way out. Now it's time for you to do it."

James' chin dropped to his chest. She was right. He couldn't handle jail. He wouldn't last more than two weeks before he killed himself behind bars. His cowardice embarrassed and inflamed him at the same time. He couldn't pay for the lives he had taken the way society mandated, so he chose to take the easy way out and kill himself. That was what he was doing, wasn't it? Choosing to kill himself instead of facing the music? He sighed in affirmation, beaten. He only hoped that his blood would satisfy Carmen and Susan's souls enough that they did not torment him in the afterlife.

CHAPTER 69

Pete got out of the car slowly, removing his flashlight from the trunk, all the while keeping his eyes on the house. It looked normal still. Just an old house sitting vacant on an overgrown lot. He felt silly for reacting the way he had in the car, but something had happened to him, had taken over his mind for a moment in time. Remnants of his fear lingered as he stood in front of the house, looking at the door that had transformed into a mouth in his hallucination.

A light was on in one of the front rooms, its dull ray back-lighting one of the boards that barricaded the windows. Had that light been on before? Pete couldn't remember. Seeing it frightened him more than anything he had experienced yet.

Pete turned back to the car and leaned down to Andrea's open window. He said,

"Wait for me here, okay? Once I find James, I'll come out and get you." He straightened up and turned to walk away when Andrea grabbed his arm and held it tightly.

"Be careful," she whispered. "Someone is in there. That light wasn't on when we pulled up. If it's not James..." Andrea didn't finish her sentence.

Pete nodded and looked back at the house, adrenaline lighting up his extremities. He breathed deeply, sucking the cold air in, filling his lungs with it. He hoped the air would invigorate him. Instead, it mingled with the chill left over from his hellish daydream, its consistency that of mercury, thick and metallic. He swallowed hard before turning back to Andrea.

"It's probably him. I'll be right out."

Pete tapped the outside of the door and walked towards the house. He turned back once to look at Andrea. Her face was full of concern. He offered a weak smile and walked up the porch steps to the front door.

CHAPTER 70

"It has all been set up for you, James," Lillian said as James climbed the first step of the stepladder. Her face was stuck in the death mask, her last expression on earth, as she watched her grandson mount the steps, confronting his own mortality.

James took the second step shakily, his knee protesting as he lifted his foot onto the platform. He looked up at the joists, much closer now than they were before. He reached his good hand up to them, extending his arm, straightening it painfully. He banged his hand against the lowest joist and it remained firm under the knock. It was solid and sturdy. He sighed as he brought his hand back down, the knowledge of how he would end his life weighing heavily on his shoulders.

"The beam is strong enough to hold you, James. It will be quick." Lillian's voice was reassuring. She looked at him with sensitive eyes. She had been where he was, knowing the time had come to say goodbye to the world she knew and take her life. She knew what he was feeling.

"It will be all right," she added.

James looked at her and smiled, the grin thick with sarcasm and terrible acceptance. His hands fumbled with his belt buckle, his fingers shaking as they worked. He unlatched the clip, let the pin drop away from the hole, and pulled the belt through the loops. He winced as his right elbow shared the work with his left, taking the belt from around his waist. It hurt, but he relished it. It would be one of the last sensations he would ever feel.

CHAPTER 71

Pete walked up the porch steps and saw a board lying on its back with rusty nails jutting upward. He kicked it away from the door and turned the doorknob. The squeaky door opened slowly, revealing an empty room. The dim light from the uncovered bulb shone from the other side of the living room, casting a brown cone ray on the bare hardwood floor.

The house was quiet. The only sound Pete could hear was his rapid breathing.

"James!" Pete called out in the empty room. He turned his head right and left, looking for movement in the shadows.

"James, man, are you in here?"

Nothing. Pete sighed as he rubbed his temple, his back just inches away from the front door. His right hand was still holding the doorknob, as if it were a safety blanket.

"Come on, James. Let me know where you are and I'll come to you."

Still nothing. Pete looked around the shabby room and felt fear stirring in his stomach. He stood still in the room, waiting for his eyes to adjust to the darkness that surrounded him. His imagination played with him, showing him figures standing in the shadows that filled the corners of the room, made the hair on the nape of his neck stand up at the thought of eyes peering out at him, seeing him as he stood in front of the door. His hands felt clammy and his forehead was moistened with perspiration. His blood had run cold. His fingertips were icy. Pete lifted his hand off the doorknob and rubbed it together with the other one, tucking the unused flashlight under his arm as he tried to warm his hands.

He was tempted to walk outside and get back in the car, to put some distance between them and the ominous house. He would tell Andrea that he hadn't found James, that he wasn't in the house. They could drive back to New York and wait for James to come home. Pete shook his head and exhaled loudly. Andrea would know he hadn't searched the house. He hadn't been gone long enough to cover one floor, let alone three. He had come this far. He couldn't turn back now.

Pete breathed deeply and crossed the living room, forging ahead, and ignoring the fear of things lurking in the dark that nagged in his head. He saw a stairwell on the left side of a long hallway. The other side was dark. Sighing, Pete flicked on his flashlight and started up the stairs.

CHAPTER 72

J ames held the belt in his hands, the buckle dangling limply on the left. He looked at the joist above his head again and a lump formed in his throat. Was he really going to end his life this way?

Yes, he was. He had to. There were no other options. His mind clouded with thoughts of Andrea and his child, a daughter he would never see. He hoped that, by doing this, he was making life easier for them. Maybe his daughter wouldn't be damned to have the same fate he had. He would do everything he could to stop it from beyond the grave. He would fight for his daughter's life.

He imagined Andrea during her pregnancy; she would be radiant. Maybe she would move to Virginia to be closer to her sister. Maybe she would find someone new, raise his daughter to know another man as her father. Sadness engulfed him as he imagined his little girl calling someone other than him Daddy. It made him sick to think that another man would sleep with his wife and raise his child. The worst part was that he knew it would be better for them if he were gone. Their lives would be normal if he was out of the picture. Another man might be able to provide them the stability that they deserved. All he could give them was the shame of having a husband and a father that was rotting in jail.

It was better this way.

James slung the buckled end of the belt over the joist, standing on his toes to catch it on the other side. He raised his right arm with concerted effort. His elbow screamed against it, but he ignored the pain and tugged both ends of the belt, testing the strength of the joist one last time. It held firm. He brought his damaged arm down gingerly, feeling every pop and strain. His right hand dropped heavily on his thigh; his elbow was unable to hold the wrist and hand up any longer. A crunch came from within his pocket as his hand hit it. He put his hand in and pulled out a creased sheet of paper and pen. The letter.

James held the paper in his hand, turning it over as he tried to think of something to say. Nothing would suffice. Nothing would ever make Andrea understand why he had to do it. He thought again of writing Pete, confessing everything, but doing that was out of the question. How could he expect Pete to keep the letter away from Andrea? He would want to, but the contents would be so devastating, so damning, James wondered if Pete would be able to do it. Telling Pete that his best friend had not only slept with his wife but had murdered her as well as another woman would be more than he should be expected to handle. He would need someone to lean on—they both would. Why should James complicate their grief with his confession? Maybe they would never find out, he thought. Maybe the investigation of Susan's death would prove inconclusive. Maybe Carmen's case would grow cold. He decided that the fantasy sounded much better than the reality. He would take his sins to the grave.

James put the pen and paper back into his pocket without writing a word. He thought of how the words from his father's suicide note haunted him throughout his adult life.

For protection. For me.

He had marveled at the poetry of it and, at the same time,

hated it for its simplicity. He couldn't decipher it. It was what it was. James had been forced to accept the eccentricity of what was in his father's mind in those last moments, his thoughts so discombobulated they were only able to form those two concise and troubling sentences to sum up his actions. Or were those words the product of imputable clarity? He didn't know. He never would. His father's words left him hollow. The lack of closure stayed with James for the rest of his life. He didn't want to do that to his daughter.

A muffled sound came from upstairs, sounding almost like a voice. James stopped, standing as still as he could, and listened. He didn't hear the sound again. He turned his attention back to the joist, trying to regain the courage to finish what he had set out to do.

There was very little slack on either side of the belt. James would have to get closer to the joist if he was going to do it right. He planted his good foot on the platform and put the other foot on the stepladder handle. He extended his good leg, stretching it as straight as he could, savoring the strain in his muscles.

He stood up on his pointed toes, pressing himself upward as his hand fumbled with the belt buckle. His hands were sweating as he tried to work the end of the belt into the buckle at his throat. The pressure against his Adam's Apple was unbearable even with him bracing the bulk of his body weight with his legs on the stepladder. His mind couldn't help but imagine the all-encom-passing pain that awaited him when he no longer had a foothold to share the weight.

After what seemed like hours, he slid the pin into the last hole of the belt and looped the excess into the holder. His hands instinctively reached for the joist, its sides made slick from the moisture on his hands. Tears streamed out of James' eyes as he looked at the subbasement, its walls being the last thing he would see. He was alone again, his grandmother leaving him to die by himself as she had. A cry of fear and of sadness escaped his lips and echoed off the walls. This was it. He clinched his teeth and slid his feet off the stepladder.

His feet kicked out spastically as the pressure increased on his throat, toppling the stepladder over onto its side. The drop didn't break his neck the way he had hoped it would. Instead, his neck pressed into the belt buckle, crushing his larynx. The unyielding leather was choking him slowly; the blood rushed to his head in torrents, flooding his ears with the sound of rushing water. His tongue protruded out of his mouth as he tried to pull air into his lungs. His hands clawed at his neck, trying to loosen the belt, the pain from his elbow all but forgotten. He barely felt his nails digging into his skin, ripping at it as they tried to get between his neck and the belt.

James' eyes faded in and out of focus as they began to bulge out of their sockets from the pressure. His grandmother stood beneath him now, watching him suffer. Her smile was sinister and animated, the remnants of sympathy he had seen in her eyes drowned out by the anticipation of his end. His father was there too, his mouth turned up in a vampirical grin that exposed sharp canines. He savored his son's last moments like a full-bodied wine.

There were other souls in the room also, men and women that James didn't know dressed in the clothing of their period; some in tattered cloth and makeshift burlap, others in regal garb indicative of royalty. They stood together, their appearance oddly iridescent in the dimly lit room. The low rumble of their chatter, like the incessant buzzing of bees, rose to James' ears. They huddled together, their eyes trained on him like spotlights, enjoying the show that was his death.

One man stood in the distance, close to the back wall, behind the other spirits come to call. A ruffled collar was visible beneath his bearded chin. His eyes pierced through the shadows, almost glowing in the dark. William Boone. He nodded towards James, acknowledging his presence, welcoming him home. He turned and left the room, disappearing through the subbasement wall.

James could hear the low rumble in the room, airy voices chattering, their intonations rising and falling in excitement and anticipation. They watched him intently, morbid relish glinting in their eyes, as James hung suspended above the subbasement floor, his life drifting away under the strangle of the belt.

CHAPTER 73

Pete descended the stairs after having searched the top floor and finding nothing but an old ornate mirror in the hallway, broken glass in one of the bedrooms, and left behind furniture in the other. He had stopped in front of the mirror at the top of the stairs and looked at himself. His clothes were wrinkled and disheveled. His eyes were tired, the lids drooping slightly. He ran his hand over his face and sighed. The house seemed exceedingly quiet, as he looked in the mirror, like some sound, some monotonous undertone that had been running unbeknown to him, had been silenced. Pete turned his head, the silence seeming sudden.

He turned back to the mirror when he was satisfied that he hadn't heard anything and regarded himself again. His body was fatigued. The drive had taken more out of him than he thought. His mind drifted back to the daydream he had in the car and he shivered unconsciously. He looked at the window through the mirror, its frame mounted high above the stairwell. A branch knocked against it while he watched, surprising him. He jumped at the sound it made and looked back at his reflection. The image had changed. It was moving, was wavy, like a drop of oil in water. A low moan had interrupted the silence, droning on as though it had always been there. Pete's eyes were merging together in the center of his head and his nose and mouth had become one grafted piece. His forehead pulsed, first one side, then the other. His frontal vein was painfully distended, visibly protruding from his forehead. The moaning filled his ears, driving him mad. Pete gasped and blinked rapidly, trying to clear his vision. When he looked again, the image was normal. The house was silent again, the moaning jaggedly cut off. Pete was panting now, as he looked at himself in the mirror, not wanting to look but having to make sure. He cast one more glance at it before he turned around and ran down the steps. *I'd better hurry this up,* he thought to himself, hating the spooked feeling that sat like a rock in his chest.

The main floor didn't show any signs of James having been there either. The kitchen, dining room, and living room were also empty. Pete opened every door on the main floor as he had upstairs, finding mostly closets and storage areas. The last door he opened revealed another dark stairwell leading to the basement. Pete tried the switch at the top of the stairs and nothing happened. He shined the flashlight down the stairs, hoping to find some clue that James was in there. Nothing but the stairs was illuminated by the light. He inhaled deeply as he ventured down into the darkness.

The room was empty as most of the house had been, the discarded liquor bottles and brown paper bags that littered the floor were the only indication that anyone had been in the house for decades. Pete hoped he could get out of the house before the squatters came back, not wanting to get into a confrontation over turf.

The flashlight beam fell onto another door at the opposite end of the room. Pete crossed the room cautiously, shining his flashlight in every corner, illuminating every shadow. He didn't want to unwittingly awake a squatter and get into an altercation. That would be all he needed with Andrea sitting alone outside in the car.

Pete tried the knob and found it unlocked. As the door squeaked open on rusted hinges, Pete felt a presence. He spun around, casting the flashlight beam across the room. No one was there, but he still felt the odd sensation that he was not alone. He bounced the flashlight around the room one more time, seeing nothing. He turned back to the door, the hairs on the back of his neck standing on end.

Another darkened stairwell laid behind the basement door, leading to a subbasement common in older houses. Pete used to play in his grandmother's subbasement when he was young, hiding there for hours without being bothered, so he wasn't surprised to find one in that house. The cool, stale air rushed up at him as he stood at the top of the stairs. He cast one last look over his shoulder, surveying the room before he descended the stairs.

CHAPTER 74

The pressure on James' neck was starting to fade. He knew that the pain wasn't dissipating, he was just losing the sensation. He had passed the moment of exquisite tenderness when he felt all of his pain pulsing together, intermingling. The intensity had passed. The culmination of his suffering had boiled over into sublime nothingness, releasing him from its vice-like grip. He was dying. He had stopped trying to pull the belt away from his neck. His nails were caked with his own blood and skin. His arms hung limply at his sides. His legs had stopped kicking, the muscles relaxing as he dangled like strange fruit from the tree of death.

He looked at his grandmother, her upturned face gruesomely jubilant as she witnessed his dying moments, waiting to welcome him into the fold. His eyes started to glaze over, fogging as he watched her smile grow wider. Maybe this is what people saw at the moment of death, he thought with the last of his lucidity. Horrible visages of dead relatives ushering them to hell. The little voice in his mind chuckled one last time as it put the stylus on the old, popping record, pumping the melodic voice of Peggy Lee in his ears as she crooned the words to *Is That All There Is?*, lulling him to his final sleep.

A beam of light cut into the room. He tried to clear his eyes, to focus on it while he could. The souls in the room turned toward the light. They backed away from it, dispersing quickly, making a path that led from the far wall to where James hung in the center of the room. He watched as the ray got bigger and bigger, coming towards him. Maybe there was a light at the end of the tunnel after all.

Pete entered the room behind the light and saw James almost instantly. He was hanging from a joist in the exposed ceiling, his belt wrapped tightly around his neck. Pete was pinned in place. Seeing James hanging in the center of the room, the stepladder he had used cast aside and lying abandoned on its side, sent shivers up his spine. He had never seen a dead body before, except for ones that had been cleaned up, clothed in their Sunday best, and placed in a coffin. He had never been at anyone's side on their deathbed, sitting with them as they drifted away. Death was neat to him, open or closed casket. He had never seen what death really looked like, the desolation of it all. He felt queasy at the sight, his stomach curdling as he looked at James, his neck turned black and blue from the taut belt, his limbs hanging flaccidly at his sides.

Pete stepped closer to James and saw that his eyes were open, rolling in their sockets as they tried to focus on him. His mind leapt into action, pushing him forward to wrap his arms around James' legs. Pete squatted, preparing to lift James up and relieve the pressure that his bodyweight had placed on his neck. There might still be time to save his life. But then, Pete stopped. This was what he wanted, wasn't it? James would be out of the way and he would be able to make his move on Andrea. James would pay for cheating with Susan with his life, leaving Andrea and Pete free to do whatever they wanted.

Pete let go of James' legs and took a step backwards. James' body swung back and forth from the jolt, the belt cutting deeper and deeper into James' neck. The skin above James' eyes was turning green from the lack of oxygen. Bubbling spittle spilled over James' bottom lip, running down his chin slowly as he swayed. It wouldn't be long before James was dead.

Pete looked up at his friend wondering if he could hear him.

"Are you still there, James?" Pete asked. James stared back at him, looking lifeless.

"I don't know if you can hear me, but I wanted to thank you for making it easy for me. Don't worry about Andrea, I'll take real good care of her and your baby, but—. Oh, I'm sorry. You didn't know Andrea was pregnant, did you?"

James' anger surged inside him, but he made no facial expression at the remark. He was fading, Pete's voice sounding distorted to him, overshadowed by the sound of his slowing heartbeat thumping dully in his ear.

"The way I see it, we're even now," Pete continued. "Susan died taking my baby with her. Now you'll die and I'll raise your baby like it was my own. It'll be just the three of us, James. Our nice little family. Just like I had planned."

An evil laugh emanated from Pete, the sound was rich and full.

"I hope you can find Susan when you get there, buddy. I'm sure she'll be happy to see you, since she was crying over you before she turned off Main Street. At least that's what it looked like from the coffee shop I was sitting in. Maybe you and Susan can make a life together in hell."

James looked down at Pete, barely conscious, but hearing everything that was being said. Pete had wanted this, had wanted him to die. He had the chance to save him and he didn't. Pete had seen Susan just before she died. How? He said he was in the city when it happened, nowhere near Nyack.

James realized at that moment that it had all been a set up. He didn't kill Susan. He didn't know how he knew it, but the feeling resonated so strongly in his mind that he accepted it as truth. He didn't know if Pete had killed Susan or not, but he had lied about his whereabouts when it happened. All the guilt James had been feeling since Susan's death was unfounded. He didn't kill her! The cops weren't on to him. The case had probably not been reopened. Pete had been playing some terrible game, moving people around on a board like chess pieces.

James' mind abandoned anger and reminded him of Carmen. Sweet, innocent Carmen who died for no reason: a victim of his instability. He had killed her in cold blood. He couldn't absolve himself of that crime. He had taken a life and for that he had to pay.

James wanted to kick at Pete, to hurt him before he died, but he didn't have the strength. As his eyes went dark and all feelings of pressure and pain were obliterated, James heard Pete say,

"Goodnight, Jimmie."

James spent his last conscious moment wishing he could kill just one more time.

EPILOGUE

Pete and Andrea drove back to the house Thursday morning in silence except for the occasional sniffle and sigh. James' body had been released from the hospital, and they had spent all morning making the arrangements for his funeral. Andrea couldn't get out of the house and on with the simple chores that make up everyday life without help. She was still in shock. Her sister hadn't gotten in from Virginia yet, so Pete offered to go with her to the oddly cheerful Smith and Sons Funeral Home.

An appropriately melancholy funeral director led them through the contract and into the casket room. Pete faltered then, the memory of Susan's funeral flooding his mind as soon as he entered the room full of open caskets. Bronze, copper, wood, even theme caskets littered the slender showroom floor. Deer standing in an emerald-green forest, surrounded by tree trunks that reached up to the sky were painted on one, cherubs floating beneath the body of the beloved, guiding them to Heaven on another. Pete felt claustrophobic and dizzy. He reached out to steady himself on one of the coffins, his hand grazing the satin pillow inside as a film of sweat coated his body.

As he stood, trying to regain control of himself, Susan's face appeared in front of him. Her radiant eyes were staring up at him, the silk pillow where she laid her head every night was wrinkled and askew. She was smiling at him. He could feel her hands tracing his body and resting on his buttocks. He could hear her telling him that she loved him as he entered her, spreading her legs further and further apart. Her eyes closed in ecstasy as he drove harder and harder into her. He smiled at the memory, at the look on her face. Slowly, the image disappeared and he could hear Andrea talking to the funeral director. Her voice was low at first, then it rose to an abnormally loud pitch, bouncing off the walls, echoing throughout the caskets, filling the room. Pete looked over at Andrea and saw her talking, her voice teetering on the edge of collapse. Her voice was elevated, high pitched, and electric. It was mixed with Susan's laugh and the sound of rustling leaves. And there was something else. Pete's mind strained towards the sound, trying to pick out each element. An odd buzzing droned in the background, behind all of the other sounds, muted and blaring all at the same time.

Someone was crying in the funeral home. The sound penetrated the walls, cascading from above him and raining down on his skin, the drops warm like summer rain. Pete only realized that it was he who was crying when Andrea turned to give him a tissue. His tears fell from his eyes and into the empty casket before him. He caressed the pillow that lay in the casket, wishing that he could caress Susan's face one last time.

He slept with Susan's silk pillow for weeks after she died, never changing the case, even after the smell of her hair had faded from it. He clutched the pillow, soaking up her scent, hoping that it would last him a lifetime. The day of her funeral he almost couldn't get out of bed. He rose to dress, throwing the comforter to floor. He put on his pinstripe black suit and tie like a zombie. His mother had laid out his clothes for him the night before. He wasn't able to focus on even that mundane task. Once he was dressed, he sat on Susan's side of the bed and cried. His mother and brother had to wrench him from the bed. He wouldn't leave the room until he had removed Susan's pillowcase, folded it up as small as he could, and put it in his breast pocket.

God, how he had loved her.

Pete didn't hear the words spoken over the closed casket that sat amidst flowers and wreaths sent from family and friends. He could only stare at the box, where her head would be if he could see it. He thought of her smile, her voice telling him that it would be okay and that she loved him. His thoughts were invaded time and again by what he thought her face looked like then, in death. He wasn't able to identify the body at the morgue because he wouldn't have been any help to the doctors. All he could do was provide the name and number of the dentist that had been taking care of Susan since she was a child. So, what he saw in his mind, the image of her ruined face, could never be validated. He would never see her again, not after that morning when she drove to Nyack and out of his life. He couldn't say goodbye to her encased in the bronze box that would be her bed forever. He could only sit and stare unwaveringly at the coffin, fighting the screams that welled in his throat every time his mind conjured up the image of her skinless, charred bones.

The police had ruled Susan's death an accident, gas deposited on the engine, causing it to ignite. It was a tragedy, a senseless twist of fate, such a terrible loss of life. Everybody accepted that, everyone around him mourned the life of a woman who died too soon. But he knew differently. Susan had died for a reason, just like James had, and he was the only one left who knew what it was.

Pete walked Andrea into the house, went in the kitchen, and put on a pot of water for tea. Andrea sank into the reclining chair in the day room and stared out at the back yard. He watched her from the kitchen. So beautiful. Her skin was smooth and soft. Her shapely body was hidden from view, but he knew that underneath the baggy, nondescript clothing she had donned that morning, was a beautiful bikini worthy body. He smiled at the thoughts he entertained. As she sat looking out of the window mourning the loss of her husband, Pete's eyes roamed the room. She was all alone and confused in her big house in Monsey, New York. Pete had no intention of letting Andrea be alone or letting that big house be empty for very long.

Susan's face flashed in his mind. How foolish she had been to think that he would truly forgive her. That he would raise that bastard child as his own and live life happily ever after. He chuckled at her naïveté. He would have divorced her as soon as he had found another woman. Why not? She had already better-dealed him, hadn't she?

He made the deal with her because he could, plain and simple. She was so mortified when he confronted her, so pathetic with her pleading. So, he capitalized on the situation. He played a card from his hand and waited to see if she would follow suit. He didn't owe her anything, not after what she had done to him. So, if she was going to be gullible enough to think that he was capable of forgiving and forgetting, why not milk it and see what happened?

Part of him was ashamed of the way he treated Susan that day. They had been in love once, hadn't they? How could he treat her so ruthlessly? Time had washed the love away and shown him the situation in black and white. Susan had cheated on him with his best friend. She obviously hadn't been thinking about the love they'd shared when she climbed into bed with James. Why should he?

And that's what remained, the sour taste building in his mouth until he had to discard it. So, he did.

But James' death was different. It caught him off guard, unlike Susan's—his hatred for her had boiled inside him until it blew. Pete hadn't known, not up until the very end, that he wanted James to die.

Pete hated James for what he had done, as he had hated Susan. He had wanted him to pay. But death?

It didn't matter anymore anyway. What's done is done, as he was fond of saying. Besides, everything worked out the way he wanted it to anyway. Who cared what road they had to travel to get there?

The irony wasn't lost on him. As he stood in the kitchen, pulling out mugs and sugar for the tea, he thought about the turn of events. A turn in his favor. James had the audacity to carry on a relationship with his wife, virtually under his and Andrea's noses. He wanted Susan, so much so, that he did whatever he had to do to be with her. When she died, his life slowly unraveled. And now he was with her. In hell. It was Pete who stood in James' house now, with his wife. Soon she would be his, just like Pete's wife had become James'. His child would be Pete's to nurture and love. Life was funny that way.

Pete brought the tea over to Andrea and put it on the tray stand. She didn't look in his direction.

"Andrea? Honey, it'll get better."

She turned her head to him slowly, tears blurring her vision.

"I just don't understand. He was happy. We were happy. Then those dreams came. Those terrible nightmares. He used to scare me with what he told me about them. Where did they come from?"

"He was sick, Andrea. He was sick, just like his father had been. It wasn't about you or anything you did."

"He didn't show signs until a couple of months ago. It all seemed to happen so fast. How could something like this just show up? Just happen?" Andrea's hand had been tracing the rim of the steaming mug of tea absently, but now she turned to face him. Pete saw her eyes, ringed in pink and shimmering with tears. He hurt for her.

"The dreams were so vivid to him, Pete. So real. He stopped believing they were dreams after a while. I tried to tell him that they were, of course. As traumatic and disturbing as they were, they were still just dreams. Somewhere along the way I stopped believing they were dreams too."

They were silent for a while, Andrea's admission hanging thickly in the air between them. Pete fidgeted in the hush, the staggering weight of reality sitting squarely on top of him, crushing him.

"You did everything you could, Andrea," Pete blurted out, saying something, anything to break the silence.

"I could feel the difference towards the end," Andrea said, turning her head to look into the backyard, her eyes unseeing as she reflected on the last months of her husband's life.

"It was tangible. It was oppressive, like the dessert sun. What I felt was second hand, though. I can only imagine what James felt." Andrea paused to take a sip of her tea. She continued, "I think I met one of his demons."

"What are you talking about, Andrea?" Pete asked incredulously. She was starting to sound mad, her comments atavistic of James' history, the irrational words resonating in his ears like nails scratching a chalkboard. He was suddenly very afraid for her.

It was one thing to wish that you could have helped your husband, could have stopped him from carrying out his death. But to claim to have seen a glimmer of what had driven him out of his mind? The thought alone chilled Pete to his core.

He realized distantly that his concern wasn't as wholesome as it might appear at first glance. His own agenda could be besmirched if Andrea continued to travel down that road of despair, pining for her dead husband and blaming herself for not seeing the signs sooner. Her grief would be time consuming anyway, without the smidgen of guilt that was introducing itself as her thoughts became more frenzied. Pete didn't want to let her slip into some immense melancholy, delaying their inevitability even further.

A little voice, like that of a child running past him in the park, said spitefully, "She'll dream too."

He had to do something to shake her out of it.

"You couldn't have seen anything from James' dreams, honey. This whole thing was in his head."

Andrea shook her head slowly, still watching the day unfold with blind eyes.

"I saw something from his dream manifest itself in him." She paused, not for effect, but because the realization of what happened was more than she could bear. Her chest heaved as she breathed in deeply, trying to suppress the sob rising in her throat.

"I saw it in him that day he fell in the shower. He was battling something and I saw it. It won, Pete." Her hand fluttered up to her mouth, the unconscious movement of a woman trying to control herself. "It won."

Pete sat silently letting Andrea cry for what seemed like an hour. He was about to say something soothing, something to coax her into drinking more of the tea and getting some sleep, when Andrea continued.

"How terrified he must have been. How incredibly afraid. And all I could do was watch it happen to him."

Andrea succumbed to her sobbing now, rocking back and forth in the chair slowly as the emotion drained from her. She hugged her arms tightly to her chest as she cried, wishing that she could enfold James in her embrace one more time. Her grief was immense, rivaled only by her shame.

"I loved him and I let him handle it by himself. I let the demons come out of him and take him back with them," she sobbed wetly. "I let this happen."

"No, no, Andrea," Pete cooed in her ear. He put his arms around her shoulders and held her as tightly as she held herself, trying to ward off the hysteria he envisioned brewing inside her.

"Whatever this was, it had always been there. It was just quiet, waiting for the right moment to come out. Something triggered it, I just don't know what. We'll never know what happened with James. He didn't give us enough time to find out. There was nothing you could have done to stop this, Andrea. You have to believe that.

"They were just dreams in the beginning," Pete continued as Andrea's cries died down. Her body still trembled against his chest.

"That's how it started for him and probably for his father too. Dreams are only as important as people make them out to be. James, his father, and probably other generations before them placed great importance on them. Something triggered the dreams to start in James, just like they had with his father. Some trauma or turn of events, something in his life prompted the sand in the hourglass to fall. It was inevitable, Andrea."

"That's just it. He didn't do anything but go to work and come home. We weren't fighting. Pete, I just don't understand this."

Pete left her in the dark about the affair. What she didn't know wouldn't hurt her.

"He must have been suffering for a while. It could have stemmed from finding his father all those years ago. He might have been holding it in all this time, and any small thing could have erupted the dormant feelings. There was nothing we could do."

Pete felt Andrea's body tense as she drew in a breath. She responded so sharply, Pete was caught off guard. She lifted her head from his chest, her face flushed. Anger spat like spittle out of Andrea's mouth. He could almost see the child in the park laughing at him.

"Don't tell me there was nothing we could do! With all the advancements in psychiatry, you're telling me that there was nothing that could have been done to stop him from – from..." She couldn't bring herself to give life to the words that stuck in her throat. She wouldn't allow herself to. Somehow, she thought, the horror of James' death—the way he chose to die, alone in an abandoned house in morbid tribute to his ancestors' legacy, would subside if no one spoke about it. She laid her head back onto Pete's chest. He wrapped his arms around her as he had before, warming her, making her feel safe amid the madness that was her life.

"If only he had talked to us," Pete said gently, almost whispering. His lips grazed Andrea's ear fortuitously as he spoke and he felt himself stir despite the circumstances.

They stayed that way for a while, both of them pretending to look into the backyard at the beautiful fall day, its sunrays oblivious to James's fate. The day carried on with its own transition, the season preparing for its impending death. Their idleness affected a calm over them, seeming to quiet the din in Andrea's mind, and satisfying Pete's need to smell the perfume that wafted from the base of her neck, tantalizing his nostrils mercilessly.

Andrea's face cleared for a second as she thought out loud, "The bad dreams started not long after Susan died."

Pete remained silent, hoping that Andrea wouldn't speculate about the potential connections. That subject should never be broached, he had decided long ago. The cost of its discussion was far too great.

Andrea fell silent again, not saying anything for a long time. The sound of her breathing was rhythmic, hypnotic in its regularity. Pete found his eyes closing slowly, his eyelids suddenly heavy and thick.

Andrea's breathing changed unexpectedly, jolting Pete out of his slumber. She breathed in deeply, almost gasping for air. Then it evened out again, her chest barely rising and falling as she inhaled and exhaled. She was fighting for her sanity, her very life.

She turned to Pete with wide, barren eyes. Her face was frighteningly blank as she stared at him, the look of finality playing in her eyes. She said in a monotone voice that seemed to be coming from all around them, breaking the silence like a low hum from an old speaker,

"If you die in your dreams you *do* die in real life."

Pete looked out at the sunny afternoon and watched a squirrel gathering leaves to build a nest in the tree that overhung the deck. As the squirrel worked, Andrea succumbed to more sobbing and tears; her head resting against Pete's chest. A smile tickled the inside of his mouth.

Washington DC
Herndon, Virginia
Sterling, Virginia
McGaheysville, Virginia
Tampa, Florida

Peering into the darkness
I have a sense of one
with me
searching also
for themselves
but finding me.
- The Dark, by elle wood

Afterward

Nyack, New York. The depiction given in this book paints the village as a picturesque river town on the cusp of contemporary culture yet tucked far enough away to still be considered secluded. That image is correct. The small town feel of Nyack is endearing. Antique shops and boutiques line the streets and people casually mill about on any given day, window-shopping and taking in the unique atmosphere. The pier overlooking the Hudson River is my favorite spot in the village.

I used a little creative license around town. There is a Main Street, but that is common of most small towns in the United States. The bed and breakfast nestled on the residential street, the gateway to Victorian and Cape Cod homes from antique row, though befitting, does not exist. So, the next time you are in Rockland County and decide to do some antiquing on the Hudson, stroll Main Street in Nyack to see what you might find. The café on Main Street? The bookstore on the corner? Maybe the Italian restaurant just up the street from Mitchell Manor? If you decide to dine there, please be sure to tell them that James and Susan say hello.

Silver Spring, Maryland and Monsey, New York are also real

towns; the latter is my hometown. Monsey didn't get much attention this time around but will at a later date. Silver Spring, Maryland, a town like many others on the East Coast, successfully merges the residential and the business culture that is separated, in most cases, by a four-way stoplight.

The Boone house can be found anywhere: in rural Maryland or Virginia, in suburban New York or Connecticut. Even in your town. Lillian could be lurking behind the fogged windows that look out onto your street, watching as you get into your car each day and drive away. Do you know your genealogy? Is your family tree up to date? If not, Lillian could be waiting for you.

Sterling, Virginia

The End

About the Author

L. Marie Wood creates immersive worlds that defy genre as they intersect horror, romance, mystery, thriller, sci-fi, and fantasy elements to weave harrowing tapestries of speculative fiction. She is the recipient of the Golden Stake Award, a MICO Award-winning screenwriter, a two-time Bram Stoker Award® Finalist, a Rhysling nominated poet, and an accomplished essayist. Wood has won over 50 national and international screenplay and film awards. Wood has penned short fiction that has been published in groundbreaking works, including the anthologies *Sycorax's Daughters* and *Slay: Stories of the Vampire Noire*. She is also part of the 2022 Bookfest Book Award winning poetry anthology, *Under Her Skin*.

Her nonfiction has been published in Nightmare Magazine and academic textbooks such as the cross-curricular, *Conjuring Worlds: An Afrofuturist* Textbook. Her papers are archived as part of University of Pittsburgh's Horror Studies Collection. Wood is the founder of the Speculative Fiction Academy, an English and Creative Writing professor, a horror scholar with a Ph.D. in Creative Writing and an MFA in Speculative Fiction, and a frequent contributor to the conversation around the evolution of genre fiction. Learn more about L. Marie Wood at www.lmariewood.com.

A group of friends head out to enjoy a much-deserved night out and paintballing is on the menu. But the team they are playing against has something entirely different in mind. The friends find themselves in a battle for their lives in unfamiliar terrain against well-equipped opponents whose motivations are both irrational and lethal.

Considered, "… a true trip into the darkest depths of what mankind is capable of at its worst," by Midwest Book Review, this story is a classic tale of prey combined with slasher film "edge-of-your seat" vibes with a little modern-day relevance to keep you unsettled.

Blackened Roots is a unique collection and will be a must-have for zombie lovers. Blackened Roots takes the zombie mythos back to its roots. Drawing from a variety of cultural backgrounds, Blackened Roots imagines a world of horror and wonder where Black protagonists take center stage – as zombies, as hunters, as heroes. From a haunting recipe to sibling rivalry, a singing zombie cowboy, a slave ship, and disobedient gods stories, Blackened Roots is a groundbreaking Afrocentric zombie anthology celebrating the rich cultural heritage of the African Diaspora.

Patrick thought he knew what awaited him in the afterlife. He's learning the hard way that he was dead wrong. He is hunted by a race of giant beasts, the likes of which have never been seen by living eyes, and he is surrounded by the newly-dead from worlds beyond knowing. In this Realm, nothing and no one can be trusted.

Patrick's choices will create echoes in the world of the living. He may be the key to salvation in this Hell known as The Realm, but it may come at the cost of his family.

With his legacy on the line, can he make the right choice?

https://www.mochamemoirspress.com

About Mocha Memoirs Press

Established in July 2010, Mocha Memoirs Press's mission is to amplify marginalized voices in speculative fiction genres (science fiction, fantasy, horror). We publish bold, fearless fiction that pushes boundaries and smashes gatekeepers.

We invite you to review our catalog to review the diversity in our stories. You can access the catalog at https://www.mochamemoirspress.com. Join our newsletter **here.**

You can also find us online:

Instagram - @mochamemoirspress

TikTok-@mochamemoirspress

BlueSky-@mochamemoirspress.com

Twitter (X)- @mochamemoirspress

Facebook facebook.com/MochaMemoirsPress